Praise for Marcia Clark's
KILLER AMBITION

"A refreshing and suspenseful portrayal of high-stakes trials, criminal lawyers on both sides of the aisle, and the strategies behind their every move.... Rachel and her posse of girlfriends, colleagues, and their love interests are engaging enough to hope for their continued growth and success in investigations that are equal to Rachel's, and author Marcia Clark's, many and formidable talents in the courtroom."   —Paula L. Woods, *Los Angeles Times*

"*Killer Ambition* builds real drama out of its tabloid crime and makes Knight a likable crusader for truth in Tinseltown."   —Josh Emmons, *People* (3 out of 4 stars)

"Legal thrillers don't get much better than this.... Boasting a feisty protagonist, a winning supporting cast, and steadily escalating courtroom drama, *Killer Ambition* finds Clark at the top of her game."

—Michele Leber, *Booklist* (starred review)

"Suspenseful and gripping.... The best yet in the series. Marcia Clark's own expertise enables her to realistically portray the drama and vicissitudes of a criminal prosecution."   —*Publishers Weekly* (starred review)

MARCIA CLARK

KILLER AMBITION

A NOVEL

MULHOLLAND BOOKS

LITTLE, BROWN AND COMPANY

NEW YORK BOSTON LONDON

Copyright © 2013 by Marcia Clark
Excerpt from *The Competition* copyright © 2014 by Marcia Clark

Mulholland Books / Little, Brown and Company
Hachette Book Group
237 Park Avenue
New York, NY 10017
mulhollandbooks.com

The publisher is not responsible for websites (or their content) that are not owned by the publisher.

Printed in the United States of America

Originally published in hardcover by Mulholland Books / Little, Brown and Company, June 2013
First Mulholland Books / Little, Brown and Company mass market edition, March 2014

10 9 8 7 6 5 4 3 2 1

In Loving Memory of Tristan Sayre
(1992–2010)

*"There are things that we don't want to happen but
have to accept, things we don't want to know but have
to learn, and people we can't live without but
have to let go."*

—*Author Unknown*

KILLER
AMBITION

PROLOGUE

Rocky mountain peaks glowed lonely and austere under the nearly full moon. But the trail that led to God's Seat, a throne-shaped outcropping high atop Backbone Trail, wound darkly under thick canopies of branches and overhanging boulders. One false step on that narrow path meant a thousand-foot drop and certain death, but the two lone figures walking single file up the trail moved at a heedless pace.

The night was still except for the crunch of their footsteps on sun-baked earth: one confident and driving, the other stumbling gracelessly forward, blinded by terror, steps punctuated by weeping, a nearly inaudible murmuring—*This can't be happening...Can't...No, no, no, no. Please, let me wake up. Please, please. This is just a dream.* At the top of the ridge, beside a waist-high boulder, the larger figure stopped and threw a shovel to the ground, the clang of metal hitting rock.

"Dig."

The smaller figure stared at the shovel, then abruptly doubled over, stomach heaving convulsively as the vomit rose up too fast to control. The larger figure watched for a moment, then, with cold disdain, flashed a vicious-looking blade. "You hear me? Pick up the fucking shovel and—"

"Okay, okay," came the reply, as clammy, trembling hands took the shovel and thrust it into the earth. *Okay, okay...okay, okay...* repeating it over and over, mantra-like—wheezing with the effort to breathe through a fear-constricted throat.

"Faster."

Slowly, the hole grew deeper and longer. *Okay, okay...This will be okay. Someone will come. Someone will come. Okay, okay...*

And then, miraculously, someone *did* come. A soft rustling, the sound of slow, tentative steps approaching. And, as if in a dream, a moonlit face emerged from the darkness.

Three Nights Earlier

Hayley and Mackenzie spilled out of the chauffeur-driven Escalade and into the throng of twenty-somethings in front of Teddy's, the "it" club in the Hollywood Roosevelt Hotel. Long sparkling earrings and sequined minidresses on spray-tanned body beautifuls, well-toned pretty boys in carefully torn jeans and three-hundred-dollar T-shirts—the air heavy with the tension of feigned indifference, as though each and every one of them wasn't desperate to gain entrée into the exclusive club. Hayley led the way through the crowd, her blonde head thrown back, stiletto heels hitting the ground with confidence. Mackenzie trailed behind, nervously pulling down her tube skirt as she instinctively reached for Hayley's hand. Her eyes focused on the ground to avoid the angry glares of the waiting crowd. The jackhammering of her heart made her breath come in short, shallow gulps.

When they reached the door, the bouncer, slender and sinewy, a spider tattoo wrapped around his neck, raised a skeptical eyebrow from beneath the worn brim of a black hat. Mackenzie wiped a nervous palm on her thigh before relinquishing her license. But Hayley, with a sexy-lazy smile, smoothly dipped into the cleavage of her leopard-print halter top and flipped her license out between two fingers. As always, Mackenzie watched with awe and envy, knowing she'd never master that kind of breezy nonchalance.

The bouncer briefly scanned their IDs, then handed them back with a dismissive head shake. "Not even close."

Mackenzie's heart stopped. *Busted.* But then Hayley stepped in and shoved a card under his nose. She looked him straight in the eye. "You sure?"

The bouncer frowned and peered at the card, then took back Hayley's license and gave it a second look. Suddenly, his face broke into a lopsided grin. "Your dad know you're here?"

Mackenzie felt giddy with relief—and foolish. After all this time she should surely know better. Clubs, private parties, restaurants—hell, even the *Vanity Fair* after-party on Oscar night—all happily opened their doors to the daughter of megastar director Russell Antonovich.

"My dad *sent* me," Hayley joked, with an intimate look that brought him in on it.

Chuckling, the bouncer lifted the rope, then reached back and opened the door, unleashing a blast of music. "Have a nice night, ladies," he said.

Hayley grabbed Mackenzie's hand and led the way through a wall of dancers whose bodies glowed under pulsing multicolored lights, their only guide through the near-impenetrable velvet darkness. A hand shot up and waved to them from a crowded horseshoe booth next to the DJ—the sweetest spot in the house. They inched their way over and squeezed in, Mackenzie practically sitting in Hayley's lap. The walls seemed to vibrate with the thunderous bass, making conversation impossible. But it didn't matter. They weren't there to talk and they wouldn't need to place orders: hors d'oeuvres were served continuously, and they always had bottle service. Tonight's offering was Patrón Silver, and she and Hayley had doubles in their hands by the time they sat down. A cute curly-haired guy—was his name Adrian?—moved forward with a sexy smile and pulled Mackenzie out onto the dance floor. She didn't sit down again till unknown hours later when she and Hayley collapsed into the back of the Escalade.

Now

Could that really have been just three nights ago? From her perch high on a hill in Laurel Canyon, Mackenzie barely noticed the spread of twinkling lights, the crawl of traffic across Sunset Boulevard and up La Cienega. She glanced to the west, where, just a few miles away in the Hollywood Hills above Sunset Plaza, Hayley's dad had his "party house." It was a favorite hang of theirs when her dad wasn't around. They loved to skinny-dip in the infinity pool that stretched from the edge of the hilltop and flowed under a heavy plate-glass wall, right into the living room.

Laughing, partying, playing, sharing. The past year had been the best of Mackenzie's life, and she owed it all to Hayley. Tears sprang to her eyes, turning the red and white lights on the streets below into long, blurry streaks. She pulled the photo, normally enshrined on the mirror in her bedroom, out of the back pocket of her jeans. It was a picture of her and Hayley at Colony, loose, boozy smiles, arms looped around each other's shoulders. Her first night out with Hayley. And her first step out of the purgatory of "new girl" and, even worse, "poor girl" at the Clarington Academy prep school, aka high school for rich kids. Mackenzie got in on an academic scholarship, but she was a charity case and everyone seemed to know it. For the first few months she'd slunk through the hallways, a lonely, miserable misfit. Until one day, in gym class, she and Hayley had discovered a mutual hatred of field hockey. That's all it took. Her life, her whole world changed overnight. How could that have been just a little over a year ago?

Mackenzie clutched the sides of her head and tried to breathe. Hayley had said not to worry. That it would be okay. That she'd call and she'd explain everything. But for now, don't tell anyone. Don't tell.

But that was three days ago. Three days, with no word from Hayley. Was she supposed to wait this long? What if something had gone wrong? Should she call someone? But maybe nothing was wrong and her call would just screw everything up. It'd be all her fault and

Hayley might never forgive her. What was she supposed to do? Mackenzie dropped her head, hugged her knees, and squeezed her eyes shut against the tears. It would be okay. Hayley would be okay. Hayley was always okay. She *had* to be.

1

"I'm guessing by your expression that dinner went pretty well after all," Bailey said. *Her* expression had an obnoxious "told-you-so" tinge to it that made me want to lie. But I knew there was no point. Bailey was not only a top-notch detective in the elite Robbery-Homicide Division of LAPD, she was also one of my very best friends. She would see right through it. Still, I didn't have to give it up all at once.

I gave a noncommittal shrug, hung my purse on the hook under the bar, and slid onto the cushy leather stool. "It went okay."

It was ten o'clock on a Monday night, so the after-work crowd had largely cleared out of the Biltmore Hotel bar. The only exception was a well-dressed middle-aged couple on one of the velvety couches against the wall. They were enjoying Manhattans with a leisurely attitude that told me they didn't have to worry about a morning commute. Though I didn't recognize them, I guessed they were staying in the hotel. Being a permanent resident of the hotel myself, I could usually tell who was a guest and who had just dropped by for a drink.

Drew, the gorgeous bartender, who'd been my buddy ever since I'd moved into the Biltmore a few years ago, gave me a knowing smirk. "Just okay? I don't think so." He tilted his shining black head toward the mirror behind him. "Take a look at yourself, girl."

Even in the dim light I could see the sappy expression on my face. Damn. Drew and Bailey exchanged an amused smile. They'd been together for about two years now—the longest stretch either of them had ever managed with a single partner. Most of the time, it was a beautiful thing. But there were stomach-turning moments like this, when their "oneness" made me want to bang their heads together. Hard.

Bailey turned back just in time to catch my nauseated look—and ignore it. "And in case you were worried, you're not alone out there. Graden was actually whistling." Bailey made a face. "All day."

Since Lieutenant Graden Hales was Bailey's boss, she knew he never whistled. But I refused to give her the satisfaction of seeing how good it made me feel. I looked at her, deadpan. "Funny how annoying little things like that can be."

"Isn't it?" Bailey deadpanned right back at me.

Graden and I met a couple of years ago when he worked the case of Jake Pahlmeyer, a dear friend and fellow Special Trials Unit prosecutor, who was found dead in a sleazy downtown motel room, not far from the Biltmore. We'd begun dating, and I was just starting to believe Graden and I would go the distance when we had a major blowout over a violation of privacy;

specifically, his violation of my privacy. He'd done some digging, otherwise known as "Googling" me, and found out that my sister Romy had been kidnapped when she was eleven years old. And was still missing.

He hadn't known that Romy's abduction was my closely guarded secret, one I'd kept from even my besties, Bailey Keller and Toni LaCollier, also a Special Trials prosecutor. But my breakup with Graden had forced me to tell them about it. Bailey and Toni had been sympathetic to my upset—well, actually, fury—at what I called the trampling of my boundaries, but they'd made no secret of the fact that they thought I'd overreacted... wildly. "He surfed the Web, Knight," Bailey'd said. "Hardly an act of high-level espionage," Toni'd added. I knew they were right, but knowing something intellectually and dealing with it emotionally are two very different matters. It'd taken me a while to come around.

But I did get there. At least enough to recognize that my reaction was over the top, and that I wanted to give Graden another chance. So we'd been taking baby steps, getting together for coffee breaks and lunches over the past few months. Tonight had been our first real date since the breakup—or, as Toni and Bailey called it, breakdown. I'd been a little apprehensive. Would he try for a sentimental play and take us to the site of our first date, the Pacific Dining Car? Or to the romantic hilltop restaurant that had become a mutual favorite, Yamashiro? I'd hoped not. I wasn't ready for any trips down memory lane.

"So where'd you go?" Drew asked.

"We went to Craig's—"

Drew nodded sagely. "My man, Graden. Excellent choice."

It really was. The leather and white tablecloth steakhouse in West Hollywood had that same Sinatra–Dean Martin feel as the Pacific Dining Car—great food and a comfortable ambience for real dining and conversation—with none of the emotional undertow of having been "our" place. It wasn't cheap, but money was no concern for Graden, who'd made a fortune on Code Three, the video game he'd designed with his brother.

Bailey studied me for a moment. "You look ridiculously sober. You stuck with water, didn't you?"

I nodded.

"Didn't trust yourself?" she asked.

"Of course I trusted myself." I cadged a cube of cheese off Bailey's plate. "I just want to keep a clear head."

"Time to put a stop to that," Drew said. "What'll you have?"

I ordered a glass of pinot noir, and Drew moved off.

"So...you didn't trust yourself," Bailey said.

"Nope, not for one second."

We laughed, and when Drew set down my glass of wine, we toasted.

"To knowing your limits." Bailey raised her glass, and I clinked it with mine.

"To that."

We took a sip.

"And he really didn't see anyone else?" I asked.

"Not unless she worked the cleaning crew at the station. From what I saw, he was in the office night and day. I'd guess he was keeping himself distracted."

"Know what I'd guess?"

But I never got a chance to say, because Bailey's work cell phone rang. If Bailey was next up on the roster, she wouldn't have been drinking, so it couldn't be work. I listened, hoping to get some information, but all I heard was "Yep" and "Got it" and "Let me write that down." Finally, Bailey ended the call and drained her water glass in one long gulp. Then she took my glass of wine—still practically full—out of my hand and set it down.

"Hey!"

"O'Hare's sick, so I'm up. Got a kidnapping call. Russell Antonovich."

Russell Antonovich. A name attached to so many blockbusters even I, who knew nothing about Hollywood hotshots, recognized it.

"Someone kidnapped him?"

"No." Bailey made sure no one was near us, then lowered her voice. "His teenage daughter, Hayley. Antonovich delivered the ransom and was supposed to get her back within the hour. That was two hours ago."

Bailey motioned to Drew that she'd call, and we headed for the road.

2

Bailey got off the 405 freeway and headed east on Sunset Boulevard. I was about to ask where we were going when she turned onto Bellagio Road—which led to the heart of Bel Air. If I were a billionaire director I'd live there too.

Bel Air is in the foothills of the Santa Monica Mountains, and it's the highest of the three legs known as the Platinum Triangle—the other two being Beverly Hills and Holmby Hills. The most expensive homes in the world occupy real estate in that wedge of land, and the majority of those homes are in Bel Air. The biggest and most lavish are usually closest to Sunset Boulevard, but you'd never know that, because massive trees and dense shrubbery hide all but the gated entries, and even those gates are tough to find, hidden as some are by deliberately overgrown leafy climbers.

Which explains why Bailey was frowning and muttering to herself as she scanned the road for house numbers. But when we reached Bel Air Country Club, she made a U-turn and pulled over. "Do me a favor and look for this number. The navigation says we're there, but I don't see a damn thing." She handed me a scrap of paper with an address and headed back down the road. One minute later I told her to stop and peered closely at a set of massive black iron gates that were almost completely obscured by towering elm and cypress trees. The tops of the gates met in an arc, and there in the apex, woven into the iron scrollwork, was the number.

"This is it." If I hadn't been parked in front of it and looking hard, I'd never have seen it.

I pointed out a discreet black metal box mounted on an arm in the brick wall, and Bailey pushed the button. A voice that sounded like a British butler's said, "Yes?" Bailey identified us, and he told us to hold out our badges. I couldn't see any cameras, but I didn't imagine he'd have asked us to do that just for giggles, so I held them outside the window, not sure where to aim them. After a couple of seconds the gates swung open, and Bailey steered up the brick lined road.

Los Angeles has some of the most outrageously opulent manses in the country and Bailey and I had seen our share over the years, but nothing compared to this. The road opened to a bricked-in area that was the size of half a football field, in the middle of which was a massive Italian Renaissance–style fountain, complete with cherubs' and lions' heads that spewed water. Towering over the grounds was a palatial two-story Tudor-style house all in that same matching brick. It was tastefully covered in ivy that obediently climbed where it best accented the archways and latticed windows and formed a large *L* around the perimeter of the front area. Judging just by what I could see from the outside, that "house" was at least thirty-five thousand square feet if it was an inch.

Bailey parked and we both stepped out of the car and took in the view.

"Damn," said Bailey under her breath.

"A quaint little 'starter.'"

By the time we'd made it up to the arched brick entry, the door was open and a slender man in his fifties, with thinning hair combed neatly back and dressed in a cardigan and dark slacks, beckoned us in.

"Right this way, please."

We were eventually ushered into a room that was sectioned off by furniture groupings of leather couches, ottomans, and cherrywood tables. Large wall-mounted flat screens hung on opposite walls. The room was big enough that both could be watched at the same time without anyone suffering noise interference. I supposed it was what the Realtors called a "great" room. Cozy.

Several people had gathered and the room buzzed with tension, though no one was moving. It was an odd sensation, as if everyone were vibrating in place. A tall wire whip of a man approached me with a smooth, athletic stride. Something about him looked familiar. I studied the brows that arched expressively over green eyes, the full lips, the faint spray of freckles across the bridge of his nose, and the dampish, freshly showered–looking dark red hair that curled down the sides of his neck. When recognition hit, shock made the name spring from my mouth. "Mattie!"

A brief look of annoyance was quickly replaced by a self-deprecating smile; it got me at first, but there was a too-polished feeling about the expression that said he'd probably been working it from his earliest child-star

—

days. "Right." He held out his hand. "Though I actually go by Ian Powers."

We shook, and I collected myself. "Sorry," I said. "I just wasn't expecting—"

Ian Powers held up a hand. "Hey, don't apologize. At my age, I'm only glad that people can still recognize me."

It was somewhat remarkable. Though he definitely didn't look it, Ian Powers had to be in his forties. I knew it'd been more than thirty years since he'd starred as the eight-year-old boy in the sitcom *Just the Two of Us,* about Mattie, a charming, wise-beyond-his-years boy and his single father. I remembered watching the show when I was a kid, though by then, the show had long since been in reruns. It was weird to see the vestiges of that sweet little-boy face in this fully grown, casually elegant man.

"I take it you two are the detectives?"

"Actually no. I'm Rachel Knight, deputy district attorney."

"Detective Keller." Bailey put out her hand. "And your connection...?"

"I'm Russell's manager."

Ian led us to the left side of the room, where a short man, no more than an inch taller than me, dressed in a baseball cap, faded jeans, and a forest green Henley, sat on the arm of a plush burgundy couch. "Russell, this is Detective Bailey Keller and, ah—"

"Deputy District Attorney Rachel Knight," I filled in. Clearly, I was already making quite the impression.

Russell stood and rocked on his toes—I'd bet so he could look down on me. But he'd have needed a step stool to look down on Bailey, all five feet nine inches of her. He took her in with a sidelong glance that avoided his having to look up at her, and didn't offer his hand to either one of us. He took a deep breath, expelled it through his nose, then started to dive in. "Got the first message about—"

Bailey held up a hand and looked around the room. "Mr. Antonovich, before you get into it, can you tell me who all these people are and why they need to be here?"

With a pained expression he said, "Russell, okay? Call me Russell." His tone was peremptory, almost impatient, and his voice was high enough that if I hadn't been looking at him I'd have thought he was a woman. "They all pretty much live here." He pointed to a willowy blonde who looked to be in her mid-twenties and easily twenty years his junior. "My wife, Dani. That's her assistant, Angela," he said, nodding at a trim young girl with a mop of curly brown hair who was pouring bottled water into a glass for the missus. He pointed to a sturdy-looking girl in overalls and a matching baseball cap. "My assistant, Uma." I noticed she was the only one in the room who was shorter than Russell. I was sure that was no accident. An older woman came in carrying a trayful of plates bearing finger food. Russell followed my gaze. "That's Vera, the cook." No last name—unless you counted "the cook." In fact, none of these people had a last name. Not as far as Russell was concerned anyway.

"And that...?" I asked, pointing to a young man wearing jeans that sagged below sea level who was sitting on an ottoman at the other end of the room.

"Jeff, my runner. Assistant too, sometimes."

And then there was the butler who'd answered the door, and all the others it would take to keep this place going. If we kept taking attendance, we wouldn't get to the case until sometime next week. Bailey had apparently reached the same conclusion.

"I'll need a list of everyone who's been in the house today and who's in the house now," Bailey said.

"Right, got it, got it."

"When did you first realize your daughter had been kidnapped?" Bailey asked.

Russell pulled off his baseball cap, which now showed me it was his substitute for hair. The hem of tight straw-colored curls just above his ears was all that remained. He rubbed his head and then his face. With the cap off, I could see the worry and fear etched in his features. Suddenly the celebrity director was just the frantic, distraught father of a child in danger. And in that moment, the picture of my father's face filled my memory: the panic and confusion in his eyes, turning to frozen shock when, sobbing and hysterical, I told him of the stranger who'd taken Romy while we were playing in the woods near the house. I brought myself back to the present with a stiff jerk. That was Romy and my father. Not Hayley or Russell. This daughter still had a chance of a safe return.

"I got a text message with the photograph of Hayley. It came in before noon from Hayley's phone. She was at my place in the hills—"

"Hollywood Hills?"

Russell nodded. "Sent it to my private cell phone. Only my family has it. But I didn't see it till after I got home. Said that photo was proof of life and that the demand would come later. Warned me not to call the cops."

"You still have that message and the photo?"

"Yeah, of course. Got 'em right here." He pulled his cell phone out of his hip pocket and handed it to Bailey.

Bailey and I read the message on his phone: I've got your daughter. She'll be safe if you do as I tell you. If you call the police she'll be killed. I'll be in touch with my demand.

"A little while later, I get an e-mail telling me to bring a million in cash to a place in Fryman Canyon."

"Could you tell where the e-mail came from?"

"The e-mail address was Hayley's, but—"

But all the kidnapper had to do was get her password to send from her e-mail address.

"Was there a photo of Hayley in the e-mail?" I asked.

"Yeah. A video of Hayley was attached, telling me just to do what he says." Russell again rubbed his head and then his face. His next words tumbled over each other, half regretful, half defensive. "So I did. I know I should've called you guys, but I was afraid to take the chance. Thought if I did what they asked, Hayley'd be back and..."

"And I understand you've already delivered the ransom?" Bailey asked.

Russell tried to take a deep breath, but it caught in his throat. He dipped his head. "Yeah." He could barely choke out the word.

"How did you get your hands on a million dollars that fast?" I asked.

At that, Russell looked up, his expression confused. "See, that's the other thing. Only the family knows I keep that much cash around for emergencies. Hayley had to have told them—"

"And she was supposed to be released within an hour after that?" I asked.

Russell nodded.

"Where exactly?" I asked.

"At the mouth of Fryman Canyon, on the valley side. Told me to go back home and wait for the call." Russell's face bunched up and he blew out an exasperated huff. "Look, I already told all this to the captain, so why are you sitting here?"

"We have officers searching Fryman Canyon," Bailey said. "Unless and until we find someone who can give us more to go on, everything that can be done is being done."

Bailey turned back to Russell's cell phone and pulled up the proof-of-life photo. A petite blonde girl with a feminine version of her father's mouth, dressed in a pink-striped jersey blouse that exposed one fetchingly bare shoulder, stared back at us. Her expression was fixed, serious. I looked across the room at Russell's wife, Dani. I saw no resemblance. Hayley seemed to be leaning against an iron fence, through which I vaguely made out a hillside thick with greenery.

"Let's see the ransom demand," Bailey said.

Russell held out his hand for the cell phone, then scrolled and handed it back to Bailey.

The ransom demand was short and clear:

One million dollars in cash in a duffel bag. Go to Fryman Canyon. Take the small path on the left for fifty yards, then turn right. Walk until you see two trees with white string tied around the trunks. Leave the

bag between them. Go home and wait for the call. If
you bring in the police, Hayley's dead.

We watched the video. It was even shorter but no less
clear. "Dad, just do what they say and everything will be
okay. Please." It was only a few seconds, and maybe it
hit me as hard as it did because I hadn't expected it, but
it was enough to reveal a soulfulness, a pureness of heart
in the young girl.

"When was the last time you saw Hayley?" I asked.

"Thursday. Or...was it Friday? Friday, I think. They
didn't have any classes on Friday, so she and Mackenzie
wanted to hang out there." He pointed to the photo of his
house in the hills. "I dropped in to check on them, make
sure they had food, whatnot."

"How old is Hayley?" I asked.

"Sixteen."

That seemed awfully young to be floating around a
party house in the Hollywood Hills with a buddy and no
supervision.

Russell read my expression. "Her mom doesn't live
far from there."

Of course. Russell and the mother were divorced.
That explained the lack of resemblance to Dani, who I
assumed was Wife 3.0.

"So you let Hayley stay there on your custody
nights?" I asked.

"We don't really have custody nights per se anymore.
Hayley pretty much stays where she wants."

Unfortunately, not tonight.

3

"We'll need a list of the names and numbers of all of Hayley's friends, especially the girl she was supposed to hang out with, Mackenzie...?"

I prepared to memorize the name. She'd be number one on our interview list.

"Struthers," Russell said. "Mackenzie Struthers—"

At that moment a woman came rushing into the room, blonde-gray hair flying, sweater hastily pulled on and hanging off her shoulders. Jeeves followed close behind her, shaking his head.

The woman cried out frantically, "Where's Hayley? What's happened to her? Russell!"

Having seen Hayley's photo, I didn't need an introduction to know that this was Raynie, Hayley's mother. Russell hung his head and put his hands behind his neck, physically ducking the verbal assault. Bailey and I went over to her and introduced ourselves, then told her what we knew. Raynie covered her mouth as she repeated, "No, oh no, oh no."

Her breathing was labored and she paled so suddenly

I thought she might pass out, so I gently took her elbow and guided her to a nearby couch. She sank down, covered her eyes, and swallowed.

"When did you last see Hayley, ma'am?" I asked.

After a few moments she answered, "When she went to stay at Russell's other house. That would've been Thursday. She said she was going to be with Mackenzie—"

"I assume Mackenzie's a good friend?" I asked.

Raynie nodded. "One of her closest buddies."

"Wait, now I remember," Russell said. "I checked in with her on Friday. She was just fine."

Raynie turned to Russell, and her expression hardened. "*You* checked up on her? Or did you send your assistant?"

Russell looked away. Obviously this was a long-standing issue between them. A not uncommon one in the entertainment industry, where many more children are raised by nannies than by biological parents—though no one ever admits it.

"Look, if you did send an assistant who's not on the premises, we'll need his or her name," I said, to cut off the feud before it became a real distraction. In my experience, family members often like to dwell on irrelevant beefs like this because it gives them an accessible target. Not that I blame them.

Russell, looking embarrassed, turned and called to Dani to come over. She and Raynie exchanged warm greetings. It was an interesting—and refreshing—change to have the ex and the current be so easy with each other.

Russell asked Dani, "Who checked in on Hayley? Was it Uma?"

Dani shook her head. "Angie." She called out to Angela, who hurried over.

"I didn't see Mackenzie there at the time," said Angela. "Hayley just said they were going to hang out, maybe go to a club—"

"What club?" I asked.

Angela stuttered, "Uh, I-I'm not sure…Teddy's?"

"Did she say when they were going? Were they going that night?" I asked.

"Sh-she didn't say. I-I'm sorry."

"No worries, Angie," I said, sorry myself for having pounced on her. "You've been very helpful."

"You know how to reach Mackenzie?" Bailey asked. Angie and Raynie simultaneously confirmed they did. Bailey called a uniform, gave him the information, and told him to go get a statement from Mackenzie. Then she turned back to the group to ask the usual question about any possible enemies Russell might have. She got a less-than-usual response.

"You're kidding, right?" Ian, the manager, gave us both an incredulous look. "He's one of the biggest directors in the world. Every actor who didn't get a part, every writer whose project he passed on, every production company he turned down—there's probably thousands who'd love to skewer him."

"*And* who are crazy enough to do it by kidnapping his daughter?" I asked.

Ian shrugged. "It's a town full of narcissists and sociopaths. You do the math."

Though true, the diagnosis wasn't helpful. At that moment Jeeves, or whatever they called their butler, entered, followed by a uniformed police officer.

"Find anything?" Bailey asked him.

"Not so far."

"Then let's get rolling." Bailey turned back to Russell. "You're going to take us to the drop site."

At nearly midnight there was no traffic to contend with. We flew up Benedict Canyon, headed east on Mulholland Highway to Laurel Canyon, and got to Fryman Road in record time. This ransom drop was as close to a crime scene as we could get at this point, and the fact that it was in a wooded canyon meant that any evidence it might yield was disappearing by the second.

"You took Fryman Road?" Bailey asked.

Russell, who was seated in front of me on the passenger side, nodded. He'd taken off his baseball cap and was kneading it between his hands. "Take Fryman to the end. We'll have to walk from there."

Fryman Canyon is beautiful during the day, but nightfall shows its other side. The towering trees blocked what little ambient light managed to reach the mouth of the canyon, and even the moon was barely visible between the dense mass of branches and leaves. Standing at the entrance to the park, I could see only a few feet of fire road. The rest was a deep, impenetrable darkness. I was glad to see the other patrol cars pull in behind us.

Russell led the way. The patrol cops fanned out and encircled us. The smell of damp earth and pungent growth filled my nostrils and we moved slowly, our flashlight beams illuminating the road ahead, but the path under our feet was left in shadow. Unwanted visions of a bloodied, battered, and possibly dead Hayley kept flashing through my mind. The moment I pushed one away, another took its place.

After a few minutes, Russell turned left on a path so narrow and overgrown I might have missed it even in daylight. The path took us straight uphill for another five minutes, and my wedge heels, comfortable enough in normal conditions, were starting to slip on the steep, grassy terrain. No one spoke as we made our way through the canyon, and every so often I could hear the rustling of creatures scurrying about in the brush just feet away. I told myself it was probably prairie dogs or rabbits, maybe a coyote, but I knew that mountain lions and bobcats had been sighted there. To say nothing of the more dangerous animals of the two-legged variety. Officers surrounded us, but I knew it would take only a second for man or animal to launch a surprise attack—too fast for any officer to be able to react in time. With each furtive sound, I could feel the skin on the back of my neck tighten and my heart beat a little faster. Finally Russell stopped at a small clearing to the right of the path.

"I left the duffel bag right there." He pointed to a spot between two trees. As described in the ransom note, both had white string tied around their trunks.

I had to admit it was a good hiding place. If you didn't know where to look, you'd never find it. We moved forward and Bailey shined her flashlight where Russell had indicated.

There was nothing there. Russell lunged forward, but Bailey pulled him back.

"We'll need to process this place for evidence, Russell. Please step back—"

Russell's body sagged and he sank to his knees as though his spine had melted. He let out a harsh bark of a sob and cried out in anguish, "Hayley! Oh God, Hayley!"

But the canyon swallowed his words as quickly as they fell from his lips. We all stood rooted but unable to watch as he dropped his head and cried. The air was heavy with the weight of unspoken belief that Hayley would never be found alive. For reasons I couldn't explain, the passive acceptance of doom made me clench my fists in anger. They might be right, but I refused to believe we were too late. At least, not yet.

4

The next morning, Bailey and I planned to get out to Russell's house in the hills bright and early. It was only seven thirty a.m., too early to reach my boss, Eric Northrup, at the office, so I called him on his cell phone.

"Hey, Eric, it's me."

"Not at this hour it isn't."

I have been forced to admit, repeatedly, that I am not morning's freshest flower. I come in as late as I can get away with. But in all fairness, I also stay later than anyone else. Since deputy district attorneys are public lawyers, we get paid a flat rate regardless of the hours we put in. So more work does not mean more pay. Toni once totaled up my hours and figured out that my actual rate of pay was about a buck seventy-five an hour. Before taxes.

"That's very funny, Eric. So funny you probably won't care about a possible new case Bailey picked up last night. And you'll be laughing so hard you probably won't mind that Vanderhorn will hear about it before you—"

"Okay, okay. Shoot."

The threat of getting holy hell from District Attorney William Vanderhorn for not bringing him up to speed on a big media case predictably got Eric's attention. I filled him in on the night's events.

"I'll call Vanderhorn and make it official for now," he said. "But if this turns into a fileable case, he'll be all over it. You might want to rethink taking on this one, Rachel."

District Attorney Vanderhorn and I got along...well, in truth, we hated each other. He liked his deputies subservient, fawning, and ubiquitous. I liked my bosses smart, trusting, and hands-off. So it was a perfect storm of disappointment for both of us. To top it off, Vanderhorn was in love with Hollywood, not just because it was a big source of campaign support, which it was. But also because he loved rubbing elbows with the stars, and the sheer glitz factor. This meant that Hayley's kidnapping case would be a chance for Vanderhorn to ingratiate himself with all the right people. So Eric was warning me ahead of time that I'd be in for a nightmarish tour of duty with Vanderhorn riding me like a Preakness pony.

"Thanks, Eric. I'll keep it in mind."

If we never found a suspect, I wouldn't have to make any decisions. But for now, I couldn't let go. I wanted to find Hayley, even if we never nailed the kidnapper.

I headed downstairs to the lobby and found Bailey sitting in her detective-mobile in the circular drive. Angel, the doorman, was talking to her through the passenger window. I walked out of the air-conditioned hotel into a wall of heat. Only eight o'clock in the morning and it already was eighty degrees and felt like it was about ninety.

"Hey, Angel, they ever going to let you get a summer uniform?" I asked. He wore the same wool slacks and gold-braided jacket all year long. It pained me to look at him.

"Sure, Rachel. Didn't you see the memo? Starting tomorrow, we all get to wear Speedos. I can't wait." He pointedly looked down at his size-forty slacks as he opened the passenger door for me.

Angel shut the door and patted the roof, and Bailey took us out to Fifth Street and northbound on the 101 freeway. Southbound traffic was virtually at a standstill, but the northbound side was blissfully wide open. I almost felt guilty as we sailed down the freeway in full view of those poor slobs mired in commuter quicksand.

"You got your buddy working on the cell site locations?" I asked.

"Yep. With a little bit of luck, she'll be able to triangulate the source of that first text message sent from Hayley's phone. And we're pulling all of Russell's and Hayley's cell phone records."

"But that's only going to help with the first message. The actual ransom demand was an e-mail." Which meant it didn't necessarily come from a cell. There hadn't been any standard sign-off like "Sent from my iPhone," so we couldn't yet tell what device it had come from.

Bailey gripped the steering wheel. "I know."

I shifted in my seat and tried to control my agitation. I could feel time passing, the seconds turning into minutes, minutes into hours, the hours into days. Although it hadn't even been twenty-four hours since the ransom note was sent, Hayley's peril increased exponentially with each passing moment. The tightness in Bailey's voice told me she was feeling it too.

We got off at Highland and took Sunset Boulevard west. Prosaic strip malls, dry cleaners, and thrift shops gave way to giant billboards touting the latest movies, television series, and vodka, and chic little shops selling belts that cost more than a month's salary. Bailey turned north and we headed through narrow winding streets into the Hollywood Hills. High atop one of those hills sat Russell Antonovich's "party" house: a low-slung Spanish-style with tiled roof and arched wooden door. As was the case with so many of the homes perched on hills like this, the house looked tiny from the street. But I knew from past experience that most of it stretched backward, propped up on stilts, cantilevered out over the hillside. One of the gardeners was blowing leaves and grass cuttings off the neighbor's sloped driveway. We would've gotten a windshield full of it, but Bailey stopped short and honked. The gardener waved and aimed his wind gun elsewhere.

A uniformed officer standing guard in front of the door was talking to a Hispanic woman who looked upset. We introduced ourselves and asked the officer what was going on.

"She's the maid. Guess they forgot to tell her we sealed the place."

I held out my hand to her and introduced myself and Bailey.

"My name is Maria Sosa," she said in heavily accented English, giving my hand a tentative shake. "What happened?"

"I really can't say at the moment, I'm sor—"

"Is it Hayley? Did something happen to her?"

"We...don't know just yet." I shouldn't have said that much, but Maria's concern for Hayley was so sincere, I couldn't completely shut her out with a non-answer. "How long have you been working here?"

"Three years. *Ay,* it would be terrible if something happened to Hayley. You must help her," Maria said, her eyes filling with tears. "She's a good girl, you know? A little wild sometimes, but always nice. She try to help me learn English..." She wiped her eyes with the back of her hand.

I gave her a moment to collect herself. "When was the last time you saw her?"

"Thursday."

"Was that the last time you were here?"

"*Sí.* I work Monday to Thursday."

"Was anyone else here with her?"

Maria nodded. "Her friend, Mackenzie. The little sad one."

"Why do you say she's sad? Did something happen?"

Maria shrugged. "I don' know anything really. She jus' seem like that to me."

Interesting. "Was anyone else here?"

"No."

I took her full name and phone number and told her she wouldn't be able to clean the house for a little while and that I'd tell Russell she'd been there. I hoped he'd pay her until we released the house. After all, it wasn't her fault she couldn't get in to work.

"Any idea when the criminalist is coming?" the uniformed officer asked.

Bailey looked at her watch. "Within the hour."

"You get Dorian?" I asked. Dorian Struck was the best criminalist in the business. In her twenty-odd years she'd seen it all and tested most of it. But she was a notoriously tough old bird who was a tyrant when it came to preserving her scenes. If she caught us stepping into the house before she'd processed it, she'd have our heads on spikes.

"I think so."

Dorian was always in demand, so she wasn't always available. But a high-profile case like this could put the whole crime lab under a microscope. Pun intended. I was willing to bet big money her boss would make sure she got here. Dorian herself never cared one way or another. High-profile, low-profile, it was all the same to her. All she cared about was the evidence.

Bailey turned to the officer. "We just want to take a quick look. We won't go inside."

The officer gave her an incredulous stare, then shook his head. "If Dorian catches you, you're on your own. They don't pay me enough." The officer opened the door and stepped aside.

We stood on the threshold and leaned in as far as we could without falling. The tiled foyer led to a sunken living room that had a panoramic view of the city, as well as a swimming pool that ran from the middle of the room, under the glass wall, and out to the edge of the backyard. I'd have loved its sheer craziness if I didn't know how well rats could swim. I supposed Russell kept an exterminator on permanent retainer. I couldn't help but wonder whether that was a metaphor for his life in general. I recognized the iron fence surrounding the perimeter of the property as the one Hayley had been standing in front of in the photograph. I made a mental note to check whether there was enough background in the video to tell whether she was still here when it was recorded.

"What the hell do you two think you're doing?"

"Shit," I whispered.

Bailey rolled her eyes and we jumped back, away from the threshold. Dorian had arrived.

5

She pushed her sunglasses on top of her gray crew cut and planted her short, squat frame in front of us, hands on hips. "You two been in there already? 'Cause if you have..." The look in her eyes finished the sentence.

"Absolutely not," I said.

"I wouldn't let her," said Bailey—the obnoxious, kiss-ass traitor.

I shot her a sidelong look. "I'd never—"

Dorian cut me off with a wave of her hand. "I've got no time for this, Tweedledum and Tweedledee. You want the house and backyard?"

"Yeah." Bailey explained what we were looking for and where the investigation stood at this point.

"Okay," Dorian said. "Now feel free to get going. I sure as hell don't need you here."

We saluted and left. As Bailey pulled away I asked, "What was that 'I wouldn't let her' business all about?"

"Just earning a few credibility points for future use—"

"At my expense—"

"You're not the one who has to pull favors to get her.

Sometimes you got to take the hit for a higher cause. There's no 'I' in 'team,' Knight."

"Yeah, but there is one in 'kiss-ass.'"

"You'll thank me the next time we need her and I have the suck to pull her out of rotation."

She was probably right about that, but it didn't stop me from privately vowing to get even sometime soon. Bailey's smirking glance told me she knew what I was thinking. It's not always a great thing having someone know you that well.

We rode through the traffic in silence for a few moments, then suddenly Bailey gave a short laugh. "What a trip. Ian Powers was little Mattie—"

Russell Antonovich's manager and business partner.

"And he still knows how to turn on that cutesy smile," I said. "So you watched the show too?"

"Never," Bailey said. I gave her a look. "Okay, once in a while."

We turned left at Outpost Drive and I enjoyed the view of the charming, old, and very pricey neighborhood as we headed over the hill and into the Valley to Clarington Academy, where we planned to brace up Hayley's bestie, Mackenzie Struthers. The uniform who'd questioned her late last night hadn't gotten much of anything out of her. It was our turn to try.

"Want to call the principal and have Mackenzie ready for us?" Bailey asked.

"Nope. I got her cell number from Raynie. I'll call her when we get there. The less lead time, the better."

"Good point."

I had no particular reason to think Mackenzie would lie to us. But my experience with teenagers has taught me that they invariably keep secrets from the adult world and they consider it an honor to guard those secrets closely. I don't think it's nefarious, I think it's just tribal loyalty. With a little time, I could probably earn enough of Mackenzie's trust to get her to open up. But with Hayley's life hanging in the balance, time was the one thing I didn't have. I needed to know it all and I needed to know it right now. The less time Mackenzie had to ruminate and sift through what she did or didn't want to share, the better.

And I had the element of surprise on my side because Hayley's kidnapping wasn't public knowledge yet. We'd decided to keep it all under wraps for the moment in the hope that it would induce the kidnapper to release Hayley. But that strategy was a short-term option; we wouldn't be able to keep it quiet for long. Someone was bound to leak, and soon. There were dozens of employees, assistants, all their friends, and then there were cops and all *their* friends, and...you get the picture. And even if no one leaked, we couldn't afford to wait more than a couple of days without running the risk that we were exposing Hayley to greater peril by keeping it quiet. If she didn't turn up in the next day or so, we'd have to change strategies and put the story out there to ratchet up pressure on the kidnapper to let her go.

Bailey badged our way into the principal's office—which was casually yet tastefully decorated like no public school principal's office I'd ever seen—and explained in as little detail as possible that we were there on official business that didn't involve any student misconduct. The principal looked confused, but he was cowed enough not to ask questions. He gave us the run of the school grounds. Bailey and I moved outside the building, where we wouldn't be overheard, and I called Mackenzie on her cell.

Raising my voice by at least an octave, I said, "Hey! Where've you been? I been lookin' for ya!"

"At the track," Mackenzie huffed, out of breath. "I gotta make up—uh, is that you, Jess?"

Bingo. I'd managed to sound like her buddy Jess. Whoever that was.

"What?" I asked. "You're breaking up..." I pretended we got cut off and ended the call. "You see the track?" I asked Bailey.

"Dead ahead."

Bailey led the way as we trotted quickly toward the track, which was just behind the principal's office on a big, well-tended field. Luckily, there was only one girl running laps with a cell phone in her hand. She was average height, about five feet five, but her long, gangly frame made her seem taller. And it was clear that running was not her "thing." Her legs flailed out at the knees and her hands flopped as she bounced down the track, and even from the distance of one hundred feet, I could see she was red-faced and winded. Of course, in this heat even a strong runner would be boiling. When she neared us, I flagged her down. "Mackenzie!"

She didn't respond at first, and I noticed she had earbuds on, so I waved my arms and called to her again. She glanced at me but didn't immediately stop her slow, ungainly jog until Bailey held up her badge. That got her attention. She came to a dead halt, eyes bulging, as she pulled out her earbuds. Though Mackenzie was sweating, she blanched and almost stumbled as she moved toward us.

"Come on, sit over here." I gestured to a shady section of the bleachers. Mackenzie watched us warily, but she followed us without a word and sat down. "We need to talk to you about Hayley. We're looking for her."

An expression of alarm crossed Mackenzie's face. "What happened?"

"That's what we need you to tell us, Mackenzie," Bailey said, in her stern "just the facts, ma'am" voice.

"I-I already told the officer last night. I don't know anything—"

I positioned my body so the sun wouldn't blind me and looked at her steadily. "But you two were together on Thursday. You went to Teddy's with her. And we know you were staying with her at Russell's house in the hills."

At the mention of their night at Teddy's, Mackenzie swallowed so hard I could practically hear the gulp. The fact that I already had that much information hinted that I knew a great deal more, and as I'd intended, it rocked Mackenzie's bearings. Now was the time to offer reassurance and gain some trust. I shook my head. "We're not here to bust you for clubbing. We just need to know when you last saw Hayley and whether anything...unusual happened."

Mackenzie worked her jaw silently for a moment, absorbing this. "I...you're right, we went to Teddy's on Thursday. But I went home on Friday morning. I haven't seen her since then."

"Will anyone at home verify that? Your mom—"

"My mom's dead." She tried to make it sound flat, casual, but the strain in her voice undermined the effort.

Thus Maria's observation that she was the "sad one."
"I'm so sorry, Mackenzie," I said gently. She didn't look up, so I moved past it quickly to give her an escape. "Your dad. If I call him, he'll say you came home on Friday?"

"Yeah." Her unstudied monotone told me it was true. "I had to go home. I had a job interview at a plant nursery called Pretty Maids on Melrose. You can check if you don't believe me."

"I believe you, Mackenzie. Did you two hang out with anyone new at Teddy's?" I asked.

Mackenzie frowned, then shook her head as she tucked a hank of her long, straight brown hair behind her right ear.

"Did your boyfriends go to Teddy's with you?" I knew better than to think that any boyfriends were along for that ride; bouncers are a lot more reluctant to let fake IDs pass for guys than for girls. But I was fishing for information about any guys who might've had access to Hayley.

"I don't have a boyfriend…"

I took a shot in the dark. "But Hayley does. Was he there?"

"No."

Though I didn't want to scare her off by getting too pushy, I was starting to lose my patience with this choppy exchange. "Listen, Mackenzie, you must've figured out that something serious is up. A cop showed up at your house last night and now we're talking to you. Obviously Hayley's not in school and no one seems to know where she is. As far as we can figure, other than her dad, you're the only one who's seen her since Thursday. So it's very important that you tell us whatever you know, whatever you saw, that might help us find her. Understand?"

Mackenzie stared over my shoulder. She looked frightened but, oddly, not shocked. She knew something she wasn't telling, that much I was sure of.

"Was Hayley unhappy? Did she run away?"

Mackenzie bit her lip and blinked rapidly. "I—don't think so. She never said so. I mean, she's had her stuff with her mom and dad, but who doesn't?"

No argument there. "And you have no idea where she might've gone? Maybe a friend's house?"

"I don't know, but I don't think so." Mackenzie clasped her hands together in her lap and stared down at them. "I—I wouldn't make her mom suffer like that if I knew where she was. Raynie's so nice..."

"But not Russell?" I asked, though I knew her answer might not have had anything to do with Russell. Having lost her own mother, it made sense that Mackenzie would focus on Hayley's mother. But I was trying to find a way to pry her open.

Mackenzie shook her head. "No, no, Russell's cool. Way cooler than my dad. I mean, he lets us use his house in the hills, his town car, stuff like that. But he's not around as much as Raynie, you know?"

I did know. Hayley had the cool dad. That he was also a world-famous director was not as important as the fact that he facilitated their lifestyle and partying. I wondered if it had occurred to her yet that Russell's "coolness" might've been what put Hayley in harm's way. Probably not. No teenager believes there's such a thing as too much freedom.

The sun had moved since we'd sat down and now threatened to fry the left side of my face. I shifted to the right to get under the shade of a large jacaranda and pondered my next move. I wanted it to be a cold shower. I could feel the sweat beading up under my blouse and my hair sticking to the back of my neck. "What about Hayley's boyfriend? Could she be with him? Or maybe he knows where she is?"

Her face darkened. "I don't know if she's with him, but if she isn't, he'd probably know where she is. Hayley tells him everything."

Was that a note of jealousy? "They're pretty close, huh?"

"Yeah."

"How long have they been together?"

"Not that long. About two, three months, something like that. At first they were just friends, but then it was like all of a sudden they were joined at the hip. I never got to see her without him."

Definitely jealousy. "You know where he lives?"

Mackenzie shook her head.

"Do you have his cell?"

"Yeah." Mackenzie had a guilty look as she pulled out her cell phone and began to scroll. I had a feeling I knew why.

"Do Hayley's parents know about this guy?"

Mackenzie shook her head. "No one knows about him. Except me and a few of the girls we hang with." She handed her phone to me.

I looked at the entry. "Brian Shandling." I handed the phone to Bailey so she could get the information. "I'm guessing you knew him better than the others, am I right?"

"Probably."

"Because you were closer to Hayley than anyone else."

Mackenzie nodded. "Pretty much."

"How old is Brian?"

"Eighteen? Maybe nineteen. Yeah, I think he's nineteen."

"You have a picture of him?" I gestured to her cell phone.

Mackenzie picked up her phone and accessed her photos. After a few seconds, she held the phone out. "That's him."

The photo showed a nice-looking guy, tallish and slender, with dark brown eyes, curly brown hair, and one of those charming crinkly smiles that says "I'm a nice guy who sends his mom flowers on her birthday." He had an arm around Hayley, who was snuggling into his chest with a happy smile. It was a sweet picture. They looked like the kind of kids you rooted for, the ones who gave you hope for a nicer, kinder generation. My heart sank at the thought that one of them might be in grave danger.

"I'm going to forward this to Bailey's phone," I said. "Okay?" Not that I needed her permission, but it felt like the civilized thing to do.

"Yeah, sure."

"Does this guy go to college? Have a job?"

Mackenzie shrugged. "Don't know." But her eyes darted away from mine as she answered. Another possibility entered the equation.

"Is it possible Hayley ran away with Brian? Would she do that without telling you?"

Mackenzie picked up the earbud wire and looped it around her fingers. "I don't know...I wouldn't have thought so before. But now..."

The unspoken end of the sentence: Since Brian the Interloper had come between her and Hayley, all bets were off. But that made me consider a less savory possibility.

"What do you think of Brian?"

"He's okay, I guess."

"Is he the kind of guy who might hurt Hayley?"

Mackenzie jerked up, her expression stunned, and shook her head vigorously. "Never! No!" She frowned. "I kind of felt like he got between me and Hayley, and she's my best friend in the world, so, you know..." Mackenzie shrugged, then looked directly at me for the first time. "But there was nothing bad about him. He's a really good guy. Even to me. I just didn't like that after he showed up, there was hardly any time for just me and Hayley."

Pretty forthright and fair-minded of her to admit all that. And the sentiment felt genuine. I'd been considering the possibility that Brian had kidnapped Hayley to make some fast money—and I wasn't about to let go of that theory just yet. But if Mackenzie's assessment was accurate, it was a less likely scenario than the alternative I'd been considering: that Hayley had run away with Brian and cooked up the kidnapping scheme to give them some starter money. It was an ugly possibility, and one that spoke to some serious problems between Hayley and her parents. But it did have the virtue of ensuring Hayley's survival. At least until we brought her home and her father got hold of her.

"When did you last see Brian?"

"The last time I saw him was when he met us at Starbucks after school on Wednesday."

"And there was nothing unusual about Hayley when you left her on Friday morning?"

"Yeah. I mean, no. She didn't tell me...I mean, I didn't know of anything wrong."

Uh-uh. That last answer was a big clam. Something unusual had gone down, and whatever it was had her plenty worried. But short of holding her upside down and shaking her by her heels, we had no way of making her tell us. She wasn't worried enough to spill the beans. Not yet, anyway.

6

I quizzed Mackenzie a little while longer about Hayley's habits and haunts, got the names of the girls in their crowd, but learned nothing else of any great moment. Then we got the principal to pull his records on Hayley, Mackenzie, and the rest of the crowd. There probably wasn't much of use to us there, but you never know. And I have yet to regret collecting too much information.

"Let's reconnoiter," Bailey said.

"What?"

"Let's go sit in the car, blast the AC, and figure out what's next."

My sticky blouse and wet hair made that sound like a capital idea. "Reconnoitering it is," I said.

Bailey cranked up the AC and I lifted my hair and held my head near the vent to catch the cool air. Mackenzie's demeanor had set off alarm bells in my head. From what I could see, Hayley's disappearance was no shock to her. But if I was right about that, and Hayley's disappearance was planned, then something must've happened that wasn't part of the plan. Or at least she was afraid that it had. "Maybe it's time to let the captain call the press. After all, it's been more than twelve hours since Russell delivered the ransom money. Don't you think the kidnapper should've released her by now?"

Bailey rubbed her temples. It was a big decision. If we didn't go public with the story, we might miss out on a citizen sighting that could save her life, but if we did, it might just spook the kidnapper into killing Hayley.

"Let's take the middle step: report her missing without saying anything about a kidnapping," Bailey said. "Mackenzie already knows that much anyway, so it's probably long since been Facebooked and tweeted all over their school."

"Yeah, that way, our kidnapper might believe Russell hasn't told anyone, and he'll feel safe enough to release her. I agree, let's do it."

Given the circumstances, it seemed the best alternative. "You let the parents know," Bailey said as she pulled out her cell phone. I got through to both Russell and Raynie within seconds and both quickly gave their approval. "Whatever it takes," Raynie said. "I guess so, yeah," Russell said. When I finished, Bailey was still on the phone, so I leafed through the school records.

When Bailey ended the call, I suggested we try contacting Brian. She hit the number and put the phone to her ear. I could hear it go to voice mail. "Hi, you've reached Brian, leave me a message, I'll getcha back. *Beep.*"

Bailey left a message telling him to call.

"So maybe they did run off together?" I asked.

Bailey frowned. "It'd be nice, wouldn't it? I mean, not *nice,* necessarily—"

"No, but shaking down your own father is a lot nicer than being kidnapped, assaulted, and maybe killed." Everything's relative.

Bailey picked up her cell again. "I'm calling in boyfriend Brian's info, see what we can get on him."

While she did that, I considered my impression of Hayley. I shared it when Bailey ended her call. "I know it's a little soon, but I get the feeling that Hayley's a decent sort."

Bailey gave me a sidelong glance. "Why? Because she deigned to be nice to Scholarship Girl?"

"And Mackenzie has a job—something none of those kids seems to have...or need."

"Makes her an unusual choice for a bestie in that crowd—"

"Especially for a major leaguer like Hayley Antonovich," I said. Bailey nodded. "No, I got to admit, Hayley's definitely not the spoiled rich kid I expected."

At least not so far. My ruminations on Hayley were interrupted by the thumping bass of a car stereo that was getting louder and louder. It hit full blast as the car pulled in a few spaces away. The vehicle was a brand-new red Mercedes black-top convertible, and the driver, a boy with Justin Bieber hair who couldn't have been more than sixteen years old, was rocking out and talking on his iPhone. The song ended and he cut the engine and got out, still talking. "Yo, dude, check it out, you can come with me." He hit the remote to lock the car and continued as he walked away. "The folks got a house in Virgin Gorda, man. Infinity pool, seven bedrooms, bring the sex box."

"Gag," Bailey said.

"Xbox. It's a video gaming thing."

Bailey watched him saunter to class. "I know. And I meant gag."

At that moment the principal came out and headed toward the faculty parking lot. I noticed that lot was filled with Hondas, Toyotas, and Fords. Not a Mercedes or BMW to be found. "Want to hit up a few other friends while we're here?" I asked.

"Sure. Maybe get some more information on our buddy Brian."

I got out of the car and called out to the principal. "Mr. Vogel!"

He gave us his blessing to go and talk to any of Hayley's friends we could find and escorted us back into the school.

"You have a list of names?" he asked.

We gave him the three names we'd gotten from Mackenzie that matched up with the names Hayley's mother had provided. It was a tight little group of girls who'd apparently been together since grade school. Mackenzie was the only newcomer. Mr. Vogel set us up in his conference room. Another first: a high school principal with his own private conference room.

We'd hoped for a break, but we would have settled for just one or two new ideas about where Hayley might've gone or where we might find her boyfriend, Brian. What we got was shock, tears, and a blurry string of "I'm not sures" and "Ask Mackenzies." But two things struck me: Hayley's friends were truly nice kids who seemed to have a lot more going on than Mr. Sex Box. One was a World Health Organization volunteer who planned to join the peace corps, another was a science buff who was aiming for a career in green technology, and a third had her sights set on a pediatric practice that would include charity work in underprivileged neighborhoods. The second thing was that everyone sincerely seemed to have undying love for Hayley.

"No one's a better friend than Hayley...she's always had my back, since we were in kindergarten...I'd take a bullet for her, seriously."

Not a catty remark, bitter gibe, or hint of reservation from anyone. But no immediately helpful information either. The only thing we managed to establish was that no one had seen Brian since Wednesday, and the last they'd seen of Hayley was in school on Thursday. A smidgen of light came from bestie Jordana Bloom, the future pediatrician. Her flowing gauzy maxi dress and sparkly flip-flops were a marked contrast to the cutoffs and capris the other girls had worn, and I admired her style—not to mention the fact that she looked a lot more cool and comfortable than I felt.

"We didn't see a whole lot of Brian," she said. "But he seemed really nice."

"So he didn't hang with you guys?" I asked.

"I don't think he could afford to."

"Hayley wouldn't pay his way?"

"Oh, no, she would have. Brian wouldn't let her. Once, we were all going to go to Gold Class Cinema, and he said he couldn't make it. Hayley told him she'd take care of it, and he, like, said, 'NO.' Not mean or anything, just, like, that was it. I could tell he didn't want her paying for stuff for him."

Gold Class Cinema is a movie theater with first-class airplane-style recliners that make into a bed, and full food and alcohol service delivered right to your seat. It could set you back an easy fifty bucks a pop. So I got why a guy of even average means might find the experience a little rich for his wallet.

"Did he have a job?" I asked.

Jordana's brow furrowed. "I think he worked...was it in the Galleria?"

I couldn't help her, since of course I was the one who'd asked the question.

Jordana continued, "I think...yeah."

"So if Brian's such a good guy, how come Hayley never introduced him to her parents?"

Jordana looked pained. "I don't know. Maybe because she was afraid they wouldn't think he was good enough for her? He was older, he wasn't in college, didn't have any money...I don't really know. I'm just guessing."

"But there was nothing...skeevy about him? Or dangerous?"

Jordana leaned back as though I'd thrown something at her. "No. No way."

I knew we should wrap it up. Jordana didn't have anything more for us, and I didn't want to have to offer more reassurance than we could honestly give her at this point, so I decided to see if there was any meat on the bone of my elopement theory. "Did Hayley get along with her father?"

Jordana seemed surprised by the question. "I guess. I mean, we never talked about him like that."

"So she never talked about her father. Or her mother?"

She shrugged as though the question had never occurred to her before. Probably because it hadn't. "Stuff he was working on, but that's all."

I supposed it made sense. At her age, parents were wallets with legs. And these were big wallets. We thanked Jordana and headed back to Bailey's car to "reconnoiter" again.

Bailey cranked up the AC and picked up her cell. "I want to make sure the photo of Brian made it to the station and give the update on what Jordana told us. See what they've come up with so far." She tapped in the number, then swore softly. "For some reason, I'm suddenly not getting any signal. Let me try outside." She got out of the car and walked a few steps away, then began to speak. After a couple of minutes, I leaned forward to see what was going on, but her back was to me. It was another five minutes before she returned to the car. But when she got in, she stared out through the windshield for long minutes without speaking.

"What?" I finally asked.

Bailey continued to stare out the window as she spoke. "Brian Shandling does not exist. It's a fake name."

7

The wheels in my brain skidded to a stop. The entire landscape had changed. If Mr. Nice Guy was a fraud, then my theory—or more accurately my hope—that Hayley might be shacked up with her boyfriend on an island in the Bahamas was a pipe dream.

"They ran the name, found an apartment address, a couple of credit cards, and a driver's license with a photo that matches our guy, but the DOB comes back to a dead two-year-old in Utah. I've put an alert out for him and for any activity on his credit cards," Bailey said.

"Did he have a car?"

"A white Toyota Corolla. I've got an alert out on that too."

Bailey started the car and pulled out of the parking lot.

"Did you have unis door-knock the neighborhood?" I asked. Any activity over the past few days at Russell's house in the Hollywood Hills could provide a crucial lead.

"Yeah. No one heard anything weird. The closest

neighbor's assistant was home waiting for a FedEx package, and he remembered hearing car doors slam at the house on Monday morning, but no screams, no sounds of struggle. Nothing unusual."

Damn it. We needed to catch a break here. We didn't have time for these friggin' dead ends. I tried hard to keep myself from imagining what might be happening to Hayley at this very moment. "What's up with all these assistants?" I asked irritably. "Why couldn't this neighbor just sign the notice and leave it taped to the door like the rest of us?"

"Yes, let's blame the assistant for not breaking the case for us. That makes perfect sense."

I hate being busted for irrational crankiness. I was about to come up with a suitably cutting remark when I noticed that Bailey was driving like we were responding to a robbery in progress. "Why are we heading back to Hollywood? Shouldn't we at least stop by the Galleria while we're out here and see if we can figure out where Brian works—or, rather, worked?"

"Because I've already got someone tracking down his employment records, and it occurred to me that it might be more important to hit his apartment first."

She was right, so I shut up and tried to hang on to my stomach as Bailey flew down the winding Laurel Canyon Boulevard. Laurel Canyon climbs from Studio City in the San Fernando Valley up and over the ridge and snakes down the other side into West Hollywood. It's a storied canyon that was once home to a variety of megatalents, like Frank Zappa, Jim Morrison, Steven Tyler, and Joni Mitchell, and currently home to my bestie Toni LaCollier, who lived at the top of the hill off

Kirkwood—though in all honesty she couldn't carry a tune in a bucket. Toni was already a Special Trials prosecutor when I got transferred into the unit. We'd bonded so fast we agreed that we had to have been sisters in a past life. Her tiny house in the canyon hadn't been much when she bought it—a lot of the houses in the area had gone to seed—but Toni had the gift of artistry and style. Within six months, she'd turned the run-down "fixer" into a unique little gem.

The canyon retains a lot of bohemian-type charm— the Country Store, where everyone shops for munchies, still sports a hippie-style psychedelic sign—but the main canyon road, originally designed to handle only Sunday cruising, has become a primary artery for the burgeoning Valley population that travels into Hollywood. As a result, the road turns into a parking lot at least three times a day.

Luckily, we'd missed the morning-drive slog and Bailey made it into West Hollywood in less than twenty minutes. Brian's apartment was in one of those typical nondescript buildings—a box with square windows in the heart of Hollywood on North Vista Street. The building across the road had tiny balconies where tenants grew plants and stored kids' toys and bicycles, evidence that humans lived there. Brian's building didn't have any of that. The only visible signs of individuality were the differing curtains, and one hanging crystal ornament. It probably made a nice rainbow when the sun hit it. I miss unicorns.

Brian's landlord was frowning suspiciously at the uniformed officers who'd shown up to secure the place. He was short, and his wifebeater T-shirt strained to cover a paunch that looked like a second-trimester pregnancy. The plaid Bermuda shorts and black socks with slippers completed the look nicely.

"If Drew knew about the hunks you ran into on the job, he'd go out of his mind," I said.

"Yeah, I'll bet Graden would lose a lot of sleep too."

Bailey introduced herself to the landlord and held out her badge. He took it and squinted for a moment, then pulled a pair of filthy glasses out of his shorts pocket, put them on, and scrutinized the identification before handing it back to her.

"And you? Who are you?" he asked me in a heavy Middle Eastern accent.

"Rachel Knight, deputy district attorney. I'm a prosecutor in the Special Trials Unit."

"Easy to say. Let's see some ID, Ms. Special Attorney."

"Look, Mr.—," Bailey began, her voice showing the strain of holding back words she'd regret.

"Gardanian. And I own the building, so I have the right—"

In no great mood to begin with, and out of patience, I brandished my badge and held it under his nose, just to shut him up. He took it and gave it the once-over, then handed it back to me.

"Okay." He waved us in, then shuffled back into his apartment.

A uni who was a classic mesomorph with bulging biceps—the type I used to think was dreamy back in high school—gestured for us to follow him down the hall to Brian's apartment. He flashed us an amused look as we fell in behind him.

"He give you guys trouble too?" I asked.

"He tried to shake us down," the uni said. "Claimed the tenant took the only key and he'd have to charge us for the time and trouble to get another one made."

"You're kidding."

"Nope. So I told him not to worry, we had a skeleton key that would work on all doors. Then we showed him our battering ram. All of a sudden he remembered he kept a key for emergencies."

We got to the end of the hall and he gestured to the open door on the left.

"You cleared it?" Bailey asked. "No one here?"

"Empty. From the looks of it, I'd say whoever lived here isn't coming back."

Bailey and I walked in. The apartment had that damp mildew smell that old, poorly maintained buildings get. The threadbare but richly stained sofa and badly nicked wooden coffee table in the living room told me this had probably been a furnished apartment. I realized that we shouldn't be tromping around in what might be another crime scene.

"Shouldn't we get everyone out of here and call Dorian?" I asked.

Bailey sighed. "Too late. I couldn't take the chance that Brian might be holding Hayley here, or that she might be..."

I nodded. If there's a victim who's potentially wounded or in danger, you don't call the criminalist and wait to process the scene. Bailey had rightly called in the cavalry. But that meant that by now at least a dozen officers had already barged in and checked every nook and cranny, so our being here wouldn't make a whole lot of difference. But that didn't mean I wanted to be in the zip code when Dorian arrived.

Bailey and I kept our hands to ourselves to at least avoid adding our prints to the hundreds left by all the unis as we made our way through the tiny one-bedroom. And I saw that the uni was right: the place was vacant. The closets and medicine cabinet were standing open and empty, and there was nothing on the pine nightstand or dresser. I noticed that the bed was made neatly, but the cover was mussed—as though someone had sat on it.

"Did any of you guys sit on the bed?" I asked the uni.

"Not that I saw. But I'll check and confirm."

"Has anyone door-knocked the tenants?" Bailey asked him.

"Jennings, Kowalski, and Lopez took the duty. I think there's only, like, twelve units, so they're probably about done now. I'll tell 'em you're here."

Bailey nodded and I watched him walk away. She caught me enjoying the view. "You still shopping?" she asked.

"No, Sister Mary Catherine. But there's no law against looking, is there?"

Bailey smiled. Her cell rang and she moved to a corner to take the call. I went to check out the kitchen. Using a dish towel, I opened the refrigerator. Not much there. Just a pint of milk, a half-eaten loaf of potato bread, and a near-empty jar of peanut butter. That told me Brian hadn't left in haste. He'd eaten down his food reserve, knowing he was going to leave. But he also might've been too poor to keep a lot around. Bailey was still on the phone when the uni came back. I thought it might be time to find out what they called him when he was at home. No harm in asking a guy's name, right?

"Hey, Ms. Knight—"

"Call me Rachel. And you are...?"

"Justin." He held out his hand. "Justin Wagner. Nice to meet you."

As we shook I noticed he had brown eyes and really long dark lashes. Memories of the cornerback I'd crushed on in high school came flooding back and I had to force myself to focus on the task at hand.

"Did we get any response from the tenants?" I asked.

"Yeah, Kowalski got something. He's out in the hall. You want me to bring him in?"

I glanced at Bailey, who was still on the phone. "No, that's cool. I'll talk to him."

Justin turned to lead me out and said over his shoulder, "Oh, and none of us ever sat on that bed."

Kowalski delivered on the cliché with a Marlon Brando, thick-shouldered build, though he looked a little too buttoned-down to do the whole "Stella!" routine. I introduced myself and asked what he had, and he hooked his thumbs under his Sam Browne and stood "at ease" with legs apart as he spoke. "The old lady on the next floor in 2A, Iris Stavros, said she saw Brian on Monday, around noon. He was with a short blonde girl."

We'd show her a photo to make sure, but it had to be Hayley. And noon. According to the time stamp on Russell's text, that would've been after the proof-of-life photo was sent but before the e-mailed ransom demand.

"How did she happen to see them?"

"They were coming in as she was going out. She said she was on her way to the store to get some milk." He glanced upward as if to make sure Iris wasn't listening, then lowered his voice. "You ask me, she was gonna buy something a little stronger."

Iris Stavros might turn out to be an important witness. If she also turned out to be a heavy drinker, it'd be a real problem when she hit the stand. I'd have to do a lot of checking before I put her on a witness list. "Did she notice any signs of struggle or force, anything unusual?"

"No. Matter of fact, she said she'd seen the girl around here many times in the past couple of months. Seemed to her that they were boyfriend and girlfriend."

But none of that meant Hayley hadn't been kidnapped. Brian could've been hiding a gun, in which case Hayley wouldn't have dared to struggle. Or maybe at that particular time, Hayley hadn't known she was being kidnapped. She didn't necessarily have to know that Brian took the photo of her at the Hollywood Hills house in order to use it later as proof of life. In fact, it would've been smart of him to keep everything looking normal for as long as possible. That way he wouldn't have to worry about controlling Hayley until it was absolutely necessary.

"Did you ask her how well she knew Brian?"

"Said she'd known him a little less than a year, but that he seemed okay. He'd help her with groceries, that kind of thing. She didn't say he was a 'nice young man,' but that was the gist of it."

"Thanks, Stanley."

He frowned. "Name's Evan."

"Right, I was just kid—"

Evan squinted at me. "Stan's my brother."

Of course he was.

8

Bailey joined us in the hallway, a worried look on her face. Without preamble, she tersely ordered the unis to stand guard on Brian's apartment until our criminalist got there, then headed for the car. I trotted to catch up and jumped in as she gunned the engine.

I quickly brought her up to speed on what I'd learned, aware that whatever she'd just heard on her phone call wasn't good, because she was taking it out on the gas pedal. Bailey listened to my report without comment as she whipped down Hollywood Boulevard. I wrapped up my assessment of Iris Stavros and asked, "Want to tell me why we're traveling at warp speed, Captain Kirk?"

"The news release paid off, sort of. We got a tip from a guy at a cybercafé in Silver Lake. Claims he 'sniffed' someone sending a ransom note."

"Sniffing," the hacker's term for spying on someone's Internet mailings, is incredibly easy to do in a cybercafé. Don't ask me how they do it, I'm a computer Luddite. I only know about it because Graden is a computer whizbang, and he'd told me stories from some of the hacking cases he'd handled.

"That's all? I mean, that's great, but…" The call had taken a lot longer than it should have for just that.

"Brian, or whatever his real name is, had a lot of jobs before he landed the gig in the Sherman Oaks Galleria. The first sign of him in L.A. was about a year ago. He was a busboy at the Pinot Gris. Three months later, he turned up as a waiter at the Hungry Pig. Two months after that, he applied for a security job at a Bank of America a few blocks away from the Hungry Pig. He hung on to that job for four months, and then he landed his job as a jewelry store manager in the Galleria."

The progression was unremarkable. They were the typical low-level jobs young adults took to make ends meet until they figured out a career goal. And the move from security guard to jewelry store manager made perfect sense to me. I shrugged. "Doesn't seem all that unusual." But Bailey's expression looked ominous.

"Not until you factor in the locations. Except for the Galleria, every single one of those jobs was within walking distance of Russell's studio. And the Galleria? That was just a stone's throw from Hayley's school."

I tried to make the pieces fit, but no matter how I turned them around in my mind, they refused to fall into place. "I would've said that sounded like Brian had been stalking Hayley for the past year, but he spent most of his time circling Russell's studio."

"Right. And we can check with the parents, but I doubt Hayley hung out at daddy's studio much."

"No." Not at this age. She had her own world. And so did daddy.

Bailey pulled up to the cybercafé, charmingly named Head of Steam. It looked like any Coffee Bean, just with more tables. As we searched the room for our tipster, I got a strange and unappealing glimpse into the future: everyone there was transfixed by a computer screen, and most wore headphones. Though there were signs of life as we know it around the cash register, the rest of the café was eerily quiet; the primary sound was the clicking of laptop keys, the conversations virtual, not verbal. Was this where we were headed? Eye contact traded for Skype, personal discourse traded for e-mails or, worse, blogs? Thankfully, further depressing predictions were curtailed when our tipster spotted us and waved us over.

Pierced nose and lower lip, greasy black hair combed up in back and into long spikes at the sides of his face, skinny jeans that had room to bag on even skinnier legs, and black high-top sneakers. It came as no surprise to me that his name was Legs Roscoe. With the preliminary introductions completed, we got right down to business.

"I was just hanging out—"

"Sorry to stop you, but do you remember what day it was?" I asked.

"Yeah, it was Monday. Had to be well after five o'clock."

"And how do you know that?"

"Because my last class ends at four and traffic's a bitch that time of day. So I couldn't have gotten here much before that." Legs dipped his head. "I, uh, didn't mean to 'sniff' anyone, it was just an inadvertent thing. I don't usually run into any—"

I held up my hand. "Don't sweat it. We're not here to bust you."

This seemed to calm Legs down considerably. He nodded vigorously, practically bowing at the waist in his seat. "Cool. Thanks. Cool. Well, so I catch the drift that this dude was saying he had this girl and not to call the cops—"

"Did you catch anything about money?" Bailey asked.

Legs sniffed and used a paper napkin to wipe his nose. I wondered whether the nose ring got in the way when he had a cold. I decided not to ponder that question.

"Nah, I guess I just caught the tail end of it. Reason I noticed, though, was the girl. You know, the one whose picture was just on the news? She came into the café while he was typing. Real pretty. Dude seemed pissed that she was there."

"What made him seem pissed?" Bailey asked. "Did he grab her? Yell at her?"

"No, nothing like that. He just seemed, I don't know...annoyed? He didn't let her sit down. Soon as she showed up, he packed up his laptop and they left."

"Did he hold on to her arm? Push her?" I asked.

Legs looked off to the left. "Not that I remember. And tell you the truth, I didn't think much of the whole deal. Seemed like a goof. The only reason I called you guys was because of the news flash about the girl."

"So she didn't look scared or upset?" I asked.

"Not to me. I mean, she wasn't laughing her ass off or anything. But she didn't look freaked."

"Do you think you'd recognize the guy if I showed you a photo?" Bailey asked.

Legs shrugged. "Couldn't hurt to try."

Bailey pulled up Brian's photo on her cell and held it in front of Legs.

He gave the photo a hard look, then nodded. "Yeah, that's the dude. No question."

"Thank you, Legs," I said. Bailey took his contact information and we stood to leave.

"So I assume the girl's been kidnapped," he said.

"Not necessarily," I semi-lied.

"But you'd appreciate it if I didn't say anything about this conversation, wouldn't you?"

The abrupt shift caught me off guard. I looked at him for a long moment. This was pretty savvy for any civilian, let alone the pierced counterculture specimen in front of me. "I can't stop you from talking, but yeah, it wouldn't hurt if you'd keep it to yourself."

"Got it."

We started to leave, but I turned back, too curious to let it go. "You said you had a class on Monday that got out at four o'clock. What class was that?"

"Not a class exactly. More like a weekly consultation. I'm finishing my Ph.D. in neuroscience."

"So it'll be Dr. Legs Roscoe soon."

"Actually, Dr. Lawrence Roscoe. But yeah. Hopefully."

At times like this I love my job.

9

We waited till we were in the car to discuss our latest find, courtesy of Dr. Legs.

"If Brian sent the ransom note from that café, and this was a righteous kidnapping, then how could he let Hayley float around like that?" Bailey asked.

"My question too. The only thing I can think of right now is that maybe he hadn't made that video with her yet. Until Brian had her record that video, she didn't necessarily know what he was doing. But the fact that he hustled her out of there shows he didn't want anyone to see them together, that's for sure. And we know he was somewhere else when he made that video and sent it with the ransom note."

Bailey stared out the window for a few seconds, then nodded. "It's possible. We'll have to see whether we can figure out where the final ransom e-mail and video were sent from." She checked her cell. "Russell's and Hayley's cell phone records are in. Still waiting on Brian's."

"They're at the station?"

Bailey nodded. "Yeah. And our computer whizbangs

are checking to see what they can get on the ransom e-mail, see if they can track down the computer it was sent from...so far, nothing," Bailey said. "But now that Legs put Brian and that ransom note together, it's less of a priority."

True. Regardless of where Brian was when he sent the note, the important thing was to prove he'd written it, and Legs did that for us. "Be nice to find Brian's laptop, though."

"Probably won't happen until we find Brian."

I couldn't argue with that point either. And I agreed with Bailey that we should get a look at those cell phone records sooner rather than later, but I knew that once we headed downtown, we'd probably be done for the day unless something else broke. "How about we check in with Hayley's mom before we go back to the station?"

"Okay, but then we'll need to get back and hit those records."

The tension in Bailey's voice matched my own anxiety level. Every passing minute made Hayley's safe return seem farther and farther away. But now that Brian was looking like our number one suspect, I wanted to see for myself whether either parent knew anything about him. Mackenzie didn't think Hayley had told them about Brian, but I couldn't rely on that, and I had a hunch that if Hayley had told either parent, it was more likely to be her mom.

Bailey floored it to Raynie's house, which was, indeed, close to Russell's house in the hills—just five blocks away. It was a low-slung modern home set into the hillside with an entire wall of sliding glass doors that opened to two feet of balcony and an expansive view of the city. And just like Russell's—and so many of the houses in this hood—it was propped up on stilts. Those things always made me nervous, and it didn't matter that I knew they were set in granite and probably more earthquake-proof than the courthouse.

Raynie greeted us at the curb as Bailey drove up. "Just pull in here." She pointed to a small space on the street a few feet from her front door. In the hills, all space, including parking space, was at a premium; all of the roads were steep, winding, and narrow. Raynie had her hair up in a loose bun and she wore a long white cotton skirt with multicolored embroidery around the hem and a turquoise tank top. She looked fresh as a daisy, a perfect counterpoint to my straggly hair, wilted gray slacks, and rumpled jacket. I reminded myself to pick a lighter, cooler ensemble tomorrow. I couldn't get away with Raynie's boheme maxi skirt stylings, but a dress of almost any kind would be a vast improvement over a pantsuit in this heat.

We followed Raynie inside. The house was an oven. The windows that looked out over the city also let the sun bake through. No doubt those windows could provide a stunning view, but today, all they showed was a city hazy with smog, a dark yellow–tinged basin of indistinct concrete, metal, and glass. Raynie picked up a remote, and at the push of a few buttons, the electronic blinds covered the windows. Instantly the room felt ten degrees cooler.

"Sorry," she said. "I forgot to turn on the air and close the blinds this morning." She paused and swallowed. "It should cool down pretty quickly now. Can I get you anything to drink? Ice water?"

We accepted gratefully. Raynie gestured for us to have a seat on the white leather sectional couch and brought us each a glass. The walls were adorned with pictures of Hayley from birth to the present. Some were of Hayley alone, some included her friends, and others were with Raynie. None were with Russell. Not that I was surprised. A husband who decamps for a younger trophy isn't someone whose picture you need to see every day. What did surprise me was that I hadn't noticed photos of any kind at Russell's house. At least not anywhere I'd been able to see.

I dived right in. "Did you know if Hayley was dating anyone?"

Raynie took a sip of water, then held the glass in her lap between her hands and stared down at it. "She didn't bring anyone around, but she did mention having met a boy recently."

"Do you remember when she mentioned it?" I asked.

"I want to say a month ago?"

"She say when she'd met him?"

"No. Just that he was a really good guy and that he wasn't like the other boys. That he had more...substance to him. And something about him having had a tough childhood, I think." Raynie stopped and shook her head. "I'm sorry. I wish I could tell you more. I know you'll think I'm a bad mother for not pressing her for more details. But I always seemed to learn more by just letting Hayley talk than by questioning her. And in all honesty, I expected I'd meet him pretty soon if it was really serious."

"She ever mention the name Brian?"

Raynie's eyes widened. "No. Is that the boyfriend?" She looked from me to Bailey. "Is *he* the kidnapper?"

I looked at Bailey, who nodded. We had to tell her what we knew about Brian. Bailey filled her in. Raynie sat stunned for several long moments, then she leaned forward and covered her face with her hands. When she collected herself and sat up, she looked three shades paler.

"Do you know of any reason why someone would target Russell, or Hayley?" I asked.

"I'm sure a lot of people have an ax to grind with Russell. You don't get as big as he has in this town without collecting a raft of enemies. But Hayley?" She shook her head slowly. "I can't imagine who'd have an issue with her."

"Do they get along?" I asked. "Hayley and Russell?"

Raynie sighed. "Since the divorce...not so much. Hayley really held it against him." She grimaced. "I think that's why she spends so much time at his house in the hills. It's kind of an 'in your face' thing. Russell feels guilty and keeps trying to make it up to her by spending money on presents and being the 'cool dad'—"

"Meaning permissive?"

"Exactly. So she takes advantage. She uses the party house, his SUV limo, his credit card, as much as she can. I think it's her way of punishing him, and I don't like it. I've told her that if she's upset with him, she should talk to him about it, not use him that way." Raynie paused and gave a sigh that felt more like resignation than disappointment. "Bottom line, no, she isn't his biggest fan."

If I pulled that thread to its source, it'd lead me to believe that Hayley could've been in on her own kidnapping. The fact that we had no evidence of a struggle or any kind of force used against Hayley lent some support to that theory. And I have to admit I liked that possibility because it meant Hayley probably wasn't in danger.

Raynie's mouth stretched into a grim line. "I should've known there was something wrong when Hayley wouldn't tell me his name." She stopped and frowned. "By the way, how old is this boy?"

"Nineteen? We won't know for sure until we find out his true identity."

"Well, that's one reason she didn't bring him around," Raynie said. "I'd never have let her date someone that much older."

"Do you know all of Hayley's friends?" I asked.

"Until just now I would've said yes. I guess all I can say is that from what I know, she's had the same girl-friends since fifth grade—" Raynie abruptly stopped as her lips trembled.

I patted her hand.

Raynie took a deep breath. "The waiting...it's...I just want her home." Her voice faltered on the last word. She squeezed her eyes shut and turned away.

When she'd recovered, I went back to the subject of friends. She gave us the names of the same three girls we'd already interviewed at the school.

"Hayley never was one for the big crowds or cliques," Raynie said. "That whole clubbing scene was just an act she was trying on. Like I said, partly a way to get back at Russell. The real Hayley is more of a homebody. Not a lot of friends, but they're for real; girls she'd go to the end of the world for. And, I think, vice versa."

"So she doesn't have any other friends? Girls who go to a different school, maybe?" I asked.

Raynie thought for a moment. "I don't know whether they stayed in touch, but Hayley used to be pretty close to Brittany Caren."

"The actress?" Bailey seemed taken aback. "Brittany Caren, as in the star of *Circle of Friends*?"

Raynie nodded.

Now the name rang a bell. "Wasn't she in a few films too?" I asked.

"Yeah, Russell casts her a lot. We've known Brittany since she was a kid, when Russell was a co-producer on *Circle*. Hayley was a huge fan. She used to come to the set and watch the taping. Hayley was a lot younger, so to Brittany, she was just a kid. But Brittany was incredibly sweet to her. She'd always invite Hayley to hang with her in her trailer. It sent Hayley over the moon." Raynie smiled softly at the memory. "When Hayley got older, they'd go shopping together, see movies. Brittany was the older sister Hayley wished she'd had." Raynie paused, then added, "And I think Brittany felt the same way."

"So there are no siblings from a prior marriage for either of you?" I asked. "Hayley's an only child?"

Raynie nodded. "Not by choice. We tried for another baby, but..." She sighed.

I nodded.

"Any idea when Hayley and Brittany last got together?" Bailey asked.

"It wasn't recent. Brittany kind of fell off the rails, as you probably know if you've seen the tabloids. It was so sad. She went from a sweet, lovely girl to a drunken pill head. When they canceled the show, everyone knew it was because of her."

"But she's still doing movies," Bailey said.

"Only because Russell keeps casting her—no one else will, she's a walking nightmare. He probably feels sorry for her. But knowing Hayley, I'm sure she tried to stay in touch, show her loyalty. She's not the type to cut off a friend, no matter what. She'd want Brittany to know she's still there for her." Raynie's eyes grew wet and she dropped her head briefly before continuing. "How often they see each other, or whether they still get together in person, that I don't know."

We got Brittany's contact information and address, and since there didn't seem to be anything else we could learn at the moment, we thanked Raynie and said our good-byes.

"Does Russell know about Brian yet?" she asked as we headed for the door.

"No, but we'll tell him soon," Bailey said.

Raynie nodded ruefully. "Better you than me."

I thought that was probably true.

10

As Bailey drove us back down the hill, I looked at the address Raynie had given us. "Brittany lives in Hancock Park." Which was on the way downtown.

"Go ahead and call, see if you can get her. But I'm going to need to get an update from Harrellson pretty quick, so we won't be able to stay long."

"What's Harrellson doing?" Don Harrellson, a great detective and a funny guy, was one of the team Bailey had assembled to help with the investigation.

"He's checking into Russell's associates."

Meaning Russell's possible enemies. "I guess it has to be done, but what enemy would risk a possible life sentence to get back at him?"

"If we limited our investigation to rational possibilities, our solve rate would be two percent."

Hard to argue with that one. I fished out my cell phone and squinted at the number Raynie had written on an orange star-shaped Post-it. The late afternoon sun was hanging low enough to shoot a white-hot laser through the windshield, practically blinding me. I had to put on my sunglasses to read the number. I got Brittany's voice mail. "Hi, it's Brittany. Leave a message...or don't. *Beeeeep.*" I chose the former and gave her my number and Bailey's and told her to call ASAP.

When we got to the station, Harrellson was at his desk in rolled-up shirtsleeves. "Having fun out there in Tinseltown, girls?"

I don't usually like being called a girl. But it's all in the attitude. Harrellson gave the word an ironic twist that made it funny instead of condescending.

"Probably not as much fun as you're having," I said.

"Well, not everyone appreciates the joy of banging their head against a brick wall the way I do. Our boy Antonovich has helpers and advisers crawling around his house like it's an anthill, and they all thought they had to "advise" yours truly about the galactic importance of His Supreme Highness Antonovich and the nefarious ways of jealous Hollywoodites. Man oh man, did they. Between that shark fin of a manager, whatsisname, Ian Powers, with the big swinging dick attitude, and his security adviser, Duncan Donuts—"

"Donuts?" Bailey laughed.

"Nah, Duncan Froehman. They had a lot to say about who I should look into and how I should do it. Got to the point I offered them a ladder—"

"A ladder?" I asked.

"Yeah, so they could climb out of my ass."

I barked out a laugh but Bailey was all business.

"So what'd you get?" she asked.

"*Nada.* Just a boatload of genius suggestions from Antonovich's advisers about pretty much everyone in the film business and half the folks in television. Apparently everyone who labors to fill screens large and small is envious of Mr. Blockbuster."

"I'm about to check out the cell phone records," Bailey said. "Maybe they'll give us something we can work with."

"Already done, jefe," Harrellson replied. "I made a copy and highlighted a few calls that might be worth checking out. Antonovich's record has a million different numbers, but there are some calls after the first text message from our bad guy we should check out. The girl was pretty consistent. Same numbers every day. Only found one stray number that wasn't a store or a club."

He handed the pages to Bailey, and I moved next to her so I could see. On Russell's cell phone bill, Harrellson had highlighted a few calls that were made after the first kidnapping message—but before the ransom e-mail was sent. I held out Russell's phone records. "Do you recognize any of these highlighted numbers?" I asked.

Harrellson glanced back at the pages. "Not yet. But from what I've seen, a lot of these clowns have multiple numbers and they may not all be listed. So it'll take a minute to run 'em all down."

We moved on to Hayley's phone records for the past month.

One highlighted number jumped out at me. Hayley had made a call to Brittany Caren just three weeks ago. Bailey and I exchanged a look.

Bailey pulled out her cell phone. "This time, I make the call." She punched in the number. And got Brittany's voice mail. Then she punched in another number.

"Russell, this is Detective Keller. I've been trying to get hold of Brittany Caren, but I keep getting her voice mail. Can you put me in touch with her?" Bailey listened for a moment. "I don't know that she does." Bailey listened again. "Yes, that'd be great. Thank you."

Five minutes later we were back in the car and headed to Hancock Park.

11

"So how'd you get her to pick up the phone?" I asked.

Bailey was threading her way through the traffic, taking surface streets because after three o'clock, the freeways were anything but free. Especially the 101. It crawled like a giant metal beast with thousands of agonizingly slow-moving parts.

"I didn't. Russell did. Don't ask me how."

But we soon found out how. A young man whose Neanderthal-bouncer aesthetic clashed almost audibly with the Mediterranean tile-roofed mansion showed us into a massive living room. I found that the clashing aesthetic was a continuing theme. It was a house at war with itself. The outside had promised earthy simplicity and lots of open space. But the inside delivered a mishmash of styles that cluttered every available square inch. The only thing any of the furniture, window treatments, and objets d'art had in common was a high price tag.

Heavy velvet drapery held back with gold-braided and tasseled tiebacks fought with giant Aubusson rugs. Overstuffed beige chenille sofas, pink leather ottomans, and barrel chairs covered in powder blue and rose fabric that nominally matched the rugs but clashed with everything else; vases, mini-sculptures (both ceramic and bronze) that cluttered every horizontal surface. If it's true that a room sets a tone, then this one set off a screeching cacophony.

The bouncer gestured to the other end of the room, where two women, presumably Brittany and her mother, sat side by side on a love seat.

Had I seen her out on the street, I might not have recognized the once famous star. Brittany Caren had packed a lot of miles into her twenty or so years. Her long blonde hair was dull and overprocessed and her soft brown eyes had an unfocused, weary look. And she was far too thin—her cheeks were hollow and her arms protruded from her sleeveless silk blouse like winter twigs. But still and all, I could see what had set her apart: that indefinable "something" that turns all eyes to her, and only her.

Whatever you called that "something," it had skipped over Brittany's mother. Mom was thickening through the middle, but she had good legs that were crossed primly at the ankle, the pose most likely dictated by her tight, above-the-knee skirt. Short blonde hair and a less than stellar face-lift topped a bright green and hot pink ensemble. No mystery about who was responsible for the interior design that was making my eyes cross.

Bailey took the lead. "I'm Detective Keller and this is Deputy District Attorney Rachel Knight. Thank you for seeing us on such short notice."

Mom waved us toward the chairs with an irritable "You're welcome."

"And your name is?" I asked the mother.

"Patricia Caren. Russell said this was important, so I made time for you. But Brittany has an early call, so let's make this brief."

I bit back the answer that would've gotten us thrown out and turned to Brittany. "Do you know that Hayley Antonovich is missing?"

Brittany leaned forward and knitted her brow. Her frown showed concern, but there was a vagueness to her expression that made her look as though she were trying to see me through a cloud of smoke. "I—no. I didn't." She turned to look at her mother.

Mom broke in. "I did tell you, sweetie. You probably don't remember." She turned to us. "She works very hard. She has a lot of lines in her next scenes, so sometimes it's hard for her to tune in."

The words were protective, but the tone was condescending and controlling. We hadn't been here ninety seconds and already I was restraining the urge to smack Mother Caren. I turned back to Brittany, who practically swayed in her seat. It was pretty obvious that Brittany's condition had nothing to do with hard work.

"What...what happened to Hayley?" she asked.

"She's missing, Brittany. We're trying to find her."

"Oh, no...Hayley...that's horrible." Brittany teared up and bit her lip. "I love her. What happened? What can I do?"

"When was the last time you spoke to her?" I asked.

"Uh...no...I don't remember exactly. Maybe a few months ago?"

Not according to the cell phone record. "Could it have been a few weeks ago?"

Brittany squinted with the effort to remember, but then her gaze drifted off. She was silent for so long, I thought she might not have heard the question, but at the last minute she rallied.

"Um…it could be." She gave me a wobbly smile. I smiled back, hoping to encourage her.

"Do you remember what you guys talked about?"

"Now, how would she remember that?" Mrs. Caren interrupted. "She's got way too much on her plate to re-member whatever they might've gossiped about."

On second thought, a smack wouldn't be satisfying enough. I needed the satisfaction of a good solid punch to the midsection. "Why don't we let Brittany tell us?" I turned back to the daughter. "Brittany?"

Brittany glanced at her mother, then looked over my shoulder at the piano. "N-no. I'm sorry."

For Brittany, a train of thought was only loosely joined to begin with, so the uncoupling didn't take much. I tried to come at it from another direction. "Did you and Hayley get together in the past month or so?"

Brittany tilted her head to one side, her expression thoughtful. "We might have…I seem to remember seeing her at some point. I just can't say exactly when."

"Do you know *where* you saw her? Maybe she came here?"

This time her answer was immediate. "No."

It was the quickest, most definitive answer we'd had yet. I had a feeling I knew why. "Where else might you have seen her?"

Brittany opened her mouth, then gave a sidelong glance at her mother. I took the hint.

"Patricia, you really don't need to stay," I said as diplomatically as I could. "Besides, you both could wind up testifying, and if that happens, you being here now could pose a problem for me in court."

My standard—and true—advisory to all witnesses. Defense attorneys loved to thrash witnesses for having heard each other's version of events because they could claim the witnesses had altered each other's memories. Of course, that really wasn't a concern here. We weren't talking about eyewitness descriptions of a robbery suspect. But I didn't have to tell Patricia that. The truth was that Brittany would be a lot more forthcoming if we were alone.

"Testifying?" Patricia's eyes widened. "To what? It's perfectly obvious Brittany doesn't have any information that could be of use to you." Her eyebrows dipped into what would've been a frown if her face hadn't been frozen by megadoses of Botox.

She looked angry enough to throw us out. I didn't want her to end the interview, so I reassured her. "I'm not saying I intend to put either one of you on the stand—we don't even have a case yet. But I always have to prepare for the possibility. And interviewing witnesses separately is standard practice."

Mother Caren cooled off a few degrees, but not enough to capitulate. "I'm sorry to hear that, but Brittany doesn't do interviews alone." She turned to Brittany and patted her hand. "Isn't that right, dear?"

"Ms. Caren, this is a criminal investigation, not a movie promo for *Allure* magazine. It is inappropriate to have you here while we talk to Brittany," I said, keeping my voice as low and level as I could.

Patricia Caren narrowed her eyes at me. "You can either talk to her with me here or not at all. Your choice."

Mommy Dearest ruled this roost with an iron hand. That's why Brittany had been so certain she hadn't seen Hayley at the house. She probably never brought anyone here if she could help it. It didn't matter that she was legally an adult, or that she had paid for everything and everyone in this house. Brittany was mommy's prize pony and mommy was going to keep her in the race. I'd have to capitulate for now. I sat back and Bailey took over.

"Do you happen to know whether Russell had any enemies?" Bailey asked. "Anyone who held a grudge against him?"

We knew that Brian was our kidnapper, but we didn't know whether he was in league with someone else. Since Warden Patricia wouldn't leave, and she—like Brittany—had known Russell for a long time, Bailey had wisely decided to use the opportunity to grill her too.

Patricia gave a bark of a laugh. "Anyone who held a grudge? There're probably thousands. Every actor—"

I'd heard this litany enough to repeat it in my sleep. I shook my head. "We're talking about something out of the norm. Very few actors or producers are going to do something as crazy as kidnap his daughter just because he didn't hire them or buy their script."

Patricia gave me an incredulous look. "You don't know much about this town, do you?"

I knew enough to say I was sick of hearing about "this town." And all the people in it. Besides, I'd lived here long enough to know that although there were vampires in the industry, there were a heck of a lot of smart, talented people who were just decent, hardworking folks.

At that moment the bouncer came in and announced that the script had been delivered. Should he sign for it?

Looking annoyed, Patricia sighed and stood up. "I'll be right back."

Brittany had been leaning on the arm of the sofa, staring off, but I noticed that when she'd heard the bouncer mention a script, her brow had furrowed.

"You okay, Brittany?" I asked. A thought of some kind? Was it possible?

Brittany nodded. "Yeah. You got me thinking about Hayley...and the script...it reminded me. Back before Russell was a big director, when he was a co-producer on my show. It was when he'd just sold his first film script, *Wonderland Warriors*—you've heard of it, right?"

"Maybe," I said. The name was somewhat familiar.

"It was huge. *Wonderland Warriors* was what made Russell. Tommy said Russell stole that script from him."

"Tommy? Who's that?" Bailey asked.

"He was a writer on *Circle of Friends*." Brittany peered at us hazily. "You've heard of *Circle*, right?"

We both nodded. "Of course," I said, eager to get her to refocus on this Tommy guy. "So Tommy said Russell stole the script for *Wonderland Warriors*?"

Brittany nodded. "Yeah. Tommy always wrote by hand on a legal pad. He was kinda strange. But I always thought he was a pretty good writer." She started to drift off again, so I quickly reeled her back in.

"What happened when Tommy accused Russell of stealing his script?"

"It got really gnarly. Tommy—"

"Do you remember his last name?"

She squinted for a second. "Maher. Tommy Maher."

"What did he do?"

"They got in a big fight. Tommy got moved to the other end of the lot—"

The rapid click-clack of heels on marble told me Patricia was on her way back. Brittany's expression told me she'd noticed that too.

"Did Tommy file a lawsuit against Russell?" The theft of a script was no little thing—especially if the script had been the star maker Brittany said it was.

"No. I don't think—"

Patricia had the ears of an owl. As she entered the living room she said, "Don't think what?"

"Nothing," Brittany said. Her face had closed. We'd reached the end of this line.

I tried another tack. "Did Hayley ever talk to you about a boy named Brian?"

At this, Brittany looked puzzled. "Brian? No, I-I don't think so."

Patricia walked over but remained standing. "I never heard her mention the name either." She reached down and took Brittany by the hand. "Now if you don't mind, Brittany's got an early call—"

I stood and pulled out a card. "Brittany, thank you. I know you and Hayley were very close at one time. If you remember anything else, will you get in touch?"

Brittany nodded. "Of course. I want to help any way I can." She took the card and held it in front of her as though she didn't know what to do with it. Bailey added her card to mine and gave one to Patricia too. I knew Bailey did it just to tweak her. I also knew both cards would land in the trash before we made it to the car.

"Thank you both for your time," Bailey said.

Time flies when you're trying to pry information out of a zombie and end-run the zombie's keeper. It was six thirty by the time Bailey and I left the Carens'. Too late to knock on any more doors.

"Feel like a drink?" I asked.

"I feel like day-old bacon. I'd *like* a drink. Maybe several."

"Brittany looked like she had several before we got there," I said. "If I had a mother like that, I would've been dipping my pacifier in vodka."

"She's a classic Momager—"

"And a classic something else." I thought back on Brittany's vague expressions and floaty demeanor. "But I think it's more than booze. That girl's a pill head too."

Bailey nodded. "So I guess the stories are true."

"Sadly, some of them are."

Bailey headed for the 101 freeway south, taking us back downtown.

12

We decided to have dinner at the Biltmore bar—or rather, Bailey decided we'd have dinner at the bar. She said it was because it would be faster, less hassle.

"Admit it," I said. "You just wanted to come here so you and Drew could coo and slobber all over each other."

"You really want to say that in front of the person who makes your martinis?" asked Drew, who'd walked over to where we were seated.

"Ignore her, she's in a cranky mood," Bailey said. "We'll have the usual. How was your day?"

"Same-o. But it looks like the loan's coming through. Just waiting for the broker to okay the deal on the space," Drew said.

Drew was on the brink of realizing his dream of opening his own upscale bar. Though his place would be within walking distance, nothing beat the convenience of living an elevator ride away. Yet another perk I enjoyed as a permanent resident of the Biltmore.

"How're you doing? Any leads?" he asked Bailey.

Bailey ran a hand through her short blonde hair and sighed. "Nothing that blows my skirt up at the moment."

Drew gave her a lascivious look.

I pointed to Drew and Bailey. "No. You may not do that in front of me—" Drew went off to fix our drinks when my cell phone buzzed. It was Graden. The sound of his voice immediately brought a smile to my face. I turned away to take the call. We exchanged brief updates on our day—something I'd sorely missed during our breakup.

"I know you'll be running hard on this case, but if you catch a quiet pocket, want to do dinner sometime this week?" he asked.

"Love to. If my elopement hunch plays out, this could wrap up pretty fast. Want to play it by ear for this weekend?"

"Sounds perfect. And you'll let me know if you need anything in the meantime?"

The cool thing was, he didn't just mean he'd pick up my dry cleaning; he meant knocking around investigative leads and ideas. It was one of the nice perks of dating a smart cop. But it also had a downside. Graden had an obsessive need to know everything about everyone. Bailey and Toni said it was what made him such a great cop, and there was no doubt they were right. But that particular trait was about as incompatible with my privacy issues as you could get. Graden swore he could rein himself in for my sake. Only time would tell. But right now, things were good and getting better by the day. When I ended the call and turned back around, I saw that Drew had delivered our drinks and was about to put our steaks down.

Both he and Bailey were looking at me with raised eyebrows.

"What?" I asked.

"Good phone call from the boyfriend, I see," Drew said.

"I seem to remember someone saying something about cooing," Bailey said.

I had to laugh.

"Seriously though, you guys are doing pretty well, right?" Bailey asked.

"Yeah, why?"

"Because I think you should consider letting Graden check out those reports Lilah mentioned in her last text."

Lilah Bayer, née Rossmoyne, was a sociopath responsible for three murders that I knew of, not to mention the near demise of myself and Bailey. We'd set a trap for her majordomo, Chase Erling, that nearly cost us our lives. But the trap had worked. We got Erling. Unfortunately, we didn't get Lilah. She'd managed to hop a private plane to parts unknown. But on her way out of town, she texted me, claiming to have found two reports filed one month and six months after Romy's abduction, reports that might prove my sister was still alive. The text was an implicit threat and message: if I backed off and didn't pursue her, she'd get me more on Romy's whereabouts—if I didn't...you can fill in the blank with just about anything, including a biochemical attack, because for Lilah there was no such thing as overkill.

Bailey, taking my hesitation as resistance to the idea of drafting Graden to help with Lilah's leads on Romy, added, "Graden has the resources, and the time—which you don't. And take it from me, he doesn't get out in the field as much as he likes." She gave me a long-suffering look. "It's driving some—who shall remain nameless—crazy."

Bailey knew that since the DA investigators had their hands full chasing down leads on Lilah herself, I'd been doing the legwork to track down the alleged reports on Romy. So far, I'd come up empty. I'd thought more than once about asking for Graden's help, but after our fight, I hadn't been sure how he'd react. Hearing Bailey suggest it now, though, I couldn't imagine him being anything but happy to help. "I think it's a great idea, actually."

"Oh." Bailey looked surprised. Whether it was because I'd responded rationally, or given her props, I'd never know.

"Yeah, I'll ask him about it tomorrow."

"Speaking of tomorrow," Bailey said. We talked about our plans for the next day as we ate. Tired from too many hours chasing down too few leads, Bailey and I were both ready to collapse by the time we finished dinner.

"You should probably crash with me," I said. "It's too late and you're too wiped to drive home."

Bailey yawned. "I am thrashed. Okay. And I'm never saying no to room service for breakfast." Drew was at the other end of the bar filling a drink order for a waiter, so Bailey blew him a kiss and we headed for the elevator.

A permanent room at the Biltmore didn't come cheap, and it would've been way out of my league but for a sweetheart deal I fell into by happenstance. A few years ago, I'd prosecuted the man who'd murdered the Biltmore CEO's wife in the underground parking lot of the hotel. During the trial, the CEO had given me a room so I could stay near the courthouse. After I got the conviction that put the killer away for life without parole, the CEO offered to let me stay on as a permanent resident for a deal no sane person could refuse. And so I'd moved into the Biltmore for good. Last year, he'd upgraded me to a suite with two bedrooms because it got so little use. That meant it was easy to accommodate overnight guests, like Toni and Bailey. It hadn't yet meant Graden.

We headed for our respective bedrooms, and Bailey warned me we'd be starting the day bright and early. The downside of Bailey as an overnight guest was that when she said "early," she meant the crack of dawn. She'd yanked me out of bed in the past, and let me tell you, it's bracing. I set my alarm for six thirty to make sure I didn't give her the chance to do it again.

I woke up before my alarm, which tells you how much I didn't want to relive the Bailey Shake. I put on my robe and walked onto the balcony to sample the weather. The sky was an unmarred powder blue and there wasn't even a hint of a breeze. An early harbinger of yet another cooker of a day. Damn. I'd planned to wear a dress, but that's such a pain when I'm running around in the world, as I knew I would be today. I pulled out the lightest pair of cotton slacks I could find, a sleeveless buttoned blouse, and a light cardigan to combat the blast of air-conditioning I'd be in and out of all day.

When I came out to the living room, Bailey, who'd left some clothes behind when she'd had an extended stay at my place during our last case, was already dressed and digging heartily into her breakfast. It was a tantalizing stack of pancakes with a side of bacon. Bailey is tall and lean and one of those obnoxious people who can eat anything and not gain weight; and she loves to rub my nose in it every chance she gets. Toni and I have plotted her demise on many an occasion. I noticed that Bailey was dressed in similar attire to mine, except she wore a jacket to hide her shoulder holster. Personally, I preferred to carry my gun in my purse. It accommodated everything from my little .22 Beretta to my .44 Glock.

"Did you order for me?" I asked. I poured myself a cup of coffee from the large pot on the table.

"Yeah, your pathetic little egg whites and stewed tomato are over there." She pointed to a silver dome on the side table.

I sat down and spread a napkin on my lap. "What do you think of the story Brittany told us about that writer, Tommy Whatsisname?" I uncovered my sad little egg whites, scooped up a forkful, and tried to look ecstatic.

"Tommy Maher," she said. "So now we've got someone with a possible motive."

"If that script really did turn into a mega-blockbuster, I could see how someone would go nuts enough to want to destroy Russell."

"But it's been what? Ten years since that movie came out?"

"At least. Yeah, that's an awfully long time to wait for revenge."

"Still, we may as well see where it takes us. I looked up the show Brittany starred in at the time: *Circle of Friends*. They shot it at the Warner Brothers Ranch Studio in Burbank. We can go talk to them and see if anyone remembers the story."

"You want to call ahead and make sure they get us a 'drive-on'?" I said as I slithered my fork toward Bailey's pancakes. I was getting into position to sneak a bite while she made the call.

"Look at you, using the lingo," Bailey said. "Been there, done that. And I see you, Knight, so put down the fork."

Seeing my crushed look, Bailey relented and pushed her plate forward. "I'm done anyway. But make it snappy, we've got to get moving."

Ten minutes later, and a little high on carbs and syrup, I was in the car and we were heading for the freeway.

The Warner Brothers Ranch Studio is a little gated city. The head of security had arranged a parking space for us and sent out a guard in a golf cart to escort us to his office. Bailey and I had discussed whether we should just ask Russell about what happened with Tommy. But if this argument had some significance to the case, it would be better for us to find out all we could from uninvolved—or less involved—third parties before we heard Russell's side of things.

The guard drove us to a building at the far end of the studio lot and stopped in front of a door marked HEAD OF SECURITY. The nameplate under that title said NED JUNGER. We knocked on the door, and a ruddy-faced man as wide as he was tall—and he was at least six feet two—answered.

"Detectives," he said.

We shook hands, and mine disappeared into his gigantic paw as I told him I was a prosecutor. No sense getting off on the wrong foot by pretending to be someone I'm not. This time at least. He gestured for us to take a seat in the wire-framed chairs in front of his desk, and he settled into his own much larger and cushier chair behind it.

I told him what we'd heard about Tommy Maher and Russell. He nodded.

"I remember that. I'd just started here. That was, what, ten years ago? But I heard about it. You thinking that has something to do with Hayley being missing?"

"We don't know," Bailey said. "We're just checking into all possibilities."

"Sure. Though it's hard to see the... well, why don't I just tell you what I know and leave you two to connect the dots?"

Ned leaned back and held on to the arms of his chair. "Russell came up with that screenplay, and right away there was talk about it being a blockbuster. *Wonderland Warriors.* You ever see it?"

We admitted we hadn't. I could see Ned was winding up to tell us a story that was probably recycled for every newcomer on the lot.

"Movie wasn't half bad. Kind of a kid thing, but adults liked it too. Can't go wrong when you hit the whole family that way. Action-type film like *The Transformers* but with a fairy tale attached to it, like *The Princess Bride.* Anyway, the buzz started right off the bat about this great script and the big deal Russell would be getting. For a young TV writer—hell, for anyone—it was a huge deal. You ask him, he'll tell you."

Bailey nodded encouragingly and Ned continued.

"So Tommy gets wind of it and goes apeshit. Starts

yelling that it was his script, that Russell stole it from him. Now, Tommy always had been a bit of a loose cannon. Wasn't the first time he'd complained about someone taking credit for something he'd done. Got into a lot of fights in the writers' room over people stealing his story ideas—"

"Maybe they did," I said.

"Sure, maybe they did. Problem was, he cried wolf one too many times in the past. So when he got all nuts about this script, no one really paid attention." Ned sighed and sat forward. "But that film script was the end of him. Tommy started coming to work drunk, sometimes even got drunk while he was at work—and he wasn't a nice drunk. Got more and more belligerent. Then, one day, he got into it with Russell over some network notes and decked him. Just 'boom'! Coldcocked 'im, knocked Russell on his ass." Ned shook his head. "After that, they moved Tommy out to the edge of the lot—"

"Why didn't they just fire him?" Bailey asked.

"He was under contract. Easier to put him in Siberia and let his contract run out at the end of the season. 'Course Tommy had to know that was coming."

"So did he ever sue Russell over the theft of the screenplay?" I asked.

"No." A look of sadness crossed his face. "Day after the holiday party for the cast and crew, he went home and blew his own brains out."

"Damn," Bailey said.

"Did not see that coming," I said. I guessed we could probably scratch Tommy Maher off our suspect list.

Ned leaned forward and poked the keyboard of his

computer with his thick finger. As it whirred to life, he said, "There was a blurb about it in the papers. See if I can pull it up for you." He scrolled for a few minutes, then turned the monitor so we could see it. "Article doesn't tell you much, but that's the holiday picture of the cast and crew on the set." Ned pointed to the right side of the screen. "Tommy's the guy on the end."

Bailey and I leaned in to get a better look. There was something about him that I couldn't put my finger on. I tried to analyze what it was. He was of average height and size, not the look of a big bruiser who'd have the guts to knock someone down. But everything else about him fit that bill: the sour expression, hunched posture with hands shoved into his pockets; every bit of him telegraphed misery and barely restrained anger. I could see that guy getting wound up enough to coldcock someone. Or even commit suicide. I remembered one of the forensic shrinks saying that it takes a violent person to commit suicide.

I'd been staring at the photo as these thoughts circled, but then the something I couldn't put my finger on suddenly became clear. "He looks like Brian."

13

We read the obit. Sure enough, it said that Tommy Maher was survived by his wife, Estelle—and his son, Brian. Brian Shandling was Brian Maher. Had to be. It all fit. Brian taking jobs around Russell's studio, using a fake name, getting next to Hayley. The article also mentioned that Tommy had a sister, Janice, who was an author and lived in upstate New York.

"Mind sending me this article?" Bailey asked.

"Sure." He carefully punched a few more keys. I tried to imagine what it was like to type with fingers that big. "Done. I'm going to take a wild guess that this business with Tommy Maher's important?"

"Might be," Bailey replied.

He nodded. "Okay. I'll ask around, see if there's anyone who knew him."

We thanked him and, to my annoyance, Bailey declined the offer of a ride back to the car.

"What's up with nixing the ride?" I groused, once we were outside. "I dug that little golf cart. Reminded me of Autopia."

"I hated that ride. Those cars were too slow."

"But the golf carts are faster," I said as we got to our car. "So we're not passing up the ride next time. Got it?"

Bailey rolled her eyes. "When was the last time you hit the gym?" I folded my arms and refused to answer. Bailey nodded. "Exactly."

But all joking aside—or more accurately all joking now possible—we were fired up. Finally we had what felt like a real lead.

Bailey and I got into the car and she pulled out her cell. "I'm forwarding the article to you. I'll put out the alert with Brian's true name, you call in and get the info on the wife and sister."

We made our respective calls. "I've got a suggestion," I said when we'd both finished.

"Space Mountain?"

I gave her my steely-eyed look. She yawned in terror. "Since we're on the Valley side of the world, why don't we hit the jewelry store where Brian was last employed?" I said.

Bailey started the car. "A surprisingly good idea."

"You can't teach it. It's a gift."

Twenty minutes later, we were riding the escalator up to the shops at the Galleria. From the moment we stepped off, we were surrounded by clusters of teenagers—boys on one side, girls on the other, with occasional meetings between the two that generated squeals and hugs all around.

"You remember hugging that much when you were a kid?" I asked.

"Yeah, that's me. I'm a hugger," Bailey deadpanned. "Ask me, it's just the guys looking for a way to cop a feel."

"Perhaps today's youth are simply more effusive in their displays of affection."

"Or perhaps boys are always looking for ways to cop a feel."

"Or that."

But seeing the kids, their clothing, and maybe just the way they walked reminded me of an earlier hunch. I approached a cluster of girls. "Any of you go to Clarington?"

A girl with pink fringe for bangs looked me up and down before answering. "We all do." The other girls nodded.

"What about those guys?" I asked, nodding toward a group of boys ten feet away.

"Yeah, them too. Why?"

"Just taking a survey."

"What do I get?"

I looked at her quizzically.

"For answering your questions," she added impatiently.

"My undying gratitude." I walked back to Bailey, who was waiting in front of the jewelry store, and tried not to grumble about "kids today."

"What's got your knickers in a twist?" Bailey asked.

"Misspent youth. Theirs. And like we thought, the Clarington kids hang here."

Bailey opened the door and we walked in.

"So maybe Brian took the job to get next to Hayley," I said.

"Or he found a better job as a manager here and just got lucky when she floated by." Bailey looked at me, her expression amused. "Sometimes a cigar really is just a—"

"Whatever."

The security guard was chatting with the salesgirl, who was wiping down the glass counter.

"Is your manager here?" Bailey pulled out her badge.

The girl's eyes widened momentarily. "Yeah, he's in the back."

She excused herself and went to the back room. The security guard held out his hand to Bailey. "Stephen Wareby."

"Nice to meet you, Stephen." They shook. "And this is Deputy District Attorney Rachel Knight."

Stephen looked less impressed to meet me, but he reluctantly shook my hand as well. I decided it'd be smarter to sit this one out and let Bailey take the lead.

"Do you know Brian Shandling?" she asked.

"Yeah. He's the manager who's usually here."

"What do you think of him?"

Steve shrugged. "He's okay, I guess. He—"

At that moment, the stand-in manager came out, his hand extended. "Adam Meisner. What can I do for you officers?"

"We're looking into a matter involving Brian Shandling. Do you know him?" Bailey asked.

"No. I usually work in our store at the Beverly Center. I'm subbing for him."

"He took some time off?"

"Yeah. Said he was going to visit an aunt in New York, I think."

"Did he mention her name? Or say when he'd be back?"

"He didn't mention her name, but he said he'd be back next week."

Bailey's phone began to ring. She looked at the number. "I've got to take this. Sorry." She stepped away and I asked Adam if Brian had a good reputation with the company.

"I guess so. I mean, he didn't get fired or anything, but you'd have to ask Human Resources. I'm just a manager, like him, so..."

Bailey came back, looking like she was in a hurry. "Adam, thank you for your help. We'll be in touch if we have any other questions." She shook his hand and pushed me toward the door.

Bailey led the way through the mall and I trotted to keep up. She's got a good three inches on me and a really long stride, so that wasn't easy. Plus, I wasn't all that anxious to leave the mall's air-conditioned clime.

"What'd you get?" I asked.

"Turns out our boy Brian had credit cards in his real name. He bought two plane tickets to New York. I'm going to make some calls and get our airport division to check and see whether those tickets were used, and if they were, if the passengers fit the description of Hayley and Brian. And I'm going to have all the lots checked for Brian's car."

"Two tickets. So maybe—"

"Hayley's alive. Exactly."

"Okay, while you work the airport angle, I'll see if we've got a line on the aunt or the mother."

We ran down the escalator and all the way to the car. Bailey pulled out of the underground parking lot to a spot on the street where we could get a signal and work the phones.

I got a number for the aunt, Janice Maher—which

meant she was either unmarried or not willing to change her name—but got no answer, so I left a message. A records check by one of our DA investigators revealed that Brian's mother, Estelle, had died of a heart attack three years ago.

When Bailey ended her call, I told her what I'd learned.

"But if the aunt's in pocket, we'll catch up with her soon enough."

It felt like we'd been running for the past two days straight, and I was a little high on adrenaline. I wanted to *do* something.

Bailey saw my agitation and gave me a firm look. "Now we wait, Knight. Not your strong suit. But we need some answers first and that may take a day or so."

I nodded and sat back, letting my jets cool. "May as well make the best of it—"

"Yeah. Call Toni."

I pulled out my phone, but the battery was almost gone, so I borrowed Bailey's cell.

Perch was a bar and restaurant that occupied the top two floors of a building that overlooked Pershing Square, which was across the street from the Biltmore. Both floors had rooftop bars, and especially in the summer, it was heaven to have drinks up there at night. A summer day in L.A. can be hot as blazes, but it's a semi-desert, so at night the temperature can drop as much as thirty degrees. That can make outdoor dining a chilly affair. Not tonight. Tonight the air was so soft and balmy, it almost felt tropical. A perfect night for martinis on an open rooftop, where we could watch stars twinkle above and the city lights sparkle below, all around us. As we sipped our drinks, Bailey and I brought Toni up to speed on the case.

"So, girl hates dad and wants to pay him back for dumping mom and going for a younger version," Toni said. "Girl meets boy who also hates her dad and wants to pay him back for stealing a script from his father. It's a match made in heaven."

"Young love is a beautiful thing," I said.

"Think they're having a blast in the Big Apple on daddy's ransom money even as we speak?" Toni said.

"We don't have confirmation that they actually boarded a flight yet. But I'm hoping—"

"It'd be the best thing if that's how it works out," Toni finished.

I nodded and lifted my martini glass. "To rebellious teens, who are alive and well—"

"—and playing on daddy's money," Toni added.

Bailey grimaced, but we all clinked and sipped.

It was good to finally exhale. In fact, we exhaled so much, we lost interest in going to a restaurant and wound up back at my place with room service.

We talked and laughed until it was too late for Toni to go home, so she crashed on the pullout bed in the living room. I fell into my bed, tired but relaxed, and set my alarm for the civilized hour of eight o'clock.

14

I must have been dreaming about flying, because when I woke to the ringing of a bell, I felt as though I'd come crashing out of the sky.

I opened my eyes and reached out to hit the "snooze" button. But the clock said it was only four a.m. Then it hit me that the sound I'd heard wasn't my alarm, it was Bailey's phone. I'd forgotten to give it back to her last night. I forced my eyes to focus—not easy when you've been flying in your sleep—and answered. "'Lo?"

"I'm sorry to disturb you, Detective Keller. This is Officer Bander, Airport Division. We've located that car—"

Car? Which...? Then my brain kicked into gear. Brian's car. I probably should've told Officer Bander that I wasn't Bailey, but I wanted to hear the news.

"Where?"

"In Parking Lot C, a remote lot. What do you want me to do?"

I couldn't give orders...well, I *could,* but I shouldn't.

"Secure the lot and tape off the area around the car. Don't let anyone near it until I get there. I'm on my way."

As I ended the call, I thought I'd done a pretty good job impersonating Bailey. Then I ran to wake up the real article. We dressed quickly in jeans and sweatshirts—it'd be cold out there now—and I left a note for Toni, who was still fast asleep.

When we got into the car, Bailey threw me her phone. "You're so good at being me, put in the call to SID and get a criminalist to meet us there. Try for Dorian."

The streets were empty at that hour, and Bailey practically took us there on two wheels. Though I'd fastened my seat belt, I had to hold on to the dash while I made the call to keep from falling all over the car.

The vast Parking Lot C, a cheap option because you had to take a shuttle to the airport from there, was brightly lit. But at this hour, the lot was still and quiet, which gave me the eerie feeling that we were the only survivors in a postapocalyptic world. Bailey drove slowly as we looked for signs of life. Finally, at the far corner of the lot, we saw the blue and red flashing lights of police cars. As we drew nearer, I could see that crime scene tape had been put up to enclose a white vehicle within a twenty-foot radius.

Bailey parked and we walked up to one of the officers guarding the perimeter and identified ourselves.

He lifted the crime scene tape for us and we ducked under. "Officer Bander's handling the scene. He's right over there." He pointed to a short man who was standing near the trunk of the car.

When we got closer, I saw that he was much younger than his voice had sounded on the phone. Bailey and I introduced ourselves again and she asked whether he'd seen anything inside. He handed her his flashlight—one of those super-heavy big black ones that double as a weapon—and I watched as she played the light around the interior of the car.

"I don't see anything," I said. "You?"

Bailey shook her head, and I stepped back to give her room as she circled the car with the flashlight. She paused and trained her beam on the trunk area. Still focused on the trunk, she asked, "Who found the car?"

"I did," Officer Bander said. "I started with the closest lots and worked my way out."

That was one hell of a lot of canvassing. There were a ton of parking lots. Just covering the closest lots at the terminal would've taken a couple of hours.

"And did you stay here after you found it?" Bailey asked.

She was making sure the scene hadn't been contaminated—at least since Bander had found the car.

"Yeah. I called you right away and had the area cordoned off, just like you said. I'm the only one who's been this close to the car since I saw it."

Bailey looked around the lot. "How long since you called for a criminalist?" she asked me.

"About thirty minutes."

"Did you try the doors?" she asked Officer Bander.

"No."

Bailey bent down and shined the flashlight under the car. I was about to move in closer and join her, but just then, a beat-up Cadillac pulled up close to the tape. The driver rolled his belly out first, and when he approached us, I recognized the ruddy complexion, heavy cheeks, and small blue eyes of criminalist Ben Glosky. Bailey and I had him on a previous case involving a pedophile who'd done us all the favor of shuffling off this mortal coil. Ben wasn't Dorian, but he was pretty good.

Ben flashed his ID and struggled under the tape. "Dorian said to tell you she'll be here in a few and not to pull the same crap you usually do. She also figured you'd need someone who could unlock the doors without damaging anything."

"You're a locksmith?" I asked.

"Before I joined SID."

I guess it shouldn't have been such a surprise. It's not like he'd said he used to train poodles for TV commercials.

Ben gloved up, put on the regulation shower cap—though the few hairs slicked back on his head were unlikely to go anywhere—and slipped his shoes into booties. Then he took a small metal case out of his car and set it on the ground next to the driver's side door. Bailey held the flashlight for him as he examined the interior through the driver's side window. Ben took the flashlight from her and walked around the car, studying every inch. Bailey moved with him and pointed out various spots on the car. Then he crouched and shined the light under the car, as Bailey had done. He went back to his kit and took out a packet of sterile swatches, distilled water, an eyedropper, and long tweezers. Slowly, he moved around the car, lifting samples as he went.

When he was done, he handed the flashlight back to Bailey and motioned for her to follow him over to the driver's side. Bailey stood behind him, blocking my view, so I couldn't see what he did from where I was standing, but two seconds later the driver's door was open. One second later, the trunk flew open.

And there, lying in a pool of blood, was Hayley.

15

As many bodies as I've seen, as many crime scenes as I've visited, after a while, you get to be immune. But the sight of Hayley Antonovich curled up in a fetal position in that trunk hit me like a lead-handed punch to the head. Tears filled my eyes and my throat tightened with sadness and disbelief. I quickly turned away and blinked until my eyes cleared. Crying at a crime scene was unthinkable.

When I turned back, I saw an ashen-faced Bailey watching me carefully. "You okay, Knight?"

I nodded, but didn't speak. I didn't trust my voice.

Bailey pulled out her cell, no doubt to call the coroner. When she'd finished the call, she ordered everyone to move farther back from the tape, then she came to stand next to me. I could feel her still watching me with a look of concern. If Bailey saw it, others would too. I needed to get a grip. So I swallowed hard and blocked the sight of Hayley from my mind.

"Did he buy those two tickets to New York just to throw us off?" I asked. "Or do you think he's working with someone else?"

"I was wondering the same thing. But he bought the tickets using his real name, so if he was trying to throw us off, wouldn't he use the one he'd made public out here?"

"Or maybe he was sharp enough to know we'd figure out he was using an alias and he used his real name to buy the tickets—make it look more genuine."

"That's pretty smart for a nineteen-year-old kid," Bailey said.

"And pretty tangled," I agreed. "But not impossible."

Bailey sighed. "What is?"

We both fell silent, trying to manage the pain of the unwanted discovery. I'd been so optimistic. Too optimistic. That wasn't my style. But this wasn't the time or the place to figure it out. Bailey would ordinarily be the one to make the notification to the family, but since I was in from the jump on this one, I thought I should probably go with her.

"Brian doesn't know we've found her already." I glanced at my cell phone. It was five fifteen a.m.—eight fifteen in New York. "In about half an hour, I'm going to try reaching the aunt again. When I do, I'm going to tell her we're looking for Brian *and* Hayley."

"So she won't try to cover for him if he's been in touch?" Bailey set her jaw and looked back at the trunk. "It's not a bad idea. But it's a now-or-never move. Once we make notification to Hayley's parents, the news'll go global."

Bailey looked at the ground and sighed. I knew she was dreading it. So was I. The coroner's wagon pulled up and a guy in high-water pants and a nylon Coroner's Office jacket jumped out.

It was Scott Ferrier, the coroner's investigator who was my longtime "friend with benefits." The benefits in our case being his willingness to slip me reports on the sly in return for free lunches at his favorite restaurant, Engine Co. No. 28.

No sooner had Officer Bander lifted the crime scene tape to let Scott in than Dorian pulled up in a brand-new forest green Tacoma. Still a pickup, but a lot snazzier than the faded old jalopy she used to drive. There was something comforting about seeing Scott and Dorian. It was like having family show up.

"Hey, Scott." I waved and stepped closer as he set his bag down next to the trunk and took out a camera.

"Rachel!" He waved back before he turned and started taking photos.

Dorian moved next to the car with her kit, a large toolbox with tray insets that allowed her to store every little thing in its own compartment, perfectly organized, not a single cotton swab out of place. Dorian put the *D* in OCD. We both watched as Scott finished taking the pictures. Dorian wouldn't be able to touch the trunk until he was done. The coroner, or his investigator, has sole jurisdiction over the body. Until he's through, everyone else waits.

I greeted Dorian with a simple "Hey," which was more than she was in the mood for. Never much of a talker, she was even less inclined to shoot the breeze after having been awakened before five a.m.

"Nice wheels," Bailey said.

"It'll do."

Scott had finished photographing Hayley and had gloved up, preparing to deal with the body. He pulled

out the long steel needle to take the liver temperature—
one method of determining how long the victim had
been dead. I turned away. A few moments later, Scott's
assistant rolled the gurney up to the car and Scott carefully examined Hayley with his flashlight, looking for
evidence that might be disturbed when he moved the
body.

"Dorian!" he called out. "Take a look here."

Dorian, who'd already gloved up and put on her
shower cap, moved forward with her kit and peered in.
She bent down, pulled out some tweezers, and carefully
plucked something too small for us to see from the body.
Dorian placed it in a small coin envelope and set it into
one of the little compartments in the toolbox. Scott finished his examination and told Dorian she could start on
the rest of the car. He and his assistant then lifted Hayley
out of the trunk and into the body bag that was on the
gurney.

Her beautiful blonde hair was tangled and matted
with blood and her pale pink sleeveless T-shirt was
soaked in it. Her eyes were half closed, and I imagined
her bleeding out, dying slowly in that trunk, alone. The
lump re-formed in my throat and I quickly turned to focus on Dorian, who'd begun examining the driver's side
of the car with a flashlight and a magnifying glass.

"Hey, Dorian," I called out. "It's a long shot, but can
you let us know if you find a laptop?"

"No. I figured I'd just put it on eBay." She shook her
head in disgust and muttered something about "inane
questions."

Bailey almost cracked a smile. I heard the *zip* of the
body bag and the wheels roll across the asphalt to the

wagon. Only after I heard them slam the rear door did I risk speaking to Scott. "Can you tell cause of death?"

"Stab wounds. But no murder weapon in the trunk that I could see."

And I doubted very much that Dorian would find it in the cabin of the car either. One of the many reasons why I prefer gunshot wounds for a cause of death. Between the casings and the bullets, you have something to work with. Knives can never be matched the way a gun can. And criminals don't get attached to knives the way they do to guns, so they don't mind dumping them.

Bailey gathered all the officers together and asked them to canvass the grounds for a knife. They all nodded solemnly.

When they'd left, I heard Dorian mutter, "Yeah, good luck with that."

We were going to need it with a lot of things now.

16

Exhausted and depressed, Bailey and I headed back to the car.

She drove off the lot and pulled onto Sepulveda Boulevard. When she got to a stoplight, she turned to look at me. "You okay, Rachel?"

"Yeah. I'm just…" My voice broke and I felt tears spring to my eyes again. I turned to look out my window.

Bailey was silent for a moment. The light changed and she pulled forward. When she spoke, her tone was gentle. "All the homicides you've been to, Rache. I've never seen you this broken up."

"I guess I was really thinking she'd be okay…" I stopped before my voice could break again.

"But it's a kidnapping. Sure, we were both hoping it'd be different, but kidnappings end this way pretty often. That's why we run so hard and fast on them. You know that as well as I do. But for some reason, this one knocked you down hard. What's going on?"

The question was more than fair. What *was* going on with me? I'd been so wedded to the theory—no, *expectation*—that Hayley would be okay that I hadn't even allowed myself to consider any other possibility. That was completely unlike me. Finally, the light dawned. Romy. The hope of finding Hayley alive left me a sliver of hope that the same happy ending could come true for my sister. Finding Hayley in the trunk of Brian's car delivered a crushing blow on both levels. I told Bailey.

"Makes perfect sense," she said. "So what do you want to do?"

"Get back to work."

Bailey gave me a little smile. "That's my girl."

I returned her smile as best I could and turned my thoughts back to the case. I'd been planning to do something. After a few moments, I remembered what it was. "Can you get me to a quiet place where I can call the aunt?"

"How about we hit a place for breakfast and you can call from the car?"

Just minutes ago I would've gagged at the thought of food. But suddenly the idea of breakfast felt comforting, and I heard my stomach grumble. "Is there an IHOP around?"

Bailey raised an eyebrow. This wasn't my usual fare. "If not that, then at least its equivalent."

A few minutes later she pulled into a Coco's and went inside to score us a table. Trying not to get distracted by the enticing smell of grease and bacon, I punched in Janice Maher's number. By the third ring I was preparing to leave another message when I heard a click. A distracted-sounding voice said, "Yes?"

I introduced myself and explained that I was calling

because Hayley hadn't been seen in the past few days and her parents were concerned. "We have evidence that Brian bought two plane tickets to New York, and told his boss that he was going to visit his aunt in New York for a week. So we thought he was probably intending to visit you. We wouldn't ordinarily bother you with this, but Hayley is only sixteen and, naturally, her parents are very concerned."

I deliberately didn't tell her Hayley's last name, because I thought she might recognize it. I hoped that if I kept it low-key, the aunt wouldn't feel she had to lie to protect Brian.

"Well, now I'm concerned too," she said, without hesitation. "I haven't heard from Brian for about a month. In fact I was about to call him and check in. No one's heard from either of them?"

"Not for the past four days." Could that be right? Only four days? It felt like weeks.

"Do you suppose they ran away together? I can't believe Brian would do something like that. It's completely unlike him." I'd expected that reaction, but she seemed genuinely concerned, and sincere. "Have you spoken to his friends?" she asked, her tone worried.

Based on what we'd learned so far, he didn't have any. I wondered how well she knew her nephew. No time like the present to find out. "If you have the names of his friends, I'd be glad to take them down."

"I...I don't. He never told me about any friends. Only people he worked with."

I thought we probably already had those, but I took down the co-workers' names she could remember anyway.

"Did Brian stay with you after his mother died?"

"Yes. He was only sixteen at the time, so I brought him out here to finish school."

"But he wound up in L.A.—"

She sighed. "Yes. He said he wanted to be a television writer, like his father. His plan was to save up the money to go to college out there and see if he could break in by getting a job as a production assistant. I told him that it's a very hard road, with lots of competition, but Brian was determined."

"Even though . . . ?"

"You know about that," she said flatly. "I never knew for sure whether that man really did steal Tommy's script. But Tommy became a complete basket case over it . . ."

"I'm so sorry, Janice. I can only imagine how awful that must've been."

"It was. It was a terrible thing." Her voice shook a little. "What killed me was that he was a really terrific writer. In fact, I always thought he was better than me. I kept telling him to get out of Hollywood and write novels. But he wouldn't listen." Janice gave a heavy sigh.

"I hope you don't mind. I'd like your opinion regarding things we've heard about Tommy."

"All right." But her voice was wary. I'd probably feel the same in her position.

"People who'd worked with him on the show said he complained a lot about other writers lifting his stories and his lines—"

"He wasn't the paranoid type, if that's what you mean. If he said it, then I'd bet it was true. Now, I'm not saying he couldn't have been mistaken at times. But there was probably some truth to it."

"Did he talk to you about the show, or the other writers?"

"Not much." Janice paused. "As you can tell, I wasn't a big fan of Hollywood. He didn't want to hear me tell him yet again that he should get out, so he didn't talk about it much. But of course, he did tell me when that man stole his screenplay."

"So he didn't complain to you about the other writers stealing his lines or anything?"

"No. He called them untalented hacks, but he didn't say anything about stealing from him."

I hadn't considered the possibility before, but now I wondered whether those stories of Tommy's constant accusations were just hype generated after the fact to explain his suicide.

"Had you ever known him to be suicidal before?"

"Never. Oh, he could be morose. He certainly had his moods. But suicidal? Not even a hint of it. That's why I had an investigator look into his death. I thought it might be a homicide that'd been covered up to look like a suicide."

I thought people read too much crime fiction. Then it occurred to me that Janice might be a thriller writer, so I kept that thought to myself.

"What happened?"

Janice gave another heavy sigh. "He couldn't find any evidence of homicide."

"So you have no doubts?"

"He did a very thorough job. Trust me, I made sure of it." Janice gave a short, dry bark of a laugh. "I wish I did have doubts. But, no, I don't."

Neither did I. I'd read the reports on Tommy's death

and there was no indication that it was anything but a suicide.

"Did Brian know the story?"

Janice sighed again. "Not while his mother was alive. She refused to discuss it. Estelle considered the whole business of that script a sickness, and after Tommy died she was too angry to discuss it. All she wanted to do was get away from it all. She didn't care anymore whether Tommy was right or wrong. In my opinion, she was profoundly resentful—watching him unravel month by month, and then in the end...well, you know. The truth was, she hated everything and everyone associated with that script. And that meant Hollywood. Her way of dealing with that was to move them out to Arizona and never speak of it."

I don't know whether I'd have done the same thing. But I sure didn't blame her. "And after Brian moved in with you, did you tell him about his father?"

"Eventually, yes. Brian was a little guy when Tommy died. Barely nine years old. All he knew was that mommy seemed angry all the time and he believed it was his responsibility to make her happy. A task doomed to failure. Add that to his confusion over why daddy had abandoned them and you have a very sad child. Estelle was smart enough to get him therapy, and heaven knows she loved him dearly, so in spite of it all, he grew up into a sweet boy. But I could tell he was still confused about what had happened to Tommy. So I had to tell him the truth. I explained to him how and why it all happened, that his father was just too sad to go on living and his mother was angry about losing him because she loved him."

"And that helped?"

"It seemed to. He'd periodically ask me questions about what had happened, what his dad told me, what he'd done about the theft of the script. Brian even bought the DVD of the movie. He watched it over and over again."

So many things were clearer now. "Did he ever tell you that he wanted to avenge his father, clear his name by proving he'd originated the idea for the movie?"

"No. I mean, he was upset at the idea that someone might have stolen his father's script and that it had pushed his father . . . over the edge. But he never spoke of wanting to do anything about it. I mean, what could he do? The whole issue is long in the past now."

I didn't want to tell her that Brian had indeed found a way to do something about it. So I wrapped it up, thanked her for her time, and gave her my number. She assured me that if she heard from Brian, she'd be in touch immediately. "He's a lovely, gentle soul. Please believe me, he would never hurt anyone." My silence provoked her to add, "I know, someone in the family always says that, and then you find the body." The remark was so unwittingly accurate, it left me speechless. Janice exhaled and said, "Don't worry, Ms. Knight. If this girl is with Brian, I'm sure she's just fine and she'll turn up soon."

The bitter irony made my throat tighten. I barely managed to choke out a "thank you" before ending the call. When I got out of the car, the smell of greasy food filled my nostrils. It turned my stomach. I opened the door to the restaurant, intending to tell Bailey I'd wait outside, but she was already standing at the register.

"Man, you eat fast. Don't you believe in chewing?"

A waitress behind the counter brought over a bag that gave off the smell of bacon and something sweet. Bailey handed it to me. "I ordered yours to go."

Bailey finished paying. "Our pal Brian is on the move. He just bought a ticket to Paris using Hayley's iPad."

17

Bailey hustled me into the car and pulled out onto Sepul-veda Boulevard. For some reason my appetite returned with a vengeance. I was aiming a forkful of the hash browns at my mouth, but we hit a dip in the road, and it missed and bounced off my chin instead. Flicking a piece of potato out of my bra, I asked, "Where exactly are we rushing to?"

"The station. Got to call my contact with the cell site info."

Bailey's contact might be able to tell us what cell sites the iPad accessed when Brian bought the plane tickets. And, hopefully, that would lead us to Brian. "Think he's dumb enough not to know we can trace the signal?"

"He might think he can outrun us—"

And he might be right. Thus, Bailey's rush. "Do we know what name he bought the ticket under?"

"I didn't ask. We can do it at the station."

As Bailey navigated the morning traffic, I tried to stuff some food down. But after a few sudden stops and sharp turns, I gave up. I decided I didn't want to be Exhibit A for a new definition of pancake makeup.

We headed straight for Bailey's desk, and while she made the call to her contact I poked through her in-box. It looked like we already had a few reports from Dorian. Bailey fished them out and scanned them.

"Anything?" I asked.

"Dorian found no evidence of forced entry or struggle at the party house."

That's what we'd named Russell's house in the hills. "We didn't expect to. Did she recover any trace evidence to put Brian there?"

Bailey scanned the page again. "Doesn't say in this report. But I know she lifted some prints." Bailey flipped to the next page. "She notes plant debris on Hayley's body that looks similar to some debris on the undercarriage of the car—"

"So he took her with him to the ransom drop in Fryman Canyon."

Bailey nodded, then handed the reports to me. "We'll need to find Brian's prints on something official so we can give Dorian something to compare to whatever she lifted at the house."

I scanned the reports, then ran out to the vending machine to get some water. And since I was wearing old jeans, a faded sweatshirt, and no makeup, I of course ran into Graden.

He, on the other hand, was a sight for very sore eyes. His crisply pressed lieutenant's uniform showed off his lean, well-muscled frame, and his perennial light tan enhanced the wide cheekbones, sandy brown hair, and hazel eyes. Graden Hales was a man who very seldom got turned down. Surprisingly, that popularity had not turned him into an ass.

I told him about finding Hayley. "You'd think I'd know better than to get my hopes up by now."

Graden shook his head, his expression sad but resigned. "You never will. No one does. Hope dims over time, but it never completely goes away." He kept it light, but I heard the serious message underlying his words. It occurred to me that he might be referring to us.

The odds of getting back with Graden had been pretty slim. Even though I could now accept that my reaction to his Googling me wasn't rational, the hell of being "that girl" in the small Northern California community after Romy's abduction was still fresh enough to make me cringe. And so when my mother and I moved to Los Angeles, I kept my traumatic family history from everyone—including Bailey and Toni. My childhood therapist and now friend, Carla the Crone (as I'd called her), had always told me that my secretiveness was unhealthy and very likely stemmed from my irrational feelings of guilt for not having saved Romy. Though I recognized the truth in what she said, and in Bailey's and Toni's urgings that Graden shouldn't be thrown out as untrustworthy, it had taken all I had to make myself give him another chance. And he knew it.

"Listen, I've got to get some work done around the house this weekend," he said. "You around early next week?"

"It's hard to say, the way things are going. But if I am, you want to—"

"Yes."

"You don't know what I was going to say. I might've been about to ask if you wanted to paint my room."

"The answer's still yes," he said, with a smile that warmed me from head to toe. "But I get to pick the color."

Graden headed off to his meeting, and when I got back to Bailey's desk, she was just ending a call.

"And?" I asked.

"The iPad's in New York."

"How're we going to get out there in time to—"

"We're not. I put in calls to NYPD. I'm e-mailing them all the info, photos of Brian, all that jazz. They've put out the alert."

"So I guess it's that time," I said. Time to notify Raynie and Russell of Hayley's death. I couldn't even begin to tell Bailey how much I dreaded this meeting, but her expression told me I didn't need to.

"You don't have to do this, Rache."

"Yeah, I do." I couldn't let Bailey go it alone. And I couldn't let my own history get in the way of doing my job.

Bailey sighed heavily. "Do you want to get the parents together or tell them separately?"

I flashed back on the scene at Russell's house. "They all seemed pretty easy with each other. It might be best for them to have everyone together."

Bailey stood up. "I agree. And besides, it's bad enough having to give this news once."

No argument there. Bailey dropped me at the Biltmore and went back to her apartment in Larchmont Village so we could get cleaned up and look professional when we delivered the news.

We arranged for everyone to meet us at Russell's house and we were ushered into the living room, where the parents were seated on separate sections of the couch that was in front of the fireplace. There was a heavy tension in the room. I knew they were steeling themselves against the pain of hearing what we'd come to tell them. The words we were about to utter in the next few seconds would change their lives forever. It made me wish there was a giant life clock I could reach into and push back the hands, take us all to a time when Hayley was here, safe. Raynie jumped up to offer us something to drink, and when we declined, she offered us something to eat. I recognized the defense mechanism, a way to delay the blow. Because maybe if it was delayed long enough, it wouldn't come. But of course, it had to. Bailey told them, as gently as she could, that Hayley had been found dead in the trunk of Brian's car.

Russell roared, "Brian? Brian who?"

He was trying to distance himself from the fact of Hayley's death, but it was a valid question nonetheless. I told him. And when I explained who his father was, I watched Russell carefully. He blanched and then his eyes fixed on a point across the room in a hundred-yard stare.

"How in the hell did he and Hayley…?" he asked, looking bewildered.

"We think Brian sought her out," I said.

Russell covered his face with his hands, then rubbed his temples. He choked back a sob and began to pound the arm of the couch. "No, no, no!" He spit the words out as though they were rocks that'd been stuck in his throat. Then he suddenly jumped to his feet and began to storm around the room. "That goddamn crazy asshole! That psychotic son of a bitch raised a fucking lunatic of a kid! I want that piece of shit obliterated!"

Throughout all this, Raynie keened like a wounded animal, arms wrapped around her midsection, rocking back and forth. "No, no, no, no!" Her agony was almost too painful to witness. She folded forward and hugged her knees, head on her lap.

I could see that Bailey was feeling the heartbreak as deeply as I was. We did what we could to console them, but nothing can make you feel more useless than trying to assuage the pain of losing a child. It was a tragedy like no other. The death of a son or daughter upends the universe—parents predecease children, not the other way around. And I knew that the hole we'd just torn in Russell's and Raynie's lives today would never be fully healed.

Before we left, Bailey and I promised to do everything in our power to bring Brian to justice. Raynie nodded and whispered, "Thank you."

But I knew what she was thinking. We could catch Brian, we could take him to trial, we could get him convicted and locked up forever. But we could never bring Hayley back.

18

We headed back downtown in silence. In the past few hours, the sky had gone from a deep, penetrating blue to an ominously heavy cloud bank of blacks and grays. We drove through a darkness that made mid-afternoon feel like the dead of night. I rolled down the window and the thick damp breeze clung to my face and crawled down my neck. A weird stillness filled the air, as though the planet were waiting for something.

At the corner of Fifth and Broadway, a man in a black top hat, dressed in jeans and a black blazer, waited at the light. He was sitting on a piece of canvas stretched across the frame of a walker, except the walker had four wheels and a basket. When the light changed, he popped up and pushed the contraption across the street, whistling the chimney-sweep song from *Mary Poppins*.

Bailey and I watched him. "Fellini wasn't really stretching much, was he?" I said.

Bailey's mouth twisted in a half smile. I knew it was all she could manage. "Want to head over to the coroner's?" she asked.

"Sure. And we need a specialist to look at that plant debris."

"Dorian's probably already got someone." Bailey got back on the freeway and headed for North Mission Road. "I've been wondering whether the aunt…"

"Janice."

"Right. Whether she was lying? Now that we know Brian's in New York, since he used Hayley's iPad there…"

I'd been thinking about that too. "She sure didn't sound like she had anything to hide. But then again, you never know."

Bailey nodded. "Just wondering."

"Did you ever find out what name that ticket to Paris was purchased under?"

Bailey smacked the steering wheel. "Damn. I'll check into it when we get back."

The coroner's office was a bust. The pathologist who was assigned to our case, Dr. Vendi, wasn't available, and Scott was out in the field, so I couldn't bribe him into giving us a look at any preliminary notes. Bailey left instructions to bag and tag the plant debris for analysis, just to be on the safe side, and we drove back to the Police Administration Building.

"Graden said he'd tell the brass about Hayley," I said.

"I'm sure there'll be a presser of some kind pretty soon, then. You better get ready."

The murder of a superstar director's daughter was big news, and that meant both Bailey's shop and mine would be under siege. "I'll make the call when we get upstairs." It really wasn't a DA's bailiwick to talk to the press before there was a suspect in custody, but Vanderhorn would want in on it anyway. Thanks to yours truly, he could legitimately claim that the DA's office was working closely with the LAPD. Just as Bailey was pulling into the parking lot, the clouds opened up and big fat drops began to splatter the windshield.

She looked up at the sky. "I got a feeling this one's going to be the real deal."

As if to prove her right, a deafening clap of thunder boomed and a jagged streak of lightning cut across the sky.

"Damn, it's the apocalypse," I said.

"And not a bit too soon."

As we headed for Bailey's desk, I was, for a change, presentable and ready to run into Graden. Of course that meant there was no way I was going to see him.

Bailey picked up a manila envelope that was on top of her in-box stack. "Looks like we got Brian's birth records." She handed the envelope to me and picked up the phone.

I pulled out the records and saw the little tiny footprint. No one could have predicted that innocent little foot would turn out to be the foot of a vicious killer.

"He bought the Paris ticket under 'Shandling,'" Bailey said.

I put down the birth record. He'd purchased the tickets to New York under his real name. "Why would he use the alias?"

"Maybe because it doesn't matter anymore, because he's outta here."

"I suppose. Or maybe it's a deliberate mislead? Like, in case we hadn't caught on to his true name yet, he used his alias again to make us believe he's going to Paris?"

"But if he's trying to distract us, why not buy two tickets and make it seem as though Hayley's still with him?" Bailey asked.

"Not worth the expense?" I shrugged. "I don't know."

"Too many possibilities," Bailey said. "Not enough answers."

"Have we made any progress on trying to nail down where the e-mail ransom note came from?"

"I'll check. But it doesn't matter. We already know Brian sent it. The most we'll get is his IP address."

"I'm just hoping for something to back up Legs Roscoe—"

"What? He's rock solid. A little weird maybe, but solid."

"Some corroboration wouldn't hurt. Anyway, what about the calls on Russell's cell—the ones after the kidnapping? Any progress on those?"

"Not yet. We're working on it."

Damn. I could feel Brian slipping farther away by the minute. Another boom of thunder exploded outside and now the rain fell in torrential sheets. The downpour was so heavy, I could hear it pounding the pavement below. Workers who were just five steps from their offices got drenched before they could reach the door.

I looked up at the heavy gray sky. I usually prefer bright, sunny days, no matter how hot. Not today.

19

Hayley's murder was the lead story on the evening news. Hairsprayed news anchors on every channel salivated as they blasted the headlines across the country. I knew it was a harbinger of things to come if the case ever went to trial. But I didn't get time to worry about it.

Forty-eight miles northwest of downtown, the canyons and hills above Malibu, still only thinly covered by shallow-rooted grasses and young shrubs after the rampant wildfires of last summer, shed layers of earth under the pounding rain. Mudslides sent filthy rivers pouring across all four lanes of Pacific Coast Highway. At the end of the highway closest to Santa Monica, the ebbing ground dislodged rocks and heavy boulders, one of which hurtled off the California Incline with meteoric force and landed on the roof of a car, crushing the driver's skull. The car spun sideways, forming a blockade, and four vehicles behind it piled into each other like dominoes.

Farther north, high up in the mountains above Mulholland Highway, where the rain fell as though the clouds had torn apart from the weight, the water found a barren stretch of an old sunbaked trail. Pounding down the newly formed channel with a mighty force, it tore through a small, incongruous mound of freshly turned soil. And exposed an outstretched hand.

The shallow grave was discovered by a biker, and the first responding officer, having heard about Hayley, had the good sense to call Bailey—a phone call that sent us screaming down the freeway and winding up the Santa Monica Mountains within the hour. Those steep, narrow roads would've made me nervous on a clear day, but on a day that was still dark with the threat of another downpour, and asphalt that was slick with rain and oil— not to mention the occasional patches of thick mud—my heart jackhammered so hard I had to remind myself to breathe. Each hairpin turn gave me a view of the thousands of feet I'd be falling to my death if Bailey made one wrong move. By the time she pulled in behind the patrol cars parked against the side of the mountain, my stomach was in my throat and I had to get out and take several deep breaths to keep from puking.

"Where the hell are we?" I asked when I felt like I could pass for normal.

A tall, dark-haired uni with a runner's body who'd come out to escort us answered, "God's Seat, on Boney Mountain." He leaned down and peered at me. "You okay?"

Apparently I was wrong about passing for normal. "I'm fine."

"It's a tough ride. Especially for the passenger."

And especially when the driver ignores the brake. I appreciated his kindness. And as we followed him down the trail, I also appreciated the fact that I'd been at home when Bailey called, which gave me the chance to change into jeans and hiking boots. We were easily two thousand feet up, and the torrential rain had left the path slippery as ice.

We paused at a split in the mountain that afforded a view stretching from the ocean to the valley. It was almost eight p.m., but there was still some daylight left and it was peeking through the heavy cloud bank. I could see why they called it God's Seat. Even under dark, cloudy skies it was breathtakingly beautiful. After a few moments, our guide moved on and we eventually came to a small clearing encircled by crime scene tape. In the center of the taped-off area was a partially washed-out mound of dirt; the rain was still trickling across the path it had forged. Protruding from the earth was a waxy forehead and nose and an outstretched arm. But I couldn't see enough to make out a face.

As I stood on my tiptoes to get a better look, a deep, gravelly voice that sounded vaguely familiar drew my attention.

"How long you gonna keep me here? You know, I got work to do, just like you guys."

On the far side of the taped-off circle, I saw a big guy wearing a black bandanna around his head Hulk Hogan–style. Even from twenty feet away, I recognized Dominic Rostoni, highly successful custom motorcycle dealer and white supremacist gang leader. Bailey and I had run into him on our last case, and I knew he lived just off Mulholland in Calabasas—not all that far from this place. This mountain was probably a great ride for bikers.

Bailey was conferring with the officer who made the first response. I tapped her on the shoulder and pointed to Dominic.

"What're the odds?" she asked.

"Pretty good, when you think about it."

Bailey did, for about a second, then nodded. We made our way over to his side of the crime scene.

"Hey, Dominic," I said. "Long time no see." I didn't offer to shake hands.

He looked up with a frown, then his expression cleared. "Yeah, I remember you. Hey, can you tell these guys to let me go? You know where to find me."

"You found the body?" I replied.

"Yeah. Came up for a smoke."

I further assumed he didn't mean cigarettes. Just the thought of navigating these roads on a motorcycle while high on...anything, gave me vertigo.

"You touch anything?" I asked.

He looked offended. "What you take me for? An idiot?"

The true answer was "Yes, you neo-Nazi asshole." But sometimes the truth does not set you free. I did believe he was smart enough not to mess with a dead body unless he was the reason it was in that condition. And, obviously, he must've called the cops as soon as he found it, because I doubted they'd be doing routine patrol here in this weather.

"What were you really doing out here, Dominic?"

"Really, I was just out for a ride."

"Right after a storm like this." I raised an eyebrow.

Dominic sighed and looked away for a moment. "Wife and I had a fight. I needed some cooling-off time.

Soon as the rain stopped, I went out for a ride. Didn't expect to wind up here, tell you the truth..."

"And you called the cops?"

He nodded and glanced toward the mound of dirt. "Poor kid. Got one of my own, you know."

I didn't know. And I wasn't thrilled to hear that these cretins procreated. I restrained the impulse to ask what his kid was doing with his life. I didn't want to hear he'd joined the "club."

"You come here pretty often?"

"Maybe once a month."

"You happen to notice anything else unusual?"

Dominic shook his head. "Even if there was, with this weather it'd be long gone anyways."

Anyways. Didn't he say that last time too? This stuff made me nuts. "*Anyway,* Dominic. There's only one. Right?"

He snickered briefly. Guess I had mentioned it last time.

"Yeah. *Anyway,* I didn't see nothin' out of the norm."

I wondered if he was smart enough to use the double negative on purpose, just to mess with me, but decided that was probably giving him too much credit. Besides, bad grammar was the least of his deficits. I looked at Bailey, who was suppressing a smile with only partial success.

"Your information still the same?" she asked him.

"Yeah. 'Course."

Bailey gave the officer next to Dominic the high sign. "You can let him go. And thanks."

The coroner's wagon pulled up as Dominic's bike gave a throaty growl. He steered out to the road and touched two fingers to his forehead in a salute, then roared off. I didn't recognize the coroner's investigator who jumped out of the wagon. He was a smallish black man with a neat mustache and goatee.

Bailey and I introduced ourselves as he stood outside the tape and gloved up.

"George Harrison."

I wanted to say "You're kidding, right?" but his serious expression gave me the answer. Without another word, he ducked under the tape, and Bailey and I followed him. He immediately turned back and frowned at us.

"I'm going to have to ask you to stay back until I'm done."

"Mr. Harrison, how long have you been with the coroner's office?" Bailey asked, her tone on the borderline between irritation and genuine pissitivity.

"With this office, four months. In Seattle for five years, and in New York for ten." He said it without a hint of self-importance; it was just a statement of fact. That itinerary explained his accent—as in, he had none whatsoever. That was a lot of years on the job for someone who looked like he was in his twenties. Our skepticism must've shown, because he added, "Black don't crack."

The slang was so out of place in his King's English voice, I chuckled in spite of myself and I saw that Bailey did too. George gave us a little smile and unwound a bit. "You can watch from over there right now. When I get ready to wrap him up, I'll let you in for a closer look."

Bailey and I stood back and watched. George was one hell of a thorough worker—calm, careful, slow, and steady. After what felt like hours, he gestured to us.

"Take a look, but stay back." He left to get the body bag and gurney.

I scanned the area around us briefly and imagined what it would be like to be alone up here in the dead of night. Scary, desolate...and worst of all, isolated. No one would ever hear you scream. Bailey and I picked our way carefully across the river of loose rocks and mud that had streamed from the grave. As our steps brought us closer, I steeled myself for a sight that was likely to be gruesome. But nothing could have prepared me for what lay inside the crime scene tape. The body of Brian Shandling, né Maher.

20

As I stared at the pale, wet face, body frozen in rigor, his aunt's words repeated in my head: "gentle soul," "sweet boy." Her words had fallen on cynical ears at the time. Now, I was more inclined to believe they were true. And if they were, this was yet another child who'd been ripped from the world before he even had a chance to live. I wasn't ready to deal with the tragedy of another young death this soon. My only path of escape was to focus on the evidence.

"George, can you give me an estimate for time of death?" I asked.

"Just a very rough one. I'd say he's been dead for about three days now."

Three days. That would put his death very close in time to Hayley's. We'd get a tighter frame when the autopsy was done for both of them—though, contrary to popular belief, it wouldn't be down to the minute, or even the hour. Usually, the best a coroner can do is narrow the time of death down to a window of a few hours. Even then, an estimate as narrow as a couple of hours requires more information than a pathologist can gather on his own. For example, stomach contents can be helpful, but without certain information like a witness who can say when the victim last ate, or how fast that victim digests, or how much physical activity the victim engaged in after the meal, and so on—the coroner can't give a precise time of death. Since no one we'd spoken to so far had seen Brian after Iris Stavros had a glimpse of him on Monday, we weren't likely to find anyone who could say when he last ate. We'd need other information to prove conclusively that he'd died shortly before or after Hayley. I motioned for Bailey to join me and we moved outside the crime scene tape to a spot where we could talk.

"You could've told me who the victim was," I said, more than a little irritated at the way I'd been blindsided.

"Sorry. It's just that the cop wasn't sure." Bailey glanced at me. "It's just...I didn't want to jump the gun..."

...given the way I'd reacted to Hayley's death. "I get it." I gave her a grim nod. "I'm going to step out on a limb here and say Brian didn't buy that ticket to Paris."

Bailey nodded. "And it seems a lot less likely that he killed Hayley. But he was definitely in on the kidnapping—"

"And we know he sent the ransom note, so there's a good chance Hayley was in on the kidnap-ransom scheme."

"Agreed. But now we know someone else has to be involved—"

"Someone who was trying to make it look as though Brian was still alive and planning to leave the country—"

"So they could frame Brian for Hayley's murder," Bailey said. "Now we know why that ticket to Paris was purchased under Brian's alias."

While Bailey and I were talking, I saw Dorian arrive. This time she started by taking soil samples from the area and collecting leaves from the shrubs. That reminded me of Fryman Canyon. I went over and greeted her.

"Hey, Dorian. Glad it's you out here."

"Makes one of us. What do you want?"

Dorian's gushing could be so embarrassing. "I was just thinking that we also had a scene at Fryman Canyon. I don't know if you remember, that's where the—"

"—ransom was dropped. Of course I remember. I already took samples from there. Any other brilliant thoughts you'd like to share?"

"Nope, all good."

Since Dorian didn't seem in need of any further assistance, I looked around and noticed that George and his burly assistant had already loaded the body into the wagon and George was about to get into the driver's seat. I walked over to him.

"Can you give me some idea as to cause of death?"

"There was an obvious puncture wound in the left side of the neck, and a deep slice across the carotid. Probably drew the knife from behind from left to right."

So cause of death for both Hayley and Brian was knife wounds. "Can we ask Steve to compare the wound tracks to another victim's?"

"Hayley Antonovich?"

I nodded.

"Good idea. I'll put in the request. Steven testified in a case I had up in Seattle. Great witness."

Steven Diamond is the coroner's criminalist who knows and does just about everything you can think of. One of those things is to determine what kind of blade created a wound. That's a pretty unique skill that, as far as I know, no one can do as well as Steven, because he compiled a database of wounds that were known to have been made by specific knives. As a result, he might be able to get fairly precise about what kind of knife was used to inflict our fatal wounds. In this case, with two victims killed close in time, I was hoping Steven could tell us whether the same, or at least a very similar, weapon was used on both of them. And that would help to prove both kids—I couldn't help but think of them that way—were murdered by the same person. It would never be as precise a match as bullets or casings would've given us, but it was a heck of a lot better than most criminalists could do with knife wounds.

George got in, started the van, and slowly pulled out. I didn't envy him having to maneuver that bulky vehicle on these wet, winding roads. Come to think of it, I wasn't all that wild about doing it in a car. My thoughts wound back around to Fryman Canyon and the ransom money. I found Bailey talking to one of the unis and motioned her over.

"Did anyone check Brian's bank accounts? Or find out if he had a safe-deposit box?" I asked.

"No safe-deposit box, and his bank account had twenty-seven bucks and some change. No ransom money anywhere. Until now, I just figured he had the money on him."

"So maybe our third party was in on the kidnapping plan and killed them both so he could grab the money—"

Bailey nodded. "And get rid of the witnesses." She gestured to the rest of the team, who were packing up to leave. "Let me wrap up here and we can take off."

It was nearly ten o'clock now, and the darkness that had settled over the mountain was pierced only by the sliver of light from a crescent moon. The air temperature had dropped at least thirty degrees, and the hulking black hostility of the terrain was starting to get to me. I thought about Brian drawing his last breath in this harsh, lonely wilderness. Had he still been alive when the killer shoveled the dirt over him? The thought left me short of breath and achingly sad. My cell phone rang, breaking into my morbid reverie. Startled by the sound, I reflexively took the call.

A voice cried out, "I j-just heard about Hayley!" Choking sobs intervened before the caller could continue. "It's all my fault! I'm sorry, I'm so sorry!"

It took me a moment to identify the voice through the tears. "Mackenzie?"

"She told me she'd be okay! And I believed her!"

"Take a deep breath, Mackenzie."

A sharp, ragged intake of air, then, "Sh-she told me . . . she said everything would be okay—"

"You mean Hayley?"

"Y-yes." Sniffling and a few hiccups. "She said she'd be gone for a while and I wouldn't be able to reach her. I might hear something that sounded bad, but I shouldn't worry, and I couldn't tell anyone. She said don't tell, just don't tell. She said she and Brian had a plan and everything was going to be great. But she didn't tell me—" The rest of the sentence was cut off by more racking sobs.

"—what the plan was?"

"No. She just said not to tell anyone. So I didn't. She said not to..." Mackenzie trailed off.

"Mackenzie, you are not to blame. Do you hear me? You didn't know what she was planning." But Mackenzie was now crying and hiccupping uncontrollably. "Mackenzie? Is your dad there?"

"Yes."

"Does he know about all this?"

"Yes."

"Will you please put him on the phone? And stay right there, okay?"

"Okay." Then, I heard her call out, "Dad!"

Seconds later, a male voice said, "Yes?" We exchanged names and then I asked Mackenzie's father to watch her closely and not to leave her alone. I'd talk to Mackenzie myself, in person, and try to get her to understand she shouldn't blame herself for any of this. He promised to stay at her side day and night and said he'd get her to her therapist tomorrow.

If anyone understood survivor's guilt, it was me, and thankfully, I could tell that Mackenzie's father would do what had to be done. I didn't know whether Mackenzie would do something crazy. I just knew I couldn't take any chances. I wasn't about to see yet another young life be destroyed by this nightmare of a case.

21

I pulled Bailey aside and told her what I'd just learned.

"So Hayley and Brian were definitely in on it together," she said.

"And most likely were killed by the same person—"

"Or *persons*—"

"—who had to have known about their plan in time to grab the money and kill them," I said. "No way any of Hayley's buddies would've done it."

"No. We've got to dig into Brian's life—find out who he was hanging with."

But whoever it was had deliberately laid a false trail for us. I decided two could play this game. "Do you think we could keep Brian's death under wraps for a while?"

"And hope our mystery man keeps dropping false clues?" Bailey asked. I nodded. "Brian's aunt will keep for a little while. And I can warn these guys"—she tilted her head toward the officers on the scene—"but I can't promise how long—"

In a case like this, no secret was going to keep for

long. And we couldn't let Janice find out about her nephew from the press. "But it's worth a try, right? With a little more time, our mystery man might poke his head above the radar—at least once more." And with a little luck, he'd poke it up nice and high, where I could snap it off.

Bailey gathered all the unis together and gave them the word not to file any reports or talk about what they'd seen until she gave the okay. They all nodded their agreement, though I noticed a couple of skeptical expressions.

I was exhausted in a way that was as much emotional as physical. Bailey too seemed a lot worse for wear, which was unusual for her. Through many all-nighters, she was always the one who looked disgustingly fresh when the rest of us seemed ridden hard and put back wet. But now her eyes, her mouth, her shoulders, all sagged, as if pulled down by fifty-pound weights. She wrapped up with the remaining officers and we trudged down the muddy, rocky trail to her car.

As we wound our way back down the mountain, I tried to dredge up names for any of Brian's friends. No luck. I remembered that even his aunt hadn't known of any. "The only places I can think to check are his jobs. He didn't go to school here—"

"No," Bailey said. "And I've been trying to figure out where he might've gotten the idea to stage the kidnapping—"

"You mean other than from himself—"

"Yeah, I don't make him as the mastermind somehow. If you ask me, this was Hayley's idea."

It did have that teenagey melodramatic touch. But

something about the whole kidnapping scheme bothered me. "If what Brian wanted was to avenge his father, then why only ask for a million dollars? Why not go for it and ask for half the profits on that film?"

"How would he know what that was? He was just a kid. He did what was easy. Hayley told him Russell kept a million in the house. He asked for that."

I stared at Bailey. "Since when did you get to be such a softie?" Bailey was usually the one who landed on the most sinister motives for every move—whether that move was made by a child molester or a ninety-year-old who cheated at Bingo.

Bailey shrugged. After a few moments she said, "It's just a feeling. Okay?"

"You're entitled to 'em," I said. "And I don't disagree with you."

Bailey dropped me off at the Biltmore with a warning that she'd be back to pick me up at eight o'clock tomorrow. I nodded wearily, got out and patted the roof, and Bailey sped off.

One hot shower later, I was in bed. Five minutes after that, I'd fallen asleep with all the lights on.

22

I'd set the alarm early enough to have breakfast and read the paper, but I accidentally hit the snooze button twice. The next time my eyes opened, it was seven thirty. I jerked myself out of bed and ran to the shower, hitting the TV remote on my way so I could check the morning news. I needed to find out whether word of Brian's death had leaked. I cranked up the volume and scrubbed up quickly, listening as I braced for disaster. The hot water felt good on my shoulders and I'd just begun to relax when a familiar voice made me spin around and push open the shower door. I leaned out just in time to see Vanderhorn's face behind a microphone. I grabbed a towel and ran over to the television.

Preening in the limelight, as usual, he affected his "I perform a somber duty" face. "We are continuing to develop leads and are working closely with officers who, I assure you, are going around the clock—"

A reporter interrupted him with a shouted question asking for new information. I held my breath. Vanderputz *shouldn't* know about Brian, but...

"Ah…"

I could see he was aching to say something that'd get him more airtime. I squeezed the towel between my hands, wishing it was his neck. He continued.

"There is nothing more I can tell you at this time. But I believe in the public's right to know, and the moment we have any new development…"

They let him finish the sentence, barely, before cutting away to tease sports and weather. I hurried back to the shower, light-headed with relief. Crisis averted. This one, anyway. I still needed to check the Internet.

I dressed and did my hair and makeup in record time, but just as I opened my laptop, Bailey called to say she was downstairs. Damn. I grabbed a cold bottle of water, wrapped half of my toasted bagel in a napkin, and sprinted for the elevator.

"You checked the Web for leaks?" I asked as I got into the car.

Bailey nodded. "So far, so good."

We went back to Brian's past jobs and asked more questions. All of his bosses and co-workers said the same thing: he was a good worker, a nice guy, but he didn't hang out with anyone on a social basis and they didn't know of any friends. The only person he'd ever mentioned was his aunt, Janice.

As we walked back to the car after the last stop, we passed an outdoor newsstand set under an awning against the wall of a building. I glanced at the newspapers displayed on the middle shelf. Every single paper had some mention of Hayley's murder on the front page. Most featured a color reproduction of a particularly winsome pose above the fold. Not just one but three different tabloids carried a full story. Though I shuddered to think what was in those stories, I bought them all. I had to know what kind of misinformation was already being spread. We'd asked our respective offices to keep a tight lid on the details of how and where Hayley'd been found, but we knew that wouldn't stop the lower-echelon workers at either the police station or the DA's office from leaking stories—true or false—to reporters for fun, attention, and profit. I didn't know whether we'd ever have a suspect to take to trial, but if we did, I would need a jury that hadn't been tainted with lies and spin.

We got into the car and Bailey pulled out. I opened one of the papers to start reading, then realized it'd probably make me nauseated—and I don't just mean from motion sickness. I folded it back up. It could wait till I got back to my office or the station.

"You have the guts to go hit SID and see if Dorian has anything?" I asked.

"Sure, I'm in the mood for a good ass-kicking."

"Maybe if we bring her some lunch..."

"Dorian doesn't eat," Bailey said.

But I did, and I was hungry. Two tacos and a quesadilla later, we were rolling into the parking lot of SID. We found Dorian staring into a microscope at her bench. When we got within ten feet, she looked up and grimaced.

"What?" she said.

Ordinarily, I'd start with a "Hey, how ya doin'?" but not with Dorian. I'd bet Dorian's mother doesn't do that with Dorian.

"Anything on anything?" I asked.

She jerked her head in the direction of her office and started walking. We followed. Her small, spartan office was decorated in early modern anal-retentive. Her desk was spotless, the in-box placed at precisely one inch from the edge on both sides, and of course empty. Dorian unlocked her computer and tapped a few keys. "Brian's apartment: no evidence of struggle, hair consistent with Hayley's was found in the bathroom and the bedroom, and prints that matched his and Hayley's were found in all rooms. Couple of toothbrushes found in the bathroom. Preliminary tests indicate they were used by Brian and Hayley. I'll have a final answer when we get back DNA. No clothing in the closets, and other than a used tube of toothpaste—which I haven't printed yet—there were no other items in the bathroom or the medicine cabinet—"

"So Hayley stayed there with Brian."

Dorian ignored me, tapped more keys, and squinted at the screen. "Next, Brian's car. This is just the first look, so we'll have more when I get time to finish. I found Brian's hair and prints in the car, of course. Hayley's hair and prints too. Possibly some fibers from the blouse she was found in as well. It was a lightweight knit that shed a fair amount, which is helpful. Now here's the part I know you're waiting for: I found a small smear of blood on the outside of the trunk. Seems to be a mix of Hayley's and someone else's."

"Not Brian?" I asked.

"Not based on the profile I've got so far. When I get back the DNA, I'll be able to tell you for sure, but at this moment, it looks like a third party's blood."

Bailey and I exchanged a long glance.

"Do you have a plan for the soil samples?" Bailey asked.

"I don't 'plan.' I already sent 'em out to a guy who's the guru on particulates." Dorian looked up from her computer. "And I can tell you, he isn't as accommodating as I am about your 'need it now' jazz."

Less "accommodating" than Dorian? I couldn't begin to guess what that might mean.

"Given your findings on the car trunk, do you think we should go back out to the mountain?" I asked.

"I would. It's dry now, and I'd like to take another look, in the light." She turned to Bailey. "You putting in the request?"

"As of now."

I was buoyed by the possibility that we might have the DNA of the killer. Then I considered who our killer might be from a logical standpoint. I didn't like where my train of thought was taking me, but maybe Bailey would find a way to knock it down.

"We're pretty sure at this point that Brian and Hayley engineered this kidnapping scheme," I said. "But obviously someone else got into the mix. Brian didn't have any friends, so if someone was in on it from the start, that person didn't come from his end—"

"And we know it couldn't be anyone in Hayley's circle."

"But here's the question: Why would Brian and Hayley have even wanted to bring in a third party?"

"No reason I can see," Bailey said. "She knew how to reach her dad, how much money he had, all the important stuff. It didn't take much to set up the drop in Fryman Canyon—"

"They didn't need any help. So I'm betting our killer was an uninvited guest at their party. That means he had to have found out about the kidnapping while it was in progress."

"You two want to blab, take it outside," Dorian said. "Some of us work for a living."

We started to apologize, but Dorian had already turned back to her computer. When we got to the elevator, Bailey started to speak but stopped when some others joined us. After we got out of the building, she said, "What about Legs? He 'sniffed' the ransom note before it was sent."

"True. But I have a hard time believing that the guy who called us with the tip—"

"Yeah. Hard to believe, but you never know." Bailey shrugged.

"He just doesn't fit the bill." The skinny, pierced, and tatted soon-to-be doctor of neuroscience was a tough sell as a killer. "But you're right. I guess we should at least check his alibi."

"I'll put Harrellson on it," Bailey said. "Assuming it doesn't turn out to be Legs, who else could've found out about the plan in time to jump in?"

"Other 'cyber-sniffers,' I guess—"

"Jeez, I don't know. Legs Roscoe was enough of a coincidence. How many others could have jumped in at just the right time?"

"But it wouldn't hurt to try and run down everyone who was in that cybercafé," I said.

"I'll add it to the list."

I moved on to consider other possibilities. Only one came to mind. "Assuming it wasn't some random person at the café, all we're left with is someone who was close enough to Russell to find out on his end…like someone who was in the house when the kidnapping message came in."

Bailey pulled out of the parking lot and didn't answer for a few moments. "That fits. And God knows Russell's place always seems to have a boatload of people running around in it."

"Good thing we decided to keep Brian's death under wraps."

But life is all about balance, as Toni's boyfriend, Judge J. D. Morgan, always says. That good thing was balanced by a nasty bad thing: since no one knew about Brian, I'd have to get Vanderhorn's permission to interrogate Mr. Moviemaker's inner circle. It'd be like slamming my hand in the door, only not as much fun. Then it occurred to me that there was a better option— at least for me. My boss, Eric.

23

I asked Bailey to stop by the courthouse so I could make my pitch to Eric in person. He was thrilled to talk to Vanderhorn for me, though his display of joy was subtle.

"Don't you think you're in a better position to explain why you need to dig into Russell's entourage?" he asked.

"No. I think you are. Even an idiot like Vanderhorn will get it if you talk slow. And you know he likes you more—"

"He likes acid reflux more than he likes you, but that's not the point. He'll listen because he'll hear the name 'Antonovich.' And he'll want a complete explanation for why a potential major campaign contributor has to strap on a poly and answer questions about his daughter's murder. I'm bound to run out of answers."

"We're not going to poly him...yet. And if you get in a bind, just call me. I'll fill you in."

"'Yet'? I was just kidding. Knight, what the hell are you up to?"

"Nothing. I was just kidding too." I crossed my fingers. I don't know why I still do this when I lie. But at least I don't throw salt over my shoulder...anymore. Waste of good salt if you ask me. "Come on, Eric. I don't have time to fiddle around with Mr. Potato Head and I really need to get this ball rolling. Whoever murdered these two children is going to be in the wind if we don't move fast."

"Fine. But do me a favor. Start on the periphery and go easy until I give you the all clear."

"Okay, but don't let the idiot tell his new best friend, Russell, that we're looking his way. We need spontaneous answers."

Eric sighed. "Keep your cell phone close. I'll be in touch."

When I got back to the car, I filled Bailey in. "So we'll start with the bottom rung," I finished.

"We'd start on the fringe of the circle anyway."

"Housekeepers, runners, security—"

"Then personal assistants, manager, personal friends, and—"

"I'd do the personal assistants last, just before Russell, Raynie, and Dani," I said. "They know more than anyone else."

Back when I was a baby DA in the Beverly Hills branch court, I caught a burglary case in which the victim was a lead actor in a primetime detective series. Burglary was the most common felony in Beverly Hills. The burglar turned out to be the piano teacher for one of the actor's children. That case had been an eye-opening primer on how "the other half"—really more like the other one percent—lived. Everyone had a personal assistant. Some of the assistants even had assistants. And all of them were treated like furniture. The residents were so used to having assistants around all the time, they became invisible. So the most intimate of conversations about sex, deals, money, and custody battles took place in full earshot of the assistant. Luckily, most assistants were pretty loyal and damn scrupulous about not leaking what they heard. Or maybe they were just scared. But one thing was for sure: assistants were a fount of information and we'd learn a lot if we could get any of them to talk.

Bailey announced us on the intercom and the gates swung open smoothly. A young man in faded jeans and a T-shirt emblazoned with the title of Russell's last film, *Princess Warrior,* met us in front of the house.

"Mr. Antonovich will be back in about an hour, but he said you could wait inside. We've got a lot of people in and out all the time, so it'd be better if I took care of your car."

Bailey wasn't wild about the idea, but she tossed the keys to the kid. "I need easy in and out," she ordered.

The door was answered by a guy in a crew cut and an FBI-style suit. I say FBI-*style* because I didn't see the standard earpiece and I knew the FBI hadn't been called in on the case. He put out his hand and gave his name in a serious voice. "Kenneth Krup. You'd be Detective Keller and DDA Rachel Knight?"

I barely resisted the urge to say "affirmative." I didn't remember seeing any security types like this on our last visit. It seemed a little late for Russell to bring in the troops now. Bailey confirmed our identities. "This way," he said.

Back to the great room, which still truly was. "Make yourselves comfortable. I'll send Sophie in to get whatever you need." He turned on his heel—which must've been rubber, because it squeaked on the highly polished wooden floor—and left us. A mixture of light green and floral smells gave the room a garden-like atmosphere. I didn't have to look far for the source: there was a gigantic arrangement of white dahlias and lotus flowers on a low table in the far-right corner of the room, and Chinese vases filled with hydrangeas, roses, and calla lilies on glass shelves, coffee tables, and side tables. Maybe it was the size of the room, maybe it was my state of distraction, but I hadn't noticed the floral display the last time we were here.

I leaned toward Bailey. "Think Sophie would bring us a couple of dry martinis?"

"I think Sophie would bring us a couple of male strippers if we asked her to."

I considered the idea. "We should probably get some interviews done first."

Bailey shrugged.

One second later, a slight young woman, no more than five feet one, dressed in a black cotton dress and white apron and looking like she was in her late teens, entered the room. I made the deductive leap that this was Sophie. Sophie asked what she could get us. We said water would be nice. She inquired whether we wanted tap or sparkling; we opted for tap. When she returned with two glasses, I asked in what I hoped was an offhand manner how long she'd been working there.

"Three years."

"Pretty long time." Especially for someone who looked no older than twenty. "What are your days?"

"Tuesday through Saturday," she said.

"So you get Sundays off. That must be nice."

Sophie shrugged. "Sure."

I was trying to make this sound conversational so she wouldn't get scared off, but Sophie was edging away from us. I'd have to get to the point.

"Do you ever work on Mondays?"

"Around the holidays and awards season, or if Frankie calls in sick, or if there's a party and they need extra help. But then they pay me extra."

"As they should. Glad to hear it." And I really was. "Then Frankie usually works Mondays?"

Sophie nodded.

"So you weren't here last Monday?"

"No. And thank goodness because the twins were home sick and I didn't have anyone to stay with them."

That meant she hadn't been here on the day of the "kidnapping." Also, she probably wasn't eighteen. "You have twins?"

"I'm twenty-seven." She smiled at my stunned expression. "I know, I'm lucky."

"Good." I hate it when people with baby faces complain, "I still get carded at bars." Yeah, that really sucks.

Sophie zipped off to amaze others with her youthful appearance.

"I'm going to go out on a limb and guess Sophie isn't our guy," Bailey said.

"Ruthless killers come in all packages, you know."

Bailey raised an eyebrow.

"She could be the mastermind, and her devoted protégé did the killing."

"A devoted protégé who also doubles as a babysitter for her twins," Bailey said. "Of course, why didn't I think of that?"

24

We were able to eliminate others just as easily—Vera, the cook, who basically only spoke Hungarian, and had been busy in her wing of the house all day and well into the evening; Annabelle, the "interior plant designer"—I kid you not—who maintained the indoor flora on Tuesdays and Fridays; and Dani's personal trainer/yoga instructor, Shakti, who had taken Monday off to do a spiritual cleansing. Call me a skeptic, I just don't believe someone whose last name is Schwartz had "Shakti" on her birth certificate.

After about half an hour, I noticed that the Antonoviches took their air-conditioning seriously. It'd crept up on me and I didn't realize I was cold until I found myself suppressing shivers. So when Eric called during our interview with Annabelle to tell me we had the all clear to go after the major players, I used it as an excuse to step outside. I took an extra five minutes after ending the call to work the bluish tinge out of my fingers.

But now, just twenty minutes later, I was freezing

again. I wanted to go out and take another sun break, but Russell chose that moment to show up with his manager, Ian Powers, and their respective assistants, Uma and Sean. The director rolled in with an earpiece in his ear, a cell phone in his hand, and his assistant glued to his side, monitoring the conversation on her own cell while scribbling notes on a small pad. When Russell ended the call and gave us a curt nod, I could see he looked haggard, but he radiated even more nervous energy than I remembered from our last visit. I guessed he was coping by staying busy. Bailey told him why we were there and said we'd start by talking to Uma. He sat down on the nearest couch, leaned back, and folded his arms across his chest. "Okay."

"Separately," I said.

Ian, who'd remained standing, examined me coldly, as though I'd just told him I had a screenplay I wanted to send him. "Why's that?"

I wasn't obligated to explain it to him, but Ian had been Russell's manager for over ten years and was used to standing between Russell and all things unpleasant. So I chalked up his attitude to protective habit and told him. "We need to make sure that each witness gives us his or her best memory without being influenced by anyone else's opinion or recollection."

Russell's features tightened, a mixture of confusion and irritation. "But what is there for anyone to remember? I was the one who got all the messages. They won't know anything."

Since I had no intention of telling him what we suspected, I breezed by the meat of the question. "We just have to follow procedures and cover all the bases, Russell. If they have nothing to say, we'll be done pretty quick."

My tone was polite but unmistakably firm. Russell gave a loud, exasperated sigh. "Fine. But I've got sensitive materials for my next film in the study, so you'll have to use the guest room."

Oh heavens, no, not the guest room. "That'll be fine. Uma, can you lead the way?"

She dipped her head and cast a baleful look at Russell, like a chastened pet, and led us down the hallway to a large bedroom decorated in hues of forest green and ecru. It had French doors that opened onto a courtyard featuring a waterfall fountain made of a dark slate-type stone and a black marble Buddha. Very feng shui.

Uma gestured to a corner near the French doors where a love seat faced two wingback chairs. Bailey and I took the chairs, and Uma, who I could now see habitually curved her head and shoulders down, like a walking comma, scurried onto the love seat. Had working for Russell bent her into this obsequious posture, or had she always been this way? Bailey tried to put her at ease, explaining that we didn't suspect her of anything and just needed to gather information. Uma dipped her head a couple of times. "I get it, not a problem."

"Can you give me a rundown of what you did on Monday?" Bailey asked.

Uma recounted their day at the studio: meetings and more meetings, phone calls and more phone calls with producers, writers, agents, casting directors. At about six o'clock, they came back to the house.

"Do you always ride home with Russell?"

"Yeah, pretty much. He rolls calls on the way home and he prefers if I'm in the car with him while I listen in."

"Listen in?" Bailey asked.

Oh, poor naive Bailey, who didn't know the ways of Hollywood. All assistants listened in on their bosses' phone calls. Though it was never announced and the uninitiated might never know unless the boss, in the middle of the phone call, told the assistant to make a note of something. The benign reason for this systematic eavesdropping is so the assistant can take notes and keep the "to do" list up to date. The not so benign reason is to protect the boss in case the actor/producer/writer/agent later claimed something was promised that hadn't been. Uma gave Bailey the former reason. Of course.

"So you listen and take notes while Russell drives?" Bailey asked.

A perplexed look from Uma. "Um, Russell doesn't usually drive."

Of course not. He has a driver.

"And his driver's name is?"

"Lee. He dropped us here but then he left, so he never came in the house."

"But you did, right?" I asked.

"Yeah. And I remember that after we got home, Russell said he couldn't find his private cell phone, hadn't seen it all day. I found it for him. He'd accidentally left it in the car."

"And it's unusual for him to forget his phone somewhere?" I asked.

"No, not really. He's got so much going on." Uma licked her lips nervously. "I just remember that because when he checked the phone, he looked really weird."

"Weird?"

"Um…upset?" Uma paused. "Shocked, kind of."

"Did he tell you what was in the message?"

"No. I mean, I know now, but at the time, I didn't."

"Who else was around?" I asked.

Uma frowned. "I'm pretty sure Angie was here—"

Angie, assistant to Russell's wife, Dani. "So Dani must've been here," I said.

"Yeah. I don't remember seeing her, but she was probably around somewhere. She usually takes Angie with her if she goes out."

That Russell would have an assistant—or even more than one—made sense, given his workload. But it was hard to fathom what his wife would need one for. I supposed it was something everyone who was anyone had to have—like a Prada purse.

"Anybody else?" Bailey asked.

"Maybe Jeff? Yeah, I'm pretty sure Jeff was here."

Jeff, yet another of Russell's assistants. But one step below Uma, the main assistant. This assistant business was complicated.

"Did you see Russell again after he went into his study?" I asked.

Uma looked off to the right. Supposedly an eye shift to the right is a sign of truthfulness. Assuming the person being evaluated doesn't already know about those "secret" cues.

She slowly replayed the events in her mind. "Yeah. But it was later. He said he had to go out for a little bit and asked me to stay with Dani."

"Did he tell you where he was going?" Bailey asked.

"No."

"Did you see him leave?" she asked.

Uma paused for a moment. "I didn't see him walk out the door, but I didn't see him around the house for about an hour. Maybe a little more."

"And when Russell got back, how did he look?" Bailey asked.

"Kind of tired. Depressed."

"Did he say where he'd been?" I asked.

"No. He just went back in his study and closed the door. I wanted to ask him if I could leave, but he was in a bad mood and sort of out of it, so I decided it'd be better to wait. And I've crashed here before, so..."

"When did you see him again?" I asked.

"Maybe an hour before you guys got here. I guess Dani had been in the study with him, because they both came out and she was crying and he was wired, like he wanted to jump out of his skin. He'd sit down, then jump up, pace around, and leave the room. He couldn't sit still."

"Did he say anything to you?" Bailey asked.

"He asked all of us if we'd seen Hayley since Thursday."

"And had you?" Bailey asked.

"No. None of us had."

"Do you remember anything else he said? Or that Dani said?" I asked.

Uma shook her head. "I don't remember Dani saying anything to us. She just kept telling Russell to call, and I could tell she was upset with him but, like, trying not to show it. Because he was already such a mess."

"Who'd she want him to call?" Bailey asked.

"I guess the police. Because the next thing I remember is you guys showing up."

It seemed a fair guess. And a pretty complete rendition from Uma's point of view. We thanked her and let her go. After she'd left, I suggested we go fetch our next victim.

25

Russell's assistant Jeff was really just a lowly runner—a gofer's gofer, who occasionally got to do the work of an assistant—but I could see that he had much bigger aspirations. He was a xeroxed copy of Russell. Same faded jeans, same baggy T-shirt, and the same worn-out baseball cap, emblazoned with the name of the same team: the Oakland A's. Jeff even walked with the same bouncing stride. And more important, he was almost an inch shorter than Russell. Clearly he was destined for great-ness.

He even flopped down on the couch just like Russell.

"What time did you get here on Monday?" I asked.

"Let's see…I left the studio at six forty-five, so I had to have gotten here by seven thirty."

He enunciated with gusto, every word uttered as though he were savoring a new, delicious piece of chocolate, and he had one of those loud, booming voices that so often seem to come from small men. A six forty-five departure would put him out of the running, since Russell read the first kidnap message around six o'clock, and the ransom message came in not too long after that. But it was an easy enough thing to check studio records. I tossed out a question that would give me an idea right now whether he was telling the truth.

"You have security at the studio, some kind of log that says when you come in and when you leave, right?"

Jeff's eyebrows took wing. "You don't believe me? Why would I lie?"

You tell me, Jeff. But I restrained my *Dragnet* impulses. "I'm not saying I don't believe you. We're talking to a lot of people, and when you mentioned the studio, I wondered about security, that's all. Take a pill, Jeff. It's just a question."

He looked rattled, but he didn't dare refuse to answer. "We have security that logs us in and out. I know when I left because I had to pick up a package from Mila to bring to Russell."

"Mila?"

"A producer. It was a script."

Better and better. Now we could confirm Jeff's alibi with Mila. He didn't have any more information to add to what Uma had told us about the events later that evening, so we let him go. I was tempted to tell him to surrender his passport and stay close just as a joke, but I thought he might stroke out.

"A little high-strung, no?" I said after he'd left.

"He was practically playing a tune he was vibrating so fast. But I'd say he's off the list."

"Agreed. Time to move up the food chain."

Ian Powers affected an exaggeratedly imperious bearing that made me think of "The Emperor's New Clothes." He walked in slowly, with a studied casualness, then calmly settled into the love seat. The way he leaned back and spread his arms across the top of the sofa said "lord of the manor." I wondered whether the posturing was partly an unconscious effort to counteract the shadow of the "little Mattie" persona. Powers confirmed that he had indeed been Russell's manager since Russell was a co-producer on Brittany's show, *Circle of Friends*.

"Then you were representing Russell when Tommy Maher accused him of stealing his screenplay," I said.

Ian leaned forward, and for just a brief second, his features darkened. But just as quickly, they rearranged themselves into an expression of mild irritation. "It was tragic, really. I would've been glad to listen if Tommy had any proof to back up his claim—hell, I would've taken him on as a client." Ian gave a short bark of a laugh at his own semi-joke. "But he didn't. Just a lot of wind and noise. If you ask me, he saw his career tanking and got desperate, so he tried to horn in on Russell's screenplay. Maybe he thought Russell would pay him off with nuisance money. I don't know. But obviously, he was unhinged. You know he committed suicide—"

"Doesn't that work both ways?" I asked. "Some might say his suicide proved that he was telling the truth and no one would listen."

Ian nodded. "I suppose, but...I guess you had to be there. This wasn't the first time he'd claimed someone had stolen credit for one of his ideas. And he was a basket case. He even attacked Russell at one point. Did you know that?"

"So I've heard," I said.

"And now his sick, twisted son has killed Hayley."

At this, Ian looked aggrieved. "I guess it's true that the apple doesn't fall far from the tree. Do you have any leads?"

"A few," I said. "Were you with Russell on Monday?"

"Not till after you two got here."

But it was within minutes of our arrival, as I recalled. Ian saw my expression and nodded. "Russell called me. I can't remember exactly what time, but I do remember telling him to call the police." Ian shook his head. "I don't know what he was thinking. Why he didn't call immediately when he first got the message that Hayley'd been kidnapped..."

Interesting that he was taking the credit for telling Russell to call the police. According to Uma, it had been Dani, Russell's wife, who'd begged him to make the call. "And where were you when you got that call?" I asked.

"At home."

"And after that?"

He gave me a weary look. "The same. Until I called him a while later and found out he'd paid the ransom and..." Ian pressed his mouth closed and turned his eyes away.

That wouldn't usually impress me as far as alibis go, but we'd already heard from everyone who was present that Ian hadn't been in the house when Russell saw the first kidnapping note. I knew I'd have more questions for this guy later, but right now we were under the gun to find a killer who might at that very moment be headed for some country that wouldn't let us extradite. I looked at Bailey, who shook her head. We thanked Ian and let him go.

"Dani?" Bailey suggested.

"Yep."

Dani had that soft, angelic look many try to engineer but few can pull off. Delicate, natural-looking blonde curls framed a heart-shaped face with small features and wide blue eyes. For all that, she had a down-to-earth quality that probably made her a great friend. The kind who'd tell you the guy you'd fallen for was a shit heel, but still hold your hand when he proved her right.

"When did Russell tell you about the kidnapping?" Bailey asked.

Dani's brows knitted and she looked down at her hands, which were twisted around the ends of a silky fringed scarf. When she looked up, her eyes were filled with tears. "After he got the first kidnapping message. I feel so terrible. I told him to call the police right away, but he was scared. He thought the guy would kill Hayley. He kept saying he'd do anything, he'd be glad to just pay any ransom. But I should have made him call…" She shook her head and looked down again.

"Dani, we can't know what would've happened if Russell had called the police. Don't beat yourself up, okay?" She nodded but looked unconvinced. "So you were there when he got the ransom demand?"

She nodded. "I-it sounds stupid now, but we were actually sort of relieved. Russell could easily pay it, and we thought that once he did, we'd get Hayley back." There was a hitch in her voice as she said the name "Hayley," and she tried to take a deep breath, but it got stuck and I saw tears fall on her hands. "S-so, I went along with him paying the ransom and not calling the police."

"Dani, did you know Brian at all?" I asked.

"No. Hayley had only just begun really talking to me. When I first moved in, she wouldn't even be in the same room with me. I'd walk in, and she'd walk out. But after a couple of years she started to thaw, and in the past year, I have to say, we were really getting along. I think she saw that I truly liked and respected her mom and I knew what my place was in her life." Dani looked out at the fountain, her expression one of heart-twisting sadness. "Maybe she told Raynie about him. But not me."

"Did you know about the fight between Russell and Brian's father, Tommy?" I asked.

"That was before my time. In fact, I had no idea about any of it until this...but why would he kill Hayley because of something her dad did? Why not go to Russell, or a lawyer, show him the proof and see what he can get?"

"Maybe because he didn't have proof?" I suggested.

"Then how could he be sure enough to kidnap Hayley—and *kill* her, for God's sake?" Dani swallowed rapidly and struggled for control.

I couldn't tell her the truth, and I didn't want to offer her any useless platitudes. We thanked her and let her go with a promise to keep her posted.

"Any guilt about not telling her that we found Brian?" I asked Bailey after Dani had left.

"Nah. Can't see how that would make her feel any better."

"Is there any point in talking to Russell again?"

We'd spoken to him several times since Hayley's death, and although our conversations were of the casual, updating variety, we'd already asked all the questions we could think of.

"The only thing we haven't done is ask him about the fight with Tommy," Bailey said.

"But what's he going to say? 'Yeah, I stole his screenplay'? And even if he did say that, what difference would it make? He never knew who kidnapped Hayley. We saw those ransom notes. They didn't mention anything about Tommy or Brian—or anyone else for that matter."

The picture of Russell's grief-ravaged face flashed before my eyes.

"You're right. There's no point."

We'd done a great job of eliminating everyone. Now we just had to find a way to include someone.

26

By the time we finished with the Antonovich entourage, the sun was well over the yardarm. I learned that saying from Judge J. D. Morgan, who uses it to signal to his court reporter that it's time to knock off and go have a drink. It was still plenty warm outside, but I didn't mind after shivering in the too-frosty air of that refrigerated mansion. Bailey got her car keys from the kid in the *Princess Warrior* T-shirt. He turned out to be Lee, the driver, so we took the opportunity to do a little more questioning.

"Hey, Lee, are you Russell's only driver?" Bailey asked.

"Unless I'm sick or something."

"Were you here last Monday evening?"

"You mean the day of the kidnapping?" I nodded. He sniffed and gazed off for a moment. "Yeah. I drove him and Uma home from the studio that day."

"And how long did you stick around?" I asked.

"Guess about an hour or so. Just long enough to make sure the cars were all cleaned up and ready to go."

"So you didn't drive Russell anywhere after you drove him and Uma back here?" Bailey asked.

Lee sniffed again. A sign of a coke habit? Or just an air-conditioning cold? "Nope."

We thanked him and headed out. I opened the window to enjoy the warm air. But it took just ten minutes for the blanket of heat to make me feel like I was suffocating. When Bailey cranked up the air, I closed the window and enjoyed the cool artificial breeze.

"Damn," Bailey said. "I was hoping to get over to the coroner's today."

"Kinda soon to hope for anything on Brian."

"No, I was hoping for info on Hayley. At least some preliminary findings."

It'd be a few weeks before an official report could be ready, and at seven o'clock, it was too late to find the pathologist for an informal chat. But it was a perfect time for a friendly phone call. I dialed and let it ring, expecting to get voice mail.

"Rachel?"

The wary note in Scott's voice told me he had a feeling what was coming.

"Scottsky! How you doin', my man?" He loves when I call him "Scottsky." He's tried to tell me otherwise, but I'm pretty sure he doesn't mean it.

He exhaled sharply. "What do you want, Rachel?"

"Other than the pleasure of your company at Engine Co. No. 28?"

"I can't help you with Brian. I didn't do his case."

"I'm looking for Hayley's reports. I'll take anything you've got."

"Meet me at the Jack in the Box across the street to-morrow morning, eight o'clock."

"On Saturday?" I pleaded, "Make it nine—"

"I've got things to do. Eight or nothing."

I sighed. "Fine, eight it is." I ended the call.

Bailey was smirking. "Too early for ya, little buddy?"

"What happened to 'Thank you, Rachel'? 'Nice score, Rachel'?"

Bailey offered none of the above. "Ready for dinner and a potato-based beverage?" she asked.

It's one of the great mysteries of life how someone figured out you could make vodka from a potato. Or, for that matter, bread from growing stalks of wheat. If I'd been a pioneer, we would have been sober and starving.

Since we were on the Westside and too hungry to wait till we got back downtown, we opted for Craig's—that great steak and martini place Graden had taken me to. We got a table against the wall and the waitress asked what we were drinking.

"Just water, thanks," I said.

Bailey was driving and I didn't want her to have to watch me drink.

"Give her a Ketel One martini," Bailey said. "Very dry, very cold, straight up, olives on the side."

When the waitress left, I said, "You didn't have to do that. I don't mind keeping you company."

"But now you owe me."

"Oh, no," I said, raising my hand to flag down the waitress.

"You're going to send back your drink without even knowing? What if it's just a free drink at the Varnish?"

I looked at her suspiciously, but I lowered my hand. "Okay, what's the payoff?"

"Remember our interview with Uma?" She looked me dead in the eye. "That stays our little secret."

The interview in which Bailey showed her woeful ignorance of the ways of Hollywood heavyweights—thinking Russell would drive his own car, or talk to anyone on the phone without an assistant listening in. I'd never forget those priceless gems and I'd make sure she never did either. But few things are better matched than a hot day and a cold dry martini. Only Bailey would force me into a choice like this. But when I looked up at the waitress, I knew what I had to do.

"I'm so sorry, I'm going to have to exchange that for a glass of iced tea."

The next morning bright and early Scott and I picked up alarmingly bad coffee and a darn good ham and egg croissant from the drive-thru across the street from the coroner's office. I parked in the lot and he ate while I scanned the preliminary findings on Hayley. After I'd finished, we spent a few minutes chatting about our respective offices and inept management—a universal bonding issue—and Scott promised to get back to me with a date for his payoff at Engine Co. No. 28.

I'd arranged to meet Bailey at the station, where I found her scowling at her desk, doing her least favorite thing in the world: paperwork. I didn't feel sorry for her. Unlike me, she got paid overtime. "Come on, turn that frown upside down, it's not that bad—"

"Say that again and I'll shoot you."

I waved the report in front of her. "If you shoot me I'll bleed all over Hayley's report."

She pushed back from the computer and held out her hand. "Let's see."

She scanned the few pages quickly. "Plant debris and soil on Hayley's clothes, in her hair..."

"It could be from Fryman Canyon. She might've gone with Brian when he tagged the spot and then when he picked up the money—"

"Assuming he ever got his hands on the money."

"Good point. I'd bet he didn't, since it's still missing." Hayley might've gone with Brian to Fryman Canyon. But I had another theory about where Hayley'd been. I tried to remember our last conversation with Dorian. "Did Dorian say she was going to have the soil on both bodies analyzed? Or just Brian?"

"You can ask her in person if you want. I think she's going back up to the mountain today and I wouldn't mind going up there myself and taking a look around in daylight. Want to come?"

"This time I'm driving."

"You're not authorized to drive a county car. Besides, I got you there in one piece last time, didn't I?"

That didn't mean I had to keep pressing my luck, but there was no point arguing.

"Did Scott give you copies of his photos of Hayley?" Bailey asked.

"Yeah. But I don't have the photos of Brian." And I hadn't had the chance to cultivate a mutually agreeable working relationship, meaning a bribery setup, with our new coroner's investigator, George Harrison.

"I think the officer who was first on scene took some

pictures." Bailey turned back to her computer and began to tap keys, then abruptly stopped. "I was going to ask him to e-mail the photos over, but I don't want to risk anyone seeing them. I'll give him a call and see if he can meet us up there."

I'd been worrying about this. With no suspects and no new details, I'd hoped the press would lose interest. It hadn't. Instead, there were endless articles filled with rank speculation about who'd killed Hayley, why, and what evidence would be needed to prove it by "experts" desperate for the spotlight. That meant reporters, tabloid and otherwise, were crawling all over the case, looking for a leak. With that kind of constant pressure, every passing minute meant we ran the risk that Janice would hear of Brian's death on the news before I could get to her.

It hadn't even been two days since we found Brian's body. But all it took was one person to let the wrong word slip at the right time. "We're going to have to release the info on Brian pretty soon."

Bailey nodded grimly.

I went back to the Biltmore to change into hiking clothes. Twenty minutes later we were on the road, and I was bracing myself for Mr. Toad's Wild Ride up Boney Mountain.

27

It was just shy of eleven a.m. when we reached the top of the mountain, but the sun was already blinding. And at that altitude, we had no cloud or even smog cover to filter the burning rays. I took off my cotton jacket and put on my shades before getting out of the car. The heat wrapped around me like cellophane and the hot air singed my nostrils and throat as I sweated my way up the dusty hill. Although it had been only a couple of days since the torrential downpour ripped open Brian's grave, the area was already baked dry. The only remnants of that drenching rain were puddles and muddy patches that were shaded under trees and rocks.

Bailey had offered Dorian some unis to help with the search, but Dorian had declined. Graciously, of course: "Bad enough having to deal with you two clowns stomping all over the place." Now that I had the chance to look around, I could see that there was a lot of ground to cover. Thankfully, she'd brought some of her own assistants, who were already sweating in their official coveralls. Of the several main trails on the ridge, only one led to Brian's grave. But there were plenty of narrow, off-trail pathways that gave access to the spot where Brian had been found, and every inch of them had to be examined for evidence.

Dorian, who looked cool as the proverbial cucumber, had broken the area into grids and appointed her own people to lead the way through each one of them. She grudgingly allowed us to join the search but gave us strict orders: "Follow Herrera, and I mean exactly behind him."

Bailey and I inched along behind Herrera, who must've been Dorian's favorite, because he seemed to be examining every millimeter of every single leaf, stone, and branch as he moved through his part of the grid. The air was heavy with the smells of sage and scrub oak, and salty perspiration kept trickling into my eyes, blurring my vision. It would only take a few seconds to veer off course, and in that steep, rocky terrain, one wrong step could send you hurtling to your death. I swiped my damp hair off my forehead and tried not to think about it.

After about half an hour, Herrera stopped abruptly, which caused Bailey to halt in her tracks. I'd been looking at the reddish dirt and pondering the clay content at the time, so didn't notice that our little procession had braked. I bumped headfirst into Bailey, who nearly fell into Herrera. He gave her a stern look and then pointed.

There, speared on a thin branch, was a small piece of pale pink fabric—I couldn't be one hundred percent sure, but it seemed to be the same color as Hayley's blouse. If I was right, that would put Hayley at the site of... Bailey and I exchanged a look. Finally, we might have a real break. We took photos, then Herrera carefully deposited it into a paper bag. He took out a pair of garden clippers and snipped off the last six inches of branch and bagged that too.

After a few moments we began to inch forward again. Now, energized by what I hoped was a find, I took closer note of every branch and leaf we passed. I saw that there were broken branches here and there—as good a sign as we were likely to find that someone had recently been here. I pointed them out to Herrera, who held up his camera to show that he'd caught it. I didn't want to stop, but my mouth was dry and my skin felt gritty with dried sweat. I pulled out a bottle of water and let Bailey and Herrera continue to move forward. At the painstaking pace Herrera was moving, I'd still be able to catch up if I didn't budge for another three hours.

My neck was aching from the strain of concentrating on every shrub, pebble, and grain of dirt. I straightened up and pulled back my shoulders as I glanced at the stretch of mountain ahead. It looked as though the route we were taking was winding back toward the road. A scenario began to form in my mind, and I started to study the ground carefully as I walked.

Ten minutes later we snaked around an outcropping, and I looked up to see that we were just fifty feet from the road. Herrera stopped to take more photographs and Bailey pulled out her water bottle. I pulled mine out of my backpack, but it slipped from my hand and rolled under a bush. As I bent down to get it, I noticed a bright spot in the branches of one of the bushes—an artificial color that didn't belong there. Poking my head in for a closer look, I saw that it was pink, and possibly rectangular.

I stood up and called out to Herrera. "Here! I've got something!" Probably just Barbie's Dream Car, but I wasn't going to take any chances.

Herrera turned back and carefully retraced his steps. He bent down and looked at the object through one of the biggest magnifying glasses I'd ever seen. I was entranced by that giant magnifier. I decided that I wanted one of my own, and made a mental note to drop a hint to Bailey about it—my birthday was coming up soon. Then it occurred to me that after Toni and I got done ripping on her about the questions she'd asked Uma, she might not be in such a charitable mood. Preoccupied with important thoughts like these, I almost missed it when Herrera finally finished taking photographs and extracted the object from the bush.

It was a cell phone.

28

"Nice catch, Counselor," Herrera said as he bagged the phone.

He insisted on re-covering every inch of ground from that spot, and it took us another hour to reach the end of the path, which did turn out to be the roadway. Feeling wrung out and filthy, I walked to the shadiest area I could find and sat down on a rock. Seconds later, Bailey joined me.

"How much you wanna bet that cell phone's Hayley's?" I said.

"No bet. It is, I agree. I just hope Dorian will finish with it fast."

"All she can really do is check for prints and swab for DNA, which'll probably be a bust. The thing's been out here a couple of days now. I just wonder if it'll still work." I scanned the road and the pullout in front of us. "Think there's any point in trying to get tire marks out here?"

Bailey looked at the area where we'd emerged from the brush. "After that biblical rain, I can't see how anything would be left. But I'll ask Dorian."

We drank our water and waited as the rest of the crew headed for their cars, then Bailey asked Dorian about the tire tracks.

"Already took photos with a zoom lens. But I'm not hopeful."

I started to ask her when she'd be done with the cell phone, then clamped my mouth shut.

Dorian raised an eyebrow. "What?"

"Nothing."

"That's what I thought." Dorian turned and headed for her pickup.

"See you later."

Dorian said over her shoulder, "Not if I see you first."

I pulled on my backpack and turned to Bailey. "I hope our 'connection' doesn't make you feel left out," I joked.

As we were about to get into Bailey's car, Dorian called out to us from her truck. "You can have that cell phone the day after tomorrow."

When we reached Mulholland Highway, my phone played the default tune, "FM" by Steely Dan. I looked at the screen but didn't recognize the number. A reporter? Unlikely. Sandi, the DA's media relations chief, had been doing her job well and had managed to keep me out of the fray. A job that was made significantly easier by the fact that Vanderhorn had such big love for the fray. And so far there'd been no leaks of any real information. The press, and especially the tabloids, were trying to keep the story going by digging up background "color" about Hayley's life, but surprisingly, they'd been kind. I had the feeling that might be due to the fact that the biggest of them, the *National Inquisitor,* had set the tone by printing sympathetic vignettes supposedly garnered from her "closest buds." And since those stories were selling, the rest of the papers had fallen into step.

I decided if this was a reporter, I'd just hang up. It was my go-to strategy with the press, which explained my wild popularity. I answered warily, without giving my name. "Hello?"

A man cleared his throat, then spoke in a deep, rolling baritone. "Am I speaking to Rachel Knight? This is Sterling Numan. Dorian asked me to take a look at your soil and plant samples. Sorry to disrupt your weekend—"

"No problem." It was already fully disrupted.

"—but I thought you'd want to hear from me as soon as I had something to tell you."

It took me a moment to shift from surly to grateful. "Mr. Numan, thank you for calling."

"Dr. Numan, and you're entirely welcome. I'll be preparing a formal report, of course, but I've made some notes and I have some preliminary findings that might be of help to you. Ordinarily I wouldn't relay my preliminary findings. I prefer to wait until I've completed the analysis, but Dorian told me this is a matter of some urgency." He cleared his throat again.

"Yes, that's correct. Thank you for making an exception, Dr. Numan."

"I only ask that you bear in mind that when I complete my analysis, I may alter my conclusions—"

"I understand."

Numan cleared his throat again. "The plant debris and soil composition found on the vehicle associated with Hayley Antonovich's body—"

"The Toyota, correct?" I was careful not to say it was Brian's car on a cell phone.

"Correct. The levels of sand, silt, and clay revealed particulates most commonly found in the northwestern portion of the Santa Monica Mountain Range—"

"As in Boney Mountain?" Where Brian's body had been found, and where I'd just been.

"Yes. Trails on Boney Mountain such as the Mishe Mokwa, for example."

"Did you also examine soil samples taken from Fryman Canyon?" Fryman Canyon, where Russell had left the ransom money, was forty to fifty miles away, depending on what route you took. I needed to know whether the soil in Fryman Canyon was different from that on Boney Mountain.

"I did. And to answer the question I believe you intend to ask, no, the particulates I identified on the Toyota could not have come from Fryman Canyon."

"And what about the soil and plant debris on Hayley's body?"

"The same. The likely source was Boney Mountain."

"How much could your findings change when you complete your examination?"

"Well…" He gave a formal chuckle, *heh-heh-heh.* "One never knows what one may find, but I wouldn't expect my final conclusion to be radically different."

I thanked Numan and ended the call.

"So the soil on the Toyota and on Hayley's body comes back to Boney Mountain?" Bailey asked.

"Yep. And he excluded Fryman Canyon as a possible source."

"Which means Brian and Hayley must've driven up here."

"The question is, why?" I asked. "If the ransom drop

was in Fryman Canyon, what were they doing forty miles away on Boney Mountain?"

Bailey frowned and shook her head. We rode back downtown in silence.

"I feel like I spent the night in a ditch."

"I could use a shower myself," Bailey said. "It's almost six o'clock. I can justify knocking off for the day. How about you?"

"I don't have any better ideas."

We got to my room and headed for the showers. I changed into a fresh pair of jeans and a lightweight blue jersey tank top. We met in the living room and flopped on the couch.

"I'm wiped," Bailey said. She'd changed into cutoffs and a T-shirt.

"Yeah. I guess it's the heat." And the constant gallop we'd been doing since we caught the case. This was the first time we'd knocked off before nightfall that I could remember.

"Room service?"

Bailey's favorite thing. I'd just picked up the phone to place our orders when Bailey's cell phone rang.

"Keller."

I gave our orders to room service while Bailey took her call. Seconds later, she put down her phone.

"We got a *ping* from Hayley's iPad," she said.

Another effort to mislead us into thinking Brian was still alive? It's what we'd been hoping for.

"An e-mail?"

"No. Just the signal that the iPad had been activated."

"Where?"

"New York," Bailey said. "NYPD's running it down."

I would've loved to fly out there and chase down the asshole myself, but it would waste hours in flight time, and we couldn't afford an extra minute. We'd gotten lucky with that signal from Hayley's iPad. Now we just had to hope we'd gotten that signal soon enough.

29

Abe Furtoni, the NYPD officer who'd given Bailey the news, had promised to call in with updates the moment anything broke. Waiting for a call like that is nerve-racking, so just to give us a little diversion, I turned on the television and found a mindless reality show about rich housewives.

"You think they really live like that? Just doing lunch and backstabbing each other?" Bailey asked incredulously.

"No. Sometimes they go to parties and backstab each other."

Bailey's phone rang and we exchanged a look as she picked it up. "Keller."

After a few "okays" she ended the call.

"They've traced the signal to a deserted building near the Staten Island ferry station. NYPD's on their way to Rosebank right now. Furtoni'll call back when he's got more."

My pulse kicked up several notches, all traces of fatigue gone. Unable to sit still, I began to pace. Bailey, a sphinx in these situations, loves my pacing.

Bailey eyed me as I made my first two laps. "Why don't you go to the gym? Work off some of that nervous energy."

"I don't want to miss the call." Just saying it out loud made me pace faster. After three more laps, Bailey'd had it.

"You'll miss the call if I lock you in the closet too."

I went to the window and looked down at Pershing Square. At eight o'clock the sun had finally begun to surrender and the last few rays of light were sinking under the weight of darkness. I walked out onto the balcony to enjoy the first cooler breezes of night air. Desiree, a flamboyant cross-dresser who seemed to spend his time parading between Temple Street and Grand Avenue, strolled by in five-inch leopard-print platform shoes, black spandex short shorts, and a bright yellow tube top. I thought the yellow and brown feathers woven into his near-waist-length black ponytail were a nice touch. I would never have had the patience. This was one of his most restrained outfits. I waved and he favored me with a nod and a little smile.

Bailey's phone rang again. While she took the call, room service brought our dinners: steak and salad for Bailey, a Caesar salad and grilled shrimp for me. Too nervous to eat, I watched Bailey's face, trying to read her expression. This was a lost cause if ever there was one, because Bailey has the classic poker face. The call went on long enough that I was ready to jump off the balcony by the time Bailey finished.

"Okay, here's the deal," she began. "Three kids, late teens, had the iPad. The youngest one coughed up the story first. They were hanging with friends in Manhattan and decided to keep partying all night, so they got a room at the DoubleTree Inn in Times Square. They saw the maid's cart parked in front of a room with the door open, but no one was around. The iPad was lying out on the desk, so they stole it along with a watch and some other junk."

"And that room was registered to?"

"We'll find out pretty soon. They're on their way there right now."

"We need to know when that person checked in too."

Bailey looked at me. "Gee, really?"

"Sorry, just thinking out loud."

"No, it's cool," Bailey said. "I'm a little uptight myself."

I looked at her. "A little?"

"Shut up."

An hour—and many frayed nerves—later, she got the next call. This time it was brief. When she ended the call, she scrolled on her cell phone for a few moments, hit a key, and then looked up.

"The room was registered under the name Stuart Connor," Bailey said. "Check-in date was the day after the ransom note was sent—"

"What time exactly?"

"Early in the morning. Around seven thirty."

"So he picked up the ransom money, killed Brian and Hayley, and hopped a red-eye?" I asked.

"Yeah. I'm not a hundred percent clear on how one guy, even a big one, could overpower both Brian and Hayley on that mountain. But more than that, this Stuart guy—whoever he is—couldn't have been at Russell's house when the kidnapping note came in. Everyone who was there at the time hung around too late to have gotten out to Boney Mountain."

Russell's house in Bel Air was over forty miles away from Boney Mountain. "And everyone who'd been in the house that evening was also around the next day. No one was missing in action." Stuart Connor had been out of town for days by now. That meant only one thing. "He had to have someone on the inside tell him Hayley'd been kidnapped..." That reminded me. "Did Harrellson run down our buddy Legs Roscoe?"

"Oh, yeah. He was heading up a study group that night. Has about a dozen alibi witnesses."

So much for that. And regardless of whether this Stuart guy did the murders alone or not, he definitely was our number one "person of interest." At least for now. "How long after he checked into that hotel was that ticket to Paris purchased on Hayley's iPad?"

"A day, maybe? I'll get more specifics when I hear from Abe," Bailey said.

"Is Stuart Connor still there?"

"No. He checked out the same day those kids snatched his stuff. They're checking surveillance cameras at the hotel, see if they can catch an image of him."

I thought about that a moment. "If this Stuart character was using Brian's credit card, he might be using his ID. There was no wallet on Brian's body, was there?"

Bailey squinted. "There was...some stuff. Papers or something, but no. No wallet."

"Then we should send Brian's photo out to NYPD. See if anyone on the surveillance footage bears a resemblance. It's easier to get away with using Brian's ID if he looks at least somewhat similar."

"I'll get hold of Brian's photo—"

"And when you talk to your contact..."

"Detective Abe Furtoni."

"Right," I said. "If they find this Stuart Connor on the surveillance footage at the hotel, tell him to make a still photo out of the best frame—"

"Yeah, so we can show it around."

"And they've got an alert out for this guy at all the—"

"—airports, bus terminals, blah, blah, blah. Yes. And I was thinking we should have them check out the iPad. See if there's any info that'll help us track this guy. Maybe some e-mails..."

I looked at Bailey. "It's our case. If they mess up anything on that iPad, it'll be our asses. I say we get that thing back here ASAP and do the work ourselves."

Bailey nodded. "We should get it in a couple of days if they send it FedEx."

"To hell with FedEx," I said. "If that iPad turns out to be evidence, I'll be eating dirt through the whole trial about all the ways it could've been messed with en route. We need them to have an officer hand-deliver it to us."

"I don't think—"

"I'll take care of it." Even if I had to knock heads with Vanderhorn.

"I'll give Furtoni the heads-up so he can figure out who he's sending."

While Bailey made the call, I pictured the iPad—its lovely touch screen.

"It's probably a long shot since those kids stole the iPad and played around with it, but if we get lucky, we might be able to get prints off that iPad," I said.

"Prints will be great if he's in the system. Of course, if he's not…"

We'd be screwed—for now. But if we got him, we'd be able to prove he had the iPad. Which would prove he was involved in the murders. It wasn't a home run, but it was better than nothing. And a damn sight better than anything we'd had so far.

30

Bailey went home that night and I put myself to bed early. I'd already left a message for Eric saying I needed approval to pay for an NYPD officer to bring out the iPad. There was nothing more we could do at this point. Nothing but wait, anyway. Sunday I caught up on sleep, then I went to the office and attacked the mile-high stack of motions and messages that had piled up on my desk.

A step onto the balcony Monday morning told me it was going to be another scorcher of a day. I didn't have any court appearances, so I could do casual. I opted for a light cotton shift and sandals, and when I stepped outside, I was plenty glad I did. In just two blocks, it felt as though the temperature had already climbed by at least ten degrees. Cup Man, the street resident who loudly proclaimed non sequiturs about world affairs on the corner of First and Main with a Styrofoam cup perched on his head, was shirtless today. Stray cats slept languorously in the shade and even the homeless—usually bundled up in everything they owned—were carrying their coats in shopping carts.

I hurried up Broadway, eager to get into the air-conditioned courthouse. The elevator did its usual swoop and bump as it bounced to a stop on almost every floor on the way up to my office on the eighteenth.

I wanted to talk to Eric, but first I'd have to get past his secretary, Melia Espinoza, aka Gossip Central. Legal secretaries are generally very well paid—at least in the private sector—because they know almost as much as, and often more than, the lawyers. But the DA's office doesn't pay anywhere near what the private sector does, so the really good ones never bother to apply. Thus, the gift of Melia. I deal with her by asking her to do as little as possible. This arrangement suits her just fine.

When I stopped in the doorway, she jerked her head up. Once again, I'd interrupted her reading a tabloid rag that lay open in her lap under the desk. Since no one ever mentioned it, and Eric had never busted her, Melia thought no one knew. Every prosecutor in the unit knew. And inconsiderate bunch that they were, they imposed on her tabloid time by expecting her to do secretarial things. Like find a file, or the boss.

"Oh, Rachel. Hi! How're you doing?"

The effusive greeting left me momentarily speechless. She usually barely remembered my name, though we'd been working together for years.

"I'm fine. Is Eric around? I left him a message."

"He's in a meeting right now, but I'm sure he'll take your call. Want me to get him?"

Interrupt him when Vanderhorn might be listening? Hell no. "No, thanks, it can wait." But what was up with girlfriend? Cheery, helpful. Who was this pod person, and what had she done with Melia?

"Rachel, you know they're saying a stalker killed Hayley Antonovich. Is it true?"

The light dawned. I had the big celebrity case. Thanks to me, Melia had the hottest seat in town—right in the middle of the investigation. This made me her favorite DDA. I knew I should find a way to capitalize on this. But I couldn't think of anything I needed at the moment. I'd have to give it some thought very soon. Melia's devotion wouldn't last one second longer than the case did. "We really don't know, Melia. Could you just tell Eric to call me on my cell?"

"I will. Good luck!"

Jeez. I'd have to take the long way around the hallways from now on to avoid my new best friend, Melia. This helpful, enthusiastic version was unsettling. I'd hoped to find Toni in her office when I got in, but her door was closed and she didn't answer when I knocked. Having exhausted my opportunities for distraction, I retreated to my office and dug into the half of my desk I call an in-box.

By noon, I'd almost reached the bottom of the stack. Most of the motions didn't require a written response; they were just CYA (cover your ass) motions the defense attorneys had to make so they wouldn't be accused of rendering ineffective assistance when the case went up on appeal. I was reading through my second-to-last of these scintillating creations when my cell phone played "The Crystal Ship" by the Doors. The ringtone I'd assigned to Toni.

"Antoinette! Where the hell are you?"

"What do you mean, where am I? You're the one that's been out God knows where. So where the hell are *you?*"

"In my office, pushing the wheels of justice forward."

"Don't talk to me about slaving, white girl. I just got out of court. You ready to do lunch?"

"I'm starving to death. Meet me in the lobby."

Toni had to be back in court by one thirty, so we shared a quick salad in the lobby restaurant at the New Otani Hotel.

"What're you doing in court?" I asked.

Toni made a deprecatory wave. "Nothing fun. Just pretrial motions on my double."

Toni's defendant was a twenty-five-year-old meth freak who'd beaten his twin sisters to death with a rubber mallet.

"Is the mom still showing up?" The mother had tried to help him kick his addiction for years before finally giving up and throwing him out. She blamed herself for the killings and felt it was her duty to attend every hearing.

"Like clockwork, and it's killing me to watch her suffer the way she does." Toni blinked and looked away for a moment. "Enough about my sad stories, what about yours? Fill me in."

I caught her up on the case.

"I think you're right. There had to be more than one person involved," she said. "But do you think this Stuart Connor did the killings alone?"

"I don't know how one person manages to pick up the ransom money in Fryman Canyon, then get out to Boney Mountain, kill two kids, bury one, drive the other one down to LAX in the trunk of a car, then hop a plane to New York. Do you?"

"Of course *I* could manage it, but that's me."

I grinned. Toni probably could. "We're in a holding pattern until we find this Stuart character. But I still feel like he had a partner in all this. We eliminated everyone who was around at the time, but obviously we've missed something—"

"And Russell and Dani didn't tell anyone about it?"

"So they say. But everyone and his brother was running in and out of their house the whole time. And Russell and Dani were a mess. Who knows what they might've inadvertently leaked? And who knows where Russell might've put down his cell phone?"

Toni had a skeptical look. "Something about all this doesn't sit right with me."

This is why Toni and I always talk our cases over with each other. It's not just a friend thing, it's a practical necessity. Because when we're running hard on a case, we can get mired in the details and miss the big picture. We've helped/saved each other this way too many times to count. Now, Toni's remark made me stop and take stock. I thought about what we'd seen and heard since we first met with Russell and company. I'd assumed someone in the house had to have gotten wind of what was going on in order to know in advance where the money drop was supposed to be. That wasn't a bad assumption—in fact, it was pretty logical. But Toni was right. There was something off about the whole scenario, because Brian and Hayley wound up on Boney Mountain—not in Fryman Canyon.

I sighed and shook my head. "I agree with you, Tone. This machine is missing some parts for sure. I just don't know what they are."

"Bet your buddy Stuart does."

"If we ever find him."

My cell phone played the opening bars of "Killer Joe," an old jazz standard that was Bailey's ringtone.

"Dorian's finished with Hayley's cell phone," Bailey said without preamble.

"Pick me up." I told her where we were.

We dropped Toni at the courthouse and promised to give her updates. Dorian was in her office typing a report. We stood in the doorway and waited for her to look up.

She peered at us over her reading glasses. "Sit."

We obediently sat, and I waited to see if she'd add, "Stay." She didn't. When she finished typing, she passed the phone, now encased in a paper bag, to us.

"I've got prints, some of which I'm sure will come back to Hayley, since the settings indicate it was her phone."

At last, something had broken our way. Bailey pulled on gloves, opened the bag carefully, then removed the phone and turned it on. After a few seconds she said, "I don't see any voice mails at the time of the kidnapping or later." She touched a few other places on the phone. "But I do see text messages. A lot of them."

I leaned in anxiously and tried to read the screen.

"Here," Bailey said. She placed the phone on Dorian's desk where we could all see it.

The first text was from BRIAM—we'd verify, but it was most likely our Brian, the *M* at the end for his last name, Maher: still waiting for drop. stay in car.

The next message was from Hayley to Brian, and it was sent three minutes later: what's going on?

It was eerie, reading Hayley's last texts. Like hearing a voice from the grave. And it was painful, seeing that little pink phone—small and vulnerable, like Hayley.

Brian didn't answer. Two minutes later, Hayley texted him again: u should be done by now! Where r u?

Still no answer from Brian. Hayley texted again, this time three minutes later: what's going on???

With each text, I could feel her rising panic.

Again, no answer from Brian. Four minutes later, Hayley texted him: r u ok?

No response. Five minutes later, Hayley tried again: where r u??? what's happening??

Then, finally, four minutes later, Brian texted Hayley: I'm ok. All clear. Meet me on trail.

"That was the last message," Bailey said.

"Do you remember when Brian's phone was used for the last time?" I asked Bailey.

"I have to check his cell phone records again...I think there was a call around the time of that last message. But I'm not sure. I know there wasn't much activity after the ransom demand."

"We never did find Brian's phone, did we?" I asked.

"No," Bailey replied.

The picture forming in my mind was chilling, but it made the most sense. "We'll have to get the cell sites to make sure, but I'm betting these texts were all sent on that mountain."

Bailey picked up the phone and stared at the messages again. "A twenty-one-minute lapse between Brian's first message—"

"Telling Hayley *not* to leave the car," I said. "And his

last message. In between, Hayley texted him five times. But she got no response—"

"Until that last text, telling her to come out to the trail. But Brian never made it back to that trail."

"That last message doesn't fit."

We fell silent for a long beat.

Bailey said, "Then that last message…"

"Was sent by our killer. He murdered Brian, then lured Hayley out."

31

"**I'll get hold** of my contact and find out what cell sites got pinged." Bailey put the phone back into the bag. "Thank you, Dorian."

"It *is* my job, you know. And now I've got a shocker for you: yours isn't my only case." She waved her hand toward the door. Bailey and I picked up on the subtle cue and left.

The sun beat down from a cloudless sky and I could feel the heat of the asphalt through my sandals as we crossed the parking lot. I told her about Toni's reaction.

"I agree," Bailey said. "There is something off about all this."

"I'm sure the kidnapping was initially just Brian and Hayley—"

"That part feels right."

"And that means we have to be right about someone else jumping into the mix after the first note was sent," I said.

We got into the car and Bailey cranked up the AC.

"All we can do is keep working the Stuart Connor angle. He's the only hot lead we've got right now," Bailey said. "I've got everyone trying to run him down from our end while NYPD works theirs."

"Problem is, I don't remember seeing the name Stuart Connor anywhere around Russell's entourage so far—"

"It wasn't. Which means we hit the next group just outside Russell's inner circle and keep moving out from there."

Bailey pulled out of the lot. "I suggest we hit the studio first."

"That'll probably give us the most bang for our buck. But we're going to have to move fast—"

Bailey nodded, her expression grim. "Yeah, it's over three days since Rostoni found him. Brian's death won't keep for much longer. And once it gets out, Stuart Connor's going to know his cover's blown and take a powder."

"If he hasn't already."

"Right."

Bailey floored it and neither of us said another word until she pulled up to the security guard shack at Russell's studio. The guard, whose nametag told us he was Franklin Yarberger, was a shrunken, hawk-nosed man with weathered-looking skin who studied our badges, photos, and faces as though he were playing a game of Count the Differences. Finally he nodded. "I'll call Russell's office, let 'em know you're here."

But Bailey held up a hand and signaled for him to get closer. He leaned down and squinted at her. Bailey kept her tone low and confidential. "You know we're the ones working Hayley's murder, don't you?"

"Yeah. You seem to match up."

"Well, we need to keep this low-key. Don't want to alarm or...tip anybody. Know what I mean?"

No one, I repeat, no one, plays the "just between us cops" card better than Bailey. It worked best with the wannabe's, but I'd seen it work with retired officers too. I made Franklin as the latter. It's the suspicious eyes. Always a dead giveaway.

As Franklin looked at Bailey I could see his wheels turning, considering whether to go along with it. "Yeah, I know what you mean. Used to be on the force myself."

Like I said, the eyes give them away every time. That and the framed eight-by-ten photograph on Franklin's desk showing him in full LAPD uniform. He told Bailey how to get to the security office and pushed the button that lifted the security bar. "Park in any spot marked 'visitor.'"

We had to drive a while before we found one that wasn't occupied, and the lot was teeming with activity—people running, riding bicycles, driving golf carts. I really love those little carts. Bailey saw me look longingly as one passed us by and shook her head.

The security office was at the farthest edge of the lot. I made the mistake of yawning as I got out of the car, and hot air burned through my mouth and down my throat. Thankfully, the security office was cool. A secretary's desk faced the door, but it was vacant. Bailey called down the hall to the left of the desk and identified herself. A hefty man in baggy shorts and a grungy Raiders tank appeared at the door, his outsized belly leading the way. He was dripping with sweat; even his neat little mustache looked soaked. He wiped his face and neck with a hand towel that had been draped over his shoulder as he said, "Sorry, I was just working out. Promised the wife and doctor I'd drop fifty pounds before the holidays."

Bailey introduced us, and we showed him our badges.

"Pete Toker," he said, extending a still sweaty hand. I let Bailey shake it first, then took my turn. "What can I do for you?"

"We'd like to see your personnel records if we could," Bailey said. "You keep employee photos?"

"Sure. Everyone has to wear security badges with photos. We keep copies in their files."

"We're looking for people with criminal records. No offense, I know you wouldn't hire them knowingly—" she said.

"None taken. You never can tell what might slip through the cracks. 'Sides, if we have someone on the lot with a rap sheet, I'd like to know about it. Follow me."

The truth was, it was photos we were after. Abe Furtoni, our contact in the NYPD, had been able to isolate the video footage of our man Stuart Connor at the check-in counter of the hotel, and per our request, he'd pulled off a still shot and scanned it to us. We weren't looking for a rap sheet per se. All we really wanted to do was see if we had a match to our surveillance photo. We just didn't want Pete to start wondering who we had in our sights until we absolutely had to. By saying we were looking for criminal types, it'd look like a general, wide-angle search.

Pete led us down the hall to a room that had a small table and chair in the far-right corner, shelves that covered one wall, and filing cabinets that filled the other two walls. "We were supposed to go digital with everything a while ago, but you know, on a studio lot we're the poor stepchildren. You'll find all the current employees on the shelves and all the ex-employees in those two cabinets on the right."

"And the rest of the cabinets?" I asked.

"Just scripts and stuff from what I've seen. They were here when I got hired and I never had cause to get into 'em. You can if you want." Pete turned to go, then stopped. "By the way, thanks for not making the obvious joke about my name."

I didn't tell him it was too easy, though it was. Pete left us to our own devices and we got down to business.

32

Bailey pulled the still photo of Stuart Connor out of her jacket and put it on the table. I studied it again. It was lousy quality, a grainy black and white, typical of the cheaper variety of surveillance cameras. The guy seemed to be slender, medium tall like Brian, and had a similarly shaped head. But his hair was covered with a baseball cap that also obscured his features, so I couldn't really see much. We'd tried to match the photo to the DMV and criminal databases, but it just didn't have enough detail. I didn't expect to find a great match in these records either, but I hoped we might spot someone who was worth at least a second look.

"I'll start on the bottom shelf," I said. "You can take the next one up."

We worked methodically, looking at the photos in each file for someone who might match the guy in the video. Three hours later we had a stack of twelve "possibles." Bailey asked Pete to come in. This time he was freshly showered and dressed in the beige studio uniform.

"Can you tell us whether any of these guys called in sick or took days off in the past week?" Bailey asked.

"Let's take those to my office and I'll check. I keep the daily logs on my computer."

Pete was able to eliminate nine of them right off the bat. "Those guys have all checked in every day for the past five days. The other three...not sure. If they have off-site work to do, they might not come in, but that doesn't mean they left town or anything."

"No, but you've narrowed it down pretty well. Thanks, Pete. I'll run the other three," Bailey said.

Pete said he had rounds to make and left us, saying we could stay in his office as long as we liked. Bailey called in the information on the three remaining "persons of interest" and I thought about what we had so far.

When she got done, I shared my thoughts. "We've been thinking this was too much for one person to manage, right?"

"Right."

"But we don't know how someone got wind of the kidnapping. And we don't know why the kids wound up on Boney Mountain."

"Still with ya."

"How'd the killer get them up there?"

Bailey shook her head. "Unless that's where they'd planned to do the money drop all along."

"In which case, the ransom drop in Fryman Canyon was what, a decoy?"

"Well...at least a way to separate the kids from the money," I said.

"But how would the bad guy keep Russell from getting the real ransom note? The one that theoretically said, 'Drop the money at God's Seat'?"

The ring of Bailey's cell phone saved me from having to answer. She made notes on the little pad she keeps in her jacket pocket as she listened.

"We've got two hits," she said when she hung up. "One is for Nima Faluja." She tapped his file. "He's got a prior for shoplifting. Record was expunged a few years ago. The other is for Jack Averly. He's a dope dealer. Got two convictions. Completed probation on his second case last year."

I looked at both files again. "Really, it could be either of them."

"I might've agreed, except Nima has a pretty good alibi."

I looked at Bailey. "In jail?"

Bailey smiled.

I picked up Jack's file. He was a production assistant. Those are usually aspiring writers, directors, actors, you name it, who get their asses thrashed for more hours and less money than they could make as waiters or waitresses. But I supposed it could also be someone who just wanted to work around the "industry"—or who wanted to deal to the "industry." That'd be a fairly lucrative gig with all the highly paid, neurotic types floating around. And being a PA would be great cover for a dope dealer. "We've got an address for him, but—"

"If he's our guy, I can't see him coming back here. At least not yet."

"But he doesn't know we've got his real name, and unless he's got a passel of fake IDs, he might have to use it now—"

"I'm calling NYPD," Bailey said.

She gave all the information to Abe Furtoni and then called LAPD and did the same. "On the off chance he comes back here."

Bailey made a copy of everything in his file, and just as she was finishing up, Pete came back. His formerly crisp uniform had wilted from the strain of Pete's once again overheated body. He wiped his forehead when he came in. "Whew. Still hot as blazes out there. So what do you think? Anyone look good to you?" he asked.

"Can't tell yet," Bailey said. "But would you mind keeping this on the down low for now?"

"Not a bit."

We thanked Pete for his help and he wished us luck. "And try to stay cool out there."

There was no chance of that.

Bailey started the engine so we could get the air-conditioner running, and as I adjusted all the vents to face me, she pulled out her cell. "I'm going to see what we can find in this guy's name. Car, cell phone, residence. See if it matches what we found in his file."

"Great, but first..." I pulled out my personal cell phone and entered a number.

I waited while the phone rang. On the third ring, a voice answered. I put the phone on speaker.

"Yeah?"

"Hey, Jack," I said, doing my best "bimbo babe" impression. "I been missing ya."

I could hear a loudspeaker announcement in the background but couldn't make out what it was saying.

"Who is this?" he asked, irritated and wary.

"Don't you remember? We hooked up at the bar, in the hotel?"

"I don't remember hooking up with anyone at any hotel, lady. You got the wrong number."

The loudspeaker announcement sounded in the background again. Then he hung up. But that was okay, because this time I was able to make out the words. *"Welcome to LaGuardia Airport..."*

33

With the benefit of Jack's true name and photo in hand, NYPD was able to hit the ground running. They grabbed our boy at the gate, just as he was about to board a flight to Aruba on a ticket he'd purchased in cash. Abe and Bailey had cooked up a charge of possession of stolen property to hold him until we could get there. It was, technically speaking, a legally supportable charge. We did have proof that he'd been in possession of Hayley's iPad. Of course, that proof hinged on the word of a couple of sketchy kids, but beggars can't be choosers.

I called the office to get Eric's approval to fly out to New York while Bailey did the same on her end. I reminded Eric that since Bailey and I would be out there, the office wouldn't have to pay for an NYPD officer to bring back the iPad. That helped to grease the wheels. Bailey took me home and waited while I packed. It didn't take long. The occasion didn't exactly call for strappy sandals and a cocktail dress. We stopped at Bailey's place so she could pack, and within fifteen minutes we were back on the road and heading for the airport.

"You've got to admit, that was a pretty good move I made calling Averly's cell," I said.

"Yeah? And what if he'd been gay?"

"You saw this guy's security photo. No way he's gay. He had a cheapo haircut with no product in it, and he was wearing a baggy, washed-out T-shirt—"

"They're not all perfect and gorgeous, Knight."

"Aren't we missing the point?"

"Which is?"

"It worked."

Bailey pulled into the parking structure closest to the terminal. It was expensive, but we didn't have time to shuttle in from one of the remote lots.

We both had carry-ons, but since I wasn't allowed to keep my gun and Bailey was, I put my .38 Smith and Wesson in her suitcase. We had to fly coach, naturally, but we got lucky and had the whole row to ourselves— the virtue of taking a red-eye. I'd hoped to get some sleep on the flight, but I was too keyed up. I kept rolling through all the questions I planned to ask Jack Averly and all the possible answers he might give. I looked around, saw that the few nearby passengers were fast asleep, and whispered to Bailey, "What's he going to say about how he got Hayley's iPad? 'Duh, I didn't know it was hers'? 'Some dude gave it to me'? 'I found it on a picnic table'?"

Bailey's eyes were closed. "Give it a rest, Knight. There's no way to know what this clown's going to say until he says it."

"But seriously, Bailey, he can't deny knowing whose iPad it is. He works at Russell's studio for God's sake. And regardless of how he got it, how come he didn't return it? If he wasn't trying to use her iPad to make it look like Brian was alive, then why not give it back?"

Bailey opened one eye. "If you don't give it a rest I'm going to knock you out."

"Fine. You get your beauty sleep, and I'll do the thinking. As usual."

Bailey pressed the call button for a flight attendant. When she appeared, Bailey said, "Would you mind getting her a Bloody Mary? On second thought, make it a double. No, a triple. And hold the tomato juice."

I sipped my incredibly strong drink and continued to play out the interview in my head until the alcohol kicked in. I didn't even realize I'd nodded off until Bailey shook me and said we were about to land.

It was nine a.m. when we got to New York, so we took a cab straight to the station where Jack Averly was being held. Detective Abe Furtoni was on hand to meet us. He was dressed in the shirt and blazer that's standard detective wear, about six feet tall, solidly built, heavy eyebrows just shy of a unibrow, and an olive complexion with a bluish tint around the jaw that said a five o'clock shadow would show up around noon.

We shook hands and Bailey thanked and congratulated him.

"You've definitely had me running these past few days," he said. "But anything I can do to help you put away the sack of shit who killed that little girl."

He led us back to the lockup, where it was standing room only, with as many as four men crammed into each four-by-six-foot cell. There was a low hum of male voices and an occasional shout. "Gimme my damn phone call!" Or "I want my lawyer!" But I didn't mind the noise as much as the smell. No matter where you go, all jails have it: that mix of sweat, grime, and urine, interlaced with the ammonia that vainly struggles to overcome it all.

"Do you have an interview room?" Bailey asked.

"We've got a room off the captain's office. It's actually a conference room, but if they're not using it, we can have it. I'll go check."

We stepped back out and waited. I tried to spot Averly through the window in the door to the lockup, but it was so filmy it was practically opaque, so all I could see were blurry figures. Two minutes later Abe returned.

"It's ours for the next half hour," he said and gestured for us to follow him.

It was a very bare room with one long conference table and wooden chairs all around it. A few framed photographs of captains and other officers hung on the wall, some of which were so old they were black and white.

"Why don't you sit over there?" Abe pointed to the far end of the room. "I've got a couple of officers bringing our boy out. They'll be staying in here with him. I hope that's okay."

A few minutes later I heard the clink of chains, and then Averly shuffled into the room. With his hands cuffed to waist chains and his feet linked together by more chains, he was a one-man band. And he looked just like his security photo: wavy brown hair that reached almost to his collar, sharp, ferret-like features, and very thin chapped lips that he licked nervously as his eyes darted between me, Bailey, and Abe.

We introduced ourselves and told him we were investigating the kidnapping and murder of Hayley

Antonovich. Abe again advised Averly of his rights and he again waived them.

He replied immediately, "I don't know anything about any kidnapping or murder."

That was way too fast. And he looked way too cool. Not good.

"How did you wind up with Hayley's iPad and Brian's ID?" I asked. I couldn't be sure he'd had Brian's driver's license, but we knew he'd used one of Brian's credit cards to buy the plane ticket to Paris, so I surmised that at one time he'd had the rest of Brian's stuff too. Unfortunately, by the time NYPD grabbed him, he didn't have anything of Brian's on him. So I was basically bluffing. But if he didn't correct me, I'd know I was right.

"I found them."

Notice he didn't say, "What ID?"

"How'd you get them?" I asked.

His eyes darted around the table, then settled on a point over my right shoulder. It didn't take an expert to know that whatever came out of his mouth next would be a lie.

"In a car." He shrugged. "I guess it was wrong, but it was unlocked, and the stuff was right there on the floor."

"So you decided to help yourself." The disdain in my voice made it very clear what I thought of this horseshit story.

"Yeah," he said with a defiant look. "I figured I could buy myself a free trip and have some fun."

"Then why didn't you take that flight to Paris? You bought the ticket, why not go?"

He shrugged. "Changed my mind. Decided I'd rather hang out here for a while."

"So you wasted the money on a ticket to Paris because...?"

"Why not? Wasn't my money."

"So you didn't know whose iPad it was when you took it?"

"No."

"But you must've realized whose it was when you used it to book the flight to Paris."

He shrugged again, nonchalant. "Not really. I didn't care."

We'd flown all this way just so this asshat could lie—badly—to our faces. "This is complete and total bullshit. You want to try again with something that resembles the truth?" There was no point pussyfooting around with this guy. He wasn't intimidated, he wasn't scared, and he wasn't remorseful. And there was no way he was going to give us anything.

He favored me with a cold little smile. "Yeah. Here's the truth: I want my lawyer."

Abe gave the high sign and the two officers escorted him back out.

"What did he have on him when you arrested him?" I asked Abe.

"His cell, his wallet—with his own ID. We haven't searched his suitcase yet."

"Can you release his cell phone to us?" Bailey asked.

"Yeah. And we can hang on to him and keep the stolen property charge alive for a while if you like."

"I like," Bailey said. "Is he calling his lawyer now?"

"Should be."

"Be nice to hang around and see who shows up, if you don't mind."

34

Abe sent a uniform out for subs while we waited. He got a meatball, I had a ham and Swiss, and Bailey had a pastrami. We'd just rolled up the paper wrappers into balls and taken turns trying to make baskets into the trash can in the corner when the sergeant came in to tell us that Jack Averly had decided he didn't want to call anyone right now.

"Lucky break," Bailey said. "Abe, can you keep him off the phone for a little while? If we're right that he's working with someone, it'd help if he couldn't send up a flare."

"I can try. But they do smuggle cell phones in here and I'd bet he's waiting to make a friend in the tank who'll let him use one."

Bailey nodded. "Your jail phones are monitored?" Most were nowadays.

"Yeah."

"Averly probably needs to call his buddy to hook him up with a lawyer," Bailey said. "But if he uses your phone, we'll know who he called."

We thanked Abe for all his help and declined his offer of a ride to the airport.

"We've got to make a stop before we head back to L.A.," Bailey explained.

We couldn't put it off anymore. It was the fifth day since Brian's body had been found—much longer than we'd intended—and we couldn't push our luck any further. We had to notify Janice of his death. Bailey had called to tell her we'd be in Manhattan, and by coincidence, Janice had meetings in the city, so she'd be staying at the St. Regis Hotel, a swanky old-school place in midtown, near Central Park. Even if I hadn't already known she was a bestselling author, the fact that she could afford those prices would have been a tip-off.

I hadn't noticed the weather because we'd been inside ever since we landed. But now, as I stepped outside, I felt like I'd been smacked with a wet towel—a very hot, cloying wet towel. Unlike the arid heat in Los Angeles, summers in New York City are sticky, humid, and airless, and the odors emanating from the sewers can turn your stomach inside out. It's why everyone runs up to the Hamptons, or Connecticut—anywhere to escape the misery. Within ten seconds, I was dripping with sweat and dying for a shower. Fortunately, we lucked out and got a cab quickly.

The doormen at the St. Regis have to wear full livery: top hat, jacket with epaulets, and gloves. In this heat, it must've been torturous. I took a photo so I could show Angel how easy he had it compared to these guys.

I hadn't spoken to Janice since we'd found Brian's body, but we did have one more contact after our first conversation. It was when she'd heard about Hayley's death on the news. Although I hadn't told her Hayley's last name, she'd put two and two together—and she'd called to tell me in no uncertain terms that Brian couldn't possibly have been responsible. At the time, I hadn't known she was right. I told her that since Brian was the last one to be seen with Hayley, we had to consider him a possible suspect. If she heard from him, the smartest thing to do would be to get him to surrender. She promised she would. I promised I'd clear him if I could.

Now it occurred to me with bitter irony that I was about to keep my promise. Janice answered the door dressed in flowing black palazzo pants and a white tank. She looked to be in her forties at most, though I knew she was ten years older than that. Janice had the same slender build as Brian, but not his soft, rounded features. Her cheekbones were prominent and she had a slight hook to her nose. But her eyes were gentle, kindly. Janice ushered us in graciously and offered us something to drink. We thanked her but declined. The posh suite had a sitting room but, as is typical of so many hotels in the city, no view to speak of at all—unless you count the offices of the building across the street as a view. Given Manhattan rates, I figured the suite had to be setting her back at least a couple of grand a night.

Janice took a seat on the couch, and we sat across from her in the small French Provincial chairs. Given what she already knew about Hayley, it took her just one look at our faces to know what we'd come to tell her. Janice put her hands to her cheeks. "No, oh, no," she said. "He's not...please don't tell me..."

"I'm so sorry, Janice," I said. I told her what had happened to Brian as delicately as I could and concluded by saying, "We think Brian and Hayley were likely killed by the same person...or persons."

Though I was sure she had considered the possibility that Brian had met the same fate as Hayley, reality and possibility were two different things. Janice dropped her head and put one hand to her chest as tears quietly rolled down her cheeks. After a few moments, she asked in a tremulous voice, "Do you have any idea who did this?"

"We believe there had to be more than one person involved," Bailey said. "We've got one suspect in custody here in New York. We're still working on finding the second suspect."

Janice nodded and looked out the window behind us. "I didn't really get to know my nephew well until his mother died. I took him in because there was no one else. I wasn't sure it would work out. I'd always lived alone, so I worried, what on earth would I do with a teenage boy? But it was the best thing, by far, that I've ever done. He was charming, sweet, and so loving. With all the loss he'd suffered in his life, he was still one of the most cheerful, generous, kindhearted people I'd ever known. He changed my life. Even got me to watch television. Brian loved *The Wire,* and he made me a fan too. And I introduced him to classical music and museums." She fell silent for a few moments, then continued as she stared out the window. "We had such fun. I remember taking him to see a modern art exhibit—he made me laugh so hard. 'Aunt Janice,' he said, 'that's not art. I could do that with a paint roller'..." For a moment, the happy memories made her smile. Then the harsh reality of the present took hold again and she bent her head as a fresh wave of tears poured from her eyes.

Janice, who seemed to me to be a lonely soul, had found real warmth and even joy when Brian entered her life. To lose it this way was an unspeakable tragedy. After a few more moments she sat up, and Bailey passed her some Kleenex. She dabbed at her eyes and asked, "Do you think this had something to do with the theft of Tommy's screenplay?"

"I do," I said. "Brian and Hayley were very close. I think Brian confided in Hayley and they faked her kidnapping. Possibly as payback."

"But...it doesn't fit. Money didn't mean much to Brian. You had to know him, to really get it. He was all heart and soul. That's why I believed him when he said he wanted to write. He had that...artistic, sensitive kind of temperament. I just don't see him asking for money."

I didn't know what to say to that. But I did know there were a lot of things that didn't make sense yet and I told her so. We talked a little longer and asked if she wanted us to call anyone for her.

"I-I'll call. I'm having dinner with a friend. Don't worry about me. Just—will you keep me informed of...everything?"

"Of course," I said. "And if you think of anything—about Brian, or Tommy—please call. Any and all information would be helpful." We gave her our cards. "Please know that if there's a trial, we'll help you fly out and find a place to stay so you can attend."

A strange look skipped fleetingly across her face, but then Janice smiled tremulously. "That's very kind of you. Thank you."

I again promised to stay in touch and told her we'd do everything in our power to bring the killer to justice. It was no more comforting this time than it had been for Hayley's parents.

In the cab, on our way to the airport, Bailey and I were quiet. Tired, emotionally wrung out, and, for the moment, stymied; there was nothing good to say. "I don't make Averly as the mastermind," I said.

"He definitely wasn't at Russell's house when the kidnapping e-mail came in. So I'd agree, at least based on what we've seen so far."

"And he doesn't feel like a mastermind. Too weaselly . . . you know?"

Bailey nodded. We dragged our carry-ons through the terminal and took seats near the boarding gate, then Bailey went to find us some food to take on the plane. It was only after we'd boarded the flight that I remembered what I'd wanted to do.

"Bailey, do you have Averly's cell phone on you?"

"Yeah." She patted the pocket of her jacket.

"Is it wrapped up?"

"It's in a plastic bag. Why?"

"Let me see it."

Bailey pulled out the bag and gave it to me. Carefully, to avoid smudging prints, I manipulated the bag so I could press the power button through the plastic. When it booted up, I found the phone icon and looked at "Recent Calls."

"Look at all those calls to and from 'unknown caller,'" I said.

Bailey frowned. "And they're on the day of the kidnapping." She scrolled back up the page. "Last one was yesterday."

"The day Averly got arrested. We need to figure out who this 'unknown' caller is. How much time do you think we have before Averly gets his hands on a contraband phone?"

"Could be any minute. Especially if he promises big money."

Which he might very well have if he collected the ransom money. Bailey pulled out her cell and made a call. She gave Averly's phone number and asked to have the unknown caller identified as fast as possible. "And if you get the answer before I land, give the information to Lieutenant Hales immediately. I'm calling him now so he'll expect you." Bailey read off Graden's cell phone number and ended the call.

The flight attendant gave the announcement to turn off "all cell phone devices," so Bailey powered down and put Averly's phone back into her pocket.

"I guess that's all we can do now," she said.

There were no Bloody Marys for either of us this time. With any luck, we were going to have to hit the ground running.

35

We didn't talk during the flight. It was packed, so the case was strictly off-limits, and we were too tired for small talk, so the moment we were airborne, we both fell asleep. But in the last hour of the flight a baby—whose Benadryl had probably worn off—woke up and began to cry nonstop. I felt sorry for the little one, but I confess, the noise was getting to me. And from Bailey's expression, I saw I wasn't the only one. "Want to send over a shot of Jack Daniel's?" I asked.

Bailey turned to face the window and closed her eyes.

Now fully, and unhappily, awake, I distracted myself by thinking about what our next moves should be. Apparently, Bailey did the same. The moment we cleared the Jetway, she leaned in and spoke in a low, urgent voice. "We're getting a telephonic for Averly's place."

It was nearly six o'clock, so the only way to get a search warrant right now was telephonically. The only problem with that idea was that it meant we'd have no choice of judge. We'd get whichever one had pulled the after-hours duty. Though I thought we had enough probable cause to hit Averly's apartment—and his car, for that matter—you just never knew when you'd get stuck with a judge who wasn't the brightest bulb in the chandelier. I started framing the pitch in my head as we raced through the terminal and out to the parking lot.

While Bailey drove, I called in and asked for the duty judge. And got Judge Pastor. A lucky break, because he was both smart and quick on the uptake. With the phone on speaker, I gave him the rundown, and when I'd finished, he immediately said, "You've got it. Put Detective Keller on." I held the phone closer to Bailey and the judge swore her in. By the time she drove up the ramp to the freeway, we had our warrant. I called the station and Bailey found Detective Harrellson.

"I need help. We've got a warrant for an apartment and a car."

Harrellson knew better than to ask on a cell phone whose place we were about to hit. "Send me the address. I'll get a team together."

I e-mailed him Averly's address and the license plate of his car. We got lucky and hit a pocket of light traffic, so it didn't take us long to get there. I noticed that Jack Averly's apartment wasn't far from Brian's place geographically. But otherwise it was a world away. Though Brian's place had been impersonal, his building was alive with working people still dialed in to the world. Averly's looked like a broken toy abandoned in a vacant lot. Worn down and used up. The lobby's glass door was dingy, the paint on the splintered wood frame was peeling and bare in places, and the carpet runner was stained to the point where it was impossible to tell what color it had been originally. Even in shoes, walking on it was gross.

Averly's apartment was even worse. Nothing more than a Dumpster with running water. A plastic ashtray overflowed onto the cheap particleboard coffee table with smoked-down roaches, and a baggie of weed lay on the floor next to a beanbag chair. Against the opposite wall, on top of an old, dusty television set, was a pizza box. The buzzing sound coming from inside it told me the flies were taking care of Averly's leftovers. The bedroom was exactly that: a room with a bed—or rather a mattress—on the floor. Not even a dresser. He'd stacked some of his clothes in U.S. Postal Service plastic bins—the kind you see left next to mailboxes on the street—and the rest he'd just thrown around the room. There was no apparent rhyme or reason to it, just a matter of whim that likely depended on his state of sobriety. I left the bathroom and kitchen to the cops and didn't even look. It was bound to be the stuff nightmares are made of. Not having to search places like that was a perk of being a DDA. I noticed the cops were happier than usual to glove and mask up before tossing this sty. And they only had to do the general combing for the big, obvious things that might link Averly to the kidnap and murders—like Hayley's or Brian's property, or the ransom money. I couldn't even think about what the criminalists would have to endure when they dug for the fine-point search.

I watched them work for a while, but the place smelled so gamy that eventually I had to get outside. Even the smog and monoxide were a vast improvement over the fetid air in that stink pad.

The luckier officers got to stand watch over Averly's car, which was parked outside in the carport. It was an old blue Mustang and in only slightly better shape than his apartment. Inside, I could see that the backseat was strewn with McDonald's bags, Taco Bell wrappers, plastic cups, and empty beer bottles. Surprisingly, the front seat was relatively tidy—just a couple of Coke cans on the driver's seat.

Bailey was standing behind the car, examining the tires. "Hey, Bailey," I called out. "We can add a charge of open container if we need to hold him longer." I pointed to the empty beer bottles. She gave me a sarcastic thumbs-up.

Just then, Dorian's Tacoma came roaring up the street.

Dorian strode up with her box of magic tricks. I'd never seen someone so short have a stride so long. As she opened her box and gloved up, Bailey came over and asked her to check out the tires and undercarriage in particular. She did it respectfully, but of course it didn't matter.

Dorian stood up and put her hands on her hips. "Wait a minute. You think you need to tell me how to do my job?"

"I just wanted to make sure—"

"Do I remind you to sign your search warrant? Get a witness's phone number? Run a rap sheet? Or—"

"I apologize." Bailey held up her hands.

"Go help them"—Dorian gestured to a couple of young officers guarding the crime scene tape around the carport— "and let me do my job."

As Bailey backed away, Dorian shined her flashlight into the front seat of the car. She'd brought a crime scene photographer with her, and he moved around the car, taking pictures at her direction. When he'd finished, she dusted the driver's and passenger's doors for prints, then pulled out a slim jim and popped the driver's door open. After photographs of the interior were taken, Dorian began to work over the seats with some kind of tape. I left her to it and walked up the street to get a sense of the neighborhood. None of the other buildings looked as bad as Averly's, though one or two came close. But overall, it was a typical lower-middle-class hood on the east side of Hollywood: struggling actors, office workers, mechanics, a smattering of families, and sketchily employed twenty-somethings splitting the rent on a studio.

When I got back to the carport, Dorian was opening the glove box, and I saw her remove a small notepad. After she'd put it into a plastic bag, I asked to see it. "Don't open the bag," she ordered.

"I wasn't going to." I looked at the writing on the top page. It was a phone number.

Bailey peered over my shoulder and pulled out her cell phone. "I'll call it in," she said, and moved away.

I went back to watch Dorian, being careful to stand out of her line of sight and, therefore, fire. Seconds later, Graden pulled up. Damn. I suddenly remembered that he'd asked me to text him when I landed.

"I was just about to text you," I said when he walked over to me.

"No you weren't."

"I know. Sorry."

Graden waved off the apology. "You'll remember next time."

"And you know this because?"

"I will shamelessly bribe you."

"That could work," I said. "With?"

"Admission to the Police Academy shooting range."

I love the outdoor shooting range at the Police Academy in Elysian Park. The entire facility was originally built for the 1930 Olympics and the buildings have old-style charm, plus the setting is lush and arboreal. In short, it was a great bribe. Damn: Graden was good.

"I'll think about it," I lied—I was already on board. "What brings you out here?"

"I wanted to see what you got."

"And?" I looked at him expectantly.

"And I have news for you guys."

"And?" I was losing patience.

"And, of course, it was a transparent excuse to see you."

"Finally, the truth."

"I'm a little rusty. I'll get better." He signaled to Bailey and she walked over to us. "I got the report back on those texts we pulled off Hayley's phone—the ones between her and Brian. They were all sent on Boney Mountain."

Bailey and I exchanged a look. We'd thought so. It was the most logical explanation for all the evidence we'd seen so far.

"Good to have that confirmed," Bailey said. "Now I've got news." She told Graden about the numerous calls we'd found to and from an unknown caller on Averly's cell phone. "I just found out whose phone they came from." Bailey paused, her expression unreadable.

"Who?" I asked impatiently.

"Ian Powers."

"Russell's manager? No way."

What on earth would a high-powered manager and co-owner of one of the most successful production companies in town be doing with a little pissant like Averly?

"Yep—way. And the number on that pad in Averly's glove box?"

"Ian's?"

Bailey nodded.

"What the hell...?" I gave voice to the only explanation that came to mind. "So he's Ian's dealer?"

"Maybe," she said.

"Averly have a rap sheet for drugs?" Graden asked.

"Minor league, but yeah," Bailey said.

"Did 'unknown caller' show up at other times on Averly's phone?" I asked. If so, it would mean they had an ongoing connection—the kind you'd expect to find between a dealer and a regular customer.

"We're still working on it."

Graden shook his head, his expression troubled. "Did you know that Powers set up a charity that sends underprivileged kids to summer camps?"

"No. How come you do?" I asked.

"The group coordinates with LAPD to target the toughest neighborhoods. The idea being to get the kids out of harm's way while school's out and they have too much time to get in trouble."

"Good idea," I said. When I'd first met Ian Powers at Russell's house, I'd had a vague memory of his name being connected to something in a legal context but couldn't remember what it was. Now it came to me. "Didn't he sponsor some legislation to protect child actors? Something about putting counselors on sets where there were child actors so they could act as monitors and prevent abuse…"

Graden squinted for a second before answering. "Sounds familiar."

I looked at Averly's car, pictured the dump of an apartment just beyond. "So what the hell is he doing hanging around a guy like Averly?" I asked.

We all stood in silence as the question hovered in the air.

Bailey's phone rang and she stepped away to take the call, leaving me alone with Graden. I had to admit I enjoyed having him involved in the case. I wondered if I'd be pushing it to ask him out for a bite tonight. Until Dorian processed her evidence, there wasn't much else we could do. "Graden, do you have any plans for dinner tonight?"

"As a matter of fact, I do," he said. "I'm taking out a smokin' hot prosecutor."

Silver-tongued devil. He wasn't *that* rusty.

36

I didn't want to be too far from home or have too much to drink, just in case something broke and I had to jump, so Graden suggested we go to "our" place, the Pacific Dining Car. The host automatically took us back to our favorite booth in the Club Car. I'd worried a return to our old stomping grounds might be unsettling, but it actually felt good to be back in familiar surroundings together. Over Bloody Marys, I gave a more detailed report on our trip to New York, and then pondered Ian Powers's possible connection to the case.

"It does make sense that Averly would deal to him," I said. "It's a lot safer to buy dope from a PA on the lot than it is to do business with someone outside."

"But it seems like too much of a coincidence—Averly, who just happens to be Ian's dealer—gets caught with Hayley's iPad, buys that ticket to Paris in Brian's name…"

"Yeah. But Ian's only link to the murders is that screenplay. The one Russell supposedly stole from Brian's father. So what's Ian's motive? Fear that Brian had proof that Russell stole Tommy's screenplay?"

Graden shook his head. "So far, there isn't any, right?"

"No. But the thing is, even if we assume there was, it makes no sense." This had bugged me from the very start. "If Brian had proof, then why wouldn't he just take it to a lawyer? Why mess around with a fake kidnapping?"

"And if he didn't have real evidence, then why would Ian feel threatened? Especially after all these years?"

"Right." I sighed.

"And, just to make your life a little more miserable, why would Brian have evidence when his father obviously didn't?"

I shook my head, frustrated. "This case...the further in we get, the less it makes sense."

But Graden and I getting back together was making more and more sense. When he brought me back to the room, our good-night kisses were more intense than ever—and it was that, as much as anything, that told me we hadn't really started over at square one. We were picking up where we'd left off. Not only healed from the fight, but closer than ever. I made myself say good night before I said the opposite, and put myself to bed in a happy daze.

I woke up early, jangling with nervous energy. Every passing hour gave Jack Averly more opportunity to get his hands on a cell phone and warn his partner in crime. That meant, like it or not, we had to push it. I phoned Bailey.

"Graden already did it," Bailey said. "Called Dorian at home at seven this morning."

My knight in shining armor. "Did she tell him what they had so far?"

"She told him what kind of idiot he was and that she already knew it was a priority."

"Then maybe she worked late last night." I looked at my bedside clock. "It's eight now. Want me to call, or should we just get over there?"

"Let's call. It's easier to take the blast from her on the phone than face-to-face."

"You'd know."

"Which is why you're making the call," Bailey said.

I reached Dorian on the first ring.

"Why am I not surprised? You know, if you clowns would leave me alone for thirty seconds, I'd move a lot faster."

"So you don't have anything yet?"

"I may have. Who's got red hair?"

I sat up, eyes wide. I started to say the name, then stopped myself. I wanted to be sure before I answered. Quickly, I mentally reviewed the images of everyone we'd met in the past week. I was right. There was only one.

"Ian Powers."

"Well, obviously I don't have any exemplars, so I can't say much more than that the hairs on the passenger seatback in Averly's car *may* be consistent with his."

This was huge. If it was Ian's hair, and you added that to all the recent phone calls between him and Averly, we'd have the beginnings of a real connection between Ian, Averly, and the murders. I felt my pulse start to quicken. "Anything else?"

"Nothing in the apartment so far. But I found soil and

plant debris on the undercarriage of his Mustang that looks a lot like what I found on Brian's car. I've already sent it to Numan. He'll have an answer for you pretty quick."

"Did you get any prints inside the car?"

"A couple of partials on the interior passenger door handle. Might be good enough to give us a match if you get someone in handcuffs."

But how to get Ian in handcuffs? A sample of his hair, if it matched, would do it, but I had no time to get all espionage-y about snatching one of his crimson locks without him knowing it. That meant I'd need to get a search warrant for his place. Did I have enough to justify one? It was a close call, and I knew judges would be nervous about granting a dicey warrant with someone like Powers, but I had no choice. I'd just have to push it and hope for the best.

Dorian had no more surprises for me, so I called Bailey and gave her the update. "I know it's iffy, but I don't think we can afford to wait for more results. We've got to go for it. If Ian's our guy, he'll be dumping evidence the minute Averly gets his hands on a phone."

Bailey was silent for a few moments. "You're right. Let's go to J.D. for the warrant."

Being a former cop, Judge J. D. Morgan, Toni's boyfriend, understood situations like this better than most.

"I'll bang out the affidavit right now," I said.

"I'll pick you up in fifteen."

She was there in ten, but I'd already made a list of the evidence, so I was waiting downstairs in the lobby, affidavit in hand, by the time Bailey got there. Feeling the pressure with every second that passed, I found myself gulping for air as I jumped into the car.

J.D.'s clerk, Siobhan Flanagan, said he was in a conference with some lawyers in chambers.

"Siobhan, it's an emergency," I said. "You know I never cry wolf."

"Sorry, Rachel. It's a seven-defendant gang murder and it's been hell getting all those lawyers in one room. He said no interruptions for any reason. Why don't you try Lavinia? I know she's in chambers."

Lavinia Moss was the youngest and also the first black female judge to be assigned to handle the high-profile cases. That meant at the very least that she was smart. It probably also meant she was politically savvy. The political part was what worried me. Judges who're focused on getting elevated to the appellate bench don't take chances on dicey warrants.

I thanked Siobhan and we trotted down the hall toward her courtroom, Department 125. I had a vague memory of hearing something about Judge Moss... where?

"You know her?" Bailey asked.

"I think I remember Toni saying she was tough but sharp."

The clerk, a young guy I'd never met, got the okay and let us into chambers. Judge Moss hadn't done much to spruce up the place other than the usual diplomas—Boalt Hall for law school, which meant s-m-a-r-t, and UCLA for undergrad, which meant smart and local. But I didn't see any glad-handing photo ops with governors. Hoping that was a good omen, I introduced myself and Bailey.

"Welcome to Department 125," she said. "So what've you got for me?"

I gave her a thumbnail sketch of the overall case, then explained the situation with a possible accomplice in custody in New York, the need for urgency, and the evidence we had so far.

"May I see the affidavit?"

I handed it to her and tried not to bounce my knee or bite my nails while she read. When she'd finished, she put the pages down on her desk, leaned back in her chair, and frowned. Little stars of anxiety burst under my skin as I thought about the time and evidence we could lose if we didn't get this warrant. It wasn't an option to hit up another judge. If the defense found out, they'd scream about it, and not only would we look like crap, we'd probably lose the suppression motion. Everything we'd seized would be thrown out.

"Now the warrant, please."

I handed her the search warrant.

"So you want to search his house and vehicles and you want to surreptitiously place a GPS tracker on his cars?"

I nodded.

Judge Moss reviewed the affidavit again, then put down the pages and drummed her fingers on her desk as she stared out her chambers window. "If Ian Powers is your guy, you know he's going to get himself a heavy hitter," she said. Bailey and I nodded. "And that lawyer is going to put this search warrant through a meat grinder." We nodded again.

Judge Moss looked down at the warrant again. Was she going to turn us down? I calculated the waiting time to get the results on the blood smear on Brian's trunk, on the hair comparison, and even the fingerprint comparison. Even a best case scenario of a couple of days would give Averly plenty of time to tip off Ian, and give Ian plenty of time to dump evidence. Judge Moss sat up and looked me in the eye. "You don't have enough."

My stomach lurched. We were hosed. But the judge continued. "At least not for the GPS. As for the search…" She leaned back and stared out the window with narrowed eyes. "Well, I never dodged a tough call before and I'm not about to start now." Judge Moss picked up the warrant. "Detective Keller, raise your right hand." I quietly let go of the breath I'd been holding. We had our warrant.

37

Bailey'd had a team standing by, so the minute Judge Moss signed, she called to give them the go-ahead and we flew out of the courthouse. Graden had said he'd meet us there. When you toss a pad belonging to a whale like Powers, it's good to have the brass on hand. Not only can they deal with the inevitable outraged threats of retaliation, but by watching the search, they can swear to whomever—be it judge, jury, or management—that everything was done by the book. The thought of getting to put Graden on the witness stand made me smile.

Powers lived in Bel Air, not far from Russell, but their manses were a study in contrasts: whereas Russell's was an ivy-covered Tudor that had a traditional feeling, Ian's was ultramodern, concrete gray, all straight lines and right angles with varied rooftops and slanted skylights and lots and lots of glass.

We made a ruse call to the housekeeper saying that we had a package to deliver so she'd open the gates without any nasty confrontations. The house was set back so far from the street, she'd have to check the surveillance camera to see that we weren't UPS. I was banking on her not bothering since it was mid-morning, a typical delivery time. And I was right. The gate swung open and we drove through.

A large outer door stood open, giving entrance to an enclosed courtyard with a retractable glass ceiling. It was halfway open right now, but I imagined they'd close it when the sun got a little higher in the sky.

A squat Hispanic woman in a maid's uniform answered the door. When she saw the contingent of cops behind Bailey and me, she glared at us. "What do you want?" she said, her tone both surly and condescending. It was a rather surprising degree of belligerence in the face of all those uniforms. Bailey raised an eyebrow, introduced us in a steely voice that would've given Muhammad Ali some pause, and showed her the search warrant.

She looked at it with suspicious eyes. "You can't come in," she said. "Mr. Powers isn't home."

"He doesn't have to be here. We'll leave him a copy of the warrant. Now if you don't mind, Ms. . . . ?"

"Vasquez." But she did mind. She folded her arms and said, "Mr. Powers says no one can come in when he's not home unless he tells me in advance."

"Ms. Vasquez, no one has the right to refuse to let us execute a search warrant. Please step aside. Then go ahead and call Mr. Powers and tell him we're here." With that, Bailey stepped forward and closed the gap, leaving Ms. Vasquez with the choice of either backing up or getting knocked flat. She very reluctantly—but wisely—chose the former option, scurrying away, presumably to call her boss, and Bailey and I stepped inside, the unis on our heels.

The front door led into a wide foyer, which opened into a great room. It had "interior designer" written all over it—but unlike Russell's, this decorating maven was a minimalist: sparse, simple furniture, with lots of windows and skylights, cool gray walls, and bamboo floors covered by thick Gabbeh rugs that provided striking spots of rich, earthy rusts, browns, and oranges. It was a little stark, but it had an austere appeal.

Bailey dispatched teams of three for each of the bigger rooms, which included an immense kitchen with two refrigerators, three ovens, and three dishwashers. Boyfriend must do some serious entertaining. Bailey and I took the study because it'd pose the gnarliest legal questions about what we were allowed to paw through. Especially since I'd written the "items to be seized" part of the warrant as broadly as I dared. I've learned from hard experience that when it comes to warrants, less is not more. Limit yourself too much and you can leave critical evidence behind. And of course, evidence left behind is evidence we'll never have the chance to get again. So I always try to think ahead to what might become important, even if it isn't obvious at the moment. But I also had to be careful. Ian was likely to have legal documents that had no bearing on our case, so I wanted to make sure nothing got touched that would get anyone's hands slapped later.

Given the rest of the house, I'd expected a glass and chrome affair for a desk, but instead this was a traditional kind of study: a heavy-looking mahogany desk with a big leather lawyer's chair behind it and two cushy upholstered armchairs positioned in front of it. An antique wooden filing cabinet stood in the corner behind the desk, and the walls were covered with framed posters of the movies he and Russell had produced over the years. There were quite a few.

"Don't see any Oscars, Emmys, or Golden Globes," Bailey said.

"Maybe he keeps his statuary in the bathroom."

"Knowing him, more likely in the bedroom." Bailey and I shared a smirk.

We were just about to get down to work when a commotion at the front door made us stop and listen. A husky female voice was demanding to know what was going on. I leaned out into the hallway and saw a stunning brunette with waist-length hair in a flowing, nearly sheer tunic-length dress and five-inch heels standing in the foyer, a Neiman Marcus shopping bag on her arm.

"Isn't it kind of early for a Neiman's run?" I asked Bailey.

"Yes, that does seem to be the question on everyone's mind." She nodded toward the officers, who were openly enjoying the view.

"Mrs. Powers—?"

"Or a much-respected girlfriend," Bailey said.

"Shall I see if she's free for lunch?" We'd need to interview her pretty quick if Ian wound up in handcuffs. I figured we might as well take a shot at her now since she was here.

"Let the unis get her info for now. We can talk to her later when we've got something to work with."

"Do the guys know how you're always looking out for them?"

"You've seen how fast I pull together search teams," Bailey replied.

I nodded. "Point taken."

We got down to work. I started with the filing cabinets, where I was most likely to find the sensitive legal papers. But there wasn't much there: contracts, old divorce documents—apparently Ian had a "prior"—and some official-looking correspondence with agents, but nothing that appeared to be sensitive, or even current. He'd probably gone paperless—the way of the world.

Bailey had pulled off all removable cushions on the chairs and sofa and leafed through every book on the shelves by the time I'd finished with the filing cabinet. We turned our attention to the desk. She took the left side, I took the right. Other than office supplies and paperweights, the most interesting thing I found was a photograph of a voluptuous copper-haired beauty in an evening gown. But she looked nothing like the slender brunette we'd seen in the entryway and in the photos that were dotted around the house.

"Something on the side?" I said, holding it up for Bailey to see. Just as she reached for it, I saw writing on the back. *To my darling son, the best manager Hollywood has ever seen. XOXO, Mom.*

Bailey took the photo and read the back. "Let's hope he isn't keeping his mother on the side."

"Gagging now."

I moved on to the bottom-right drawer. But when I pulled the handle, it wouldn't budge. I pulled again; no luck.

"This one's locked." Bailey and I exchanged a look. She gave it a yank, confirmed what I'd said, and called out to the other officers to bring in the tools.

Four minutes later, the drawer was open. And there,

under a few issues of *Hollywood Reporter,* was a laptop computer. Bailey lifted it out. "It's not totally suspicious that he locked it up."

"He's probably got just as many hot-and-cold running assistants as Russell. A lot of prying eyes," I said. "Though you'd think a password would be enough security in your own home."

Bailey shrugged. "He might just be paranoid."

"True."

"But it might be more than that. If we take it, it could buy us a lot of trouble…" And yet, if we didn't, we might regret it. Bitterly. "Your call, Counselor," she said.

I'd included my standard phrase in the description of things we were allowed to seize: "All items whether electronic or written that might reasonably contain information or writings relevant to the crimes of…," in this case, kidnapping and murder. The only real problem with seizing the computer was that we might run into privileged material. A manager doesn't have a legally recognized privilege. But if we uncovered any communications with his lawyer that involved this case, it'd be trouble. On the other hand, if we left it here…

"Yeah. Take it. It's covered." I'd figure out how to handle any privilege issues later. The first priority was to get the evidence.

Bailey changed gloves and gingerly pulled the laptop out of the drawer, then slid it into a paper bag. "You do the idiot check to make sure we didn't miss anything in here. I'm going to make sure they got Ian's hairbrush, toothbrush, and all that jazz."

"That jazz" would provide the exemplars Dorian and Tim Gelfer, our DNA expert, could use to determine whether hairs and any bodily fluids that'd been seized matched Ian Powers. As I picked up the bag containing the laptop, I heard loud male voices coming from the front of the house.

Bailey pointed to the computer. "Make sure you get that tagged and logged."

Then she walked off. And left me there, holding the bag.

38

I moved toward the front of the house where the evidence officer was stationed just as Ian Powers shouted, "I have the right to have my lawyer examine the warrant first! You can't just barge into my house this way!"

"You do not have the right to have your lawyer review the warrant first, Mr. Powers," Graden replied, his voice low and steady. If Powers thought he could throw his weight around with Graden, he was about to find out just how sadly mistaken he was. When I reached the front of the house, I saw that Graden was holding a copy of the search warrant and Powers was leaning toward him, neck muscles strained and bulging, chin jutting out, as though daring Graden to hit him.

Graden looked calm as the clear blue water in Ian's infinity pool. Good news for Powers, because one punch from Graden would've ruined his close-ups for the next few months. Graden acknowledged me with a brief nod, then turned back to Powers. "I can assure you that there will be no damage to your—"

"I'm calling my lawyer!"

Graden replied with calm indifference, "Be my guest."

Ian pulled out his cell phone and gave it the command to call his lawyer. I deliberately turned my back to him and started to hand the bag containing the laptop to the evidence officer. But then I thought better of it and stopped. If there was incriminating evidence on this laptop, Ian would go ballistic, and his lawyer would come running even faster. I could be dragged into court before I ever had the chance to see what I had. I motioned to the officer to join me outside and hugged the bag to my body to hide it from Ian as I made my way around him. Fortunately he was distracted, yelling at his lawyer. I had to get out of here fast, while I still could. When we stepped out into the courtyard, I explained the problem to the evidence officer. "So could you log it in and let me take it back to the station right now?"

"You've got to have an officer with you for chain of custody. I can't just let—"

"Bailey Keller can vouch for—"

"What's the issue here?" Graden asked.

"Walk me to the car."

I explained the situation and Graden pulled out a walkie-talkie. "Send Keller out here ASAP." He moved to my right, putting his body between me and the house to block Ian's view. "If this turns out to be your guy—"

"I know, it's gonna be hell—"

At that moment, a customized, chauffeur-driven black Mercedes roared up to the gate. Ian's lawyer. It had to be.

"Oh, shit," I said. I turned my back to the gate. "Graden, where's your car?"

"I don't have one. I hitched a ride with one of the unis."

Damn it. Where the hell was Bailey? The gates swung open and the car came roaring up the driveway. Graden walked toward it slowly, making it look casual. I turned my back to the car and moved further up the drive, forcing myself not to look back or move too fast. I heard Graden introduce himself and the lawyer demand to see the warrant and his ID. I hoped that would keep him busy for a while, but before Graden could answer, he asked, "And who's that woman over there?"

Being the only woman in the immediate area who wasn't in uniform, I stuck out. If the lawyer saw me with Ian's laptop, he'd start screaming about privileged material and demand an immediate hearing. If he got the right judge, he could tie us up in court for weeks. My back was to him, but I tilted my head enough to see out of the corner of my eye. The lawyer had started toward me. There was no place to hide, and I couldn't just run. Could I? Fortunately I didn't have to answer that question, because at that moment I heard Bailey introduce herself. "And your name is?" she asked him.

"Stanford Trinity, Mr. Powers's lawyer—"

"You planning to represent Jack Averly too?"

"My plans are none of your concern, Detective. Now let me see that warrant."

Graden interceded. "Come with me, Mr. Trinity."

I didn't hear a response, so I waited until I heard their footsteps in the courtyard before turning around. Then I silently motioned to Bailey and mouthed, "Get over here." She spread her arms out questioningly. "What?"

I waved at her with urgency and she finally trotted over to me. "Get me out of here. Now!"

She gave me a puzzled look, but hurried to get the car. When we drove off the compound and I could let myself exhale, I explained why I'd been in such a hurry to get out of there. It felt good to finally put the laptop down on the seat. I'd been holding it so tightly, it'd made dents in my chest and stomach.

Bailey had a little grin on her face. "Wouldn't it be a riot if all it had on it was Angry Birds?"

"No. What took you so long?"

"Got a call from Abe Furtoni back in New York. Our boy Averly just lawyered up."

"Let me guess: a high-priced white-collar firm."

"Exactly."

"And that's why you just asked Ian's lawyer if he was representing Jack too."

"And did you notice? He didn't ask me 'Jack who?'"

"Did Abe know whether Jack Averly got hold of a cell phone?"

"He didn't give Averly a chance. They stuck him in solitary right after we left New York. Averly must've gotten desperate, because he finally used the company phone this morning."

"And called Ian?" I asked.

"Don't know yet. But Abe only got the call from Jack Averly's lawyer a few minutes ago—"

"So Ian got a lawyer for Averly about the same time he called a lawyer for himself."

"Way it looks to me."

Any doubts we may've had about that conclusion were resolved seconds later. My cell phone played

"Dirty Work" by Steely Dan—the ringtone for my boss Eric's number. It was Melia.

"Hi, Rachel. Everything okay?"

The ridiculously cheery yet familiar tone was still jarring. I fervently hoped this would wear off soon. "Everything's great, Melia. What's up?"

"I've got a call from a lawyer in New York. Want me to patch him through?"

"Who is it?" Never before has Melia offered to put a call through to me when I'm in the field. Not unless it's Eric or Vanderhorn.

"Beldon Castleman."

It was a little depressing to know that Melia could really do the job when she wanted to. "Thanks, Melia. Put him through."

"Okay. Have a great day, Rachel."

With the next click, I was on with Beldon Castleman, Esquire. He explained in clipped, wannabe British tones that he was handling Jack Averly only as long as he was in New York, as a favor for Donald Wagmeister. "I don't know if you've crossed swords with Don before—"

"I know Don." Not because we'd "crossed swords" but because everyone knew Don. He was one of the most high-priced criminal lawyers in Los Angeles.

"We don't intend to fight extradition, and we'll be asking for the earliest court date available for arraignment when he gets back to Los Angeles."

"Not a problem, Beldon. But in the interest of fair notice, you might tell Don that if he intends to try and cop a fast plea to the receiving stolen property count, we'll be adding more charges by the time Averly gets back here."

A long-standing legal rule requires the prosecution to

file all charges related to a single event at once if they
have evidence to prove all the charges. The point being
to prevent successive, harassing prosecutions. So if the
DDA goofed and only filed the lesser charge, a defense
attorney could run in, get his client to plead to the lesser
crime, and preclude the prosecutor from ever bringing
the heavier charges. I was telling Beldon not to plan on
that happening here.

"Such as?"

I said nothing. No sense showing my hand before I
was sure.

"That's fine, I'll let Don know. And in the meantime,
I've left my number with your secretary if you should
need to reach me for any reason."

When I ended the call, Bailey asked, "How'd he
sound when you said you'd be adding charges?"

"Like he could care less." I paused. "He might've
been bluffing."

"Maybe. But if he wasn't—"

"They've already got their strategy ready."

Bailey nodded. "What the hell are they cooking up?"

"Good question."

39

When we got back to the station, Bailey called the evidence officer and asked what else they'd found so far.

"Anything good?" I asked when she hung up.

"A nine-millimeter Ruger. Bottom drawer of his nightstand."

"Registered?" I asked, hoping it wasn't. It was a puny charge, but at least it was solid.

"Yes. Which is more than I can say for you—"

"My guns are registered."

"Now. After I pounded on you repeatedly for months."

"I'd been busy. Did they get his toothbrush or anything we can use for DNA?"

"A toothbrush and a used condom."

"Great. And yuck." Gross, but great. "Have we checked out Averly's bank accounts?"

"You mean like for a deposit of at least half a million in cash?"

I nodded.

"Of course. I put in the request before we left for New York."

"And?"

"If the answer was yes, don't you think I'd have told you by now?"

Her phone rang and she answered it. "That was Numan's assistant," she said. "The particulates and plant debris on Averly's Mustang came from Boney Mountain. They look very similar to the samples that were taken from Brian's car."

"So Averly's car was up there too. Now the question is, can we put Ian in that car?"

"That's Dorian's problem," Bailey said. "We've got one of our own: like what are we going to do with Ian's laptop?"

I'd been thinking about that on the ride back to the station. "We could throw caution to the wind and just dig into it. Or we could go to court and ask to have a Special Master appointed to look through everything and make sure there aren't any privileged materials on it."

Usually the court appoints a Special Master—a lawyer well versed in legal privileges—to examine files only when they belong to a shrink or a lawyer. Getting one in this case was a bit of overkill, but I didn't want to risk losing something critical on the off chance we ran into something we weren't supposed to see.

"Doesn't it take a while to get a Special Master appointed?"

"It can. But it doesn't have to."

"What are you thinking?"

"I could probably get a judge to appoint Daniel Rose to do it right now."

"I repeat: what are you thinking?"

Daniel Rose was well recognized as both a legal

scholar and a brilliant trial lawyer; his practice used to consist primarily of giving expert opinions on whether lawyers had rendered ineffective assistance—in legal parlance, a *Strickland* lawyer. Any judge would be happy to appoint him Special Master. Bailey's concern wasn't legal, it was personal. Daniel and I had been in a serious relationship a few years ago, until I'd hit an emotional bump and ended it. Last year, after I'd broken up with Graden, I ran into Daniel at Checkers, a restaurant in the downtown Hilton Hotel. He said he planned to move into a condo not far from the Biltmore, and a few months later, he made good on his word. Since then, he'd dropped some hints that he'd be interested in getting back together. Though I hadn't taken him up on his offer, I never really turned him down either. But I figured that the ever-active courthouse gossip mill would have clued him in about me and Graden by now, so there was no need to get all telenovela about it.

"I can just ask the judge to appoint him, and then you can let him check out the computer."

Bailey looked at me warily, but conceded that might work. "Which judge?"

"I think we stick with Judge Moss."

"Probably a good idea. Plus, it'll impress her that you're being so careful."

I smiled.

Bailey raised an eyebrow and pushed her desk phone over to me. "Here."

I dialed. Judge Moss approved. I hung up and told Bailey she'd be hearing from Daniel soon.

"And you probably don't need to run into him—especially not here," Bailey said.

Where Graden could walk by and see us, and think...
the wrong thing. I nodded and started to leave, then
turned back. "If Dorian says it's Ian hair in Jack Averly's
Mustang, I'm going back to Judge Moss to get the GPS
on Ian's cars."

"'Course."

Bailey's phone rang and I moved slowly, straining to
hear who it was. I heard her say, "Just a sec.

"Do you need an escort, Counselor?" she called out
to me, eyebrow raised.

I glared at her, then turned and headed for the elevator.

40

So much had happened, it was hard to believe that it was still just early afternoon. I walked out of the station into yet another day of blazing heat; the sun beat down from a cloudless topaz sky, the light bouncing white and searing off the sidewalks. Even through my sunglasses I found myself squinting as I made my way up the street to my office. A bus belched out a cloud of exhaust just as I was about to climb the back stairs and I held my breath all the way into the lobby.

It was a good thing I got in a few deep breaths as I ran for the elevator, because the intense mix of perfume, body odor, and food in the densely packed crowd made me hold my breath again. I was lightheaded by the time I got back to my desk. As I dug through the work that'd piled up in my absence, my thoughts kept straying to the laptop, the bloodstain, the hair...everything I had to wait for. It was driving me nuts.

"How goes it?"

I looked up to see my boss, Eric, standing in my doorway. His wavy brown hair was unusually wild today, and in his rolled-up shirtsleeves and scuffed loafers, he presented the very picture of an "aw shucks" country boy lawyer. Which is why defense attorneys never saw him coming. And by the time they realized that he was the smoothest shark in the tank, it was too late.

"Yeah. We've got a lot of evidence cooking, but no results yet, so…"

"You're waiting, and loving it." Eric smiled. "Tell me what you've got."

I gave him the latest developments, ending with my decision to bring in Daniel Rose as a Special Master.

He nodded approvingly. "It's good to be cautious on this one." Not usually my strong suit, but a lot of unusual was about to come my way.

A week later, news of Brian's murder was finally announced, and it reinvigorated the press coverage, though we'd managed to keep a tight rein on the details. With no suspect in custody, media interest was a simmering cauldron—semi-contained, but ready to boil over at a moment's notice. And if we did arrest Ian Powers, the case would go nuclear.

Eric stopped by my office, looking as anxious as I felt. "I'll keep giving Vanderhorn the updates for now," he told me, "but you'll have to give me a major heads-up if it looks like Powers is getting arrested."

My expression must've shown what I thought of having to put Vanderhorn in the loop. "There's nothing he can do," Eric said. "He can't stop Bailey from making the arrest. But he does have to be prepared. The press will want a statement and—"

"The *press* will want it? Vanderhorn will trip over his own tie to get the press to take his statement."

Eric gave a wry smile. "And you should be there when he does."

Because he'd need someone around who actually knew something about the case when his good buddies in the fourth estate asked questions.

"What do you want to do with Jack Averly?" he asked.

"Unless we find proof that he's the killer, I'd let him plead out for testimony."

"Plead to what?"

"I can't say right now. I don't want to go there until I have something more on either him or Ian."

Eric stared out the window, momentarily silent. When he looked back at me, his expression was concerned. "Going after a big wheel like Powers is a dangerous thing, Rachel. If this goes to trial, Ian's defense will go after you with everything they've got. In every media outlet available. They'll make up stories to undermine your credibility and your integrity. And it'll all creep into the courtroom because they'll have the press at their beck and call. Forget about fact-checking or corroborating sources; it'll go straight out from the lying horse's mouth."

He spoke with a quiet intensity that told me this was no general warning. "Been there?"

Eric nodded. "Huge fraud case. The defendant owned several banks and he cost the customers millions."

"Do I know about this one?" It sounded familiar, but not recent.

"It was years ago. Just before I got transferred over

here to head up Special Trials. It was the day before jury selection, and I was supposed to meet some friends at a bar near my old office in Norwalk. While I was waiting, this tipsy girl starts flirting with me. The next thing I know, she's sitting on my lap, unbuttoning my shirt—it was crazy. I pushed her off and eventually she gave up and left, but the next day, there was a story in one of the tabloids about the prosecutor having an affair with a teenager. The story got picked up by the local press and it almost cost me the case—and my job."

"But it didn't. And it obviously didn't hurt your career any."

"I was lucky, not smart. The bartender knew something was fishy and he was able to identify the person who took the picture as one of the defendant's buddies. The whole thing blew up in their faces, and the press was happy to carry that part of the story too. But a fraud case is nowhere near as sexy as this one, Rachel. It's a bad combination of heavy hitters, money, celebrity, and a glamorous world. The press will be crawling all over this the moment you file, and every eye in the country will be glued."

I nodded.

"If your killer turns out to be Jack Averly, just a loser dope dealer, it'll stay manageable. But if it turns out to be Ian Powers...you've got yourself one gigantic cluster fuck."

I let the information sink in. Eric's story was chilling, but I appreciated his telling me. Forewarned is forearmed as they say, though I had no idea what I could do about it if Ian's people decided to set me up. "Thanks, Eric."

"Keep me in the loop. I'll do what I can to manage Vanderhorn."

"Will do."

Eric left, and for the first time, I stopped to consider whether I was really up for the kind of nasty ride he'd described. I was still pondering the question when my cell phone played Bailey's ringtone.

"Daniel's done with the computer. He gave us the all clear."

"Great—" I sat up, and my heart gave a heavy thud as I suddenly realized I'd forgotten something. "Bailey, what about prints? Did you call—"

"I got Ben, the criminalist who did Brian's car at the airport, to dust it before Daniel got here. We've got some nice prints all over that thing. And Daniel wore gloves, just in case."

I sagged with relief. "Thanks, Bailey." I took a second to breathe. "Did Daniel tell you whether there was anything that looked good for us?"

"Unfortunately, he said he didn't see anything to get excited about."

Damn. All that for nothing. "Okay, then let's give it to our computer whizbangs in my office. Maybe Ian's got some information hidden or encrypted or . . . something."

"I'll bring it over."

"So now we're just waiting for Dorian and Gelfer."

"I checked. They won't have anything until tomorrow. And I think Dorian blocked my number."

I was silent as I tried to figure out what else we could do besides wait. Bailey read my silence.

"There's nothing we can do right now," Bailey said.

I looked at my desk. I estimated it'd take me only an

hour to clear it off. Then what would I do? Pace in my hotel room? Even I didn't think that would help anything. "I'll call Toni." We'd been playing phone tag for a while.

But first I called the head deputy of our computer crimes section, Cliff Meisner. He agreed to take a whack at the laptop but warned, "People have gotten pretty sophisticated about hiding information, so it'll take some time."

Translation: I had to wait. Again. And I wasn't getting any better at it.

41

Bailey returned with our round of martinis. We all clinked and sipped. A cold martini on a warm summer night. My besties, Bailey and Toni, and the lights of the city spread out around us like a glittering swath of sequined lace.

"I probably should've called Graden," I said, taking in the nighttime view of downtown L.A. from the corner of the rooftop bar at Perch.

"Really, Rache," Toni said. " 'Should' makes it sound like you'd be doing it out of guilt. That ain't right."

"'Toine's right," Bailey said. She pronounced it "Twan." "Just because you have a night off doesn't mean you owe it to him. And besides, you're wiped out, edgy, and pissy. You wouldn't be able to play nice tonight. So you did him a favor."

I couldn't argue with one word of it.

"And you'll notice I'm not with Drew either."

"So I'm the only one who's normal around here?" Toni asked.

"Relatively speaking," I said. "Though given present company, that isn't saying much."

Toni waved off the remark. "How'd it go with Judge Moss?"

"How did you know?" Bailey asked.

"Black lawyer grapevine. So how'd it go?"

"She was awesome." I filled Toni in on the latest developments.

Toni gave us a smug smile. "Told you she was good. And it doesn't matter that she wouldn't give you the GPS. Powers can't afford to run anyway."

"Exactly," I replied. "But I never did get to see what kind of car he had. Did you?" I asked Bailey.

"You mean *cars,* plural. A gold two-seater custom Bentley, a black Ferrari, and a white Rolls-Royce."

I tried to picture Ian Powers in the Rolls. "White Rolls-Royce? Somehow that doesn't fit."

"It's the girlfriend's car."

"The Neiman Marcus brunette?" I asked.

Bailey nodded.

"No wife, no children?"

"Neither," Bailey said.

I remembered noticing the absence of family photos. There'd just been a smattering of pictures of his girlfriend.

Toni gave us an update on her double homicide case, which seemed to be going well. All in all, it was as relaxing an evening as it could be, under the circumstances. I made myself go to bed before midnight, hoping that the morning would bring us some answers.

As it turned out, all the morning brought was an early harbinger of trouble. It came in the form of a call on my private cell phone. I'd left for work early, hoping to beat the worst of the heat. I also figured that since my mind was so wrapped around the case, I might as well obsess in my office. I was about a block from the courthouse when my cell phone played the default ringtone. Sure that it was either Dorian or Numan, I answered without looking at the number. Instead, a man with a *real* British accent—so I knew it wasn't that poser-lawyer, Beldon— said, "Hello, Ms. Knight?"

Maybe I was disarmed by the accent, or just too distracted to think quickly enough to deny it, but I admitted it was.

"This is Andrew Chatham from the *National Inquisitor,* and I'm calling about the Hayley Antonovich case."

The *National Inquisitor*? How in the hell did he get my private cell phone number?

"I don't know how you got this number, but I'm not at liberty to discuss the case."

"But my sources indicate that you may very well have suspects in custody shortly, one of whom is a very highly placed individual in the industry."

How could this guy know that already? I quickly tried to imagine who the leak was, but there had been so many people in Ian's house—and that didn't even take into account nosy neighbors who might've seen all the police cars. I'd probably never know.

"I'm sorry, Mr. Chatham—"

"Do call me Andrew, please. I expect we'll be in touch quite a lot in the coming weeks and months. No sense standing on ceremony, is there?"

"Andrew, please don't take this personally, but I have no intention of being in touch. Do have a nice day."

I ended the call. We hadn't even made an arrest and

it was already starting. But the more shocking part was that the first call had been from a tabloid, not the mainstream press. I'd heard rumors that the major newspapers had taken so many financial hits, they couldn't compete with the "pay for play" jockeys in the tabloid world. That phone call might be proof that the rumor was true. But more important, this was an early shot across the bow, warning me that if we did arrest Ian Powers, I'd be in for the three-ring circus from hell. I tromped heavily up the stairs to the courthouse as though I were being led to the guillotine. All I could do was hope that the day would pick up from there.

I stopped at the snack bar on the thirteenth floor to get a bagel and coffee. I'd been in a hurry to get to work and hadn't wanted to wait for room service. Poor, poor me, having to "wait" for room service. I admit that sometimes I even make myself gag. I was on my way to the elevator, bagel in hand, when I bumped into Daniel Rose.

"Hey, Rachel! I'd ask what you're up to, except I already know."

"Dan, thank you so much. I can't tell you what a relief it was to get you as Special Master."

He looked gorgeous, which was par for the course. In shirtsleeves, with his jacket slung over his shoulder, he looked like an ad for Armani—except more intellectual, with his thick black hair that had just the right amount of gray at the sides and wire-rimmed glasses. And what cologne was he wearing? He smelled great.

"The chance to help out a friend...and the allure of getting the inside scoop on a hot case. It's a tough combination to resist."

His eyes were as warm as his smile, and as always, my heart lifted at the sight. But in the next moment I caught myself. I was with Graden now. And although nothing had happened between Daniel and me, it seemed only fair that I should let him know. I began to speak but was cut off by a highly caffeinated and excited Melia, who'd just burst out of the elevator.

"Rachel! I'm so glad I found you. You've had a million calls! I've got all the messages for you. And Eric needs to see you ASAP. Vanderhorn wants a meeting—"

"Okay, Melia. Calm down. I'm on my way."

Daniel shook his head sympathetically. "Duty calls. Let me know if you need me...for anything."

There was no mistaking the double entendre with the look that accompanied that line. I wish I could say it didn't faze me. The truth was, a jolt of electricity shot all the way from my head to my toes. The *ding* of an elevator saved me from having to come up with a real answer.

42

"Don't go there, Rachel," Eric said. "You'll never figure out who leaked. The only thing we can do now is push them off with a 'no comment' until we have a move to make. In the meantime, Vanderhorn wants you to give him some background on the case—"

"When?"

"This afternoon—around two thirty."

"Good. I might have answers from Dorian by then, and if they're the right ones, Bailey's going to make an arrest."

"Then it'd probably be better to get you in to see him sooner." We exchanged a look. Vanderhorn needed more time than most to absorb information. Asking him to catch the facts of a case on the fly was like asking a dog to catch a medicine ball. "Let me find out if he can move something." Eric told Melia to place the call. One minute later she buzzed him, and he picked up the phone. Eric explained the situation to Vanderhorn's secretary. Another minute later he said, "Fine," and hung up.

"He'll see us in an hour. Stop by here and we'll go together." I nodded and stood up. "And try not to look like that when we go."

"Like what?"

He ignored me. "See you in an hour."

I did know what I looked like: pissed and annoyed. I think Vanderhorn makes a horse's ass look smart and I didn't want to help him look any better for the camera. On the other hand, he was the one who'd have to field most of the questions if we filed the case. If he looked bad, we looked bad. Talk about your paradox.

I forced myself to concentrate on the work I hadn't been able to finish the day before, but couldn't stop looking at my phones, waiting for one of them to ring and hoping it would be Dorian. You know the old saying about watching water to see if it boils. So finally, with twenty minutes to go before our meeting with Vanderputz, I gave up and reviewed the reports. I'd need to dumb it all down into sound bites, so I spent the remaining time thinking of simple ways to summarize the case.

At the appointed time Eric and I arrived at the anteroom outside Vanderhorn's office, where his secretary, Francine Jefferson, sat. She was in her sixties but she didn't look a day over forty. Smart, no-nonsense, and with a peppery sense of humor. No one understood how she put up with Vanderhorn. My theory was that she'd taken him on because she loved a challenge. Now she looked at me over the top of her reading glasses.

"You jumped into it this time." She shook her head. "I don't like saying I told you so—"

"Yes you do, Francine. You love it."

"A little bit. And I know you're not going to listen,

but I'm going to say this anyway: Get out now, while you still can, because this case is going to be a bona fide nightmare."

The buzzer on her desk sounded, telling us that Vanderhorn was ready to receive.

She shook her head at me. "You know what that means."

The district attorney has the primo spot on the eighteenth floor, even though it isn't a corner office. Spacious and tastefully furnished with a leather couch, several swivel chairs, and a large cherrywood desk that had nothing on it but framed photos of himself and his lovely, shockingly age-appropriate wife and teenage daughters, it had an expansive one hundred eighty-degree view of the city. A pricey-looking telescope stood on a tripod in the corner, and I wondered whether Vanderhorn was a peeper. The happy thought of him getting busted for it was interrupted by the man in question.

"Have a seat, everybody."

Vanderhorn looked like someone who *should* command respect. At six foot three, he was imposing but not freakish, and his thick shock of white hair, strong features, square jaw, and brown eyes with just the right amount of creasing to look experienced but not old photographed alarmingly well. And did I mention that he had a year-round tan? Now, he leaned way back in his massive leather chair and steepled his hands in front of his chest.

"I understand there's a possibility that you might be asking to file charges against Ian Powers," he said, lifting one eyebrow and then the other as he looked from me to Eric. Boomer, a golden retriever that belonged to a childhood friend of mine, used to waggle his eyebrows just like that. I bit the inside of my cheek to keep from laughing and nodded. "Tell me about the case," he said.

I did, in as few words and in words with as few syllables as possible. "Right now, I'm waiting for the test results of the bloodstain on Brian Maher's trunk, the hair removed from Jack Averly's Mustang, and any prints that may have been lifted. I've also given Ian's laptop to Cliff Meisner to check out."

Vanderhorn frowned, and for a moment I thought he was about to ask something intelligent, like whether there might be any privileged material on the laptop that could cause problems in court.

"Well, I'm not sure you'll have enough even if those...items match up to Ian Powers. What's your theory?"

Oh, jeez. I took a deep breath to keep from saying something I'd enjoy but regret, and dived in. "The Mustang has already been determined to have soil and plant debris on it that are unique to Boney Mountain, where Brian's body was found. The same debris was found on Brian's Toyota and on Hayley's body."

"So maybe that proves they were all up there, but how do you prove it was at the same time?"

"With the remaining evidence. If the hair in Averly's car is Ian's, and if there are prints in Averly's car that come back to Ian, and if there is any evidence that ties Ian to Brian's Toyota, then we'll have tied both dead kids to Ian and to Jack Averly and his car."

"Did you ever find the ransom money?"

"No. But that would've been easy to hide." Vanderhorn leaned back in his chair again and looked at me through narrowed eyes. "And Ian Powers definitely could have found out about the kidnapping right away," I continued. "Russell's phone records show he called Ian within minutes after he got the first text from Hayley's phone."

"So your theory's that he found out about the kidnapping and jumped in on it? Why? What's Powers's motive?"

That, finally, was a good question. "We believe it has to do with the theft of Brian's father's screenplay."

Vanderhorn's brow knitted. "And the thinking is that this boy, Brian, had some kind of proof that his father's screenplay was stolen and that Ian killed him to keep it from coming out?"

I knew where this was going and I wished there was a way to head him off, but I was stuck. "Yes."

He straightened up in his chair and looked down his nose at me. He'd gotten hold of an actual idea and he was damn proud of it. "Well, if Brian had enough proof to make Ian Powers that nervous, then why did he resort to kidnapping Hayley? Why not just hire a lawyer? With all the potential money in a lawsuit like that, any lawyer would've been glad to take the case on a contingent fee basis."

"That is something we're looking into. Obviously we don't have the answer to that yet—"

"Don't you think you should? Before you start filing murder charges and…whatnot on this man, don't you think you should have that motive nailed down?"

I opened my mouth to answer, but Eric stepped in.

"Actually, Bill, as you know, we don't have to prove

motive, and it's very possible we'll never know the whole backstory to this thing. But if the evidence does pan out as Rachel described, I think we have to file the case."

Vanderhorn's expression said he didn't care much for Eric's reasoning. Filing murder charges on a major Hollywood figure like Powers had "campaign fund disaster" written all over it. Vanderhorn would cling to the lack of motive like a man hanging on to a slippery rock at the edge of a waterfall, to avoid losing that kind of support.

Seeing his reaction, Eric added, "We'd certainly file if it were anyone else, Bill. And if we don't, you can expect there'll be victims' rights groups who'll accuse you of playing favorites."

Predictably, the possibility of public backlash was what got Vanderhorn's attention. Hollywood was powerful, but he couldn't win an election if everyone outside of Hollywood hated him. Vanderputz was on the horns of what was, in his world, a true dilemma.

"I want to see those reports. I'll make my decision then."

That concluded the proceedings, and Eric and I headed back to our humble neck of the woods.

"Now I'm praying the evidence doesn't come back to Powers. If I have to keep dealing with crap like that, I'll go postal."

Eric shook his head sadly. "Now you did it. The gods of trial are sure to punish you. The minute you say you don't want it, that's when you get it."

I laughed. "Thanks, Eric, I needed that."

"I wasn't kidding."

"Neither was I." I waved to him and walked back down the hall to my office.

Ten minutes later, I got a call from Bailey.

"Put on your flak vest. We've got Ian's prints and hair in Averly's Mustang and Ian's thumb and index print on the trunk of Brian's car. And we've got Averly's prints on the interior driver's door handle of Brian's car—"

"So how do you see it?" I asked. "Averly drove Brian's car to the airport with Hayley's body in the trunk, and Ian drove Averly's car?"

"Possibly, but here's the best part: Remember that bloodstain on the trunk of Brian's car?"

"Of course."

"Well, it's a mixture of Hayley's and Ian Powers's—"

"Holy shit—"

"Wait, it gets better: that bloodstain is right next to Ian's thumbprint."

I sucked in a lungful of air. "No kidding?" That was one hell of a lot of circumstantial evidence. But it all hinged on the blood. Prints were great, but we'd never be able to say when they got there. Same with Ian's hair. But a mixture of Ian's and Hayley's blood. That was undeniable. Then why was I nervous? Would I feel this way if the defendant was just an Average Joe? Probably not. The thought rankled.

"Right? One hell of a case. But I gotta run. Got to bring the brass up to speed and get them ready for an arrest. I'll have the reports walked over to you so you can start filing."

Bailey sounded stoked, so I didn't want to be a buzz-kill and tell her that I wasn't flying solo on this one, that Vanderhorn would make the final call on whether to file—and that his approval was by no means a foregone conclusion. "I'm on it."

Of course, this meant I'd have to go back to Vanderhorn immediately. Two meetings in one day. Talk about cruel and unusual punishment.

43

I called Eric and gave him the news. His response?

"Told you so." I had a feeling there were a lot more "told you so's" in my near future. "Call me back when you have the reports in hand. I'll set up the meeting with Vanderhorn."

I couldn't sit still, so I went down the hall to see Melia. I had a question for her, and I wanted to ask it in person. I moved back up the hallway and found her chattering excitedly on the phone. When she saw me in the doorway, she quickly said, "Call you later," and hung up.

"Hi, Rachel!"

"Hi, Melia!" Another secretary might've caught the note of sarcasm, but that secretary would not be Melia. "I was just wondering, who've you given my cell phone number to? I just need to know what to expect." I'd deliberately framed the question to assume she'd given out my number in the hope that it'd lull her into admitting it.

"No one." She stared off for a moment, mouth partially open, as she considered the question further.

"Nuh-uh, I'm sure I didn't give it out to anyone. Why, is there someone you want me to give it to?"

No nervousness, no embarrassment. She was telling the truth.

"No, not that I can think of right now. But I expect there'll be calls from the press and the tabs if we file the case, and I don't want them to be able to reach me on my cell. You know how much I hate the press—"

"I'd never give your number to the press. Eric told me never to give out deputies' cell phone numbers a long time ago."

Then how did that tabloid reporter, Andrew Chatham, get my cell phone number?

"Uh, excuse me, I have something to deliver to Ms. Knight," said a male voice behind me. I turned to see a uni holding a manila envelope. The reports from Bailey.

I told him I was the one he was looking for and he started to ask me for ID, but Melia interceded.

"It's her."

Why that was sufficient to allay his concern I have no idea, but he handed me the envelope and I thanked him. As I walked back to my office, I noticed it was taped closed. It was unusual to seal reports this way—let alone have them hand-delivered, but this case required extraordinary measures. I reviewed all the reports, just to make sure there were no hidden surprises. I didn't see any, but I was about to go in and do battle with the Meathead, so I decided to call Dorian and make sure there were no caveats to be wary of.

"Dorian, I read everything, but I have to go and sell this case to Vanderhorn. Is there anything I should know that isn't in these reports?"

"Such as?"

"Such as the DNA result on the trunk that shows the mixture between Hayley and Ian. Is that solid? Are there any possible contamination issues the defense can raise? Did anything weird happen during the testing?"

Dorian snorted. "No, nothing 'weird' happened. And I'm not going to make Gelfer write a report saying 'nothing weird' happened, so don't ask."

"Okay, thanks, Dorian—"

"You have to *sell* this to Vanderhorn? What's he want, a videotape of the guy doing it?"

"You got one?"

She hung up.

I called Eric and braced myself for round two with middleweight chump William Vanderhorn.

Francine raised an eyebrow when Eric and I walked into the anteroom.

"Back again so soon?" She looked at me pointedly. "Already starting, isn't it? Guess I don't need to say it, do I?"

"You already did." I sighed.

We had to wait a little longer this time even though the lights on Francine's telephone indicated he wasn't on the line. My bet was that he just didn't want to see us. The feeling was more than mutual.

When we were finally allowed in, Eric handed him the reports. "It's all here. They've got prints, hair, even blood, tying Ian Powers to these murders."

Vanderhorn took the reports. I could see his eyes moving across the page, but I didn't believe he understood a word. Especially since his lips weren't moving. He set the reports down on his desk and cleared his throat. "Of course, this doesn't resolve the weakness in our proof of motive."

"No," Eric replied.

I silently hoped he wouldn't remind Vanderhorn that we might never know the true motive behind the murders. It was the logical, intelligent—legal—answer. Therefore, it would be entirely unpersuasive for the district attorney of the largest prosecutorial agency in the world.

"I think we should try to come up with more before we put this case into the system," Vanderhorn said. "You know what they say: 'Act in haste, repent at leisure.' What's the harm in taking a little more time?"

I'd never admit it, but I wouldn't have minded waiting. The problem was, it was too late for that. I started to answer, but Eric jumped in first.

"The harm lies in the likelihood that this information won't stay on ice forever. We've already got tabloid reporters running around with checkbooks who have more information than they should—"

"The public will know what we have pretty quick, I agree. But so what? If we explain that we're still investigating, don't you think—"

"It'll calm the waters? No, I don't. But even if it did, that's a minor upside you'll be trading for a much bigger downside. If we let this drag on, important witnesses will have time to cave in and sell their stories—a credibility killer—and some may decide they don't want the limelight and disappear. Others might be…encouraged to take a long vacation."

Eric fixed Vanderhorn with a meaningful look. Heavyweights like Ian Powers could find many ways of suggesting to potential witnesses that it'd be advantageous to get gone for a while. I'm not talking about threats that they might sleep with the fishes. Ian and company didn't need to get that heavy-handed. Simple implied promises of future reward—or threats of future unemployment—would be more than enough.

Eric continued, "But that's not your only problem. You also run the risk of losing Ian Powers to a country that won't extradite. Do you want to be the DA who let another Roman Polanski happen on his watch?"

The reminder of the decades-old rape case involving the famous director-defendant who fled to France to avoid imprisonment set Vanderhorn back in his chair. He shifted to stare out the window, his chin in his hand. Somehow he always managed to look as though he were posing for a photo op.

The wheels turned slowly, but eventually Vanderhorn cranked out a decision in a voice that was filled with regret. "I guess we'll have to file." He handed the reports back to Eric. "But I'm going to assign a second chair."

I usually preferred to work alone, but given the way this case was shaping up, I didn't entirely mind the idea of having a subordinate lawyer to help me with the scut work. I knew of a young deputy who'd be perfect.

"What about Amy Stolnitz?" I asked. "She's been tearing it up in court." Plus, I knew she was champing at the bit to get into Special Trials. If I got her on this case, she'd be a shoo-in.

Vanderhorn didn't even look at me. "I'm assigning Declan Shackner to act as second chair."

I looked at Eric. Who was this?

"I'll fill you in later," he said. "Thanks, Bill. We'll keep you posted."

Vanderhorn gave us both a look of thunder. "Damn right you will. Every day."

Oh, joy.

As we walked back to our wing of the floor, Eric gave me the skinny on Declan Shackner.

"Are you kidding me?" I sputtered under my breath as Eric and I walked into his office. "A baby Grade Two! What the hell good is he going to be to me? He's probably never even done a preliminary hearing on a murder case, let alone a trial this big. What the hell is Vanderhorn thinking?"

Eric gestured for me to keep it down and closed the door, a world-weary expression on his face. "You don't recognize the name?"

"No."

"Shackner, as in Morton Shackner...as in Shackner Productions, one of the biggest independent production companies in the industry. And a good friend and frequent collaborator with—"

"Antonovich and Powers."

Eric nodded. "That's how Vanderhorn's going to appease his Hollywood buddies. Total transparency. He's so fair he's putting one of their own on the case. Shows it's all on the up-and-up."

"So who cares if I get to have a real lawyer for second chair? As long as Vanderhorn looks good."

"He is consistent."

"So's a doorstop."

44

I stomped back to my office in what Toni would've called "a mood and a half." What was I going to do with some dippy showbiz kid who probably only got hired because some management jerk wanted invites to premieres? Then it occurred to me that "useless" was the least of my problems. Vanderhorn didn't just throw Declan Shackner in to be a Hollywood token. He intended for Declan to be his spy. This just got better and better.

I slammed the space bar on my keyboard and pulled up the forms to start the filing process. I decided to call Bailey and let her weigh in. She said she might as well come over and do it in person. "That way, you can be there when I negotiate with Powers's lawyer to have him surrender," she said.

"Who's his lawyer?"

"Wagmeister—"

"I thought he was representing Averly." He couldn't ethically represent both Powers and Averly—the possibility for a conflict of interest was too great.

"I'd guess it's just for the moment."

"He'll probably keep Powers and push Averly off on someone else."

"And that someone else is probably already on deck. See you in ten."

My stomach grumbled loudly. I glanced out my window at the Times Building clock. It was almost two thirty. Where had the time gone? I ran down to the snack bar and grabbed a couple of sandwiches for Bailey and me, knowing she'd probably forgotten to eat too. I wondered whether I'd be able to send my new second chair on errands like this in the future. It occurred to me that I was finally getting my very own assistant. It also struck me as a classic example of "be careful what you ask for."

"Food." Bailey dropped her feet off my desk and onto the floor when she saw me walk in with the sandwiches. "Bless you, my child."

I picked up the turkey and Swiss and gave Bailey the BLT, her favorite. Then I closed the door—something we seldom did in these shoebox-sized offices. Bailey raised her eyebrows, then nodded. "Probably a good idea," she said.

"And one we're going to have to get used to." I gestured around the building. "Lots of 'interested parties,' and now there's going to be a big market for them."

"Speaking of which, any idea who leaked to that tabloid guy?"

I shook my head. "I'm leaning toward filing the same charges on Averly and Powers," I said.

"Either one could be the accomplice, I guess. Even though we think Powers has to be the mastermind, that doesn't necessarily mean he did the killing."

"Not yet, anyway. They're still testing everything, so

we might learn differently. But for now, let's bang out a working theory so I can sort out the charges. I can always amend later."

"We don't know how he did it, but somehow Ian got wind of the kidnapping. Then, although the drop site was Fryman Canyon, they all wound up on Boney Mountain—"

"Man, I hate that part of the case." The more "somehow's" and "for some reason's" we had, the more ammo it gave the defense to argue we didn't have enough proof.

"No more than I do." We both sighed. "Anyway, I think Powers called in our boy Averly to at least help, if not do the heavy lifting, and be his ride up to the mountain—"

"Right. And based on the messages on Hayley's cell phone, my guess is that Ian ambushed Brian—"

"Ian? Why not Averly?"

"Charging-wise, it may not matter. But the evidence seems to shake out that way, and he's the only one with both the motive and the smarts. The way I see it, Ian kills Brian, or knocks him out, gets his cell phone, and sees the texts from Hayley, so he knows Hayley's in on it and she's nearby—"

Bailey balled up the sandwich wrapper and tossed it into the wastebasket. "He kills Brian, buries him, but not well because he doesn't have a whole lot of time, then sends the text to Hayley to lure her out. He kills Hayley, dumps her into the trunk of Brian's car—"

"Right," I said. "I'm not sure he planned on seeing Hayley up there—"

"Yeah, I don't think he planned to kill her. After

all, she's his buddy's daughter. He might've figured that with Brian out of the way, she could be scared off from taking things any further. But when he realized that she was there on the mountain, he couldn't let her go—"

"Because if Brian's body was ever found—"

"Which in fact it was—"

"—she'd be a bad witness to have floating around. So he kills her and puts her into the trunk of Brian's car—"

"Which gives us the blood on the trunk."

I nodded. "That's the nail in Ian's coffin as far as Hayley's murder." It's very rare for someone to kill with a knife without cutting themselves, so the fact that we had Ian's blood mixed in with Hayley's showed he likely committed her murder. "As far as Brian's murder...the physical evidence doesn't do much for us one way or the other in terms of showing whether it was Ian or Averly. But Ian's got the motive to kill Brian—"

"Yeah, so I'm with you that Ian probably did them both. Then Averly drives Brian's car to the airport and takes off to New York."

"And Ian drives back down the mountain and shows up at Russell's house," I said. "So here's my question: Is it at all plausible that Averly didn't know about the plan, and just thought he was giving Powers a ride up to Boney Mountain, then got roped into putting a body into a trunk and driving it away? If so, he's an accessory after the fact, not an accomplice. On the other hand, if he did know that the plan was to kill someone, he's an accomplice—at the very least to the killing of Brian if not both Brian and Hayley."

"Do we have to choose now?"

"We have to file something now. And if we file just

the accessory charge, and he pleads to it, we could be shut out of ever getting him for murder."

"But if we file murder charges and later have to reduce or dismiss them, we look pretty raggedy, don't we?"

"Yep."

Bailey folded her arms and stared at the floor.

"I'm going to vote we take the risk of looking raggedy," I said. "Overcharging Jack Averly won't take any options off the table, but undercharging will. Besides, it'll give us more bargaining power. If he's facing a life sentence for murder, he'll be a lot more interested in taking a deal in return for testimony."

"So two murder counts each for Averly and Powers. What about a kidnapping charge?"

"Well, the texts on Hayley's phone seem to show they got to the mountain under their own steam."

"Not for Hayley," Bailey said. "I meant for Brian. We found his body in such a remote spot. Either Averly or Powers had to have made him go out there."

"That's logical. Problem is, there's no way to prove any kind of force was used to move Brian around. But it's the difference between what I believe and what I can prove. Besides, if we do luck into some evidence, I can always add a count of kidnapping."

Bailey nodded.

"So just to play it all the way out," I said, "Averly drops the car at the airport, then hops a plane to New York—"

"Where he buys the ticket to Paris in Brian's name to throw us off—"

"Using Hayley's iPad, right. And then, when the iPad

got stolen, he had to get out of Dodge. Fortunately, I made my brilliant move of calling Averly—"

"Let it go, Sherlock." Bailey tapped the desk. "So who bought those first two tickets to New York? Brian? Or Averly, using Brian's credit card?"

"My bet would be Brian. He and Hayley were about to come into a million bucks. May as well live it up." They'd deal with Russell's wrath later. "We'll need to get into Powers's and Averly's backgrounds, build up the history between them. Show they had a connection before the kidnapping."

"Already did the background checks. Averly's you know about. Ian Powers had no time to get busted. Daddy was a drunk, and by the time he was eight, he was a child star who was supporting his whole family."

"Great. Now we're prosecuting a charity sponsor, child star, *and* a kid who pulled the freight for the family. Anything else? Maybe he flies in care packages to the starving in Nigeria?"

"Don't think he has a pilot's license, but I'll look into it," Bailey said. "As for his connection to Averly, I'll go back into Averly's phone bill and check out the pattern of calls between them. They had to have known each other for a while for Ian to feel safe enough to pull Averly in—even if he didn't let Averly in on the plan to kill Brian." Bailey pulled Jack Averly's rap sheet out of her file folder and laid it on my desk. "Here's your copy. I highlighted the drug busts in yellow. So far, I'm still on board with our theory that he was Ian's dealer."

"We should interview everyone at the studio. See if we can find anyone who'll say Averly was dealing."

"You really think anyone'll talk to us now?"

I shook my head. "But we have to try." I turned back to my computer and started to type. "So two counts of murder for each of them, plus use of the knife, arming with a deadly weapon. And it's a special circumstance of multiple murder, so it's a mandatory sentence of life without parole." I hit "Print" and the pages began to roll out.

"Meant to tell you. Just before I left the station I got word that Averly's on a plane. Should be landing late tonight."

"Great. I'll get this paperwork downstairs. With a little luck, we'll get these guys arraigned tomorrow morning." I stood up to go.

But at that moment someone knocked on my door. I opened it to find a slender young man in a black Hugo Boss suit and silk tie flashing me a thousand-watt smile. His dark brown eyes with thick, curly lashes, rosy cheeks, and fine features gave him an almost delicate handsomeness. "Rachel Knight?"

"Yeah, can I help you with something?"

He put out his hand. "I'm Declan Shackner, your second chair."

45

We learn the maxim at an early age that we shouldn't judge a book by its cover—and then we proceed to ignore it every single day. I took in Declan's three-hundred-dollar haircut and his five-thousand-dollar suit and immediately sized him up as a rich, spoiled Hollywood brat who had only to point and his doting daddy would spare no expense or power play to get it. Unfair as hell, no question. But there it is. I'd decided that since he was brought on to be Vanderhorn's spy/bun boy, I'd use it to my advantage and assign him the duty of making the daily reports. The knowledge that I'd already found a way to avoid the noxious chore brought a genuine smile to my face.

"Nice to meet you, Declan." We shook hands, and I introduced him to Bailey, whose expression told me she'd had the same reaction to our new teammate that I had.

"It's good you're here. I do have something for you to do." I explained that he'd be reporting to Vanderhorn for me and that he could start by telling the district attorney that I was filing two counts of murder.

"That's it?"

"For now. Meet me back here in half an hour and I'll give you the rundown on the case." By that time, with charges filed, the story was going to start hitting the news anyway.

Declan flashed me another perfect smile with an "Okay, great!" and left to perform his first assignment.

"So who is that kid?" Bailey asked.

I gave her the scoop.

Bailey gave a short laugh. "Well, nice move making Vanderhorn's spy do the duty."

It was a minor victory, but I take them where I can get them.

Bailey and I went down to do the filing and get an arrest warrant, and when we got back, she put in the call to Ian's lawyer, Don Wagmeister. She told him what I'd filed and offered to let him surrender Ian at the Men's Central Jail, but only if he promised to produce his client within the hour. She ended the call saying, "At an hour and one minute, I'm going to assume you've declined this offer and I'll arrest him wherever I find him."

She gathered her papers into the file and stood up. "I'd better get over there."

I was very glad to let her handle the booking herself. I hated the jail on Bauchet Street. Truthfully, I hate them all. But that one in particular is the very embodiment of institutionalized despair. "We should probably notify Antonovich and Raynie," I said.

"You might want to wait for me and do it together. I think it's gonna be a bitch."

I figured Russell and Ian were buddies, but I didn't know how tight. "You have some new info?"

"A little. I called that head of security guy, Ned, to find out if Averly ever worked at Warner's. Just trying to see how far back Averly and Powers might go."

"And this told you about Russell and Ian...how?"

"Ned said he'd have to check the records, but we got to talking about the fight between Tommy and Russell over the script again, and he said it was kind of unusual that Russell had even had a manager. He was just a co-producer at the time, and that's too low on the totem pole to justify a manager as hot as Ian was—even back then."

"So Ian was already on the rise as a manager?" I asked. "For some reason I'd thought Ian Powers was kind of a nobody back then. You know, 'has-been' child star struggling to make a comeback on the money side of things."

"Apparently not—"

"Then Tommy's screenplay was what got Russell through Ian's door?"

"All Ned knew was that after the screenplay sold, Ian sprang for a group vacation with the wives in Tortola."

I looked at her quizzically. How could Ned know that?

"Russell kept a photograph of the four of them all sunburned and drunk hanging in his office."

"Classy," I said. And after Russell's screenplay made them both rich and huge, they had all the necessary ingredients for a long-lasting friendship.

Bailey nodded. "Russell's likely to take this harder than you'd expect."

"All the more reason why we've got to move. We can't let him hear about it on the five o'clock news."

Bailey tapped her file folder against her thigh. "If you decide you want me to come, just call me, okay?"

After Bailey'd left, I looked at the clock on the Times Building. Declan had been gone for over an hour. An inauspicious beginning, I thought. Just because daddy got you into the office doesn't mean you can fiddly-fart around. I started working on my "to do" list, while I mulled over the problem of whether to wait for Bailey or not. I heard fast, light steps coming down the hallway toward my office and looked up just as Declan arrived at my door.

"I'm sorry, Rachel. He made me wait, and then he wanted to talk."

"About the case?"

"A little. But more about how he wanted everyone to know that we'd be taking it one step at a time and that if it was starting to look like we had the wrong guy, we'd dismiss on Ian immediately."

Who did the idiot think he was going to appease by that? If it were me, I'd just be wondering why he let a case he was so ready to dismiss get filed to begin with. I'd have to find a way to let Vanderhorn know this kind of talk wouldn't save his reputation in Hollywood; it would only undermine the prosecution. Perfect: I was up against a superstar manager *and* the DA.

"And who is this 'everyone' he wants you to notify?"

Declan's face flushed and he shoved his hands into his pockets. "My dad."

Surprised to see that, far from smug, he seemed to be embarrassed, I felt a flash of sympathy. And then the flash was gone. Screw this kid. How many other aspiring prosecutors, struggling to pay off their student loans, had gotten stuck on a waiting list because Declan had a daddy who could push him to the head of the line? But that thought gave me an idea.

"I've got to notify Russell and his wife that we've filed on Ian." Plus, I needed to ask Russell about the phone call he made to Ian after he got the first kidnapping message. Make sure he did in fact tell Ian about the kidnapping. "Why don't you come with me?" I'd see if having a showbiz kid around did me any good.

Declan looked at me with serious eyes. "Do you know how close Russell and Ian are?"

"Tell me while we walk."

But when we got down to the street and I started to head for the Biltmore, Declan stopped me. "Wait, where are we going?"

"To my car."

"And that's parked . . . ?"

"Where I live. At the Biltmore."

Declan tilted his head, his expression puzzled, but didn't ask me the usual questions about how or why I lived in a hotel. "Why don't you let me drive? My car's closer." He pointed to the parking lot across Temple Street.

It was indeed closer, and it cost a fortune. "Okay, thanks."

He drove a fairly new-looking silver BMW, of course. And though it wasn't custom and it wasn't a luxury model, I'd venture to say no other Grade Two deputy could afford the payments on this puppy. Declan backed out very slowly and carefully maneuvered around the island leading up to the pay window.

"This a new acquisition?" I asked.

"Yeah. I got a great deal on it because it was what they call 'slightly used.' But I'll be paying it off for the next four years, and if I don't get my Grade Three promotion, I'll need to unload it. So I've got to keep it sharp for the resale. Make sure I can get what I paid for it."

The kid wearing the five-thousand-dollar suit worried about this? I couldn't help myself, I had to ask. "Wouldn't your dad help you out if you got behind?"

Declan's expression hardened. "I don't know. I wouldn't ask."

Interesting. A rift? Or just an admirable assertion of independence? Maybe time would tell. Right now, I needed to get ready for what was coming, and it seemed Declan was the man who could help me do it. "Russell lives in Bel Air, but his wife told Melia that he'd be at the studio. It's on—"

"I know where the studio is." Declan turned right and headed for the on-ramp to the 101 freeway. "I was going to tell you about Russell and Ian. They've been super-tight for a lot of years."

"How close?"

"Close enough to travel together, party together. They always do the awards scene together."

Awards, as in Oscars, Directors Guild, and Golden Globes.

"Were the families close too?"

"Well, the wives have changed. Ian's been through two divorces—"

"And the current girlfriend, how long's she been around?"

"A year? Maybe two. Ian's girlfriend, Sacha...she's

your typical Hollywood trophy, actress-wannabe material. You know the type."

"Not personally, but I get the drift." I smiled inwardly, finding Declan much more fun and interesting than I'd expected. "What about the early days, before their divorces? Did Ian and either of his wives socialize with Russell and Raynie?"

"Yeah. Definitely. And when Russell was shooting on location, Ian would always take Raynie and Hayley out to dinner, do stuff with them to keep them company. I'd see them at my dad's house sometimes when he threw parties."

"Is it possible that Ian and Raynie...?"

Declan shook his head firmly. "Uh-uh. Raynie was true blue. And she was never out alone with Ian. It was always Ian and his wife number one...I forget her name at the moment, and Raynie and Hayley. No, it was all on the up-and-up."

Not so much anymore. But who'd want to believe that Ian, the substitute daddy, would kill little Hayley? Yet another obstacle in a case that already had more than its fair share. I braced myself as Declan pulled up to the studio guardhouse.

46

I've been yelled at by judges, serial killers, and defense attorneys, but there was no possible way I could've been prepared for the fury of the storm that was Russell Antonovich.

He'd been sitting behind his desk when I gave him the news. Now he jumped to his feet. "Have you absolutely lost your mind? Ian is like a second father to Hayley! How could you...how *dare* you charge him with her murder!"

"Russell, I know this is a shock, but if you'd let me explain—"

Declan had been standing just behind me. Now he stepped up next to me, and I saw he was about to speak, but then Russell pounded a fist on his desk. "I *know* why! It's because you want to make a big name for yourself. You're going to climb up on Ian's back with this bullshit case so you can get famous! You probably think you're going to be a big deal, don't you? Well, it won't work, I'll tell you that right now—"

Not only the vehemence but the substance of the accusation took my breath away. "Russell, you can't really believe that. You can't honestly believe I'd file a case with no evidence, just to get my name in the papers."

Russell jabbed his finger dangerously close to my chest, his eyes spitting fire. "You wouldn't be the first! There's *no* way Ian could've done this. No fucking way!"

Declan moved forward to put himself between us, and shot out a hand to stop Russell. "Hey—" he began.

But I stepped to the side and confronted Russell face-to-face. "And you have no interest at all in hearing what kind of evidence we've got? Evidence that proves he murdered your own *daughter?*"

Russell's breath was coming in ragged gasps, and his arms shook with the effort to keep his clenched fists down at his sides. But my last salvo finally got his attention. He stopped his tirade with a visible effort and narrowed his eyes. "Let's hear it."

I described it all, right down to the texts we'd found on Hayley's phone and Averly's purchase of the ticket to Paris using Hayley's iPad, and concluded with his phone call to Ian. "And *he* was the one you called when you got the text from Hayley's phone about the kidnapping. You told him about it in plenty of time for him to—"

"I told him *nothing!* And you'll never prove I did!" The fury radiated from his every pore, a palpable heat that made me draw back, momentarily speechless. For long seconds, we stood staring at each other in silence, the air between us thick and dangerous. Finally, Russell turned away, breaking the spell. The light must be dawning for him, I thought, awful as that must be. Words of consolation formed in my mind as Russell walked slowly to the window. But he spoke first.

Turning back to me, in a voice now filled with contempt as well as fury, he snarled, "How stupid are you? It's that asshole punk Averly! Jesus! Isn't it perfectly obvious?"

I blinked at the unexpected turn, but recovered quickly to fire back, "What about Ian's blood on the trunk of Brian's car? His fingerprint on the bumper? His phone calls to Averly in New York? His hair and fingerprints in Averly's car? Don't you see how—"

"What I see is a frame job that's working! This Averly character—"

"What? Planted Ian's blood? His fingerprints? His hair?"

"Averly works on the lot and Ian knows him. So he sat in Averly's car. Big deal. And Ian's blood and…and prints…" Russell sputtered for a moment as his gears spun. Finally, the gears caught. "How do we know Brian didn't try to shake Ian down before the kidnapping? How do we know he and Brian didn't get into a fight when Ian refused to be blackmailed? That kid was just as psycho as his father!"

"But if that's what happened—and Ian got into a fight with Brian that left him bloody—why not tell you about it?"

"Because he didn't want to upset me! Because he didn't think I needed to be distracted by a stupid, crazy boy who believed his delusional father's stories!"

"Okay, then why was Ian calling Averly in New York?"

"How should I know? He probably didn't even know Averly was in New York. And so what if he called Averly? That doesn't mean it had anything to do with Hayley's…" Russell stopped short, unable to say it.

"This is insane! There's no friggin' way!" Russell pulled at his hair. "I swear to God, I'll have your job for this!"

I wanted to tell him that right now I'd gladly let him have my job, but while I searched for something more productive to say, Declan stepped in.

"Russell, I understand why this would be very upsetting news," he said quietly. "But Rachel isn't looking for anything but the truth. And if she finds out that Ian wasn't involved, she'll be glad to drop the case."

I was a little annoyed at hearing, for the second time today, how happy I'd be to drop charges against Ian Powers. But Declan's words seemed to stem the tide of Russell's umbrage. When Declan finished speaking, Russell gave him a long stare, then fired a look of utter contempt and disbelief at me and turned toward the window that opened out onto the lot. He was still breathing hard, and his hands clutched the sill. When, finally, Russell faced me again, some of the beet-red color had drained from his face, but his eyes still shot angry sparks. "Your boss knows about this?"

"Of course."

"Fucking civil service lawyers." With a look of disgust, he picked up his phone and growled, "Have someone escort these two off the lot!"

I finally got to ride in one of the golf carts.

"Whew!" Declan said after he'd pulled out of the studio lot.

"Yeah." Russell's alternative scenario that made Averly the bad guy had its flaws, but it wouldn't surprise me if the defense landed on some version of that. "I hate to do this to you, but I'm going to need you to write up a report of what you heard Russell say. I'll do one too."

"Especially that Ian never told Russell about any confrontation with Brian?"

"Yes, especially that part. It's not impossible that Ian would keep something like that from Russell, but it's highly unlikely. If nothing else, he'd want to prepare Russell for any problems Brian might cause. It makes no sense that Ian would feel he needed to shelter Russell."

In fact, if Ian's defense did try to claim he was just protecting Russell, the weakness in our evidence of motive wasn't such a problem. If Brian had some proof that Russell stole his father's script, he would've gotten a lawyer. He hadn't. That meant Brian wasn't a real threat. So why *not* tell Russell that Brian had come around talking a lot of unprovable nonsense? And if Brian didn't pose a real threat, then why kill him? I admit, it was a bit circular, but it did give us something to work with. After what I'd just been through, any little bit of good news was a welcome relief.

"And while you're at it, put it in your report that Russell denied telling Ian about getting the kidnapping text from Hayley's phone," I said.

Declan looked at me. "You don't believe him?"

"Not for a minute. I think he was on his phone to Ian within seconds."

Declan nodded. "I agree. I thought he protested a lot too much." He paused. "Can we tell *when* that blood drop was left on the trunk?" Declan asked.

"Blood smear, and no. So the defense could argue that Hayley's blood got on the trunk at a different time than Ian's. But it's a loser. What are the odds they'd both swipe the same exact spot on the trunk of someone else's car—on two different occasions?"

Declan nodded. "But you can't say for sure which guy killed them."

"Not yet."

I sure hoped that would change...soon.

"I think Russell's in denial," Declan said. "He doesn't want to believe someone he thought was, like, his closest friend would do something this heinous."

"I'm sure. It's horrible enough to suffer through the death of a child. But it's a whole new form of hell to know that the murder was committed by someone close to you. He's probably dealing with a fair amount of guilt right now."

But an awful suspicion had leaped into my mind during the fight with Russell. One I didn't want to be right about. One I couldn't share with Declan. So we rode on in silence until he pulled off the freeway at Broadway.

We talked about what we'd need to do to get ready for trial as we walked back to the courthouse, and when we got up to the office, I told him that if he had any work left on his other cases, now was the time to wrap it up.

"I'm going to finish up my 'to do' list. When it's done, I'll call you and we can divvy up the work."

"Got it." Declan turned to go, then stopped and held out his hand. "I just want to thank you for letting me be your second chair. I know it's an honor I probably don't deserve, but that doesn't mean I don't appreciate it. So...uh, thank you."

We shook, and I found my attitude toward him softening. He really wasn't what I'd expected. "No, thank *you,* Declan. I was glad to have you there. That got a lot uglier than I thought it would."

*   *   *

I started to work on my list, but our discussion about Russell and his feelings of guilt had struck a familiar chord. It brought back memories of my father. He'd felt guilty too. At the time, I was so young, and so consumed with my own shame and feelings of responsibility for my sister's abduction, I hadn't been able to see that his anger, his emotional distance, and his drinking were all ways of coping with his own guilt.

But now, with the benefit of hindsight, a few more pieces of my childhood puzzle fell into place. After Romy was abducted, my father started taking me with him to go target shooting. At the time, I'd thought that was just something he'd always liked to do, and that he'd started bringing me along to make me feel better, to distract me from my loneliness.

But that wasn't quite right. My father hadn't done any target shooting before Romy's disappearance. It was only after her abduction that he bought a gun and taught me how to shoot. I was only seven years old, but day after day, when I came home from school, he'd take me out to the fields near the woods and drill me on how to aim, shoot, and take apart a gun. And that wasn't all. He'd "play games" that I only now realized were survival training. "I'm the bad guy and you're the cop, Rachel." He'd reach out as if to grab my arm. "Now what do you do?" I had to show him how I'd move out of range and pull my gun. "Now let's pretend you're walking along and I sneak up behind you. What do you do, Rachel?" I learned all the moves.

Though he insisted on perfection, and the "games" quickly got to be repetitive, I'd loved every minute. It was the only time I got to see him smile. Whenever I hit the can during target practice, or gave the right answer, or made the right move, I'd look to see his reaction. Was he smiling? Rarely. But when he was, my heart would soar. More often, his face had a sad, faraway look, or an expression that was fierce, intense…and scary. Still, I turned back to him time after time, because those rare smiles were the only source of joy in my dark, gray world. They showed me the father I used to know, the one who'd swing me by my arms as I screamed with sheer joy, who'd put me on his shoulders and gallop to play horsy, who could make me laugh with just a word or a funny face. Dad was always there for me. Until he wasn't.

In my limited child's-eye view, I couldn't see that those "games" were really my father's effort to keep me safe. Romy's abduction had taught him that the only way to fight back against a world that bred the kind of predators who would snatch a little girl off the road was to teach me to fight for myself. No one else could be relied on. Not even himself. And ultimately, I think his broken vision of himself as caretaker and protector was too much for him to bear. Which was why, over time, our "playdates" dwindled—and so did his sober moments. For the last full month before he skidded off that icy bridge, there were no more games.

47

The following morning I was up early and pushing through my closet. I had to find a suit that would look good enough for the arraignment but not make me sweat through it on my way to the courthouse. I pulled out a few possibilities and turned on the television to catch what they were saying about the case. News of Ian Powers's arrest had gone nationwide, and from the looks of things, the tsunami had hit. A spray-tanned, hair-gelled anchor announced with unrestrained zeal:

> A shocking development in the murder case of Hayley Antonovich and Brian Maher! Two suspects were taken into custody last night and the identity of one of them has rocked the film industry! Ian Powers, manager for superstar director Russell Antonovich and co-owner of RussPow Studios, was arrested last night, along with studio production assistant Jack Averly, and charged with the murders of Hayley Antonovich and Brian Maher. Their arraignments will take place this morn-

ing. We'll have live coverage inside the courtroom,
so stay tuned…

I flipped between channels. All of them made the
same breathless announcement and all promised "live
coverage of this dramatic moment." A pretty funny thing
to promise considering the fact that there wasn't much
to cover. An arraignment was a limited affair: I would
read the charges, Powers and Averly would plead not
guilty, and then we'd set a date for the preliminary hearing. At most, it should take about five minutes. But it
was a chance to watch all the players in action, and that
alone guaranteed they'd get viewers.

I'm a big believer in the public's right to know, so
if anyone wants to sit in and watch a trial, I'm all for
it. What I'm not in favor of is spin. And spin is all you
get when the media jumps in. Lawyers who are third-
rate on their best day and have never tried a lawsuit
get "face time" to pontificate endlessly—and worse,
misleadingly—about every facet of the case. As a result,
the public's right to know becomes the talking heads'
right to misinform. And then there are the stealth commentators: the lawyers and experts who are working for
the defense but don't admit it. They get on camera and
present themselves as neutral observers, when all along
they're just stumping for their side of the lawsuit.

Knowing those publicity junkies would soon pollute the
airwaves with garbage about my case put me in a foul
mood. I turned off the television and dawdled over coffee
while I read the paper. The *Times* carried the story on the
front page, above the fold—proof that the case had gone
big-time. So far, it was just an unbiased recitation of the

charges. The paper's favorite expert, a law professor of limited brainpower but limitless desire for exposure, merely observed that the charges carried a sentence of life without the possibility of parole. Pretty much straight-down-the-middle reportage. I knew it wouldn't last. The moment the trial got under way, rumor and innuendo would fill in for the facts whenever they were juicy enough. Any source would do, corroborated or not.

When I first stepped outside, I was surprised to find that it was a little cooler than I'd expected, and I thought about heading back to change. But by the time I got to the courthouse, the temperature had begun to rise. If I'd left any later, I would've been a mess. I looked through the glass doors into the lobby and saw a few cameras but not a big crowd. Feeling cheered, I hopped onto an elevator and rode up to my floor, thinking it might not be so bad after all.

When I got to my office, I called Declan.

"Want to do the arraignment with me? May as well get your name on the record."

He happily accepted.

Then I called Bailey. She accepted too, but not quite as happily. "I guess I should."

When Declan and I stepped off the elevator, I saw that I'd been lulled into a false sense of security. The few cameras I'd seen in the lobby were the latecomers. The bulk of the attendees for today's proceedings had already shown up, and they were clogging the hallway from one end of the courthouse to the other. I pulled Declan aside before we ran the gauntlet.

"Don't answer any questions. Keep your head down and follow me."

I took the lead and kept my eyes focused on the door to the courtroom. At first we got left alone. Only the reporters who regularly covered the courts knew who we were. But halfway to the courtroom, one of them spotted me. "Hey, Rachel! What've you got on Powers? Who's the real killer?"

The rest of them picked up on the cue and started shouting questions. I shook my head, said, "No comment," over and over, and wove my way through the crowd. I'd just pushed open the door when a semi-familiar voice with a British accent called to me from the anteroom.

"Rachel Knight! We meet in person at last. Andrew Chatham." He put out his hand, and I reflexively took it.

Shorter than I was by about three inches, Andrew was very slim and dapper in a blazer, white button-down shirt, and dark slacks. Kind of Fred Astaire–ish.

"Hello, Andrew. I have no comment."

"Well, that's an improvement on our recent phone call."

I looked at him, puzzled.

"When you hung up on me." He smiled without a hint of malice. I don't know why, but something about him made me smile back. "So I shall take this exchange as my victory for the day and not, as you Yanks put it, push my luck. Good day. Have a nice arraignment."

Amused, I replied, "Thank you, Andrew."

Only one camera was in the courtroom, so I surmised it would provide the "pool feed," meaning everyone would use the footage it got. I moved to the prosecution side of counsel table with Declan close behind me. This courtroom was devoted exclusively to arraignments. Instead of the usual setup with separate counsel tables at either side of the courtroom, it had one big U-shaped table that gave room for the defense and prosecution to sit on opposite sides and other interested parties— bail bondsmen, cops, or probation officers—to sit in the middle. It was also the only courtroom that had a glass-enclosed section on the defense side. That was where the prisoners sat. Mornings were always crowded in this courtroom, but today was the worst I'd ever seen, with the press and the public in full attendance, eager to get their first up-close look at everyone. The audience section—twice the size of a normal courtroom—was filled to capacity, a very rare event.

I immediately spotted Don Wagmeister on the other side of counsel table. It wasn't hard to do, since he stood six feet four and was built like a solid rectangle—a rectangle that was usually adorned with brightly colored theme ties, like sharks, the scales of justice, and the guy on the Monopoly "Get Out of Jail Free" card. I'd heard he had hair plugs, but I'd never noticed it myself. Then again, he slicked his hair back with so much goo, who could tell? I was about to go over and hand him the first batch of discovery—all the crime and evidence reports that'd been generated so far—when the judge took the bench.

The bailiff told everyone to rise. Declan and I were already standing, so we stayed that way. Judge Patrick Daley, a bird-thin, nervous man in bifocals, moved up the steps to the bench swiftly, his black robe flowing around his legs. His eyes landed briefly on the camera, then flicked away as he called the court to order. He spoke so rapidly, the sentence came out as one long word. "Everyone-be-seated-court-calls-the-case-of-*People-versus-Powers-and-Averly*." The judge paused just long enough to take a breath. "Lawyers-please-state-your-names-for-the-record...People?"

Some judges are definitely not in love with the lime-light, and Judge Daley seemed to be one of them, so he chose to get rid of us first—a very wise move. I hated it when judges put a high-profile appearance last on the calendar. It meant everyone had to suffer through a courtroom crowded with reporters that much longer. Declan and I gave our names, then the defense—with Wagmeister drawing out the opportunity for free adver-tising by announcing his name in a booming voice.

"Donald Wagmeister for Ian Powers, Your Honor."

The next voice, low and husky but firm, took me by surprise. "Terry Fisk for Jack Averly."

Terry Fisk? Unlike Wagmeister, Terry was easy to miss—at first. Barely five feet tall, with a pug nose and a square jaw that jutted out when she argued—which was often, and with vigor—she was one of the toughest in the business. Smart as they come and always prepared, she was a brawler of a lawyer who took her gloves off when she walked into court and never put them back on. If you were looking for a gentlemanly trial, you'd never get it with Terry. I'd counted myself lucky not to run into her before. Now, obviously, my luck had run out. It couldn't have happened in a worse case.

"People, please arraign the defendants."

I read the charges, then asked, "Mr. Powers, how do you plead, guilty or not guilty?"

Powers cleared his throat to declare in a voice he tried to pack with outrage, "Not guilty!"

"Mr. Averly, how do you plead?"

Jack Averly's head had been down. Terry nudged him with her elbow and whispered to him. He glanced up briefly, then dipped his head and stuttered, "Not-uh-not guilty."

Terry shot him a sidelong dark look. Notorious for demanding total control of her clients, she coached them to within an inch of their lives and expected them to repay her efforts by doing exactly as they were told. I knew that Averly would catch hell from her for that pathetic performance the moment they got back into lockup.

The judge accepted the pleas and I moved toward the defense side of counsel table as I spoke. "Your Honor, I'd like the record to reflect that I'm handing each defense counsel a copy of the discovery that we have to date." I described the reports that were included in the packet.

"It will," the judge said. "Counsel, please acknowledge receipt."

"Acknowledged on behalf of Mr. Powers," Wagmeister said as he took the packet from me.

Fisk took her packet without looking at it, or me. "I won't acknowledge that's what the prosecution gave me because I haven't had time to look at it. All I'm prepared to say is that she handed me some papers."

I walked back to my side of counsel table. "That's fine, Your Honor." I kept my voice calm but thought to myself, "Here we go." Turning over the initial discovery was a routine thing—it was never a reason for even a minor skirmish. Even for Fisk this was an unusually testy start. "I've number-stamped all the pages and I'd like to lodge a copy of what I gave to counsel with the court at this time. Let the record reflect they're numbered one through fifty-seven."

I always made an extra copy of discovery to lodge with the court just in case of situations like this, though it'd been a long time since I'd needed to. Giving the court a copy of what I'd given the defense offered some proof that I hadn't deprived them of anything. I handed the packet to the bailiff, who passed it up to the judge. He looked through the pages quickly. "The record will reflect I've received the pages and noted that they are numbered as you indicated. Now let's pick a date for the preliminary hearing."

"I'd like to go past the statutory ten days," Wagmeister said, consulting his calendar and picking a date a few weeks out.

"That's acceptable with the People," I said.

"Ms. Fisk, is that acceptable to you?" the judge asked.

"No. We're not waiving time. Mr. Averly wants his preliminary hearing within the statutory ten days."

The judge, consulting the calendar on the wall, named a date barely over a week away. "People?"

"That'll be fine, Your Honor," I said. It wasn't really so fine. Now I'd have to prepare two separate hearings. But since I intended to put on a bare bones preliminary hearing with just the physical evidence, it'd be a lot less painful than if I'd had to wrangle civilian witnesses.

"The case is assigned to Judge Daglian for preliminary hearing." The judge banged his gavel and called the next case, the relief in his voice palpable.

Bailey shook her head. "I can't believe it. Already."

One measly arraignment and the ride was already getting bumpy.

48

The press was ecstatic. If there was blood in the water at the arraignment, they could expect Armageddon when this thing went to trial. They shoved microphones in my face and shouted questions: "Did Terry catch you by surprise?" And my favorite: "Is there bad blood between you two?"

I kept my head down and refused comment as Declan and I made our way through the mass of reporters. Not wanting to give them a chance to corner us by waiting for an elevator, I headed for the stairs. But the heat made the stairwell feel like a tomb. After two floors I was panting and it felt like the walls were closing in. I pushed open the door at the seventh floor and poked my head out. The coast was clear. I heard the *ding* of an arriving elevator. We ran for it, but there were people inside, so we didn't speak until we got into our wing of the eighteenth floor.

"Is she always like that?" Declan asked.

"Pretty much. Though I didn't expect her to bite this hard at an arraignment." We stopped at my door, which

I'd taken to locking, and I pulled out my key and let us in. "On the other hand, I've never seen a lawyer who doesn't prance and strut when there're cameras around. So my advice is to get used to it."

"Can't the judge stop them?"

"To a certain extent. But not all judges want to. Some are worse press panderers than the lawyers—"

I was about to launch into all the ills of high-profile cases when Melia practically skidded to a stop at my door. I'd forgotten to close it—my bad.

"Rachel, have you seen the news?" Her voice was breathless, her eyes wide.

"What's up?"

"Come on, you can watch in Eric's office. He's at a meeting."

I wanted to ask her to just tell me what the heck was going on, but she'd already trotted back up the hallway. I shrugged at Declan and he gestured to the door. "After you, Fearless Leader."

"You may never call me that," I said as I stepped out into the hallway. "I'll explain why later." It was our nickname for Vanderputz—well, one of them.

The television was tuned to a local news channel and Melia was holding the remote. She turned up the volume as we entered the office. A young blonde who looked like a Victoria's Secret model—plunging neckline and all—was emoting into the microphone. *... the reaction in Hollywood has been one of disbelief and anger.* The camera cut away to a scruffy-looking young guy I vaguely recognized as a television actor on one of the law shows. *Well, she's obviously looking for her fifteen minutes. I mean, it's just a bogus case—The* camera cut to a forty-something woman in a black suit and leopard-print blouse. *Ian Powers and I have locked horns over many deals and many clients, so I'm not exactly his best friend, but even I have to say that this is simply outrageous. The DA's office is going to crash and burn and they richly deserve to—*The camera cut away, and this time it was a young actress I'd seen in ads for a recently released vampire movie. *Ian Powers has been my manager for years and I know him very well. Believe me, there's no way this could possibly be true and that DA, what's her name?* A voice off camera supplied my name, and she repeated it. *Yeah, Rachel Knight. Everyone knows she only filed these outrageous charges because she thinks it'll make her famous.* I felt as though I'd been smacked in the face with a frying pan. It's one thing for friends and relatives to protest a defendant's innocence, but this kind of nasty, personal diatribe against a prosecutor was unheard of. I wanted to look away, but I couldn't.

The anchor moved on to a young Hispanic man in a mechanic's uniform. *I don't know about this case or nothin', but Ian Powers came around to my hood when I was about to get jumped into a gang. He got me out of there . . .* The young man started to tear up. *He saved my life. That's all I wanna say.* He turned away, and the anchor looked after him with an *Awww* expression. I felt sick. The camera cut to a young man in a paramedic's uniform. I braced myself for another shot to the heart as he began, *Yeah, I met Ian Powers when I was—*but suddenly, the screen went black. I turned, blinking and dazed, and saw that Declan had taken the remote from Melia and turned off the television.

"I heard the drumbeats starting last night. I was going to say something, but I didn't want to distract you before court, and I guess I hoped it'd go away. I'm sorry."

"Don't be. You did exactly the right thing, Declan."

I turned to go, but Melia grabbed my arm. "I'm sorry, Rachel! I didn't mean to upset you, I just thought you should know."

I patted her hand. "Don't sweat it, Melia. I did need to know. At least now I'm ready for...whatever." But my readiness wasn't really the issue.

If I kept getting slammed this way in the press, I'd never find a decent jury. And foisting the case onto someone else wasn't an option, not after I'd pushed to get it filed. If I abandoned it now, it'd look like I didn't believe in the case, and that would just prove the Hollywood toadies right: that I'd only filed the case because I wanted to be famous, and when I saw my approval ratings hit the skids, I'd jumped ship. In short, that I was a sleazy coward. No, I believed in the case, and if it sank under the weight of public opinion, then I'd go down with it.

But now that I was playing out the ugly possibilities, I had to take it all the way. If I lost the case after this drubbing...then what? I'd be exiled to live out my days in the hinterlands, relegated to drunk-driving and shoplifting cases. My career as a prosecutor moribund. And if I left the office, who'd hire me? I couldn't even hang out my own shingle because no one would retain a former prosecutor who'd filed what some thought was a trumped-up case to gain fame and fortune—a case proven to be a sham when she lost it on national television.

It's not that I wanted to go into private practice—I didn't. I'd only ever wanted to be a prosecutor. But being a lawyer was all I knew how to do. I had no other way to make a living.

Now that I'd played out the possible repercussions, I was forced to face facts: I was staring down the barrels of a shotgun that read *career—and life—destroyer.*

49

I put my head down and tried to bury myself in case preparation. Work is always my refuge when I need an escape from misery. And since this time the source of misery *was* the case, I told myself it was doubly helpful. I could distract myself from the prospect of doom while devoting every ounce of energy to making the case as solid as possible. Win-win. Well, it was something anyway.

But it didn't work. Every five seconds my phone rang with calls from the press: Did I see the public reactions outside the courthouse? Did I realize what I was up against when I'd filed the case? Did I regret my decision to file it? I wanted to let them all go to voice mail—then erase them. But I was already losing the battle for the hearts and minds of the public, judging by that last newscast, so I needed every bit of goodwill I could muster. I answered every last stupid question and hoped I was building some kind of rapport that would get me favorable coverage.

I bounced from call to call all afternoon and completely forgot about Declan until it was almost five o'clock. It was only the sound of footsteps stampeding for the door that brought me back to earth long enough to realize I'd neglected to give him an assignment. I'd never had a second chair before, so I wasn't used to delegating.

I had to admit that the more I saw of him, the more I liked him. I was starting to think that Vanderhorn might seriously have miscalculated in thinking Declan would act as his spy. But what I didn't yet know was whether he was a decent lawyer. I pondered what I could let him do that wouldn't jeopardize anything. I had an idea and picked up the phone. Only in that moment did it occur to me that he might've left. He certainly would have been well within his rights to decide he wasn't needed. He hadn't heard from me all day. But he picked up on the first ring. Score another one for the kid, I thought. Very smart to hang out and show his dedication to duty.

"Hey, Rachel. I was hoping you'd call. Got something for me?"

"Yeah. Come on down."

Twenty seconds later he walked into my office, buttoning his jacket.

"Declan, lesson one: no formal attire requested here. Take off your jacket, roll up your sleeves. Get comfortable."

"How do you feel about my shoes?"

"Don't push it."

He smiled and sat down.

"Here's lesson number two: you don't have to wait for me to call. If you're looking for work, just come tell me. Okay?"

Declan saluted.

"Here's what I've got for you: I wrote the search warrant pretty broadly and I think it should cover Ian's laptop—"

"You find anything on it?"

"No. And we probably won't, but I gave it to Cliff Meisner to check for anything that might've been encrypted."

"So you want me to get in touch with Cliff and find out if he's got anything so far?"

"Yes, and I'd like you to do some research. Make sure we're on firm ground with the seizure of the laptop and that there aren't any limitations to what we can use if we do find anything."

"Should be pretty easy. You worried about privilege?"

"No." I told him about having gotten a Special Master appointed to examine the files before we looked at it.

"I never would've thought of that."

"You will now."

That was the whole point of having a young up-and-comer act as second chair. The younger prosecutor got to learn how to play in the big leagues from someone who knew the ropes, instead of having to learn by getting knocked around—and losing. I still think of my mentor, Harvey Gish, with tremendous affection, and admiration. You couldn't put a price on what I learned from him. He taught me to "never assume the other side knows what it's doing" and "always be sure you know more about the case than anyone else." He was referring to one of the most common mistakes prosecutors—or, really, any lawyers—make: automatically opposing what the other side wants. "Just because the defense wants it doesn't mean you should object. Always think for yourself. Who does this help more?" And he was so right. You'd be surprised how many times the defense asks to put in evidence that's much better for me than it is for them. Lessons like that showed me the world of difference between the way the run-of-the-mill cases are handled and the kind of lawyering required in the "big case." It was the practice of law on a whole different level, one most lawyers never saw.

"So what'd you think of Jack Averly?" I asked. This would be the first of many conversations we'd have about how to watch and listen closely in court.

"He looked scared."

"Scared of whom?"

Declan thought a moment. "His lawyer?"

"Well, he should've been, but no. He didn't flinch when Terry gave him that hard look. I'd say first and foremost he was scared of Ian, and secondly of jail. So, assuming I'm right, what does that tell you?"

"That Ian was the mastermind?"

"We were pretty sure of that to begin with. What I'm getting at is, strategically, what does his attitude mean to us?"

Declan shook his head and leaned forward. "I give up. What?"

"He's the one more likely to talk. Ian Powers is never going to give us the time of day—no loss, because we can't give the puppet master a deal to testify against the puppet, anyway. But Averly's a different story. He's looking at a sentence of life without parole, all because he let Ian rope him into this mess—a mess he may really not have known involved murder until it was too late. So he's a good candidate for a deal, and after seeing him in court, I have some hope that he'll take it. The only real question is: Will he plead to something substantial enough to make the deal tenable for us?"

"What do you want to give him?"

I started to answer, then realized this was a great teachable moment about something that didn't get talked about often enough. "I'll tell you in a sec, but first, I want to say this: dealing out a defendant in return for his testimony should always be your last choice. I've seen prosecutors make deals just to make their lives easier, when they could've proven the case without the testimony if they'd just put in a little more work. Never, ever do that. Before you make a deal, make sure you've done everything you can to prove your case without that defendant's testimony. And if you're sure you do need it, then make sure you get the defendant to plead to the right charges. Meaning charges that accurately depict what he did. You can't let a possible murder accomplice plead to an illegal left turn. And trust me, the jury will throw out every word he says as a liar's package that was bought and paid for. In this case, Bailey and I think there's a good chance Averly didn't know what he was getting into. That would make a plea to accessory after the fact not only a good deal for him but also a fair reflection of his involvement. And he's got at least a few of the important missing pieces we can only get from him."

My cell phone played "Killer Joe." *Bailey.*

"I've got to take this, so—"

Declan stood quickly. "I'm on it, boss."

"You can start Monday, Declan."

"I'd rather not wait." Declan waved to me and left.

"What's up?" I asked.

"You've heard the news, right?"

I sighed heavily. I'd managed to forget about it all for the past few hours. Now the memory of the ugly accusations deflated me. "Yeah."

"I'm coming to pick you up right now," she said. "I could use a drink and you can watch me if you're not in the mood."

I smiled in spite of myself. "I should get some more work done. Fisk's demanding her speedy prelim—"

"You were ready for that thing days ago. Come on, Knight."

I looked at the murder book—the binder detectives prepare that contains all the reports. My concentration was broken, so I probably wouldn't be all that productive even if I tried to get back into it. And getting some distance right now might be a good thing. Sometimes, a little breathing room gives me my best inspirations.

"Okay. But let's stay out of Hollywood."

"Gee, how will we survive? Be downstairs in ten."

I called Declan to tell him I was leaving and made him promise to get out soon too. When I got downstairs, Bailey stepped halfway out of her car and waved to me. "Brought you a present," she said, pointing to the front seat.

Toni rolled down the window and gave me a broad grin. "We're hitting the Varnish, so hurry up. They've got a drink with my name on it and it's getting warm."

The Varnish was a speakeasy-style bar, tucked into the back room of Cole's, a nineteen-twenties diner. Dark, intimate, with small booths and the best mixed drinks I've ever had, it was the perfect little hidey-hole for a persona non grata like me.

After we'd imbibed enough to let go of the day, Toni seconded Bailey's sentiments about the public reaction we'd seen.

"First of all, you've got to remember that was just Hollywood. They're probably all Ian's clients or wannabe clients—"

I shook my head. "There were a couple of working-class guys stumping for him—"

"Who benefited from his charity, right?" I nodded. "My point stands: those were all people who got something or hope to get something from Powers. There're a lot more folks who don't fit into either of those categories than those who do. Folks who won't find it so hard to believe that some manager—yes, even one who's a charity sponsor—would kill someone—"

"But people like that, and especially actors, can sway public opinion, Tone," I said. "There're a lot of people out there who like the idea of being in league with the stars."

"Yeah, but the fools who believe what these airhead actors say are not going to make it onto your jury. You'll see to that." She saw my skeptical look and held up her hand. "No, you can't weed them all out, but you're going to have a chance to push back very, very soon, thanks to Terry's demand for a speedy prelim. When you start putting on evidence, it's gonna be a brand-new day."

I had to hope that Toni was right, that getting the evidence out there would balance the picture. In any case, it was better to hang on to that hope than to dwell on the way my jury pool was being poisoned by all this bad press.

"Speaking of a decent case," I said. "What do you think of giving Averly a deal to testify?"

"Right now? Before the prelim?" Bailey asked.

"Yep. I'd like to get him on the record as soon as possible, while his memory's still fresh."

"You think Averly did either of the murders?" Toni asked.

"I can't say for sure right now. But Ian's the only one whose blood is anywhere to be found."

Toni nodded and sipped her drink. "And you don't know how Ian heard about the kidnapping, or how they all wound up on that mountain?"

"No. Averly could fill in the gaps for us. Maybe flesh out the motive too."

"The only downside I see is that it'll look like you're piling up on Powers when Averly might be just as culpable," Toni said. "Just because you didn't find his blood anywhere doesn't mean he didn't kill Brian—or Hayley, for that matter."

"But Powers has got to be the mastermind," Bailey said. "No way this two-bit-dealer PA had any part in a plan this big until Ian dragged him in."

"I agree with you there," Toni said. "I'd say it's at least worth an exploratory meeting to find out if he can give you something to make it worth your while." Toni gave a wry smile. "Cutting a deal with Terry Fisk. What fun."

I looked at my empty glass. "I think I need another drink." We all got one, and then I broached the suspicion I'd been dreading, and needing, to air. "Remember that giant screaming match I got into with Russell when I told him about Ian's arrest?"

"Like we could forget," Bailey said.

"I got this bad feeling," I said. "Like he knew Ian did it—"

"And was covering for him?" Bailey looked incredulous.

"You gotta be kidding, Rache," Toni said. "Denial's one thing, but deliberate cover-up—about the murder of his only child? Uh-uh. You know I'm always down with believing the worst, but that's just…"

"A bridge too far," Bailey filled in. "Even for me, I think. What gave you that idea?"

"We know Russell called Ian right after he got that first text from Hayley's phone saying that Hayley'd been kidnapped. So when I went out there to tell him about Ian's arrest, I'd planned to get Russell to confirm that he told Ian about the kidnapping during that call. No big deal, really. Ian's his best friend; it made sense he'd have thought it was safe to tell Ian, right?"

Bailey nodded.

"Except that the minute I got the words out of my mouth, Russell denied it—"

"So?" Toni challenged. "Maybe it's true. Maybe Russell didn't tell him."

"But he didn't just deny it. He said, hollered actually, that I could never *prove it*. Why, of all things, would he say *that?*"

They both shook their heads. The table was silent for several long beats.

"Could just be guilt," Bailey said. "Russell didn't want to believe he'd set the wheels in motion…"

But there was a note of doubt in her voice. Toni stared down at her drink.

"Right," I said. "See what I mean?"

50

It was a soul-shaking thought: that a father might cover for the murderer of his child. If it was true, Russell Antonovich deserved a far worse fate than the legal system could deliver. But at this point there was nothing we could do. We needed proof, not just suspicion, that Russell knew what Ian had done. That we did not have. I could only promise that if the evidence existed, we'd find it. And use it to put Russell away for as long as possible.

Right now, I had a more immediate lion to beard. Literally. I had to play "Let's Make a Deal" with Terry Fisk. I placed the call bright and early Monday morning, so I'd be sure to catch Terry before she went to court. "I'd like a meeting with you and your client. I want to talk about a deal."

"You don't talk to my client until we have a deal."

"Terry, your client is looking at life without the possibility of parole. I'm prepared to offer him a substantially lesser sentence that'll let him parole out in a few years. But I'm not going to do it unless I can make this offer to him personally. I need to get a feel for whether he'll give us something worthwhile—"

"No way. No one talks to my client but me until everyone's signed on the dotted line."

"You want to stand in the way of a sweetheart deal just because I want to look him in the eye when I make the offer? Because if you do, I'll want to put that on the record in open court."

There was a beat of silence as Terry considered the ramifications of what I'd just said. If I took the deal off the table because of her refusal to let me make the offer in person, and he got convicted, she'd never live it down. There was no valid tactical reason for her to refuse my request. It wasn't as though I were asking to take a statement so I could use it against him later. And if Averly was convicted of murder, even if an appellate court didn't find her incompetent, she'd be the jerk who tanked her client's chance to beat a life sentence.

"Why do you need to see him? I mean really?"

"Because I want to make sure he understands what I'm offering."

What I didn't say was that I didn't know whether I could trust her to relay the offer. It wouldn't be the first time an attorney withheld an offer to prevent a client from being a "snitch"—or, in a high-profile case, to keep the case alive so the lawyer could grab more limelight. Added to those possibilities was the potential pressure from the co-defendant's side, in this case Ian, to prevent that client from testifying, which could significantly increase the odds that any offer might be "forgotten." Though Terry wasn't the type to cave in to pressure from anyone, with a major player like Ian Powers and his supporters in the mix, I couldn't take any chances.

"No questioning."

"No."

Terry exhaled loudly. "When?"

"In one hour."

"Make it two; I've got an appearance in Judge Henley's court in fifteen minutes."

"See you there."

Bailey drove us to the Men's Central Jail on Bauchet Street, where Jack Averly was housed and undoubtedly making all kinds of new friends. The largest county jail in the world, it's a concrete mushroom of a building that squats across three square blocks and emanates a gray, hopeless despair. As we put our guns in the lockers and passed through security, I held my breath, trying to let as little of the putrid air into my lungs as possible. Bailey went to tell the guards that we needed an attorney room, and I pondered whether I had enough Febreze to get the smell out of my clothes. Terry came through the metal detector and sat down next to me.

"What's your offer?" she asked.

"One count of murder, I'll dismiss the other count. It gives him a shot at parole."

She gave me an incredulous look. "You called me here for that? Forget it." She started to get up, but I pulled her back.

"Come on, Terry, chill. Where's your sense of humor? The deal is accessory—providing he gives me the solid truth about everything. No whitewashing bull about how he didn't do nuthin' and Ian did everythin'."

Terry glared at me, but she sat back down. We didn't

speak again until Bailey returned with a guard who said he had a room for us. We entered the tiny glass-walled room and took seats around a metal table. I stared at the windowed hallway Averly would have to pass through to get to us. Within minutes I saw him shuffling in his waist and leg chains, a deputy holding his elbow. When I'd seen him in New York, I thought he had the kind of smart-assy attitude and rangy look that would give him an attractive bad-boy appeal to some. But the county jail had a way of ripping the insouciance out of even the toughest of criminals, and Averly was far from the toughest in this jungle. His eyes were wide and staring and his face looked pinched. So much for the bad-boy appeal. As the deputy chained him into his seat, he barely glanced at any of us, even Terry.

"Jack, the prosecutor says she has a deal for you," Terry said, jumping in first, no doubt to take control of the situation. "I don't want you to say a word. Do you hear me?"

He gave a sideways nod, his head tilted away from her, eyes cast down.

"Hey, Jack," I said, hoping to get him to engage with me.

"Just state your offer. This isn't a blind date," Fisk interrupted.

"It kind of is, Counsel," I said. "I have a feeling Jack didn't do these murders himself, but I don't know for sure—"

Jack opened his mouth, but Terry cut him off. "And now you're baiting him. Make your offer and do it fast or you're out of here."

Jack clamped his mouth shut, but a beseeching look

flashed across his face. He would've gladly taken the bait I'd offered, and he was ready to deal. Just what I wanted to see.

"Here's the deal, Jack: I'll dismiss the murder charges and let you plead to being an accessory after the fact for both murders. That means a possible low of sixteen months. As of right now, you're facing a sentence of life without the possibility of parole. Pretty big drop, wouldn't you say?"

"He's not saying anything." Terry turned to Jack. "Right?"

Jack ducked his head and muttered, "Guess not."

"What I'll need from you in return for this deal is your testimony. That means your complete, truthful testimony to everything you know about this case. Do you understand?"

"Yeah, I—"

Terry hit the table with her hand. "You don't speak. How many times do I have to pound it into your head?" She turned to me. "And you. No more questions, got it? He understands."

I ignored her and continued. "We'll need you to make your decision soon. Because if you take this deal, I'm going to want you to give statements to me and Detective Keller, and I'm going to want you to testify at the preliminary hearing. Please nod if you understand."

Jack threw a sullen look at Terry and nodded.

"So that's it," Terry said. "Unless you're adding a year's supply of Turtle Wax to your offer, I'd like some time alone with my client now."

"You have one week to get back to me. After that, the deal's off the table."

Bailey and I stood to go, and a guard came over to the room to let us out.

"I'll be in touch," Terry said.

The guard opened the door, and I began to follow Bailey out when Jack suddenly blurted, "I didn't kill anyone!" He cowered like a whipped puppy under Terry's glare, but found the courage to add, "I just need you to know that."

I nodded. "Thanks, Jack."

Terry glared at me. "Don't you have somewhere to be?"

I raised an eyebrow. "Just being polite, Counselor."

Bailey and I left, and as we walked out into the afternoon boiler room of a day, I breathed a sigh of relief. Even the smoggy heat was an improvement on the permanent stench of Mordor.

"Think he'll take the deal?" I asked.

"If he has half a brain. But Terry's not gonna help us. I'd say she'll hold out for a 'no time' offer."

"Wouldn't surprise me." It's what I would do.

"Think he was telling the truth?"

"Seemed so." I shrugged. "I've kind of felt that way all along. He's just a punk. I don't see him having the stones to kill. Especially not with a knife."

"Then again, you never can tell."

"Well, there is that."

51

With so little time to prepare for a preliminary hearing
that would likely be broadcast around the country—
or as Declan put it, "go wide"—we had no time for
lunch, and I wasn't planning to make any time for
dinner either. So Bailey dropped me at the office and
headed back to the station, where she'd be hunkered
down and getting ready too. When I passed by Melia's
desk, she jumped up and thrust a fistful of messages at
me. I groaned inwardly and took them back to my office. I flipped through them quickly. There were more
than thirty, and as I'd suspected, they were all from
reporters. It was already too much to handle. I could
either prepare my case or field press calls. I couldn't
do both. Much as I'd wanted to earn some brownie
points and make nice, I was going to have to let Melia
route all of the press calls to Sandi, our media relations
chief. I told Declan.

"You might not have as big a problem with public
opinion as you think, Rachel. Most of those people on
the newscast were in the industry, and they all have

something to gain by currying favor with Powers or Russell Antonovich."

Exactly what Toni'd said. "But how do they all know Russell isn't on board with us?"

"Are you kidding? Russell has minions circling him around the clock. And every single one of them knows everything about him. He likes beets, hates brussels sprouts, and throws away his socks after one wearing. He doesn't care for the Lakers, loves the Oakland A's. If that's common knowledge..."

"Yeah."

"And they like to spread any insider information to all their friends—it gives them status. So something as big as this? After the way he screamed his head off when you gave him the news? Believe me, word started spreading before we got off the lot. Which means everyone and her Chihuahua knew that the way to Russell's heart was to vilify you. And I promise you that if we lose, every single one of them will be on Russell's and Ian's doorstep, calling in their chits."

"So it doesn't matter that Ian slashed the throats of two young kids. It's all about sucking up to the big names—"

"Who can put them in films, buy their screenplays, hire their clients...yes."

Sickening. But, really, was Hollywood so unique? What about Wall Street? Or Capitol Hill? They were no better. Some would argue they were a lot worse—and they might even be right.

"How's the research coming?" I asked.

"I think you're in good shape with the seizure of the laptop. The language you put in the warrant about electronic writings covers it. The only real issue's going to be what writings you can get into evidence. But that's a relevance issue, not a Fourth Amendment issue."

"And on that note, you hear back from Cliff yet?"

"No progress there. He agrees, there's nothing he's seen so far that has anything to do with this case, but he's checking for any anomalies in...something, I can't remember the word he used—"

"Wouldn't matter if you did. I wouldn't have known what it meant." I looked down at my "to do" list. "I'm going to dig into the coroner's reports right now. Do me a favor and check on that request for Steve Diamond to compare the wound tracks on Brian and Hayley and see if he can say whether the same knife was used on both victims."

My phone started ringing. Declan flashed me a look of sympathy and went off to take care of his task. I buzzed Melia and told her to take that call and start routing all my calls through Sandi.

"What if they're personal?"

I took a deep breath and blew it out. "I don't get personal calls on the office number. They always come to my cell, Melia." But, really, how could I expect her to know that? Just because, in the past two years, not *one* personal call had ever come to my office number? Silly me.

I hung up and called Bailey. "We seized the Ruger they found in Ian's bedroom, right?"

"Yeah. And to answer your real question, we are having it looked at, but I wouldn't get my hopes up. It seemed pretty clean."

We'd already tested for fingerprints and found only

Ian's, so I figured Powers had initially held Brian at gunpoint because it would've been an easier way of controlling him if they'd had to move him up the mountain ridge to the killing ground. But Powers didn't want to use the gun to kill because bullets and casings left too much evidence. If we could come up with evidence of soil or plant debris on the Ruger consistent with Boney Mountain, it would go a long way toward proving my theory correct. And proving premeditation.

I flipped through the murder book, to the evidence report. "You ever get the hard copy of Averly's phone bill? I don't see it here."

"I should have it soon. It took a little while because I asked them to go back through all of his numbers for the past ten years."

"Okay, keep in touch."

"Yeah, sure. I'll call every fifteen minutes." She hung up. I did not believe she would.

For the next couple of days, I toiled away at my desk, working through lunch, taking my dinners in my room. Other than the occasional visit from Toni and phone call from Graden, the only people I spoke to were Declan and Bailey. Thanks to my having delegated the daily Vanderhorn reports to Declan, I didn't have to waste time cooling my heels in his anteroom—or catching more of Francine's "I told you so" looks. I had a feeling Vanderhorn was A-OK with this arrangement. By Wednesday evening, I'd gotten on top of the case enough to believe I might just be able to spend some weekend time with Graden, so I called him and asked what he was doing on Saturday.

"You could come over to my place and let me make

dinner for you," he suggested. I knew it was a concession to my desire to avoid restaurants, where I might run into less than adoring fans, or the press. But it would also put us alone in his house...with wine. I was, however, sorely tempted.

"I might not have time for a whole night out."

Graden suggested we wait and see how the rest of the week shook out. "We could always just grab a quick bite downtown."

I agreed. Did he know that my hesitation was only partially work related? I couldn't tell.

On Thursday Bailey called with news.

"I got Averly's phone bill. Wait'll you see. Oh, and by the way, it does look like he and Powers go back—"

"Great. Wait'll I see what?"

"I skipped right by it the first time, for some damn reason—"

This preamble was killing me. "Tell me already!"

She continued, rolling right over me, "—but then I realized there was something familiar about one of the numbers. I checked out the exact time and then I checked out the number—"

"Seriously, I'm going to hang up."

"Remember the texts between Hayley and Brian on the mountain?"

I exhaled impatiently. "Of course."

"Well, after the last text from Brian, there was a gap, and then there was a text telling Hayley to come out and meet on the trail—"

"That was probably from the killer. Yes, I know—"

"No, there's no 'probably.' That text was *definitely* from the killer."

I sat up and clutched the phone. "What?"

"In the same minute—probably within seconds of sending that text, the killer made a call from Brian's cell. To Jack Averly."

"Oh, my God." This was huge. It proved that Averly didn't take part in the actual killings. Powers wouldn't be calling Averly if Averly was standing next to him. And Powers wouldn't have been using Brian's cell to do it if Brian was still alive and kicking.

"That's it," I said. "Ian Powers called Averly after he killed Brian—"

"—to say he'd found Hayley?"

"Or to tell Averly what direction he'd be moving in so Averly could meet him."

We had our proof: Ian Powers had killed them both.

52

"We've got to turn this over to Terry," I said. This was critical *Brady* material—evidence helpful to Averly's defense—and it had to be provided immediately. Ian's phone call was proof that Averly wasn't present during Brian's murder, and it was a pretty strong indication that he hadn't been present for Hayley's murder either. Powers didn't need Averly's help to take Hayley down, not once he realized she was within striking distance. His call to Averly—made at the same time he texted Hayley—provided some evidence that he was telling Averly where to meet him and going after Hayley himself. The fact that there was no physical evidence tying Averly to either murder offered more support for the theory that Ian had done the killings alone. Put it all together, and Averly had a decent basis for the claim that he truly didn't know about the murder plan, which meant that he was only an accessory after the fact.

I put in a call to Terry and told her what I had. I said I'd sweeten the deal and give Averly time served, which meant that if he pled guilty as an accessory, he'd get out immediately.

"You're going to insist on making him this deal in person again," Terry said irritably.

"Correct. We should do it fast too, because if he's going to take it, I'll need to call off my witnesses and get him ready to testify at Powers's preliminary hearing."

"I can make it at two thirty," Terry said.

"Fine."

"And bring me a copy of that phone bill."

I'd make her sign an acknowledgment of receipt form too. She'd already shown she was going to play the "prosecutor is hiding discovery" game at the arraignment. I planned to make sure she paid for that gambit. From now until her client pled guilty, I was going to bury her in discovery and have her signing acknowledgment forms, on the record, until her fingers fell off.

I gave Declan the good news.

"I'm calling Mr. Vanderhorn right now," he said.

I hadn't heard anyone say "Mr." Vanderhorn in so long, I almost didn't recognize the name.

Bailey picked me up outside the courthouse and we rehashed the ramifications of this latest development.

"It was pretty sloppy of Ian to call Averly," I said.

"He's not an experienced killer, and this whole thing was put together on the fly. Besides, he did have the presence of mind not to use his own phone."

"True, that. And he was in a hurry to get to Hayley. Especially if she'd managed to get close enough to see Brian lying there."

We fell silent, imagining the scene. Brian, bleeding out near a shallow open grave. Hayley alone in the darkness, peeking through the bushes. The shock of seeing her boyfriend lying there, on the ground, dying. And then…her terror as Ian—her second father—gave deadly chase.

"I hope Averly takes the deal," Bailey said. "I'd like to hear how they all wound up on that mountain when the ransom drop was in Fryman Canyon."

Personally, I wanted to hear why Ian decided that Brian had to die. But I doubted Averly would be able to give us that. Ian wouldn't have wanted to tell him anything more than was absolutely necessary. This time, when we got to the waiting room, Terry was already there. And holding her hand out. I knew she wasn't hoping to shake, so I put the report and a copy of her client's phone record into it. She scanned the pages for the next few minutes.

"Thanks," she said when she'd finished.

For Terry, that was gushy.

We waited in silence for the next ten minutes, and then a deputy arrived to escort us.

"I need a few minutes alone with my client," Terry said.

I'd warned Terry on the phone that I didn't want her to tell him about the deal. Again, I wanted to make sure he got the offer pure and unadulterated by any spin. She saw I was about to protest.

"I gave you my word I wouldn't tell him what you plan to offer, and I won't," she said.

I nodded to the deputy, and he took Terry back to the same attorney cage we'd had last time. Jack Averly clanked in shortly thereafter. Terry's back was to me, so I couldn't see her expression, but I saw Averly tilt his head, then slouch down in his chair and nod. A minute later she signaled the guard to let us in.

I put my micro recorder on the table and turned it on. Bailey'd had one in her pocket last time, but I wanted to be open about it now. If Terry could see us recording the conversation, she'd be less likely to try and claim later that we'd strong-armed her client into a plea.

Terry again took control. "I'm going to let the prosecutor make her new offer." She nodded at me. "Go ahead."

Gee, thanks, boss lady. "First, I have to have an answer to one question."

Terry narrowed her eyes. "No, absolutely not. I told you up front, no questioning."

"This is a platinum offer, Counsel. I don't give this kind of deal every day, and I'm sure as hell not about to do it unless I'm certain of what I'm getting. If you can't even let him give us this one answer, we're out of here."

I stood to go.

"Wait, I want to hear it!" Averly flashed his lawyer an angry glance. "It's my life, not yours!" He turned to me. "Ask your question."

Terry's eyes narrowed to slits and her chin jutted out. She looked like she wanted to reach over and snap his neck. But she didn't object any further. A client doesn't control much, but he does have the right to decide whether he'll take a deal or not. If Terry tried to get in his way now, even if it was just to keep him quiet, she ran the risk of looking like she was interfering with that right. And it was all being recorded.

"When you were on the mountain, did you get a call from Ian on a strange cell phone?" Averly wouldn't have known it was Brian's cell that Ian was using, but he might well have noticed the number was unfamiliar.

Averly frowned and looked down at the table. Then his expression cleared. "Yeah, I did."

"Where were you when you got that call?" I asked.

"In my car, out on the road."

"Could you see him?"

"No."

"What did he—"

Terry slammed her palm down on the table. "That's it." She leaned forward and spoke directly into Averly's face. "If you answer one more question, you can go find yourself another lawyer!"

Averly shot her an angry look, but he obediently clamped his jaws together.

"Fine," I said. "Jack, you plead guilty to accessory after the fact and I'll agree to time served. That means you're out of here as soon as you enter the plea."

"A hell of an offer," Bailey added.

Averly gave me a little smile. "Don't you kind of *have* to reduce my charges to accessory now? I mean, how could I be a killer if I'm getting a call in my car?"

"Doesn't mean you're not an accomplice. The law doesn't require you to be present to qualify as an aider and abettor—which means you're held equally as liable as the killer. So, no, I don't 'kind of have to' reduce the charges. And you can always reject this deal and take your chances with a jury."

I stared him down, thinking, "Don't play poker with me, pal." I might not be thrilled with my case against him for murder, but he might not be thrilled with the result if he trusted his fate to twelve strangers. And unlike

Averly, if I lost, I wouldn't be facing a lifetime in the slammer.

"How long do I have to think about this?"

I looked at my watch. "Two minutes. I can make this case without your testimony, Jack. Take it or leave it, but if I walk out of here without an answer, the deal's off the table."

He nodded and stared at a point above my head. When he looked back at me, he had a superior little smile.

"No, thanks," he said.

"Excuse me?"

"I'm not taking your deal."

53

Terry stayed behind to talk to Averly. We headed out to Bailey's car.

"You know, I always had a lot of respect for Terry," Bailey said. "So I don't want to believe she'd encourage her client to give up a sweetheart deal just to avoid representing a snitch—or worse, to cozy up to Mr. Big. But I just can't believe a guy who's never done prison time and isn't a gangbanger would turn down a 'no time' deal like this."

"And I doubt there's a Hollywood Production Assistant prison gang to offer protection for their homies."

Bailey chuckled. "No, not last I checked."

"So prison time should be scaring the bejeezus out of this guy." Even if Terry told him we'd never get him for anything more than accessory, that could still mean around a year in prison, even with good time, work time. That's a long time for a virgin like Averly. On the other hand, if the incentive was right... "Averly's young—he's what? Twenty-four?"

"Twenty-three."

"He strikes me as ambitious in a sleazy kind of way. The young part makes him silly enough to think he can handle a short-term stint in prison—"

"Which is really crazy for a soft little cherry like him—"

"And the ambitious part thinks this'll move him to the front of the line when it's time for Ian to hand out his 'I love you's.'"

"Then you don't think Terry pushed him?"

"No. The bummer is, now I'm stuck going to trial against that barracuda."

Bailey grinned. "It'll be the best show in town."

We reviewed what was left to be done for Averly's preliminary hearing. Thankfully, since we had only a few days left, it wasn't much.

Bailey pulled to the curb in front of the courthouse. "I'll go back over Averly's and Powers's phone records and see what kind of activity they had before the kidnapping—"

"And I want to make sure we've got all of the bank records for both of them, any safe-deposit boxes—I know we didn't find any in California, but we should check out of state. That ransom money's got to be somewhere."

Bailey tapped the steering wheel as she stared at the afternoon crowds. "You know, it's possible Averly stashed the ransom money in New York."

"Yeah, that should be an easy search. Somewhere in New York." Bailey shook her head, and I turned my thoughts to a more immediate issue. "I was planning to add accessory charges to Averly's counts and take him to prelim on everything. But now I'm starting to think we should dismiss the murder counts."

"And just go after him as an accessory? Why? Why not wait until after the prelim?"

"Given the evidence we have now, there's a real possibility the prelim judge will dump our murder charges anyway and only hold him on the accessory counts. If that happens, it'll look like we were overreaching—"

Bailey nodded slowly. "True. And even if we got to keep the murder counts, I'm not all that excited about our chances with a jury—"

"No." I didn't believe we had proof beyond a reasonable doubt that Averly knowingly aided and abetted the murders. If I didn't believe it, then I couldn't ethically put those counts into a jury's hands. "And it might take some wind out of Terry's sails. Now that she has the phone records, she'll want to rent a Goodyear blimp to holler about how Averly's been falsely accused. If we beat her to the punch and dismiss the murder counts, it might take out some of the sting."

"What do you want to bet she's calling the clerk to set a bail review hearing even as we speak?"

I looked at my phone, half expecting it to ring with that news right now. "No bet."

Averly, like Ian, was being held without bail because double homicide is a capital crime that prohibits bail as long as the proof is evident or the presumption of guilt great. But with the new evidence that showed Averly probably wasn't personally involved in either murder, Terry would have a good shot at convincing a judge that he was at best an accessory, not an accomplice to murder, and therefore entitled to bail.

"So we may as well get out in front of it and drop the murder charges before she can make us look any worse."

"That's the way I see it," I said. "I'll call the clerk and get us set for a re-arraignment." But Terry would probably still insist on keeping our preliminary hearing date, so the new charges wouldn't buy us any more time. "Did we get any of that surveillance footage from LAX?"

We'd asked for footage of the day of the kidnapping for all gates with flights to JFK or LaGuardia airports to see if we could spot Averly.

"It wasn't in as of this morning. But we don't need it for prelim, do we?"

"No. I just want to make sure we keep after them so we have it in time to show the jury. Terry's not going to waive any time in this case, so we'll be in trial within sixty days after the preliminary hearing."

Just saying the words made my stomach knot. There were still a few loose ends that needed tidying, but we were pretty much as ready as we were going to be. What plagued me were the unanswered questions. Not only how everyone ended up on Boney Mountain, but also how Ian and Averly found out about the kidnapping to begin with. As to the latter question, I probably already had my answer. Now that I knew how close Russell and Ian were, I felt sure that Russell told Ian. The problem was, with Russell my staunch enemy, I had no way to prove it. Even if there were phone calls between them at the relevant time, there was no way to prove what Russell had told him.

The grim look on Bailey's face told me she was well aware of what we were up against.

"Well, one step at a time," I said. "First, let's get through this preliminary hearing on Averly."

I headed up to the office and printed out the new

complaint, charging Averly with two counts of being an accessory after the fact. Judge Daglian's clerk, Manny Washburn, called to tell me that we could do the re-arraignment at nine a.m. sharp tomorrow. "But don't be late," he warned. "He's squeezing you in before his regular calendar."

"I'll be there. But tell the judge Terry's going to make a pitch for bail, so—"

"She already warned us."

No shock there. I spent the rest of the day catching up on my caseload. By seven o'clock, I decided to head for home. I wanted to make sure I got to bed at a reasonable hour. It was going to be a tough morning.

I woke up on time and tried to prepare myself for the butt-slamming I was about to get from the press. No matter how I tried to spin it, reducing the charges on Averly so dramatically was going to hurt us. We'd be accused of sloppy police work, sloppy lawyering, and overreaching. But it was better to get it over with now, and on our own terms, than lose the counts at prelim— or worse, in the middle of trial. I got in at eight thirty and reviewed my notes for the bail argument. Fifteen minutes later I started to head down to court, but got stuck on back-to-back phone calls from lawyers and witnesses on my other cases. By the time I finished, it was five minutes to nine. I raced out the door to the elevator and punched the button. I glanced down at my watch over and over again as precious minutes ticked by before an elevator finally arrived. By the time I made it to the courtroom, it was five minutes past nine. Judge Daglian was already on the bench—and fuming. Manny, the clerk, was shaking his head.

"Ms. Knight, what does nine sharp mean to you?"

"I'm so sorry, Your Honor. I got stuck on—"

"Not interested. If it happens again you can bring your checkbook. Now, please give the new charging papers to the clerk and counsel and arraign the defendant."

As I handed out the copies, I noticed there were only two reporters in the audience and no cameras. Odd. I'd expected Terry to call every news outlet in town to witness this early victory. When I'd finished arraigning Averly on the new charges, Terry launched into her bail pitch.

"Your Honor, I remind the court that the defendant is entitled to reasonable bail now that the capital charges are gone. And these tremendously reduced charges prove that the People's case against my client is unraveling by the minute."

"So what do you suggest, Counsel? O.R.?" Judge Daglian's raised eyebrow made it clear that Averly's release on his own recognizance was not an option.

Terry lifted her chin, the "tell" that she was spoiling for a fight, but she reined in her baser instincts. "I'd say at most a bail of ten thousand would be appropriate."

"People? You good with that?" the judge asked.

"No, Your Honor, we're not. Jack Averly has already given us ample cause to believe he'd be a flight risk." I outlined his trip to New York, how he'd been apprehended at LaGuardia Airport, his possession of Brian's ID, and his drug history. "I'd ask for five hundred thousand dollars bail."

Terry sputtered about the "outrageousness" of my request. The judge split the baby.

"I'll set bail at two hundred and fifty thousand."

I'd figured we'd land somewhere in this ballpark, and ordinarily I wouldn't have worried that a defendant like Averly would be able to make bail. But Averly had deeper pockets floating around him than most other defendants. I scooted up to my office and called Bailey immediately.

"I'll put a tail on him," she said. "Don't sweat it, Knight."

I didn't have time to sweat it. The press had missed this development on the first bounce, but they more than made up for it now. I got an avalanche of calls demanding information. Sandi, the media relations director, decided it would be best to handle this in a press conference. The conference room off Vanderhorn's office was so crowded, reporters were sitting on the floor. For a change, I was glad Vanderhorn had asked me to stand next to him at the podium. He'd be within arm's reach if I needed to throttle him.

But he started well enough. "As I've said before, this investigation is ongoing. It is not uncommon to amend charges as new information comes in—"

A reporter shouted out, "But this is a big drop. Why didn't you know about this phone call between Powers and Averly sooner?"

Vanderhorn cleared his throat—a typical stalling tactic of his—and said, "It is our duty to be ever vigilant to the possibility that new information will change the complexion of a case, and to be willing to make any necessary alterations, as we have done—"

Another reporter, smelling blood, chimed in. "Yeah, but he's asking *why* you didn't know about that call— isn't checking the defendant's phone records one of the first things you do?"

Vanderhorn drew himself up with a deep breath, and I could tell he was getting ready to bury them in more PR blather—which would only piss them off. I stepped in. "Yes, but the call came from Brian's phone—not Ian Powers's."

There was a moment of complete silence as they all absorbed the new information. Then the questions started flying hot and heavy. "Does that mean Averly wasn't there?" and "So where was Averly when the murders went down?"

Vanderputz had barely moved to let me reach the mike—heaven forbid he step out of frame—so I was practically standing on his feet as I fielded every question for the next fifteen minutes. And even though he really had no information to give, he didn't let that stop him from flapping his gums. Every other question, he interceded with brilliant observations like "Investigations are always ongoing" and "Information comes in continuously." By the time Sandi finally ended the conference, I wanted to grab him by his tie and slap him until my arm fell off. But I was too tired.

54

That evening, as I headed down Broadway toward the Biltmore, my cell phone rang. I thought it might be my soil expert, so I answered.

A fast-talking, excited voice said, "Rachel, it's Benjamin at KRFT radio—can I put you on the air to answer a few questions about today's proceedings?"

My face grew hot with anger. I tried to rein it in as I answered, "No, Benjamin. How did you get this number?"

"Rachel, everyone has the number. We just haven't used it until now."

Furious, I ended the call on as polite a note as I could muster. My cell rang another five times before I got to my room and turned it off. If I changed my number, would they just get it again? Probably. The only thing I could do was to screen my calls and let every unknown number go to voice mail. Feeling hounded, I went to take a shower. But before going to sleep, I made sure all my friends and witnesses had assigned ringtones.

Graden and I settled on Drago Centro, a fantastic

place just a few minutes from my hotel, for dinner that Saturday night. I told him about the siege I'd undergone with the press. "Matter of fact, I just had an idea. Would you record the outgoing message on my cell? Maybe it'll cool their jets if they hear a male voice when they call."

"You sure you want me to?" Graden asked, smiling. "It might start a rumor."

Preoccupied with the case, I needed a minute to understand what he meant. "Why would they know the male voice belongs to someone I'm...uh, seeing?"

Graden held up my phone and clicked the "Record" button. "Hello, you've reached Rachel Knight's phone and this is her boyfriend, *LIEUTENANT* Graden Hales. You can run, but you cannot hide. If you harass her, I will find you." He clicked off, then clicked it on again and added, "Thank you. Have a nice day. And don't leave a message. I wouldn't if I were you."

I didn't know how badly I'd needed to laugh until that moment.

Over the next few days, I checked in with Bailey and talked to Declan about trial strategies in general. But otherwise, I kept my head down and worked.

By the day of the preliminary hearing, I was as prepared as I could possibly be. Clouds had moved in during the night, and the morning air was heavy with the promise of a summer shower. With no appetite for breakfast, I left early, hoping to beat the rain, and took an umbrella just to be on the safe side.

My phone started ringing as I crossed First Street and didn't stop the entire trip. This time I knew better than to answer. But I noticed no one left a message. Thank you, Graden. I ducked into the courthouse just as the first few drops of rain began to fall, and was early enough to avoid running into the press.

I don't usually like to wait in court, and whenever possible, I get the DDA who regularly works the calendar in that courtroom to give me a call when my case is almost up. But it's not a foolproof strategy, and I have found myself in the hot seat for being late more than once. So today I decided to take no chances. I was front and center when the bailiff opened the courtroom doors. Surprisingly, I was the only one. There wasn't a reporter in sight. Weird. The clerk, Manny Washburn, looked at me with surprise when I walked in.

"Rachel Knight, the first one in court?" He put his hand to his forehead. "I think I feel faint."

I walked over to his desk. "Must be all that Wite-Out you use on your minute orders. I'm here on the Averly case. Can I get first call?"

"No one's used Wite-Out since 1980, Rachel. And since you're the first one in, who else would I give first call to? My mother?" Clerks are often smartasses like this. It's the natural evolutionary adaptation to being around so many lawyers. "And I know what case you're here on. I've had about fifty calls from the press in the past hour."

"But I didn't see—"

"Because the judge banned 'em all. Said he wasn't going to have a circus in his courtroom. So no cameras." I let out an exasperated sigh. "Sorry, Rachel, but it's not like you're having that good a hair day."

I ignored the gibe and sat down at counsel table. I'd

wanted the public to see the evidence so they'd know that, contrary to what they'd heard from the televised ass-kissers, this case was no sham. Just this once, press coverage would've been a good thing. We'd probably still get some print coverage—the judge couldn't keep the reporters out. But nothing gets the public's attention like television.

Terry strode in a few minutes later and, with a curt nod to me, started to unpack her briefcase. Lawyers, witnesses, and the friends and family of defendants and victims began to arrive after that, and within half an hour, the courtroom was full.

Judge Daglian took the bench and began to call his calendar. When he got to our case, Terry stood. "Your Honor, my client bailed out last night. As you requested, I gave his passport to your clerk this morning. But Mr. Averly had some matters to take care of before court and told me that he'd be just a few minutes late. If the court could please put us on second call."

"I will. But he'd better be here by second call or he's going right back into lockup."

Bailey came in, murder book in hand, and sat down next to me in the attorney section. "How much longer?" she asked.

I told her what Terry'd said. "Did your guys tell you he'd bailed out?"

"No. Be right back." She hurried out of court.

Twenty minutes later, the judge called our case again.

Terry stood, her expression stony. "Your Honor, I haven't heard from my client, but I can assure you he'll be here shortly."

"Have you tried to reach him, Counsel?"

"Yes, I've left several messages. I believe he must be on his way."

Bailey rushed back in and came over to me. "Ask for a sidebar," she whispered. "I'll go with you."

When we gathered at sidebar, I told the judge that Bailey had information for him. He motioned for her to speak and she leaned in.

"Your Honor, I had Mr. Averly under surveillance. I just found out that there was a triple homicide in the area last night, so the detail was pulled off to help secure the scene. Patrol officers went to his apartment just now and knocked on the door. They got no answer. So they contacted the manager and got him to check inside—"

"I object to any search—" Terry barked.

"Doesn't matter, Counsel," Bailey said. "There was nothing to see. The apartment's empty. He's gone."

55

The judge turned to Terry. "Who posted his bail, Counsel?"

"I—don't know, Your Honor. All I know is that Mr. Averly called to tell me he'd bailed out. I didn't ask how."

Probably because she didn't want to know.

"Well, it should be easy enough to find out," the judge said. He motioned for his bailiff to come over.

"Your Honor, I think we should be putting all of this on the record in open court," I said. "I see no reason why this information should be kept under wraps."

I was plenty mad, but I wasn't about to miss the opportunity to give the defense a little bad press. If Averly was on the run, he looked guilty as hell, and that made our case look that much better—against both him and Ian Powers. Terry objected, but the judge agreed there was no reason why the public couldn't know that Averly had absconded. When he announced that Averly was at large, the entire spectator gallery erupted in gasps, and one reporter even yelled out loud, "You've gotta be kidding me!"

"Come to order!" the judge declared, fixing that reporter with an infuriated glare that would've melted a normal person. "You don't speak. You observe, with your mouth closed. Got it?" He turned to the bailiff. "I want to know who posted his bail. In the meantime, I'm issuing a bench warrant for the arrest of Jack Averly. Detective Keller, please give the information on him to the clerk. I guess for now, that's all on the matter of *People v. Jack Averly.* Next case."

As we packed up to make room for the next hearing, I studied Terry's face for any sign that she'd known this was coming. She might be one hell of an actress, but it didn't look like it to me. In fact, she looked pretty angry.

Bailey and I walked out to the elevators, trailed by reporters, all of whom were shouting questions: "What does this do to your case?" "Were you planning to make him an offer to testify against Powers?" "Who do you think bailed him out?" I brushed by them all with a "No comment" and left them to stampede Terry as she walked out of the courtroom. Over the *ding* of our elevator, I heard her say, "I have no doubt my client will return. Jack Averly wants his day in court and he knows the People have no case."

"I can't friggin' believe they dropped the ball like this," Bailey said when we got off on the eighteenth floor. Her face was white with anger.

I waited until we got to my office and closed the door. "Ian had to have been the one to bail him out—"

"Probably his money, but I doubt it was under his name—"

"I'm sure it wasn't," I said. Ian had a lot of friends—probably in both high and low places—who'd be glad to do him a favor. "But I don't see why Ian would help him run. He had to know that Averly turned down a deal to testify against him. Ian had nothing to worry about."

My office phone was ringing almost continuously. The press was in full feeding frenzy mode. I watched with a sense of vengeful satisfaction as Melia put each line on hold. She'd route them to Sandi in her own good time. Let those reporters get a taste of Melia's efficiency for a change.

"But Averly did. He knew you'd prove the accessory charges. So maybe he was freaked out about doing a few years in prison after all."

And maybe Ian knew better than to trust Averly's resolve once he found himself locked up with Bubba in a four-foot cell. I was frustrated, but there was nothing I could do now except hope that Averly stumbled and got caught. Out of the corner of my eye, I noticed it was still raining—though it was more of a heavy mist with fine, thin drops. I watched them fall for a moment. "There is at least one bright side: it makes Averly look guilty as hell, and that spills over onto Ian as well."

"True. And you want another bright side? Terry Fisk is out of our hair."

I turned back to Bailey as the realization sank in. "Man, that *is* good news."

"We've got another week and a half before Ian's prelim, right?"

"Yeah, and all I have left to do is see what I can pull out of the coroner," I said. "If it's really juicy, I might save it for trial."

Bailey stood. "Look, I want to get into it with the unis who were supposed to be watching Averly, so—"

"Go. See you later." I didn't envy those patrol officers. Bailey can really blast when she's angry. And triple homicide or no, someone really should've stayed behind to keep an eye on that jerk.

With Averly out of the picture for now, I had time to work on my other cases. But first I searched my phone for the ringer control and turned it off. Better. But I could still see the blinking lights for my two lines. I covered the buttons with a file folder. Perfect. No more sound, no more fury. I put my head down and worked until almost seven o'clock. I packed up to leave and had just reached for my cell when it vibrated. I looked at the screen. The number was vaguely familiar, so, thinking it was one of my witnesses, I answered.

"Hello?"

"Rachel Knight, how are you this lovely evening?"

The now-familiar British accent told me it was my buddy from the *National Inquisitor*, Andrew Chatham. I cursed myself for not realizing why the number looked familiar. "I'm fine, Andrew. But you know I'm not going to tell you anything, so why waste your time?"

"Because you may change your mind and I'm the sort who's ever hopeful. I can be useful, you know."

My silence told him what I thought about the likelihood of that statement. Now listening only for a chance to end the call with a graceful exit line, I juggled my purse onto my shoulder and snapped my briefcase closed.

He resumed. "Proof of my worthiness: You have not seen the last of Terry Fisk."

I stopped and clutched the phone. "What do you mean?"

"She's joining Ian's team."

56

I called Bailey and told her what I'd just heard.

"Damn," Bailey said. "Well, so much for our good news."

To put it mildly. My shoulder sagged under the weight of my purse, which now felt like it was loaded with bricks, and I could barely pick up my briefcase. I decided to leave it in the office for tonight. I was exhausted; there was no point in pretending I'd get any more work done. But tired as I was, a nervous ball of energy burned in my gut. Prosecuting someone who was not only a major Hollywood player but also one who'd been like an uncle to the victim—and one with a history of "giving back" to the mean streets where he'd been born—was a daunting task in itself. Adding a pit bull like Terry Fisk to the mix would make it an unending bloody battle to keep the evidence from getting buried under a morass of defense red herrings and a barrage of laurels for Ian Powers the Wonderful.

I was grateful to find the elevator empty and slumped back against the wall, eyes closed, as it hurtled down to the lobby. At this late hour the evening crowds were long gone, and I was nearly alone as I headed for the glass doors at the back of the building. I fished out my cell phone and turned on the ringer as I made my way out of the building.

I'd just turned onto Broadway when I heard pounding footsteps coming up behind me. Before I could turn to see what was going on, a batch of reporters closed in and shoved microphones in my face. Over their shoulders, the black lenses of video cameras glared at me.

"Ms. Knight, pundits are saying you had enough to go after Averly for murder—that you shouldn't have dropped the charges to accessory—so why did you *really* dismiss his murder charges?" And "Former city councilman Mel Berman says it's *your* fault Averly bailed out and ran! What do you have to say to that?"

A number of pungent responses crossed my mind— among them "Who cares what a former city councilman, and especially that idiot, thinks?" but I was just too damn beat. So fatigue alone was responsible for my giving the safest answer.

"As a prosecutor I'm ethically bound to proceed only with charges I believe a jury would find to be true beyond a reasonable doubt. That's all I have to say."

It was such a politically correct, neutral statement, I couldn't believe it'd come out of my mouth. This damn case might actually be altering my DNA. I pushed through the crowd and moved as fast as I could without breaking into a run. A few reporters chased me for a minute or so, yelling for my response to the pundits, but when they saw I wasn't going to give any more answers, they gave up and fell back. But I couldn't stop myself from looking over my shoulder the whole way home, wary of yet another ambush. I reluctantly admitted that from now on I'd better drive to work. I made a mental note to ask Eric to get me a parking space close to the building.

Winded and depressed, I dragged myself back to my room. It'd been a long, hard day…again. I treated myself to a glass of pinot gris with dinner and by the time I got into bed, I was so drained my eyes closed before my head even hit the pillow. But when I fell asleep, I dreamed that my legs were chained together and I was being chased by a pack of pit bulls. Zombie pit bulls. Go figure.

I didn't need to rush into the office the next day. I had no court appearances, and there were no witness interviews scheduled. I called Eric to tell him what had happened with the reporters when I'd left yesterday evening, and he got me secure parking under the courthouse. No one would be able to get to me now—at least not outside the courtroom. I'd given Declan the day off. He had to take care of a root canal. I told him that would ensure he'd still feel as though he'd spent the day in court. I got to work early, just because I needed to get busy, doing…something. It was good that I did, because at eight forty-five, I got a call from Judge Daglian's clerk.

"We just got notice that Wagmeister wants to come in and advance the case," she said.

Meaning he wanted the case moved up to an earlier date. "Did he say why?"

"No. But he said he'd be here at ten o'clock. Can you make it?"

I wanted to say no, but I'd only be delaying the inevitable. "Yeah."

I called Bailey and asked if we could push the coroner meeting.

"I'll check. So you think this is it, Terry's joining in today?"

"I do."

"Okay. We still have over a week before Powers's prelim, right?"

"Right. We've got time."

Wrong. We didn't.

This time a phalanx of waiting reporters surged toward me as I stepped off the elevator, and cameras clicked and flashed in wave after wave as I "No commented" my way down the hallway. Obviously, Judge Daglian's distaste for the media had been short-lived.

As expected, Terry was standing next to Don Wagmeister at the defense table. Ian Powers was dressed in one of his many multi-thousand-dollar suits. He looked a little tired—no doubt because the sheriff's deputies got him up before five a.m., standard wake-up time so they could get prisoners on the bus to court. But otherwise, Powers was impeccably groomed and looking very calm. A young law clerk was dispatched to hand me the written motion giving notice that Terry Fisk would be joining the defense team for Ian Powers. Usually, adding an attorney is not a big deal, and no formal motion is either required or given. The lead counsel stands up in court and says so-and-so is joining the defense team. This formal, written motion was an obvious grandstand play. Until now, Don hadn't made a lot of noise in the press. And as long as he didn't engage, I didn't have to push back to counter his spin. But I had a nasty feeling those relatively genteel days were over.

Wagmeister, wearing an unusually sedate tie, waxed unusually eloquent for the occasion. I'm sure it was just a coincidence that the cameras and recorders were all pointed his way. "I would like to advise the court that I will be joined in the defense of this case by my most esteemed colleague Ms. Terry Fisk."

Judge Daglian thanked him for the notice. "Why does this require a formal appearance, Mr. Wagmeister? As long as the fees are coming out of your client's pocket, he can have twenty attorneys as far as I'm concerned."

And he probably will before this is over, I thought, even if they don't all get paid. You'd be surprised how many lawyers are willing to donate a little pro bono time when it means an appearance on the five o'clock news.

"Yes, Your Honor, I understand, and I would not have taken up this court's time if that were the only matter. I'll defer to Ms. Fisk to present our next motion."

I watched as Terry moved to the podium between the defense and prosecution counsel tables. A wave of camera clickings followed her every step, and when she got to the podium, she took her time adjusting the microphone down to her height, giving the photographers a chance to get their shots. And they'd be the best she'd ever had, because she looked terrific. Freshly styled hair, minimalist makeup, sharp suit—it was all working for her.

"Your Honor, at this time the defense will be requesting to reset the preliminary hearing for an earlier date."

"And what date do you propose?"

"The day after tomorrow."

What? I held my breath and prayed that the judge would say he couldn't do it, that his calendar was full.

"People?" the judge asked. "Is that acceptable?"

I took my time as I rose to respond. "I have all my witnesses scheduled for the following week solely because Mr. Wagmeister chose that date—"

"If you're unable to proceed on an earlier date, that's fine, Ms. Knight. The court understands you relied upon counsel's prior representation."

Terry interrupted. "Excuse me, if I may, Your Honor. I have a suggestion. One that might alleviate the People's problem. If the People can't be ready, the defense will waive the preliminary hearing."

Ian Powers wore a little smile as he shot his cuffs and straightened his jacket. The few reporters who understood what Terry had just said began to buzz, and those who didn't know were nudging them for explanations. The buzz grew to a loud hum.

The judge banged his gavel. When the hum died down, he spoke sternly. "I've allowed all this press because I believe in the public's right to know, but I will not have the courtroom disrupted. If you have something to say that just can't wait until recess, say it outside." Two of the reporters rushed out of the courtroom, but the rest stayed put.

The offer to waive prelim was a clever move. The burden of proof at a preliminary hearing is very low. All we have to show is that there's "probable cause" to believe a defendant committed the crimes charged. When there are civilian witnesses, especially eyewitnesses, the chance for the defense to grill them early on and explore weaknesses—not to mention get statements on the record they can later use at trial to show inconsistencies—can be critical.

But in this case, Terry wasn't giving up much, if anything, by waiving. And there was a big bonus in it for the defense: if there was no hearing, the evidence of Ian's guilt wouldn't come out until the trial. That would keep a lot of bad press off Ian Powers. Some of the evidence would dribble out through pretrial motions, but it would probably only be covered by print reporters. There wouldn't be the kind of widespread publicity we badly needed to swing public opinion—or, more to the point, the jury pool—our way.

If I objected to Terry's waiver, it'd either look like I wanted the public airing—which, though true, wasn't cool, because it was an obvious effort to sway the jury pool—or look as though I wanted our evidence to be challenged, as though I didn't really believe in my case. I had to decide quickly. Was it worth getting slammed for wanting to publicize our evidence? If I let the defense waive prelim, it'd be at least two months before I had the chance to put the evidence out there in any cogent way. I decided I couldn't lose this critical opportunity. The battle for the hearts and minds of the jury pool had begun and it was time I joined it.

"As much as I appreciate the defense's kind offer, the People must regretfully decline. We would like to proceed with the preliminary hearing. If I could have a moment to check with my investigating officer about witness availability, I'll be able to tell the court whether I can make the requested date."

"Go ahead, Ms. Knight," the judge said. "I'll give you second call."

I moved to the end of the empty jury box, as far from the highly tuned ears of reporters as I could get, and called Bailey. When I told her what had happened, she erupted.

"Why the hell is the judge letting them do this?"

"He's not, Bailey," I whispered, my hand covering my mouth. "If we can't get it together, he'll deny the motion and give us more time. But it'd look a lot better if we do it without the extra time." It was all about not showing any weakness. With the press breathing down our necks, every single move would be scrutinized and every talking head would give his or her own interpretation. A request for more time would play like we had a weak case and were scrambling to shore it up.

"Well, they're almost all criminalists and techs, so it should be doable. Stand by. I'll make sure."

I stayed at the end of the jury box, my back to the rest of the courtroom, and pretended I was still on my cell so no one would talk to me. A few minutes later, Bailey called back.

"All clear. Only problem might be the coroner. But since they're being so amenable about waiving prelim—" she said.

"Yeah. They should be willing to stipulate to the coroner's testimony."

I passed the defense on my way to the clerk's desk and deliberately said nothing to either lawyer. Wagmeister put out a hand to get my attention, but I ignored him.

When the judge called the case, I said that we could be ready with all witnesses except the coroner. So if the defense would agree to stipulate to that testimony—

Terry jumped up. "The defense will be glad to stipulate. We don't intend to contest the fact that *someone* murdered these victims."

"Very well, then I'll see all parties back in this court the day after tomorrow, eight thirty sharp."

As I turned to go, I saw a reporter lean over the rail that separated the lawyers from the spectators and ask Terry for a comment.

If I got lucky, some channel would have a talking head who'd explain why I had to refuse the waiver. But I couldn't worry about that now. I had a day and a half to get ready for a hearing that would be carried on nearly every station in the country from coast to coast.

57

The day of the preliminary hearing dawned hazy and blistering. Even at seven thirty, I had to take off my jacket as I headed up Broadway. I'd needed to walk to calm my nerves, and I was pretty sure I wouldn't get ambushed by the press today. They'd be too busy lining up to get seats in the courtroom. As usual, my perennially ringing cell phone kept me company all the way. Maybe I'd miss it when the case was over...but I doubted it.

The courthouse was surrounded by satellite trucks, and as I reached the back door, I saw that there was a line of people waiting to get in and a huge crowd clustered on the front steps of the building. One young ponytailed woman held up a poster with an enlarged photograph of Ian Powers. Underneath his picture was the caption FRAMED. Another woman, who was wearing a beret, carried a poster titled NOT GUILTY. A beret? In this heat? Who could take someone like that seriously? As I entered the lobby, I heard chanting, but I couldn't make out the words—and didn't want to. A throng of reporters with cameramen filled the elevator waiting area, so I opted for the stairs. Already hot and tired, after two flights in the concrete and metal staircase, I emerged on the third floor wringing wet and out of breath. I had to find time to get to the gym. If only so I could outrun reporters.

I really wanted to keep climbing so I could avoid any run-ins with the press, but I couldn't face even one more flight of stairs, let alone make it up to the eighteenth floor. I punched the "Up" button and crossed my fingers. When I heard the *ding* of an arriving elevator on the far-right side, I ran to catch it. But as the doors opened, I saw that it was packed to the ceiling with reporters. One of them pulled up his camera, but I quickly stepped back and moved to the left, out of their field of vision. The next elevator that came was equally packed, but I didn't notice any cameras. Not much better, but I had to get to the office at some point. I slid in and tried to squeeze myself into a corner where I could face away from everyone. Just as the car bounced to a stop on the fifth floor, one of the reporters said, "Hey, aren't you—"

I scrunched back into a corner and, luckily, the push of the crowd forced him out before he could try again. By the time I got to the eighteenth floor, I was a nervous wreck. I dragged myself to Toni's office. Please, oh, please be there, I prayed. Her door was closed, not a good sign. Ever the optimist, I knocked. "Hey, Tone, you there?"

Two seconds later Toni opened the door, holding an eyelash curler up to one eye. She quickly pulled me in and closed the door.

She released her eyelashes and looked me over. "Did you hitchhike from Iowa? What happened to you?"

I told her of my short but eventful trip to the office. "Jeez, Rachel. Why don't you have a key to the freight elevator?"

Good question. The freight elevator had no public access. I should've thought of that long ago. Eric would be glad to get me a key. "I forgot, I'll—"

"Never mind. I'll take care of it for you." Toni shook her head and walked to the mirror she kept on the wall behind her desk. She put on her mascara as she spoke. "You need a blowout and some real makeup. The light in that courtroom will make you look like Morticia." I admitted I didn't know that. "How do you not know that?" she asked. I shrugged. "Okay, what do you have with you? You obviously can't use my base or concealer."

I showed her what I had. A compact and lip gloss. "I've got foundation at home, but I don't usually use it—"

Toni shook her head. "Well, you're going to use it now. It's not just a vanity thing, Rache. Looks and credibility go hand in hand, especially for women. And your prospective jurors are watching. I'll do what I can now, but we're going to have a little hair, makeup, and wardrobe session this weekend. And you're going to buy extras to keep in your office, okay? And one other thing: stop perspiring."

I nodded obediently and Toni went to work. Within fifteen minutes, she had me looking more polished than I'd ever have managed on my own. At eight twenty I called Declan and told him it was time to rock and roll.

"Wow, you look great," he said.

"I can't take any credit. It was all Toni." He looked pretty great himself, in a single-breasted navy blue Hugo Boss suit and red-and-blue-striped tie. But his cheek was twitching and he was shifting from foot to foot. I started to warn him about the press, but he held up a hand to stop me. "I saw the picketers out front. I recognized the girl holding the NOT GUILTY sign from one of my dad's films."

I looked at Declan with renewed appreciation. Not that I hadn't already been impressed with his intelligence and hard work, but his unique insider knowledge was invaluable. "It helps to hear that."

"We're playing the Hollywood game now, and that's a game I've watched since birth. Nothing is real—and everything is real. What's that line? 'King Kong was only four feet tall—'"

"'But he still scared the crap out of everyone.'"

"Only because they didn't know. Once you know, it's all over. So now you're going to show them—"

"That Ian is only four feet tall?"

"Yes, exactly."

When we walked down the hallway, I was grateful to see that the reporters were confined to a roped-off area, so we couldn't be cornered or chased. The anchors and talking heads thrust out their microphones and shouted out questions: "What do you expect to happen today?" and "Who are your witnesses?" and "Have you heard any news on Jack Averly's whereabouts?" I ignored them all.

Every seat in the courtroom was taken, every bench filled to bursting with civilians and reporters who were squeezed together like human sardines. Raynie was in the back row of the middle section. She nodded, but seemed distracted and uninterested in talking. I'd spoken to her on the telephone a few times since Ian's arrest, and although she'd been polite, her voice was controlled, her manner distant. But I understood. Ian had been like a member of the family for many years. In fact, I'd learned that he was closer to them than Hayley's real uncle—Sheldon, who was Raynie's brother. Like Russell, Raynie couldn't believe Ian had killed her daughter, but unlike Russell, she didn't seem to want to ignore the truth—if that's what it was. She just wasn't sure. I hoped that after today, she would be.

Front and center on the defendant's side of the courtroom sat Dani, Russell, and Ian's girlfriend, Sacha. Dani looked sad and stressed, but Russell sat with a stiff-necked defiance that announced he was here to support his unjustly accused friend. They were surrounded by many others, who looked like Ian fans. The air was thick with the tension that builds before a prizefight. Terry and Don were conferring on their side of counsel table, and two young law clerks were nervously standing behind them. All of them moved with the self-conscious awareness of actors on a stage.

Bailey came in carrying poster board exhibits, blowups of the relevant phone records, and, most important, the texts between Hayley and Brian, and their killer—Ian. None of this would normally be done for a preliminary hearing. But I had a public to impress, and I needed to make my evidence dramatic enough to entice the news into spinning something for our side.

"Do you have the DVD?" I asked.

Bailey pulled it out of her pocket. "Good to go."

The bailiff escorted Ian out of the lockup, and he emerged looking like he'd stepped out of a magazine. Expensive dark navy suit and tasteful tie, hair perfectly combed, he smiled and waved to Dani and Russell, Sacha, and his many supporters.

"We've got to persuade Janice to show up for trial," I whispered to Bailey. "Someone has to be here to remind everyone that Brian was a real human being before this asshole slit his throat."

"She'll be here. This was just a little too last-minute for her to pull it off."

Something about the way Bailey said it made me do a double take. "Is something up with her?"

Bailey looked around, then carefully turned her back to the spectators and whispered, "When I was trying to get hold of her so we could meet in New York, I spoke to her agent. He didn't come right out and say it, but I think he was trying to tell me she's agoraphobic."

I pulled up the memory of Janice at the St. Regis— her strange reaction when I'd mentioned flying out here for the trial. Now it all made sense. It was probably hard enough for her to make it to Manhattan. But traveling to an airport, taking a flight to unfamiliar territory, and on top of that having to deal with the stress of coming to court—it would all be far too much. I fought the sinking feeling that even the few supporters we had would never show up.

At exactly eight thirty Judge Daglian took the bench. He called the case and asked us all to state our appearances for the record. After we'd given our names and the party we represented—Declan cleared his throat nervously before he was able to choke out his name—the judge got down to business.

"Other than the stipulation to the coroner's testimony, will the rest of the testimony be from live witnesses?"

"It will, Your Honor," I said.

"You may call your first witness."

I started with Bailey, who interpreted the cell phone records. She pointed out the thirty-second call from one of Russell's lesser-used cell phones to Ian Powers's unlisted number just minutes after Russell got the first kidnap message from Hayley's phone. I also had Bailey mention Powers's call to Russell a couple of hours after the ransom note was sent, though I knew the defense would try to play it as evidence of his innocence: Why would Powers call to find out what was going on if he was the killer? But it could also play as Powers's effort to look innocent. Especially since he hadn't called sooner. I was hoping the defense would make the mistake of opening that door, so I could point that out.

But they didn't. Wagmeister played it safe and had Bailey concede that we had no proof of what Russell said when he called Ian. That there was no proof he told Ian about the kidnapping text. That since Russell was so paranoid he wouldn't call the cops, it was very likely he was afraid to tell Ian. Bailey tersely conceded all that was *possible*. I countered on redirect by having Bailey repeat that Russell's call showed there was a way for Ian to have known about the kidnapping early on.

Next up was Dorian, who described the evidence she'd collected, and gave her opinion that the hairs on the passenger seat of Averly's car came from Ian Powers.

Wagmeister did what little cross there was to do: just routine questions about how the evidence was collected and preserved. The defense didn't want to tip their hand just yet, and tangling with a strong, highly respected witness like Dorian would only make them look bad.

My fingerprint expert, Leo Relinsky, said he'd found Ian's print on the trunk of Brian's car and inside Averly's car, and Averly's prints inside Brian's car. This time Terry walked to the lectern.

"Now, Mr. Relinsky, you can't say when prints are left on an object, can you?"

"No."

"So those prints you found could've been left days, weeks, even months or years before you collected them?"

"Correct."

"And you've heard of cases in which prints were planted, haven't you?"

Leo frowned and pursed his lips. "I have heard of the very rare, bizarre case in which someone was able to lift a fingerprint with tape and place it somewhere. Mostly on television shows, but... yes."

"So your answer is yes."

He exhaled sharply. "Yes."

"Nothing further."

I didn't think Terry would really go for something as cheesy as planting fingerprints, but the press loved that kind of conspiracy junk, so it would likely get her plenty of ink and airtime. When Terry returned to counsel table, Ian favored her with a superior, congratulatory smile. The more I saw this guy, the more I hated him. I hadn't thought that was possible.

I decided not to call my soil expert, Sterling Numan. I didn't need it for the prelim and it'd just give the defense more to play with. I wanted to keep my case high and tight. So I cut straight to the chase and called Timothy Gelfer to give his conclusions about the blood on the trunk.

"I compared the evidence blood found on the trunk of the car to the sample removed from Hayley Antonovich at autopsy and found her DNA profile present. But I also found another profile in the evidence blood, which indicated it was a mix. I received samples of blood from Jack Averly and Ian Powers—"

"Not from Hayley's mother or father?" I asked, though I knew the answer.

"No. Because the profile did not share the requisite number of alleles with Hayley's sample to have come from a parent."

"Whose profile *did* match the blood on the trunk of Brian's car?"

Random coughs and shuffling had been a constant undercurrent during the testimony up till now. Suddenly, a hush fell over the courtroom.

"I determined that the other profile matched that of the defendant, Ian Powers."

"Nothing further."

Several reporters scurried out of the courtroom. Good. Chew on that.

Terry stood again.

"Mr. Gelfer, you can't tell when the blood was placed on the trunk, can you?"

"No."

"And you cannot say that Hayley's blood was placed on the trunk at the same time as Mr. Powers's blood, can you?"

"No."

"In fact, Hayley's blood could've been on that car for a month before Ian Powers's blood landed there, correct?"

"Yes, that is correct."

"Or vice versa: Ian Powers's blood could have gotten there before—maybe a month before—Hayley's fell there. Correct?"

"Yes, that is correct. Though I think it would be very—"

"Objection!" Terry said. "The witness has answered the question. Nonresponsive."

Gelfer had been about to hit a nerve. Terry didn't want logic getting in the way of her theory.

"Sustained. The question has been answered. Anything further, Counsel?"

Terry asked the judge for a moment, then leaned down to whisper something to Wagmeister. I suspected this was just a delaying tactic to let her point sink in with the spectators. Ian watched his attorneys, his expression detached, as though they were tailors debating his trouser length.

Finally, Terry straightened and said, "No, nothing further."

"People?" the judge asked.

I stood for the one question I had for Gelfer. "Were you about to say something about the likelihood of two people leaving a blood smear on the exact same spot at different times?"

Terry jumped to her feet and shouted, "Objection! Leading! And calls for speculation! Outside this witness's expertise!"

"Objection will be sustained. Would you like to try again, Ms. Knight?"

I'd made my point. And it was a logical one, not a scientific one, so Gelfer really couldn't speak to it anyway. "No thank you, Your Honor."

"Anything further for this witness?" the judge asked.

"No, nothing further."

Terry said she had no re-cross.

"Call your next witness," the judge said.

"Just the stipulation, Your Honor." I read in the coroner's conclusion that both victims had been stabbed to death. Terry stipulated, albeit through gritted teeth, and I turned to the judge. "The People rest."

Terry declined to call any witnesses and gave a brief pro forma argument to dismiss the charges. She couldn't really justify making a big show of it, since she'd just offered to forgo the preliminary hearing altogether. And thankfully, the judge didn't belabor the point by taking the matter under submission. "I find that there is sufficient cause to hold the defendant to answer for two counts of murder with the use of a deadly weapon, to wit, a knife. Shall we pick a pretrial date?"

"That's fine, Your Honor," Terry said. "But we'll need a trial date within the statutory sixty days. We're not waiving time."

Predictable. The race was on.

58

I spent the next week talking to my witnesses, going over their testimony to make sure there'd be no bad surprises, and preparing them for the kinds of questions they'd get on cross-examination. Except for Dorian. She could handle herself against ten Terry Fisks. All at once. By Friday, I was feeling like things were pretty much under control. I even thought about taking one day off. And at that exact moment, Graden called. One of those rare instances of perfect timing.

"Devon wants to bring his girlfriend over for a pool day. I thought I might throw steaks on the barbie. How's that sound to you?"

I'd only met Graden's little brother a couple of times, though what I'd seen, I really liked. He was a softer, gentler, and shyer version of his older brother. But I'd never met Devon's girlfriend. And I wasn't bathing suit ready. With all this work, I hadn't had the time to even think about getting a tan. Or finding some abs.

Hearing my hesitation, Graden said, "If you can't lose a whole day, you could just come for dinner."

I didn't know whether he'd sensed my bathing suit anxiety, but regardless, I was relieved. "That's fantastic—"

A beeping told me I had a call waiting. It was Bailey. "Graden, can you hang on a sec? It's Bailey—"

"Go ahead and take it. We'll work out the details later."

I took Bailey's call. "What's up?"

"I'm having trouble getting Dominic's subpoena served. Every time my uni goes out there, his people say he's not home—"

Dominic Rostoni, the skinhead boss who'd found Brian's body. "The Nazi asshole is resisting service? I'm shocked to the core."

"Yeah, I may have to go out there and do it myself. Also, one of our cell phone record custodians is off on maternity leave. I don't suppose you could get Fisk and company to stipulate to her? They can't really be planning any big cross on the records."

I sighed. "They're probably not, but I wouldn't expect any stipulations from this bunch. If we put her on, they won't bounce her around for long, but if we say we have a problem getting her, they'll make a big deal of it. Just tell her that once she shows up, we'll have her on and off the stand fast. Any more good news, sunshine?"

"Brittany's MIA."

"What are you talking about? The girl is filming right here in Hollywood." I'd planned to call Brittany Caren as one of the witnesses who could describe the bitter feud between Russell and Tommy Maher. The last I'd heard, she was about to start shooting her next film with Russell, and for a change it was local.

"Apparently, she had a screaming fit on the set and stormed out. No one's heard from her since. They're recasting her part."

"When did that happen?"

"Not long after we saw her, but I can't really say the timing's suspicious."

I had to agree. Having seen what a mess she was—and having heard about her reputation for walking off sets—even I had to admit that Brittany's flameout was unlikely to be related to our meeting. And in all honesty, I hadn't been thrilled about using her anyway. I had others who could describe the fight between Tommy and Russell who wouldn't show up stoned. Probably. Or at least not visibly. Brittany's disappearance was a surprise, but not a devastating one. The next one was.

My office intercom buzzed. It was Eric. "Rachel, I need a minute. Can you come to my office?"

When I got to his office, I saw that Melia's desk was vacant, so I went to his door, which was uncharacteristically closed, and knocked. "Eric?"

"Come in, Rachel."

I opened the door and saw Melia standing in front of Eric's desk. She turned and gave me a beseeching look. Eric had a funny expression on his face too, as he told me to close the door. "What's going on?"

"Apparently you've become a featured attraction." Eric held out a newspaper. "I'm so sorry, Rachel."

As I took the paper from him, I saw that it was the *National Inquisitor.* With my mug plastered almost life-sized on the front page. Splashed above it was the headline "Powers Prosecutor's Personal Tragedy." Below that was the subheading "Sister Romy Abducted at Age

Eleven." The office spun around me like a Tilt-a-Whirl. I sank into a chair in front of Eric's desk and tried to absorb it all.

Melia twisted her fingers together and spoke in a pleading voice. "I didn't buy this at the stand. It came in the mail and when I picked it up in the mail room I didn't really look at it till I got back to my desk…"

I waved her off. "It's okay, Melia."

"The whole thing with your sister! How come you never told anybody?" she asked.

I shook my head and tried to make the room stop spinning.

"Melia, give us a minute," Eric said. He stood up, leaned across the desk, and took the paper from my frozen hands. "I'll keep this for now, if you don't mind."

After Melia left, Eric sat back down. "It wasn't until I saw this article that I realized how private you are. I tried to think back over all the time I've known you, and I couldn't recall one time when you ever made mention of anything about your personal life before you joined the office."

I stared at the corner where Eric's briefcase lay, unable to make my voice work.

"I only say all this so you'll know that I have some appreciation for how particularly painful this must be. I don't know how to make this better and I can't make it go away. I can't even make it stop. This is a major tabloid, and if they put you on the front page, that means they think you'll sell papers. So there's probably more to come. The only way to get them to lose interest is for you to let go of the case. What I'm saying is, if you want off—"

"No!" I swallowed to push down the awful queasiness in my stomach. "I'm fine. Just give me a minute."

Eric looked at me, concerned. "You sure?"

"Completely." I started to stand up, then something occurred to me. "Do you think the defense did this? To rattle me?"

"If they did, they're pretty stupid. This"—he pointed to the paper—"is a favor. It's going to make you extremely sympathetic. Ian has the glitz of celebrity, with all those actors and that big director on his side, but this kind of personal tragedy grabs the public like no other."

"So you're telling me this...nightmare...is good news." I shook my head. Un-friggin'-believable.

"Yes."

But, of course, he was right. I'd have realized it sooner if I hadn't just had my bell rung. It was exactly why we always struggled in trial to get out personal details about the murder victims. Because it humanized them, made them sympathetic. I can't lie: knowing that the whole world was learning about my past made me physically ill. Humanizing or not, I'd have preferred to remain an anonymous cog in the machine, just another faceless prosecutor. But there was no way to put this genie back in the bottle.

I got up and walked to the door. "Oh, and would you mind...?" I pointed to the paper.

"Sure, of course." He held it out to me.

"No. I mean, would you mind burning it?"

Eric laughed. "It'd be my pleasure."

59

Bailey was livid. "I'm going to get that reporter's license plate and tell every cop in town to tag his worthless ass if he so much as uses the wrong blinker," she growled.

I sighed. "And then he'll write a story about how he's been targeted by the LAPD ever since—"

"Let him!"

Toni was equally outraged, but she too pointed out the upside. "You wanted to turn the tide of public opinion? Well, this'll do it. And a heck of a lot faster than evidence."

Graden had called as soon as he heard about the story. "I'm so sorry, Rachel. I know how much you hate this. I can put some security on you. Have a couple of guys with you if you decide to walk to court—"

"God forbid. Thank you, Graden. Really. But I'm sure I don't need bodyguards."

Graden sighed. "I figured you'd say that. So just make me one promise: if anyone bothers you or so much as looks at you funny, you'll tell me about it."

"I'm sure no one—"

"Promise."

"I promise."

"Dinner's at seven thirty."

Graden's house was in Pacific Palisades. If you don't live in Southern California, you probably haven't heard of the Palisades. Bel Air, Beverly Hills, Malibu—those are the big-name hoods. But as far as I'm concerned, they can't compete with the Palisades. Spread across the hills and cliffs above the Pacific Ocean, it offers sweeping views, clean air, and perfect weather with none of the traffic, noise, fog, or hassle that comes with beach living.

He had the same security gate setup that Russell and Ian had, but the driveway was a long stretch of road that led straight uphill and opened onto a beautiful expanse of lawn decorated with cherry trees and impressive abstract pieces of iron sculpture.

The house itself was a mix of modern and traditional with large, unadorned windows that gave it a light, airy feel. All that glass might have been a bad idea anywhere else, but isolated the way it was on the top of that hill, privacy was guaranteed. As I got out of the car, the scream of seagulls, the warmth of the twilight sun, and the fresh salty air made me stop and take a deep breath. The jagged shards inside my chest that I hadn't even been aware of began to melt and my steps slowed as I enjoyed the rare feeling of peace.

I could hear voices coming from the backyard and saw that Graden had left the front door open for me. I walked into an expansive living room that seemed to float over the edge of a cliff. Two of the walls were glass, and gave a panoramic view of the ocean as well as the hills. It made me a little light-headed. I'd been curious to see Graden's home. What a man does with his personal space can tell you a lot about him. For instance, a trapeze in the bedroom, or a wide array of photographs—all of his mother—would be good to know. So I took a moment to look around. Even at first glance, there was a personal feel to it that told me Graden had picked every piece himself. And that he clearly didn't believe in clutter. There were just a few big pieces: a sectional couch, a divan, a large square marble and glass coffee table, all in shades of ivory—either a brave choice or a show of supreme confidence in his housekeeper. But the quirky, whimsical art—I spotted a Mark Ryden oil and an original Naoto Hattori—and luscious, exotically embroidered throws and pillows were a perfect counterpoint. The result was a space that was comfortable, fun, and inviting. It made me smile.

But I didn't try to picture myself living there. Okay, well, maybe I did. Just for a second.

I walked out onto the patio and saw Graden at the grill, spatula in hand. Whatever he was cooking, it smelled delicious. Jeez. All that and pretty too. My stomach gave an embarrassingly loud grumble and I put my hand over it to muffle the sound. Devon and his girlfriend, who were admiring the ocean view, drinks in hand, waved to me. Graden turned to me and smiled widely. "Rachel," he said as he gave me a long, warm hug. "How're you doing?" he whispered.

"Better now."

I had a wonderful time.

Devon's girlfriend—an archaeologist—was fun, charming, and whip smart, and Graden made a salmon on the barbecue that was heavenly. But other than that one, too brief evening, I worked through the weekend. We had a pretrial motion set for Monday morning and the defense hadn't filed any written motions. That meant they were going to ambush me in court. I had to be ready for anything.

Monday morning, unable to bear the sound of my cell phone ringing all the way to work, I put it on vibrate. But my phone continued to rattle against my desk as it vibrated with new calls. I wrapped it in a cardigan I kept in the office to shut it up. Declan came in, dressed to the nines—which I'd come to realize was business as usual for him—armed with his files and all fired up. "How come they haven't filed a motion to suppress on the laptop?" he asked.

"No reason to. We haven't found anything. But I should check in with the head of computer crimes—"

"Cliff Meisner, right. I remember you said he was going over the laptop to see if there's any information we can use."

"Yeah. If it's still a 'no go' it'll be time to cut bait."

Declan opened a file and scanned it. "I got all the cell phone people lined up, and I'm working on the maps that show the cell sites accessed by each of the phones."

"Great. And you've got the DVDs of all the crime scene photos from Bailey?"

"In my office."

"We'll have to do a run-through to make sure everything's clear and plays smoothly before we get to trial."

"Wouldn't want to come off looking like we had third-rate production values," Declan said with a smile.

I chuckled. "Your dad would kill you."

Declan suddenly looked away. "Well, probably. But not for that."

I waited for him to continue, but he didn't. I wasn't going to pry. If he wanted me to know more, he'd tell me in his own time. A knock on the door offered what was probably a welcome interruption.

"Come in," I said.

A UPS man opened the door. "Could you hold this?" he asked Declan. As Declan held the door open, the man turned back to the hallway, then brought in one of the biggest floral arrangements I'd ever seen.

"Whoa! Are you sure you came to the right office?" I asked.

"Rachel Knight? That's your nameplate next to the door?"

"Yeah."

"Then I've got the right place."

The man set the basket down on my desk and it was so huge, I couldn't see over it. "Uh, I don't think this is going to work." But my voice was muffled by the foliage.

"What?" the man asked.

I stood up. "Would you mind putting it over here?" I gestured to the table on my right, then saw that it was covered with files and books. I quickly stacked them on top of each other to make room. He moved the basket. "Thanks."

"Not done yet," he said. He brought another arrangement, this time in a metal bowl. Then another one in a large vase. By the time he was through, my office looked like a funeral parlor. And I couldn't see out my window.

Declan pulled a card off one of the arrangements and

read, "'We know your sister is out there somewhere and we're praying for her.'" He started to smile, then saw my sour expression and pulled a straight face. "Sorry, you're right. This is terrible."

I shook my head.

He smiled. "It's very sweet, and it's very good news for us, so stop being such a..."

"Yes?"

"Just stop."

The press was out in full force this morning, the roped-off area packed so tightly there was no visible space between the bodies. As we passed them on the way to the courtroom, the cameramen almost fell over the rope trying to take my picture.

The courtroom was packed too, but not with friends or family. Nothing of real substance was scheduled to happen today. The people crowding the spectator gallery were just here to see the stars of the show.

We'd drawn Judge Osterman for the trial. He was relatively new to the downtown bench, so I didn't know him. J.D. took himself out of the running because we were personal friends and he didn't want any questions raised in a case this big, but I'd hoped we might get Judge Lavinia Moss. Unfortunately, the presiding judge had felt that since Judge Moss had signed the search warrant, it'd be wiser to give the case to someone else. I'd asked Toni and J.D. what they thought of Osterman, but they hadn't had any information for me either. He was too new.

Judge Osterman had a runner's lean build and a spare, ascetic look, enhanced by his habit of pursing his lips. His blue eyes bulged slightly and he combed his thin hair straight back. Overall, he gave the appearance of someone who was cerebral and maybe a little compulsive. One look at his chambers confirmed it. His desk was immaculate, all books were ordered properly in the bookcases, and all pens and pencils were tucked neatly into a leather holder that matched his desk pad. I saw no family photographs of any kind. Ordinarily I'd assume that was because he hadn't had a chance to fully move in, but in Osterman's case, I had a feeling this *was* fully moved in. I should set him and Dorian up on a date.

When I got to court, he'd already taken the bench.

"Ms. Knight, I'm aware that I came out a few minutes early, but that doesn't excuse you for being ten minutes late."

"I'm very sorry, Your Honor. We had an unexpected...arrival at the office that delayed us. It won't happen again." I wasn't about to tell him we were held up by a bunch of flowers.

"See that it doesn't. And that goes for all of you. I won't hesitate to impose fines. I will not have my staff or the jury waiting for attorneys. Now, speaking of juries, we should set the date for the start of jury selection. Tricia, what's the sixty-day date?"

Terry moved quickly to the lectern. "Excuse me, Your Honor, but the defense is requesting a start date within the next three weeks."

"Ms. Fisk, this is a life without parole case. There is a great deal of evidence, based on what I've seen thus far, and the juror questionnaires will take at least a week to read. Are you sure you can be ready in so short a time?"

"Absolutely, Your Honor."

"People?" he asked.

Damn her. It's always easier for the defense to give an early start date, because they don't have to go first, and they don't have to present any evidence at all. I would've preferred a little lead time, if only to make sure there was nothing more that could be done, but that was a luxury I'd have to forgo.

"We can do it, Your Honor. But we're still testing evidence that was seized from the houses and cars of Mr. Averly and Mr. Powers, and we won't have all our results in before trial starts. So as long as the defense is willing to go without having all the results, I'm fine with it."

"She's right, Ms. Fisk," the judge said. "You won't be heard to complain about not having enough time to retest or prepare for evidence that comes in during the trial if you insist on going that soon."

"Understood," Terry said.

"And, Your Honor, the People have filed a discovery request on the defense," I said. "We haven't received anything as of today."

"Defense?" the judge asked. "You have an obligation to turn over your witness list and any evidence you intend to introduce."

Terry stepped away and gave Wagmeister the lectern. "We're working on it, Your Honor," Wagmeister said. "As of this moment, we don't know who our witnesses will be and there is no evidence to turn over."

Defense 101. They get around the rule that requires them to turn over a witness list by not making one, and they avoid turning over witness statements by never putting anything in writing. So much for reciprocal discovery.

Terry moved back to the lectern. "I'd like to be heard on another matter."

The judge nodded. "Proceed."

"I'm not asking for a gag order, but I do think it's inappropriate for the prosecution to be telling their life stories to tabloid magazines to garner sympathy with the public, and, of course, the jury pool."

It was a sleazy low blow. But if it had to be done at all, it should be in chambers, not out in open court, where the press could eat it up.

I should've kept my cool, but I was too furious. "That is absolutely outrageous, Your Honor! No one on the prosecution side has spoken to any tabloid reporter. Nor would any of us tell personal stories of any kind to any-one, for any reason!"

Terry squared her shoulders and jutted her chin out. "I wonder what Andrew Chatham would say to that?"

"Enough," the judge declared. "I will not have ex-changes between the lawyers like this. Ms. Fisk, if any prosecutor makes comments about the case or any of the lawyers, you have reason to bring it to my attention. But I will not waste court time listening to complaints about the publication of someone's life story. If Ms. Knight saw fit to share that with a reporter, it will be her prob-lem to deal with. Not mine." The judge fixed each of us with a stern glare. "Now, do we have any *legal* business to address?"

We both said there was nothing further. The judge set a pretrial date to discuss jury questionnaires and set the trial date three weeks out.

I said nothing until Declan and I were back in my of-fice with the door closed.

"That friggin' sleaze!" I said as I swatted a flower out of the way and sat down. "And that nasty little shit Chatham!"

"You said he didn't write the article about you, though."

"His name wasn't on it, but he must've told Terry he 'talked' to me—"

"But all you said was 'No comment.'"

"He didn't have to tell her that—"

A knock on the door interrupted my flow.

"Rachel? You need to come out here."

It was Melia. I nodded to Declan and he opened the door.

"What is it, Melia?"

"You need to see this." She gestured for us to follow and ran back down the hall toward Eric's office.

She turned on the television. "I recorded it," Melia said. She replayed the footage for us.

Terry was standing on the courthouse steps, encircled by reporters. "Of course the prosecution leaked that story to the *Inquisitor*. They know the public thinks they have no case, so they're trying to win everyone over. This is a completely transparent ploy."

A reporter asked excitedly, "Then you think she made the story up? That it's all a lie?"

"No. But putting out a story like this only shows that Rachel Knight's desperate, and she'll stop at nothing to win this case."

"Are you going to ask that Ms. Knight be recused?" said another reporter.

"I don't want to waste the time. Mr. Powers is anxious for his day in court. He's an innocent victim of an unscrupulous frame-up, and we are going to prove it!"

The news cut away to a health insurance commercial and Melia turned off the television. "That's all there was," she said.

It was enough.

60

The moment my office door swung closed, Declan exploded. "That woman is a classless, lying menace! Just because *she'd* sell stories to the tabs, she thinks everyone else is as tacky as she is. We've got to call a press conference. We've got to tell them it's not true—"

"No." I was just as steamed as he was, but I had experience with this kind of trash talk and knew better. "That's just what she wants. The minute we answer this garbage, we give her exactly what she's looking for: a sideshow that discredits the prosecution and deflects attention from her guilty client."

"But won't Andrew Chatham back you?"

"Who knows? And even if he did, it'll just look like he's protecting his source: me."

Bright spots lit up Declan's cheeks as he set his jaw. "I want to beat the crap out of her." He looked at me with consternation. "I don't know how you can be so calm about this, Rachel." He sat down heavily and stared at the floor.

I smiled. "Truth? The first few times I got knocked

around by the defense, it made me insane. Matter of fact, I once got so mad at a defense attorney, I offered to dismiss the case against his client if *he'd* do the time."

"Back when you were a baby DA in Misdemeanors, right?"

"Try three years ago on a double homicide."

Declan shook his head and we both laughed.

My cell phone played "Killer Joe." "Bailey's heard the news," I told Declan.

"Frame-up?" she demanded. "Why the hell would we give a rat's ass about this friggin' clown?"

"In case you didn't notice, Terry said a lot of other ridiculously stupid—"

"That garbage about you selling your story—people who're dumb enough to buy that line aren't going to make it on the jury anyhow. But this noise about a frame-up—"

"What makes you so sure she's pointing the finger at us? Remember how many times we heard Russell's people say that everyone in the industry could be a suspect? They've got practically a whole city's worth of straw men they can prop up."

Bailey was silent for a moment. "It's pretty hard to believe that a pissed-off actor would murder a director's kid and her boyfriend just to frame the manager."

"Cops would make more sense…" Who else would've had the ability to plant blood and prints? Still, I had a feeling Terry wasn't aiming at LAPD. "We'll hash this out later. One thing's for sure, I'm going to hammer them hard about discovery. I'm not buying that they don't have anything yet. They've got to have witnesses lined up if they're going to prove Ian was framed."

"You'd think," Bailey said.

"You have time to come over? I'm going to put together the jury questionnaire and we should talk about who we want."

Most prosecutors don't consult their investigating officers about pure trial work like jury selection, but most prosecutors don't have someone as smart and experienced as Bailey.

"Give me half an hour. I've got to return a couple of calls, one of 'em to our witness on maternity leave."

"Good enough. I'll get us lunch."

Declan and I got down to work on the questionnaire. Not all lawyers are fans of juror questionnaires. And I don't think they should replace the gut feeling you get when you actually talk to jurors, see their body language, their reactions in the moment. But used correctly, the questionnaire can help us weed out the liars. That's critical in big cases, because the more high profile the case, the more we risk getting groupies who're in love with the defendant, or the spotlight, or who want to write a book—or all of the above. After half an hour, we took a break to get sandwiches and chips from the snack bar. When we got back, Bailey had pushed a flower arrangement to the side and was leaning back with her feet up on the table next to the window.

I threw her a pastrami sub and a bag of potato chips and dropped mine and Declan's on the desk.

"In general we want people who aren't impressed with celebrity," I said. "So no tabloid readers—"

"Get a list of Melia's friends. That ought to put a dent in the jury pool," Declan joked.

"And since Hayley and Brian were just kids, I'd say we like women more than men," Bailey said.

Her words hit me between the eyes. "You know, this is the first time in maybe a week that I've heard anyone mention the names Hayley and Brian," I said. Bailey nodded grimly and Declan looked pained. Too many stupid lawyer tricks and not enough time spent remembering what's really important. I'd make sure it didn't happen again.

"Old or young?" Declan asked.

"That's a tossup," Bailey said. "Young jurors might identify with the victims, but older ones will be less likely to identify with Mr. High Life Powers and his trophy babe."

"This all started with Brian and Hayley staging a kidnapping to extort money out of her father," I said. "That's more likely to turn off our usual law-and-order types, who are generally older." Even if only subconsciously, older or more conservative jurors might wind up feeling like Brian and Hayley had brought it on themselves. "Younger jurors might be a little less judgmental about it."

"Any exceptions you guys can see to our general preference for educated professionals and people with jobs?"

As a rule, the prosecution wants smart jurors—the smarter the better. And people who hold down jobs tend to feel more civically responsible than those who don't. All of these stereotypes are generalizations, of course, but we get only a few minutes with each juror, so we have to rely on them to some degree. After all, clichés are clichés because they're usually true, and jury selection is always, at bottom, a crapshoot. We just play the odds.

By three o'clock we'd settled on our prototypical best juror: female, professional, and someone who'd turn a skeptical eye on the defense conspiracy theory—which prompted Bailey to say, "God help us, we're looking for Rachel Knight."

"God forbid," Declan said with a smile. "We'd start late every single morning."

I gave him a mock glare. "What a card. I could laugh for...seconds."

After Bailey left, Declan and I finished up the questionnaire on our own. He offered to drive me home, but I wanted to walk. I needed the air and the exercise. At seven o'clock it was still fairly light outside, but the air was a little cooler and it felt good to stretch my legs. As I reached Pershing Square, I noticed a film crew was setting up for a shoot. I was passing by, looking at the area they'd roped off for the scene, when I heard someone say, "Hey, isn't that the prosecutor bitch?" A young white guy with blonde dreadlocks who was unloading lights from one of the equipment trucks craned his neck to look at me and replied, "Sure is. Hey, Ms. Prosecutor! What're you gonna do when you lose? Maybe work a food truck?" That inspired a heavyset girl in Doc Martens and cutoffs. "Say, 'ho! Whyn't you get on up here so I can show you what we think of your bullshit case—"

Shocked and a little worried, I started to back away, when a booming voice behind me cut her off. "Yo, Buckwheat, you want to talk about showing something? Get on up over here!" The girl muttered under her breath and turned away. "Yeah, I thought so," said the voice I now recognized as Drew's. "Come on, Rache, you've earned a martini on the house." He put a protective arm around me and steered me past the crew and in through the back door of the Biltmore.

"I wouldn't mind waiting if you want to go back there and 'show' her, uh...something," I said. "I can promise you no charges will be filed."

Drew smiled. "Finally, I find a perk in being friends with a prosecutor."

61

I had a martini and some welcome laughs with Drew. When I got back to my room, I saw that I had a voice mail message on my cell. The crisp tones of Andrew Chatham, my supposed tabloid co-conspirator, greeted me. "Rachel, I'm so very sorry about what Ms. Fisk said. I wanted you to know that I never told her I'd spoken to you. I do admit that I have spoken to her, and I imagine that's why she took a shot in the dark and falsely accused you that way. If there's anything I can do to clear up this mess, I'll gladly do so."

Yeah, I just bet you will. No, *gracias.*

I poured myself a glass of pinot grigio and was lying back on the couch with the remote when my cell phone played "Janie's Got a Gun," Graden's ringtone—in honor of his getting me my gun permit. I brought him up to speed but didn't mention my encounter with the film crew. On calmer reflection, I realized they probably hadn't intended to do me any physical harm. The only real danger lay in the possibility that someone had shot footage of my retreating derriere.

"Your turn," I said. "What's new?"

"I've made some progress on those reports Lilah talked about. They appear to be legit—"

Lilah, the murderous sociopath who'd sent me reports on my sister, Romy. "Why didn't anyone pick up on them before?"

"A couple of reasons. Number one reason, because I wasn't the investigating officer on the case, and number two, because the reports were from different jurisdictions, both of which were tiny and not computerized until very recently; and neither of the jurisdictions was where Romy was taken."

They hadn't realized the significance of what they'd seen. "Of course."

"So I'd say so far, so good. If our kidnapper kept Romy alive for six months, it's a lot less likely that he…"

"It's okay, you can say it: that he killed her. I've been living with the possibility that he killed her for over twenty years, I can certainly handle hearing that he might not have."

"You have the DA investigators trying to find Lilah, right?"

The DA investigators had wound up working that case with me, and in the course of the investigation, Lilah's accomplice, Chase Erling, had killed their beloved team leader. So when Lilah ran, they'd asked to take over the search for her. No one would have thought of refusing, even though she was technically an LAPD suspect.

"Yeah," I answered. "Why?"

"Just making sure. So when do you start trial?"

"We hand out questionnaires to the jury pool in a few days and voir dire starts next week."

"That's fast."

"Yeah, I've been jammed before, but never like this."

Just talking about it made my stomach hurt. After we hung up, I took a hot shower, got into bed, and watched rich housewives scream about one of them getting too drunk and another one hitting on someone's husband. It made me feel better about not being rich…or married. I was asleep within minutes.

The jury questionnaire was forty-five pages long and we had over two hundred of them. I always grade each juror on a scale of one to five, with five being best, and I flag the answers that need follow-up. It's a backbreaker of a process, but it really gets me on top of what I've got in that jury pool. I had a second copy made for Declan so he could review them all and make his own assessments. I spent the week going through each and every question-naire, page by page, and sometimes more than once to make sure I didn't miss anything.

It was a task that had me alternating between relief and misery. Mostly misery. There were some real gems—smart, well read, and solid. But there was a de-pressingly high number of defense groupies. Not that they directly admitted it. Their bias—and lack of candor—lay between the lines. A municipal bus driver who admitted in the first pages of the questionnaire that he watched every news program from five o'clock till ten o'clock every night, in later pages insisted he'd heard nothing about the case. He also said he knew he could be fair, but admitted he'd heard that Ian Powers had been framed and thought it was possible. Another potential juror turned out to have been under investigation for a string of arsons in Torrance; he said he wouldn't hold the unfair suspicion against the prosecution. I told myself that I was being unduly critical, but it felt like for every solid juror, there were ten rejects.

I wanted to believe it would all change when the jury saw the evidence, but I knew better. You can't make a jury buy logic. I fought to keep my spirits up in the days leading to the trial, but the truth was, my optimism was losing the battle against a growing dread.

Too soon, the day for voir dire arrived. I dressed in one of my "believe me" suits and left myself plenty of time to get to the office and do hair and makeup repair, as per my lessons from Toni. I'd gone back to hoofing it to and from the office. I needed the exercise, and the danger of being chased by reporters had lessened considerably, thanks to Terry's penchant for giving daily interviews on the courthouse steps. The press now stuck close to the building, where they could be sure of getting their sound bites.

Even from two blocks away, I could see the antennae of the satellite trucks that now permanently surrounded the courthouse. The sight irritated me all over again. I'd wanted Judge Osterman to seal the transcripts of jury selection, so the jurors would feel safe enough to be candid, but he'd refused. "The right to a public trial means the whole trial." The press wouldn't physically be in the courtroom because there wasn't room for them. But they'd be monitoring and reporting every word uttered in court—other than jurors' names—in a separate room that was wired for sound.

Fortunately, I now had a key to the freight elevator, so I made it up to the eighteenth floor in blissful privacy. As I passed Eric's office on the way to my own, I heard the television playing what sounded like a crowd at a rock concert. When I leaned in, I saw that Melia was watching the coverage. Curious, I stepped in to get a look. A move I immediately regretted.

The low wall that fronted the length of the courthouse building was now a shelf for vendors hawking everything from T-shirts to teacups, all emblazoned with faces—of me, of Terry, of Don, and of Ian. People were marching back and forth, carrying signs that read TEAM TERRY and TEAM RACHEL.

"What about Team Hayley and Team Brian?" I fumed.

Melia gave me a mournful look. "I know, it's terrible."

Not so terrible it made her turn the damn thing off, though.

I'd felt pretty well dressed in the navy suit with the thin silver pinstripes that I'd found on sale at Bloomingdale's. Until I saw Declan. His was a darker navy that looked like it had been made for him. There's just no substitute for bespoke.

Now that jurors would be walking the hallways, the judge had ordered the reporters to either stay in the sound-wired room or go outside. The only camera allowed inside was the one mounted on the wall above the jury, which would ensure that no photographs of the jurors would be taken. And it wouldn't be activated until after jury selection was finished.

When we walked up the courtroom aisle, I saw that

Russell was once again firmly ensconced on the defense side of the courtroom and Raynie was sitting in neutral territory, the back row of the middle section. As we set up at counsel table, I stole glances at the defense side. Terry was in a beige dress with a pleated skirt. No doubt trying for the soft, feminine touch. That would work until she opened her mouth. Don wore the standard dark suit. No fewer than six law clerks, and all wore more expensive suits than mine.

The lockup door opened and Ian sauntered out as though he were walking into an A-list party. He had a big smile and wave for girlfriend Sacha, and a smile and a nod for all his loyal acolytes, which included Russell. Five minutes later, the judge took the bench. He surveyed the courtroom with a frown and spoke to the bailiff, Deputy Jimmy Tragan. "I'll need all family members to sit in the section on the far right, away from the jurors."

The bailiff turned to face the gallery and gave them Judge Osterman's edict. Raynie reluctantly moved to the designated area, but as far away from Russell as she could get. I took that as a good sign. Then again, I might just have been desperate for a positive omen.

With the family and friends safely cloistered, the jury commissioner's emissary opened the door and our group of two hundred prospective jurors began to file in. I watched them fill the benches, looking for early signs of a bad attitude or an overly excited glance at Ian Powers. Not one nuance could be overlooked. Among this group were the twelve people who'd decide whether Brian and Hayley's killer would be brought to justice.

62

"You've all been assigned numbers and that's what we'll use today instead of your names," Judge Osterman said. "We do this to protect your privacy. My clerk, Tricia Monahan, will call out sixteen of you by your numbers, so please look at your number while she reads them. If she calls your number, kindly move up and take a seat in the jury box, starting with the upper-left corner as you face it. Trish?"

Tricia stood, pushed her glasses up her small freckled nose, and began. I pulled out their questionnaires as Tricia called the numbers. When I saw that the electronic engineer from Silicon Valley was in the first batch, I turned my back to the jury and hissed, "Damn it."

As a general rule, engineers are good prosecution jurors. Smart, logical, and dispassionate, they see through defense games and have no problem convicting. This one in particular was even better because he had sat on a murder case before—and I would bet he'd been the foreman. He was perfect.

And he was toast. Each side got twenty peremptory

challenges in this case—meaning challenges we could use without having to show actual bias or inability to serve. The trick in jury selection is in how and when you use these precious challenges.

So if my engineer had come up later in the draw, after the defense had used most of their peremptories, there was at least a chance they'd have to accept him over someone who looked even worse—like a retired cop. But now, with all twenty challenges at their disposal, they wouldn't hesitate to boot him.

"Counsel, while they're being seated, I've prepared a full randomized list of the jurors for you," the judge said. "Jimmy, would you mind handing these out?"

The randomized list was computer-generated, showing the order in which all jurors would be called up to the box. Back in the old days, the clerks used a Bingo cage and drew name cards out one by one. Nowadays, with jury pools of two and three hundred, a computer took all the names with their associated numbers and created a randomized list that showed the order in which they'd be called.

I quickly reviewed the list and flipped through some of the questionnaires to see what we were getting in this first batch and what was coming up in the next groups. What I saw put a lump the size of a grapefruit in my stomach. All of our best jurors, my "fives," were in the first batch. This meant the defense would have enough peremptory challenges to get rid of all of them. I'd be able to save up my peremptories by "passing" and accepting the jury, but the minute the next batches were called, I'd have to start using them—most of them were "ones" and "twos"—our worst. And the next batch after that...I pulled out the questionnaires and looked at the grades...just as bad. I looked through the last batch. They were better, a few "threes" and "fours," but it wouldn't matter—we'd never get to them. I'd run out of challenges and be forced to accept the jury before they could get called.

It's well known that the case is won or lost in jury selection. What's less well known is that something as simple as jurors' placement on a randomized list can mean you'll never get a shot at the ones you need. Luck of the draw plays a much bigger role in our system of justice than anyone cares to know.

While the judge read some of the basic instructions that explained their duties as jurors, Declan and I exchanged notes about which jurors had to go.

Declan thought we had to bounce the black single mother of two whose brother was in prison for armed robbery and whose father had been murdered in a drive-by shooting. Next up was a librarian who'd never married or had children and so wasn't our ideal profile—we preferred women with children—but she was relatively intelligent and well read. It wasn't worth wasting a peremptory on her, and I'd bet the defense wouldn't either. An older black man would normally have been my ideal juror. Conservative, articulate, and strong minded. But he'd said he was no fan of "this younger generation" and their "questionable values." I had two kids who'd schemed to extort a million dollars. Not a love match.

Judge Osterman had said that he'd do most of the questioning and give each side half an hour for the first round, then ten minutes for each successive round. He started by running each juror through the standard list of questions that was posted on a bulletin board near the jury box: marital status, children, employment and spouse or significant other's employment, prior contacts with law enforcement or the judicial system, any past or current situation that might affect their ability to be fair, and so on. Some of them had been covered in the questionnaire, so the questioning went quickly.

I watched as each juror answered, and made notes on tone of voice, attitude, and body language. "And now, I'm going to let the lawyers ask you some questions," the judge said. "People?"

I smiled in what I hoped was a disarming way and thanked them for being there, as though they'd had a choice in the matter. I asked them about the prosecution's problem points. Motive: We didn't have to prove it. What did they think about that rule? If they believed the evidence proved someone was guilty but they didn't understand why that person did it, could they still convict? I watched carefully as they answered. Only one seemed to be uncomfortable with the rule. A young mom, and the only obvious Ian-lover in the batch, who was addicted to the E! channel. It figured.

Then I asked, "If you heard that the victims had staged a phony kidnapping, would that make you believe the victims got what they deserved?" It wasn't something any juror would want to admit to thinking, and it certainly wasn't a *legal* reason to acquit Powers, but it was the kind of emotional issue that could make jurors look for a reason to acquit—biases that no one wants to own up to even privately, let alone out loud. The only way to handle hidden bias is to pull it out into the open. That way, there's at least a chance someone in the jury room will remind the others that we talked about this in voir dire.

I got everyone to say they agreed that it would be wrong to ignore evidence of guilt just because the victims did something they didn't approve of and—as I frankly admitted to the jurors—that the victims shouldn't have done.

Then I went through the standard discussion of reasonable doubt and circumstantial evidence. Everyone nodded as though they understood. I knew many of them didn't. That's why I always end the discussion with a hypothetical to illustrate the concepts in simpler terms. "You understand reasonable doubt is a doubt founded in reason. Not just something you might imagine." I turned to the librarian. "For example, Juror Number One-oh-eight, see that baseball on the bailiff's desk?"

The librarian glanced over at his desk and quietly answered, "Yes."

"If you saw the bailiff throw that baseball at Tricia's desk and heard glass breaking, and then you walked over and saw that the vase on her desk was broken, you'd know beyond a reasonable doubt that Jimmy had broken it, wouldn't you?"

"Well...if that's the only thing on her desk that was broken...yes."

"Exactly right. Now, it's *possible* that in the very same moment Jimmy threw the ball, Tricia's vase fell apart on its own, or that Tricia had taken out a hammer and smashed the vase herself, but would that be *reasonable?*"

The librarian blinked a few times. "Well...no, it wouldn't. At least, not in my opinion."

"So would you agree that in my example, there is no reasonable doubt that Jimmy broke the vase when he threw the baseball at Tricia's desk?"

"Yes."

I watched the others with quick glances during this exchange to see how they reacted. The older black man was looking impatient, and gave me a "duh, no shit" look. The young mother who was an Ian groupie looked perplexed—another great reason to bounce her. But the black single mother was watching me with a little smile on her face. She got it. The electronic engineer was sitting back in his chair with the forbearing look of one who'd been through the drill. Most of the others seemed interested. Like I said, a great group. It'd break my heart when the defense gave them the boot. The best I could do at this point was ask them lots of questions so I could use their answers to teach the rest of the jurors in the pool.

I turned to the young rocker with the semi-Mohawk; from his questionnaire I knew he was a stocker at Ralph's Grocery Store. I didn't intend to waste a peremptory challenge on him, but I didn't figure him to be a great pick for our side. After all, we were "The Man." But when I asked him if, knowing that Hayley and Brian had staged the kidnapping, he'd be unable to convict, he half snorted and said, "You kidding? No. Smoke him."

I had to swallow to keep from laughing out loud. Terry, of course, wasn't finding this so funny. Bye-bye, rock star. He wasn't the only good surprise: most of the others turned out to be even better than I'd expected too.

And when the defense got done, not a single one of

them would remain. By the time I'd finished my questioning, I was more depressed than before.

"Defense, you may question the jury."

Terry came out swinging—and showed me exactly what I was up against. With her very first question, I found out that even my best batch of jurors was vulnerable to the defense party line.

"Juror Number Seventy-four, do you believe that sometimes innocent people can be framed?"

The juror, a divorced father of three employed by the Department of Water and Power who looked like a beer-drinking football fan, responded, "Uh...sure."

"And have you heard of cases where innocent men served as much as thirty years in prison before the courts agreed that they'd been wrongly convicted?"

He nodded seriously. "Yeah."

I noticed she conveniently forgot to mention that those men had been freed by DNA evidence—our strongest proof of guilt in this case. I'd make sure to point that out when I stood up again.

Terry stretched the question out to the rest of the panel, and every single one of them said they'd seen such cases in the news.

"How many of you have heard about the Rampart Division of LAPD planting drugs and lying to justify arrests?"

I looked at Judge Osterman to gauge whether he'd sustain an objection. He glanced at me but looked back at Terry—a sign I shouldn't waste my breath. I sat tight and did my best to look serene.

About six of the jurors raised their hands, and I heard rustling behind me that said many in the audience would've raised theirs too.

"Would you agree that the Rampart Division's actions are an example of a conspiracy?"

The jurors answered in unison, "Yes."

Where the hell was she going with this police conspiracy junk? Why on earth would the cops want to frame Ian Powers? I was glad Bailey wasn't here to listen to this; she'd be ready to pull out her gun. Bailey and I were going to have to do some more digging to try to find out whether there was some bad blood between Ian Powers and the LAPD we hadn't heard about yet.

"Now, you all agree, I'm sure, that it's a terrible thing for an innocent man to be convicted?" Terry asked.

Firm agreements all around, "Absolutely" and "No question" and "Of course."

"And you'd never want to be in the position of believing evidence that'd been trumped up to frame an innocent man, would you?"

Again, there were headshakes all around and murmured verbal responses of "No" and "Never." Only my electronic engineer seemed immune. He pressed his lips together and watched Terry with a stony expression.

Terry moved on to the more personal issues. "You all know by now that my client, Ian Powers, is a very important figure in the film and television industry, and that he's a wealthy man."

Nods and murmurs of "Yes" throughout the jury box.

"Juror Number Twenty-eight, are you going to hold that against him?"

That, at least, was a fair question. The juror, a slight Hispanic woman who'd worked for the California Highway Patrol as a dispatcher but was now unemployed, shook her head vigorously and frowned. "No."

Declan had given this juror a thumbs-up, but I'd been less impressed. Civilian employees of police departments aren't necessarily big fans of law enforcement, and the fact that she was no longer working for the CHP worried me. She'd said she left because she wanted to go back to school. I wasn't sure I believed her. Now, watching her practically mugging for Terry, I knew this juror was trouble.

"And just to follow up with you, Juror Twenty-eight, have you ever heard of an innocent person being framed?"

Juror twenty-eight started to nod, then darted a glance at me. She cut short her nod and asked, "What do you mean by 'framed'? That someone made him look guilty? Or put him in a situation where he'd do something wrong?"

Pretty smart question, but her body language and attitude told me she'd asked that question to curry favor with me. She wanted on this jury way too much.

Terry finished with her and moved on to more mundane subjects like reasonable doubt. I snuck a look at Wagmeister and Ian. They were huddled together as though they were old fraternity buddies—the upper-one-percent fraternity. Ian was writing copious notes to Wagmeister, who nodded as he read them and patted Ian on the back. Wagmeister seemed to have slipped into the role of second fiddle rather easily, which was surprising. He was someone who'd always seemed to enjoy the limelight. On the other hand, if Ian had decided he preferred Terry to be lead counsel and he was still paying the freight, Wagmeister had no choice but to go along or get off the case.

I turned back to the jury and firmed up my decisions about who to kick first, then wrote down those juror numbers and showed Declan. Declan raised his eyebrows at my decision to kick the former CHP dispatcher.

Finally, Terry thanked the jury and sat down.

"The first peremptory is with the People," Judge Osterman said.

I stood. "The People would like to thank and excuse juror number twenty-eight."

The former CHP dispatcher favored me with a dirty look on her way out of the jury box.

"Defense?"

Terry stood. "The defense would ask the court to thank and excuse juror number sixteen."

There went my electronic engineer.

One by one, I watched the best of the pool walk out the door as the defense used one challenge after another to get rid of them. I passed as often as I dared, to save up my challenges for the coming groups, but it hardly mattered. I'd just be trading a stomachache for a headache, because they were all equally bad. And so it went that day and the next.

At mid-afternoon on Friday the judge turned to face the jury. "I know this is the least fun part of the trial for you, so for your sakes, I'm going to let you go early today and get started on your weekend." The jurors gave him a hearty thanks, which made Judge Osterman smile. The kiss-ass.

63

On Monday, as we'd been doing all along, Declan and I ate lunch in my office. I unwrapped my vegetarian pita sandwich and salted it liberally. I know salt is bad for me. But it was a lot better than a big belt of scotch—which was what I really wanted. "I can't believe the way all the jurors are biting whenever she throws that conspiracy hook into the water."

Declan nodded glumly. "And whenever she talks about the innocent guys who get nailed—"

"I've got to keep pushing back and reminding them that those guys eventually got sprung by DNA, get 'em to say they believe in it—"

"That'll help, but when you look at what we've got coming…"

That was the most painful truth of all. Our next batch of jurors included a guy who'd been busted for DUI twice and believed the cops had rigged the blood test (both times!); a woman who'd divorced her cheating husband (a former sheriff's deputy) and was now taking him to court for unpaid child support; an older man whose daughter was unfairly busted for possession of cocaine (that really belonged to her roommate); and a university professor whose best friend had been (unjustly) accused of misappropriating funds from his accounting firm and was now facing criminal charges. And it went downhill from there. The group after that one included a woman whose son was on death row and a father whose daughter had stolen the family business right out from under him—and who passionately hated everyone under the age of seventy.

Naturally, all had claimed in their questionnaires that they could be fair.

"Let's talk about the good ones that're still in our clutches. We've got the librarian, the soccer mom from cop country—"

"Cop country?" Declan asked.

"Simi Valley. Bedroom community where lots of law enforcement live. Very good for us, and the defense might like her too, because she reads *People* magazine and watches *Celebrity Ghost Stories,* so she seems like a Hollywood groupie—"

"I watch *Celebrity Ghost Stories.*"

I eyed him with mock reproach.

"It's not appointment viewing or anything, but it's kind of interesting…"

"Anyhow, I'd guess Hollywood nonsense is a fun distraction for her, not the sun in her universe. I think she'll ride with us. We've also got the single mom with the violent history—"

"You want to keep her?"

"Absolutely. She's cool and smart and she won't buy anyone's garbage. And I'm betting the defense doesn't get who she is, so they'll leave her on. Trust me on this one. What about that retired schoolteacher who taught English?"

"Not sure. I get a creepy vibe from him," Declan said.

"As in pedophile creepy?"

"I don't know." Declan finished his sandwich and wiped his mouth with the paper napkin. "But whatever. Do pedophiles tend to convict?"

I almost spit my soda across the room. "You're twisted, Declan. Yet another thing I like about you."

Back in the courtroom, the afternoon session flew. I hammered away on the virtues of DNA and did my best to find something good in what looked like a relentlessly bad batch.

By four thirty the next day, I had at least seven jurors I needed to kick and only two peremptory challenges left. This was the true heart-pounder, when I had to make the choice between the lesser of the evils. There was the owner of a paycheck advance business (the kind who prey on the poor, charging twenty percent interest for a loan against forthcoming paychecks) who openly admitted he wanted to write a book about the trial; a left-wing blogger who called me a "functionary of the male-dominated establishment" (personally, I appreciated her point of view, but legally, she had to go—and did I mention she hated cops?); and the pièce de résistance: a waiter (aka out-of-work actor) who was *very* familiar with the work of the genius Russell Antonovich and his partner, the "brilliant Ian Powers." The other four were equally nightmarish.

I asked for a five-minute break to take aim at our final round of challenges and huddled with Declan in a corner of the courtroom.

"I think that guy in the back row, the one whose mom is so sick, has got to go," Declan said. "Did you see how pissed off he was when Terry got into her spiel about the innocent men wrongly convicted? I thought he was going to come out of his seat."

"Number eighty-nine, yeah." An anesthesiologist had botched a routine hip replacement operation that left the prospective juror's mother a vegetable, albeit one who'd probably get to go home, where doctors opined she'd survive for many years. Because he'd signed a binding arbitration agreement, the most he could recover was $250,000—which he probably wouldn't get, because his mother was elderly. I had an idea that whatever he got wouldn't come close to covering the costs of in-home care. In a word, the issue of innocent people being mowed down by the machine was very real to him. I tried to find a bright side. "He's got a bachelor's degree. There's a chance our evidence could get him to see past his own life. Besides, the paycheck loan guy looks way too impressed with Powers. He doesn't care what's true, he just wants a book deal."

Declan shrugged. It was a choice between death by hanging or by poisoning. There weren't many good options here. I booted paycheck loan guy and the "waiter" and prayed I was wrong about the rest. Like it or not, by five thirty we were done.

"Congratulations, we have our jury," Judge Osterman said. "Ladies and gentlemen, would you please stand and raise your right hand."

Exhausted, I watched as Judge Osterman swore them in, wondering if I'd already made the fatal mistake that would set a murderer free.

64

I called Bailey to tell her we had our jury. "And it ain't pretty." I'd been filling her in all along, giving her the highlights—or rather the lowlights—of each day's proceedings. Bailey was still angry and incredulous about Terry's opening salvo.

"Rampart Division? Has she lost her mind?" Bailey said nothing for a few moments. "So they're definitely going for the conspiracy tack."

"Oh yeah. Terry's definitely going there, and she's taking the jurors with her." I'd told Bailey all about the alarmingly receptive audience Terry had found in our jury pool.

Though Terry had produced nothing to back up her conspiracy claim, the press had run with it as though proof were a foregone conclusion. "The only question," one commentator said, "is whether the prosecution can overcome this incendiary defense. And on that score, most agree, all bets are off."

It was, in large part, hype that was meant to make it a close race. I couldn't afford to get down about it;

opening statements would begin before we knew it. Personally, I never do lengthy openings. I prefer to promise less than I plan to deliver. It gives the unheralded evidence an added zing, and it keeps the defense from claiming we made promises we couldn't keep. I knew the defense wouldn't say much, if anything. They didn't want to tip their hand.

Over the next few days Bailey and I put in the finishing touches. Our most important being the ordering of our witness list. I usually like to call a victim's friend or family member first. It humanizes my victim—always a challenge in a murder case, since the victim can never appear, while the defendant, all cleaned up and pretty, is ever-present. And, if well coached, crying on cue. But I wouldn't be able to do it this time. Not with Russell dead set against me and Raynie still ambivalent. The night before opening arguments, I was still unsure about who to put on first. Bailey read my thoughts.

"We could start with Mackenzie," she said.

"But she's awfully young. We don't know how she'll bear up. And I don't know that I want to open our case by admitting our victims were extorting Russell. We'll have to get there eventually, but I'd like to at least start strong, put this case on solid ground before I get into problem areas. How's Raynie sounding?"

"I only really talk to her about scheduling, but from what I can tell, she's still pretty wishy-washy."

I'd never before been in the position of having the victim's family at odds with us in a murder case. "Maybe once Raynie and Russell see it all put together, they'll come around."

Bailey gave me a skeptical look. I knew she was right,

hard as it was to swallow. "Then I'll start with the physical evidence.

"How about Dorian?" Bailey suggested.

It made sense to start with our criminalist. She collected nearly all of the evidence, so I'd need her testimony before I could call the fingerprint and blood analysts—plus, she was a strong witness. But this time, since I couldn't call any friends or family for a while, I had a different plan of attack.

"Is Dr. Vendi good to go for tomorrow?"

"Yep. And I've got all her photos on disc."

We don't get to pick our coroners. It's always luck of the draw, and this time, we'd lucked out. Dr. Graciela Vendi was one of those rare pathologists who did fantastic work *and* knew how to talk to a jury. Her testimony would bring home the brutality of the attacks on Hayley and Brian in vivid detail. The defense could blab all they wanted about unnamed dark forces. Here was reality—two young people hideously slaughtered on a lonely mountain. Hopefully it would sober the jury up, get their minds right.

Bailey added, "Your guy Declan checked out the discs, said they looked good. I have to say, I really like that kid."

"Me too. But that's a total accident. Vanderputz only put Declan on so he could suck up to his Hollywood contributors—"

"And spy for him."

"Yeah. Didn't quite work out the way Vanderputz planned."

We both laughed. I raised a phantom toast in honor of my second chair.

*   *   *

With all the constant stress and worry about the crazy circus this case was turning into, I hadn't been getting much more than four hours of sleep a night, and jury selection and trial preparation had left me feeling like I'd been through a meat grinder. All I wanted to do was put it behind me and go to sleep. I hoped that with a solid eight hours under my belt, I'd wake up feeling better about the twelve select citizens we'd wound up with—or at least be able to pretend I did.

I dragged myself to the gym to work out the kinks and make sure I'd be tired enough to get into bed by ten o'clock. Then I ordered a light dinner—seared ahi tuna and a green salad—and polished off what was left of a bottle of pinot grigio. I'd just gotten into bed when Graden called to wish me luck.

"Thanks, I'll need plenty of it," I said.

"That bad?"

"I can't remember when I've felt worse about my chances this early in the game."

Graden tried to cheer me up by reminding me that anything can happen in trial—and even played back one of my own stories to make the point. "Remember? Your eyewitness fell apart on cross and the defense had a great alibi witness—solid citizen with no priors—who swore the defendant was working with him all day on the day of the murder. Even brought in the time card to prove it—"

"Except the time card showed it was the day *after* the murder." It was one of those great courtroom moments. The memory still made me smile. "I'm not going to get that kind of lucky this time, Gray. Not with Terry Fisk on the case."

We said good night and I took a health magazine—a free sample—to bed. Nothing like reading about gluten-free, fat-free, sugar-free to bore myself to sleep. In less than five minutes, the magazine slipped out of my hands and onto the floor.

The next morning, feeling rested if no less anxious, I pulled on my robe and stepped onto the balcony. I could already feel the heat building. At just seven a.m. My stomach was clenched too tightly for food, so I decided not to force the issue. I was out the door by seven forty-five and in my office by eight fifteen, a snack bar bagel and cream cheese and large coffee in hand.

"You really ought to let me do that," Declan said, nodding at my purchases, as he sat down in front of my desk.

"You're a lawyer, not a gofer."

"They're not mutually exclusive."

"Especially at the big corporate firms." I looked at Declan with curiosity. "I've seen your résumé. *Law Review,* moot court finalist, dean's list. You could've had your pick of white shoe law firms. How'd you wind up here?"

"I interned here when I was in law school and I loved it. After that, I never wanted to be anywhere else."

Maybe that was the problem he had with his father: daddy had more high-profile commercial prospects in mind for his son than the low-paid position of a county prosecutor. I was curious, because the more I got to know Declan, the less I could understand his father being anything but enormously proud to have such a great guy for a son. But being rabid about my own privacy, I couldn't bring myself to encroach on his.

"You've got the DVD for opening?" I asked.

"Right here." He patted his briefcase.

I looked at the clock on the Times Building. It was eight thirty-five. "May as well get down there and set up." Judge Osterman had issued an e-mail to all parties reminding us that tardiness would not be tolerated and sanctions would be imposed for any party not ready to proceed at precisely nine a.m.

Now that jurors would be coming to court, reporters were on orders to take their assigned seats in the courtroom. No loitering or interviewing in the hallways allowed. The judge had reserved two rows of benches for the public, who had to show up and take numbers. As Declan and I headed out of the office, Melia said they'd begun queuing up at five thirty that morning. When we got off the elevator, I saw Jimmy, the bailiff, taking the numbers from the line of lucky winners as he admitted them into the courtroom one by one.

At five minutes to nine the courtroom was packed, not even one square inch of space visible on the benches in the gallery. A loud buzz filled the air as reporters chatted and waved to each other. Raynie was waiting out in the hallway with the rest of the family and friends, at my suggestion. There was no reason for them to suffer through the grisly details of my opening statement. But Russell defiantly sat proud and tall on the "groom's" side with all the rest of the Ian Powers supporters. I hadn't spoken to Russell since the day he'd thrown me off the lot. I'd hoped he'd come around by the time trial started. I put the depressing thought out of my mind and looked through my notes while Declan finished setting up the monitors that would display our photographs to the jury.

Judge Osterman took the bench at nine o'clock on the dot and Jimmy faced the gallery. In a strong, stern voice he announced, "Come to order. Department One Fourteen is now in session. Judge Osterman presiding."

The buzz stopped abruptly and a silent tension spread through the courtroom. Judge Osterman looked down at us. "Both sides ready? Anything we need to take up before we begin?"

We all agreed we were ready to go. "Then let's have the jury."

The twelve chosen jurors and five alternates filed in. My librarian darted a quick glance at the packed gallery, then cast her eyes down nervously as she found her seat. But the black single mom seemed unfazed. She took her time moving through the jury box and relaxed into her chair, then surveyed the courtroom with an amused expression. The young man with the ailing mother moved to his seat quickly, picked up his notebook, and stared straight ahead. Some of the jurors briefly looked my way, but none of them made eye contact. The judge commended them on their promptness, made sure they had no problems or issues to address, and told them now was the time for opening statements. He reread the introductory instructions he'd given at the start of voir dire, "just to refresh your memory," then reminded them that opening statements weren't evidence but only "a brief preview of what each lawyer believes the evidence will show." Then he looked down at me. "Are the People ready to proceed with an opening statement?"

I took a deep cleansing breath that nearly choked in my throat and stood. "Yes, Your Honor."

"You may proceed."

I turned to face the jury.

Let the games begin.

65

I kept my opening simple, taking the jury through the events in chronological order, step by step, as Declan played the DVD of photos that illustrated my points. I started with the fight between Brian's father, Tommy, and Russell over the theft of the screenplay, and noted that four of them looked skeptical. I moved through the kidnapping plot and into the finding of the bodies, deliberately speaking in calm, measured tones—a counterpoint to the graphic pictures they were seeing for the first time. Brian's pale face above a bloody gash of a neck, his throat sliced nearly to the vertebrae, lying supine in his shallow grave on Boney Mountain. Hayley, the visible side of her face partially covered by bloody, disheveled hair, her left eye, half open and staring, her body curled in a fetal position in the trunk of Brian's car.

Knowing the images I'd be using for my opening statement would be horrific, I'd warned the friends and family not to be in court during my opening—all except Russell. He wouldn't take my call. So while Raynie and all of Hayley's friends were absent—Janice hadn't flown out yet and I wasn't sure if she ever would—Russell was, as always, front and center on the defense side of the courtroom. A part of me was glad. Maybe the shock value of the photographs would bring him around. They certainly got the jury's attention.

As the images of Brian and Hayley cycled through on the monitor, the jury's eyes widened. The librarian had to look away, but the black single mom's face hardened, the perfect reaction that showed she was ready to hammer the person who'd done this. I knew the defense let her stay because the group-think was that a minority was more likely to buy into a conspiracy theory. The truth was, she was the best juror I had. At least for these few moments, the jurors were forced to remember that this case was about the slaughter of two innocent young people.

When I began my opening, there was the usual low hum of activity—whispers from the gallery, jurors shifting in their seats, and business being conducted by the clerk. But by the time I'd finished, the courtroom was utterly still—no one in the jury box or even the gallery seemed to be breathing. I took what solace I could from this and thanked the jurors for their time and attention.

The judge turned to the defense. "Ms. Fisk, Mr. Wagmeister, will you be making an opening statement today?"

Wagmeister stood. "We will reserve our statement for the beginning of the defense case. But we caution the jury that what the prosecution has just presented is just a wish list. We will show substantial problems with every aspect of their case—"

This was outrageous, completely improper speechi-fying. Controlling the anger that rushed to the top of my head with supreme effort, I stood up. "Objection, Your Honor. If the defense wishes to give an opening statement—"

"Overruled," the judge said, frowning at me. Wag-meister rolled on, barely missing a beat. This kind of gift didn't happen often and he knew better than to waste a second of it.

"—and that the defense will soon present important, compelling evidence of our client's innocence. I thank you all for your kind attention."

The judge should've stopped Wagmeister's posturing little speech. In fact, he should've smacked Wagmeister for even trying it. A crappy jury *and* a weak judge. Super.

Wagmeister smiled, gave a little bow to the jury, and sat down. Judge Osterman turned to me and said, "Call your first witness."

I stood and faked a confident voice. "The People call Dr. Graciela Vendi."

Bailey escorted her in. At nearly six feet tall, Dr. Vendi was one of the few women who could look down on Bailey, and her mop of curly auburn hair made her seem even taller. She strode up to the witness stand and flashed a warm smile at the jury before turning to face the clerk and raise her right hand.

I took her through her credentials and job description. I know some lawyers like to have their expert witnesses talk directly to the jury when they testify, but I think it looks phony—like they're pretending to have a little fireside chat, or worse, trying to sell them a used car. I also think it can make jurors nervous, like the witness is watching them, gauging their reactions. Which they—hell, we all—are. But bottom line, since I'm the one asking the questions, I think it seems weird to have the witnesses look at anyone else when they're giving the answers.

"Dr. Vendi, did you conduct the autopsies of Hayley Antonovich and Brian Maher?"

"Yes, I did. And I brought my file containing my reports." She gestured to the file she was holding.

"If the defense would like to have another look at these documents before I go any further, I'd be glad to let them do so now." I always make this offer so the defense won't have an excuse to interrupt the examination if the doctor needs to check her reports to refresh her memory.

"Thank you," Wagmeister said. He walked up to the witness stand, greeted Dr. Vendi with an insincere smile, and leafed through the folder. I took the opportunity to glance at the defense table. Ian's sharp designer suit had been replaced with a low-end standard they'd probably found at Sears, and I noticed he'd suddenly developed the need for reading glasses. Seated next to him, so close she was practically in his lap, was a young blonde female law clerk—their idea of Hayley's proxy. They whispered to each other, leaning in close, lips to ears. In short, every trick in the book to make Powers look harmless and "of the people."

Hayley's friends and family, other than Russell, were still in the hallway. I'd advised them to sit this one out, since Vendi's testimony would be even more graphic than my opening statement.

"Mr. Wagmeister, is there anything in that folder you haven't seen?" the judge finally asked.

"No, this is fine." Wagmeister moved back to his side of counsel table.

I waited for the jury to focus on the witness, then I continued. "Dr. Vendi, I'm going to put the photographs you had taken during the autopsy on the monitor. Please refer to those photographs as you describe your findings. I will begin with Hayley Antonovich."

The first photograph flashed up on the monitor, showing Hayley on the coroner's table before she'd been undressed or washed. I heard movement in the gallery and when I glanced over, I saw that Russell was leaving.

Dr. Vendi looked at the photograph briefly. "I always begin with a superficial examination. I noted that there were leaves and soil in her hair and on her clothing, thin scratches that appeared to be from tree or shrub branches on her hands, arms, and legs. And of course, the severed carotid in her neck." Dr. Vendi pointed to the gaping slash across her throat that was the obvious cause of the red stain that soaked the front of Hayley's T-shirt.

"After that superficial examination, what did you do next?"

"I had the clothing removed and the body cleaned."

I signaled Declan to move to the next photograph, a tighter shot of Hayley's upper body. Cleaned, washed, and ghostly white, long blonde hair flowing, she looked angelic—except for the garish red slice bisecting her neck.

"Does this photograph depict the wound you determined to be the cause of death?"

"Yes. You can clearly see where the carotid artery was severed, and what I noted was that it was one long, extremely deep cut. There were none of the hesitation marks that would have indicated either the victim's struggle or some ambivalence on the killer's part. Nor were there any defensive wounds on the victim's hands or arms."

"Did you happen to note any bruising that might have occurred recently, just prior to death?"

"Objection!" Wagmeister stood. "The doctor can't say whether the bruising occurred during the homicide."

"I'll allow the question," the judge ruled. "It will be for the jury to determine what weight to give the answer." He nodded for Dr. Vendi to continue.

"Yes, I found evidence of bruising that appeared very fresh, which would indicate it likely occurred very shortly before death. As you know, we don't bruise after death because there is no blood pressure."

"And where did you find that bruising?"

"On her right arm."

Declan flashed the photograph that showed it.

"You can see the marks here and here." Dr. Vendi pointed to the spots around the circumference of Hayley's delicate upper arm. "They appeared to be consistent with finger marks, with someone grabbing her by the arm."

"Anywhere else?"

"On her left shoulder." Again, Declan put up the photograph. "Here, this bigger bruise on the front of the left shoulder."

"And what does that indicate to you?"

"That after grabbing Hayley by the right arm, the

killer put his left arm around her body and pulled her back."

"And then?"

"And then he or she drew a sharp object, likely a knife, across her neck from left to right."

"What, if anything, did that indicate to you about whether the killer was right- or left-handed?"

"That he or she was right-handed."

I pointedly looked over at Ian, hoping he was writing a note to his little girl prop—showing he was right-handed. But he had his hands in his lap and a serious, concerned expression on his face. I had no doubt that this pose had been choreographed by Terry. Unlike many of her other clients, Ian was smart enough to follow orders.

"The fact that there were no defensive wounds, what does that indicate to you?"

"That the victim had no chance to fight back. Most likely because she was overpowered immediately, probably taken by surprise. I can demonstrate on you, if you like."

I don't always like to do demonstrations because unless you have a relaxed, professional witness who can handle it, and just the right conditions, it can backfire. But Dr. Vendi could be trusted to do a good job of it and the conditions were perfect: Dr. Vendi was roughly Ian's height and I was only an inch or two taller than Hayley. I moved up to the witness stand and faced the jury and Dr. Vendi came down to stand behind me. She wrapped her left arm around my upper body and drew her right hand across my throat. It painted an unusually vivid picture of how Hayley had been murdered. Juror number five, a Pacific Bell repairman on disability, visibly winced. Fantastic.

"How deep was the wound track across Hayley's neck?"

"The depth of the wound track was three and a half inches."

"What does that indicate to you about the manner and means in which the wound was inflicted?"

"To me, it logically indicates that a rather large knife was used, and wielded with considerable force."

"And your conclusion about the cause of death, Dr. Vendi?"

"My conclusion is that Hayley Antonovich died of sharp-force trauma to her neck, which severed the carotid artery."

We moved on to Brian's autopsy. The similarity of his and Hayley's fatal wounds was a critical piece of evidence that indicated the murders were likely committed by the same person. I had Dr. Vendi describe this in some detail while showing the photographs that illustrated her points.

"As you can see, this victim suffered the same long, deep slice to the throat."

"How deep was this wound track?"

"A little deeper than Hayley's. This wound track went nearly to the bone."

"Would it be fair to say that Brian Maher was nearly decapitated?"

"Yes. And once again, I saw evidence of bruising on the left side of the upper arm that indicated Brian Maher was also seized and immobilized from behind in approximately the same manner as Hayley before the carotid was severed."

"Were there any differences in the style of attack?"

"Only one that was notable. There was a puncture wound to the left side of the neck that was the deepest end of the wound and shows where the knife was inserted first. It struck me that because Brian was a male, the killer might have been more concerned about disabling him as quickly as possible, and so stabbed him with great initial force before completing the cut across the throat that severed the carotid."

"Other than that deep puncture wound, did you see any notable differences in the method or manner of the attacks on Hayley and Brian?"

"No. They were remarkably similar."

"One last question: Is it common for a killer using a knife to sustain cuts to his own body in the course of the homicide?"

"Yes, very common. I'd say in at least eighty-five percent of the knife killings I see, the defendant sustains some type of cut to his body, hands, or arms. Other than the obvious fact that the killer is acting in haste and dealing with unpredictable movements by the victim, the killer is going to generate a fair amount of body heat during a knife attack. That will cause the killer to perspire, especially in the hand holding the knife. This will frequently cause the hand to slip up the handle and onto the blade. And if he or she—I say she, by the way, though I very much doubt a 'she' could've done these killings—was clutching the knife for a few minutes before the attack, that also would cause the palm to sweat and thus get slippery."

"If the killer sustained a small cut to his finger, what kind of bleeding might that cause?"

"As anyone who cooks knows, even a very small cut on a finger with a sharp knife can bleed quite profusely. So it's entirely possible that a knife as big and sharp as the one that was used here might have produced an injury that led to substantial bleeding, even if that injury was small."

"And if the killer did sustain a small injury, like a cut to a finger, would you expect that injury to still be visible three weeks later?"

Three weeks: the amount of time that had passed before Ian Powers was arrested.

"Not terribly, no. You might see a faint scar, but that would be about it. Unless it got infected."

"Even if you did see a faint scar on the killer's finger, would you be able to say that it had to have happened during the murders?"

"No. Healing rates vary depending on a number of factors. There would be no way I could be that precise about when the injury was sustained."

"Thank you, Dr. Vendi."

Other than the issue of the killer getting cut himself, there wasn't much reason to go after Dr. Vendi. Cause of death wasn't in question. I knew that Terry didn't go for the scattershot approach. She liked to zero in on the weak spot. So I wasn't surprised when Wagmeister stood up to do the cross.

"You do know that there were no injuries on Mr. Powers when he was arrested, don't you, Doctor?" he asked.

I stood up. "Objection. This witness has no personal knowledge, Your Honor."

"Overruled. She's an expert, she can answer."

Another dumb ruling. Expert or not, she can't testify to physical observations she never made.

"I don't know that, Counsel. All I know is that the jailers made no mention of any injuries in the arrest report. But they don't look for healed wounds or small scars. They only look for gross injuries so they can prove a prisoner did not sustain them in custody."

Answers like this are what make Dr. Vendi a goddess.

"Still, the arrest report doesn't mention any scars or wounds, does it?"

"No."

Wagmeister presented a photograph of a knife that had handle guards—a metal bar that separates the handle from the knife blade. "Do you see the knife on the monitor, Doctor?"

"Yes."

"If the killer used a knife like that, his hand wouldn't have slipped up onto the blade, now would it?"

"That style of handle makes it less likely, certainly. But it doesn't necessarily prohibit the hand from slipping up onto the blade. And there are many other ways for the killer to cut himself during the attack. For example, he has his left arm around the victim's upper chest, which leaves his left hand exposed. As he uses his right hand to draw the knife across the victim's neck, the blade would naturally come close to his left hand." Dr. Vendi demonstrated on herself. "You see, the left hand would be right here, near the right side of the neck. Beyond that—"

Agitated at how his one decent point was being obliterated, Wagmeister held up a hand and turned to the judge. "Objection! This is nonresponsive, Your Honor."

I was on my feet. "The answer was entirely responsive, and experts are allowed to explain their answers."

"I am aware of the rules of evidence, Ms. Knight. But I agree. Overruled." The judge turned to Dr. Vendi. "Please continue."

"Yes, I was saying that we've all cut ourselves accidentally more than once under far less stressful situations, for example, when slicing a turkey, or vegetables. Now, imagine how much more likely such an accident becomes in the course of a homicide with a struggling victim. This is why it's very, very common to see some kind of sharp-force injury to the defendant in these types of cases."

Delightful. The stronger the proof that Ian cut himself during the murders, the stronger the logical conclusion that his blood got smeared on the trunk of Brian's car that night, and not—as the defense had tried to claim—some other time. I could practically hear the wheels turning in Wagmeister's head as he tried to find a way to dig himself out of this hole. Finding none, he moved on. His next gambit was to try and get the doctor to admit it would be hard for one killer to disable two victims the way she'd described. Wouldn't the victims have had more opportunity to struggle, and therefore show more defensive wounds, if just one person had done it?

"Not if the killer took them by surprise and attacked them from behind. And neither of these victims was very big. Hayley was petite, just one hundred and three pounds. Brian was a slender boy as well. I wouldn't think it would be that hard for a fully grown adult who had the element of surprise to overcome them—particularly if he was able to attack them one at a time."

"But can you say with certainty that they were attacked at separate times, Doctor?"

"No, but I do know they were found in very different places. One buried on the mountain, and one in the trunk of a car parked at the airport."

"But if they weren't separated, wouldn't it be very difficult for a single killer to get behind each of them and do the killings as you describe?"

"If I must assume they were together, yes. But that doesn't jibe with the manner of death shown here. This was not a rage or impulse style of attack. It was a single slice across the neck of each victim—no overkill. This killer was, for lack of a better word, efficient. I say efficient because it allowed him to immobilize the victims, *and* it allowed him to avoid most of the blood spatter. I don't see someone who kills in this manner attempting to overcome two victims at once."

"But you can't say for sure that they were killed at separate times or places?"

"No. The only way I could say that for sure is if I had been there, and I wasn't."

Wagmeister decided to cut his losses and end with that unimpressive concession.

"Thank you," he said. "I have nothing further."

Terry's expression was guarded, but I could see her hands were clenched under counsel table and knew she was seething. What a cheery sight. As Dr. Vendi stepped down off the witness stand, I stole a glance at the jury: they looked solemn; some even looked teary.

"It's five minutes to noon," the judge said. "So let's take our lunch break. I'll see everyone back here at one thirty."

66

Bailey and Declan and I hunkered down in my office. Melia had offered to pick up lunch from the cafeteria, a semi-step up from the snack bar, and I'd happily accepted. In the meantime, I opened my refrigerator and offered what I had: bottled water and a couple of diet sodas. They both opted for water. I opened one for myself and consulted my witness list. "I'm thinking we pile on more of the solid stuff now. The texts between Brian and Hayley on the mountain—"

"An especially nice move after Wagmeister's genius cross," Declan said.

"Exactly." If the kids were texting, they weren't standing together. The more often I could show the defense was throwing out theories that were easily disproved by the evidence, the better.

"That won't take long," Bailey said. "I bet Terry puts Wagmeister on a very short leash from now on."

"Yeah, and that's too bad," I said. Worse, she might even do the cross herself. Which meant we'd be moving through the testimony pretty quickly. "We're going to need more witnesses to fill up the day. Let's put on Steven Diamond next." The coroner's criminalist, who'd testify about the knife, would be a great follow-up to Dr. Vendi.

"Good idea," Bailey said. "But he won't take long, and I'd guess the cell records witness won't either."

Court wouldn't recess until five, and Judge Osterman had been adamant about our filling up every minute of court time. I wanted to save the best, most reliable witnesses for last so we could end the day on a strong note. "How about the body finders? Do we have Rostoni?"

Officer Bander, the airport cop who'd found Hayley, would be a great witness, and we could get him in at a moment's notice. But our neo-Nazi was a different story. He'd been ducking subpoenas for days.

Bailey had a glint in her eye. "Oh yeah, we have him," she said proudly. "I served the jerkweed myself. One day while you guys were playing around picking a jury, I sat on his pad. Caught him when he came out to walk the dogs." Bailey shook her head and chuckled. "Big guy walking these tiny little dachshunds. But, man, small as they were, they were evil. One of 'em almost bit me."

"Too bad they didn't—you could've sued." Rostoni was well heeled for a Nazi, thanks to his custom motorcycle business. "Do you have a line on him right now?"

"I've got someone sitting on his compound, and I hate wasting the manpower. I'd be really grateful if we could get done with him."

"Get him on the road. I'll put him on as soon as he gets here, even if I have to interrupt someone else's testimony." But Rostoni and the airport cop would only take me to three or three thirty at best. I had at least an hour and a half to fill. "Let's put on Dorian." Our criminalist would probably be crossed by Terry—Dorian had collected the most incriminating evidence. But Terry didn't worry me in this instance. Dorian could've handled the McCarthy hearings.

"Nice, strong ending for the day," Bailey said approvingly. "I'll call and get her ready."

Coroner's criminalist Steven Diamond was one of my favorite experts. Careful, thorough, smart, and charming—and as neutral as they come, which of course earned him enormous credibility with juries. Steve was soft-spoken and had a gentle demeanor and an unusually delicate, respectful manner with regard to the dead. Most in the murder business, cops and coroners alike, find refuge in jocularity. Not Steve. When he spoke of a murder victim's wounds, his tone was reverential. That compassion for the victims was sorely needed in this case.

Steve had examined the wounds on Brian and Hayley and had been able to pin down the brand of knife that was likely used.

"So, Mr. Diamond," I said, "you can't tell us whether any one particular weapon to the exclusion of all other weapons caused a wound, correct? It's not like a gun?"

"Correct. With a gun, we have striae and lands and grooves that we can use to make a microscopic comparison between a possible murder weapon and the bullets or casings found at the scene of a homicide. But when a homicide is perpetrated with a knife, we cannot be that precise."

I'd use this point later on to show how carefully these murders were planned. Ian Powers had a gun—a much easier way to kill, but he chose not to use it. Why? Because he was likely smart enough to know guns leave this kind of evidence.

"In this case, can you tell whether one knife was used or two different knives?"

"Based on the high degree of similarity between the wounds, I feel relatively certain that one knife was used."

"And what brand of knife do you believe was used?"

"Most likely a Smith and Wesson, third series. The first and second series are no longer in production and haven't been for some time."

I put a photograph of a Smith and Wesson knife on the monitor. It was a vicious-looking thing, with serrated teeth on the bottom two inches closest to the handle.

"Can you describe the dimensions of that knife?"

"The knife is measured at just over eleven inches overall, with a seven-inch blade that is stainless steel."

"I notice that there's a handle guard separating the blade from the handle of the knife. Is that to keep one's hand from slipping up onto the blade?"

"Yes."

"Have you nevertheless found in your case studies that defendants who wielded such a knife have cut themselves during the homicidal attack?"

"Many times, yes. In the heat of struggle, hands do slip and victims can move about, all of which can, and frequently does, cause the perpetrator to get wounded in some manner."

Dr. Vendi and Steven Diamond—a nice one-two

punch to show how Ian could have cut himself during the murders and therefore left his own blood on the trunk of Brian's car.

"Nothing further."

This time I saw Terry put her hand on Wagmeister's arm and stand. Terry took Steve through all the expected points: no, he couldn't say it was this brand of knife to the exclusion of any other—it was an educated conclusion based on the database; yes, the handle guard sometimes did operate to keep the knife wielder from getting cut.

"And you cannot say with absolute certainty that the wounds on both Hayley and Brian were caused by one and the same knife?"

"Well...based on all the evidence—"

"Stop, Mr. Diamond. You were called as a knife expert, right?"

"Yes."

"Then please answer the question within your field of expertise. Based on the wounds and what you know of *knives,* can you say with absolute certainty that both victims were killed with the exact same knife? Yes or no?"

Steven cleared his throat. "No."

"Then it is possible that two different knives of the same brand could have been used?"

"Well...yes."

"Thank you," Terry said, and sat down.

We probably won that round on points, but Terry'd managed to kick up some dust clouds.

Next up was Barbara Meyerson, our very pregnant cell phone records custodian, who waddled in, ungainly and vulnerable, carrying a thick file folder. The minute I

saw her, I knew there'd be little, if any, cross. It'd be suicidal to get belligerent with a mother-to-be, and besides,
there was no point. The records were what they were.

But that didn't mean she didn't have dramatic points
to make for our side, and I intended to squeeze the max
out of them. I started with the phone calls between Ian
Powers and Jack Averly, to prove their connection.

"Do the cell records of Ian Powers and Jack Averly
show contact before the murders?"

"Yes." Barbara shuffled through her paperwork.
"Prior to the murders, there were sporadic calls, maybe
twice a month, for a period of a few years. None of them
were lengthy, and all of the calls placed by Ian Powers
came from a cell phone that had a blocked number. It
would show up in the records as 'unknown caller.'"

"And did you find any calls between them on the day
of the murders?"

"Yes. I have a call placed from Ian Powers's unlisted
number to Jack Averly's cell that evening."

"Just the one?"

"Yes. But the following day there were four calls between Ian Powers's unlisted cell phone number and Jack
Averly's cell phone, and another few calls over the next
three days."

"Would you say that there were more frequent calls
between them after the murders than in previous
months?"

"Def—"

"Objection," Terry said loudly. "The records will
speak for themselves."

"True, they will. Sustained," the judge said.

I gritted my teeth. Barbara was qualified to summarize what was in the records. But it wasn't a point worth fighting for. I moved on.

"Did you obtain the locations of the cell sites these phones accessed for the calls in issue?"

"Yes. The call placed from the defendant's phone to Averly on the day of the murders came from the Bel Air area to a location in West Hollywood. The following day, Jack Averly's cell phone was making and receiving calls in New York, and Ian Powers's calls were being made and received in various locations in Los Angeles."

I put a printout of the texts between Hayley's and Brian's cell phones on the monitor.

I pointed to the monitor: still waiting for drop. stay in car. "That first text was sent from Brian to Hayley?"

"Yes."

"Where was the phone when that text was sent?"

"The cell site location accessed was near Ventura, in the Santa Monica Mountains."

"Would that cell site be the one accessed if the phone was on Boney Mountain?"

"Yes."

"Was there a text from Hayley to Brian after that?"

"Yes. Three minutes later, her phone sent a text to his." She pointed to that text on the monitor: what's going on? "That text accessed the same cell site location as Brian's text."

"So that text also could have been sent from Boney Mountain?"

"Yes."

"Did Hayley's phone send more texts to Brian's phone after that?"

"Yes. Over the next fourteen minutes, she sent four texts."

"Were any of them answered?"

"Only the last one."

I took her through each of the texts Hayley had sent after that: u should be done by now! Where r u? No answer. what's going on??? No answer. r u ok? No answer. where r u??? what's happening??

Those texts—their rising panic—again gave the sad yet eerie sense of hearing from Hayley herself beyond the grave. "Was there finally an answer from Brian's phone?"

"Yes. Four minutes after Hayley's last text, Brian's phone responded." She again pointed to the monitor: I'm ok. All clear. Meet me on trail.

"Then a total of two texts were sent from Brian's phone to Hayley's, correct?"

"Yes."

"How much time elapsed between Brian's first text to Hayley and his second, which would be his last one?"

"Twenty-one minutes."

"Ms. Meyerson, if you would please consult your cell phone records for Jack Averly now." She pulled out her paperwork, scanned it, then looked up at me. "Can you tell us whether any calls—as opposed to texts—were placed from Brian's cell phone to Jack Averly's cell phone that evening from Boney Mountain?"

"Yes. Within the same minute that last text was sent from Brian's cell to Hayley's, a call was placed from Brian's cell phone to Jack Averly's cell phone."

"How long was that call?"

"Very short. Less than thirty seconds."

I paused and checked through my list of questions, giving the jury a chance to catch the significance of that testimony. "Now, Ms. Meyerson, those records don't tell you who was actually using those phones, do they?"

"No. All we know is which phone was used and where it was when the call was made."

"But according to your records, Brian's killer could have used Brian's phone to send that last text to Hayley, and then the killer could have used Brian's phone to call Jack Averly—"

As I'd expected, that one brought Terry to her feet. "Objection! Improper hypothetical, calls for speculation!"

Judge Osterman shot me a disapproving look. "Sustained. That's not for this witness to say. Ladies and gentlemen, disregard the question and don't speculate about what the answer might have been. Anything further, Ms. Knight?"

"No, thank you, Your Honor."

As I sat down, I whispered to Declan, "Think the jury got it?"

"If they were listening," he whispered.

Terry did the cross. She didn't even bother to move to the lectern.

"Ms. Meyerson, your records don't tell you who the killer was, do they?"

"No."

"Thank you very much. And congratulations. Is it your first?"

The records custodian beamed. "Why, yes, thank you."

"I know it's an exciting time."

I knew Terry had no children. Probably never even had a gerbil. And her move had cut right to the chase—very effectively minimizing the emotional impact of the texts. As I helped the witness off the stand, I noticed a few of the jurors were nodding appreciatively. Terry was gaining fans. Which made this the worst time to have to call my next witness: skinhead führer Dominic Rostoni.

He rolled in, scanning the courtroom from wall to wall as though he'd just landed on Mars. But he looked better than I'd expected: he wore his usual jeans and flip-flops, but his shirt had sleeves, and his shoulder-length white-blonde hair was neatly combed. He looked almost human, albeit not the kind of human you'd want to marry your sister. Or marry anyone at all if procreation was part of the package.

I took him through his testimony with as little fanfare as possible. Not just because I wanted to finish with him, but also because there was no need to embellish. The photographs of Brian's body in the shallow grave did that for me. All Dominic really had to do was point and say, "That's what I saw."

And that's what he did. On direct. Cross was another matter.

Again, Terry took the reins. "You're the leader of a white supremacist group, aren't you?"

"That I am."

"And your group isn't fond of liberals, is it?"

Dominic wrinkled his brow, wondering where this was going. I could've objected, but I didn't want the jury to think I was protecting a skinhead, so I sat back.

"Not their biggest fans, no."

"In fact, your group hates the Hollywood elite, doesn't it? You think they're all minority- and fag-loving liberals, don't you?"

Dominic shrugged. "They are, aren't they?"

This drew a few titters from the audience and some lip-twitching from the jurors. It was the first comic relief in the trial and everyone appreciated it, regardless of who'd provided it and how.

"And yours isn't the only group who hates the Hollywood liberals, is it?"

"S'pose not."

"Thank you. Nothing further."

"People?" the judge asked. "Redirect?"

I was about to let it go, but then I decided to try and make a point.

"Do you even know who this defendant is, Mr. Rostoni?"

"Sure. He's a big-time manager. Partner of that director, Antono...something."

Ouch. Since when did this cretin know anything about Hollywood business? My bad. I'd violated the old saw: never ask a question to which you don't know the answer. Keeping a neutral expression, I tried again. "Is that something you found out after this case made the news?"

"Nah. I knew about them 'cuz that director guy used a coupla my bikes in a film."

"So you had no problem doing business with him, liberal or not?"

"His money's still green."

I'd lucked out.

"Thank you, Mr. Rostoni. Nothing further."

"Defense?" The judge asked. "Any re-cross?"

"Briefly," Terry said, rising slowly.

"Then I take it that some of your employees or 'club' members have been to Mr. Powers's studio?"

"Probably. Delivering bikes and whatnot."

"Ever deliver to Mr. Antonovich's home?"

Dominic sniffed and thought a minute. "Not that I know of."

"It's possible though, isn't it?"

"Yeah. I guess."

"Thank you, Mr. Rostoni."

And there it was, Terry's point: people who had it in for Antonovich and Powers had access and opportunity to hurt them, know things about them—and, of course, set them up. Likely? No. But the beginnings of a basis for "reasonable" doubt? Absolutely.

The judge looked at me. "People? Anything in light of that?"

"No, thank you, Your Honor."

"We'll take our afternoon recess," Judge Osterman said. He turned to the jury. "Folks, you'd be wise to use this time to stretch your legs and get ready for our last session of the day. See you back here in fifteen minutes."

67

I pulled out my checklist for Dorian's questioning after the jury had filed out.

"Which DVDs do you want me to load?" Declan asked.

I told him, and started to review my notes. Bailey leaned in to whisper to me. "You probably want to think about giving him a witness. Just to let him feel like a real boy."

I nodded. "But not Dorian—"

"God no. Just wanted to mention it so you could keep it in mind for later."

"You're right." I hadn't wanted to throw him into this snake pit with Terry, but I could let him handle some witnesses whose testimony wouldn't draw a lot of fire. I jotted down a few names that immediately came to mind.

Dorian was a strong witness, but she was a tough one. She wouldn't be pushed one centimeter farther than she intended to go and she never stretched beyond the most restrictive explanation of the physical evidence. If she didn't see it, she wouldn't say it, and she had no hesitation pushing back in ways that made the unfortunate lawyer regret the day he was born. No one was immune, as many an unwary prosecutor who'd been dressed down by her in front of a jury had learned the hard way. The judge came out and called for the jury, and Bailey went to bring her in.

"People?" the judge said. "Your next witness?"

"The People call Dorian Struck."

Dorian strode up to the witness stand. I'd coordinated the photographs and videos to illustrate her testimony with a very bare bones "what did you see, what did you collect" series of questions. We moved through the evidence collection quickly, the only embellishment being her description in stultifyingly boring detail of the careful measures she'd taken to protect each piece of evidence from degradation or contamination. The soil and plant debris on the victims and on Brian's and Averly's cars, the fingerprints on the cars, the blood on the trunk of Brian's car, and the hairs in Averly's car. I ended her direct examination with the only analysis she'd performed.

"Did you do a microscopic examination of the hair you recovered from the driver's and the passenger's seats in Jack Averly's car?"

"Yes."

"Now, a microscopic examination cannot tell you for sure that a hair found at a crime scene matches one person to the exclusion of all others, correct?"

"Correct. It's not DNA. We speak in terms of consistency, not matches."

"Bearing that in mind, did you compare that hair from Averly's car to any party involved in this case?"

"I compared the hair to *every* party in this case who

might have contributed that specimen. That includes the victims, their friends and relatives, Mr. Powers, and Mr. Averly."

"As a result of the comparisons you conducted, what did you conclude?"

"First, I found that many of the hairs in the Mustang were consistent with the hair of Jack Averly."

"No surprise since that's his car, right?"

"Surprising or not, that's what I found."

I noticed that a couple of the jurors' lips twitched at that response.

"Were there any hairs in that car that were not consistent with Jack Averly's?"

"Yes. There were several on both the driver's and the passenger's seats that were not consistent with Mr. Averly's hair samples. I found many of those hairs to be consistent with the hair samples I myself took from the defendant, Ian Powers." She went on to describe where in the car Powers's hairs were found.

With another criminalist, I would've covered the gaps I knew Terry would go for. But knowing Dorian as I did, I left them alone. She could take care of herself and it'd come off better on cross. "Nothing further." I passed the witness to the defense.

Terry moved to the lectern. I sat back to watch the show.

"You found hairs that didn't match either Jack Averly or Ian Powers, correct?"

"Yes."

"And it's common to find stray hairs or fibers that can't be identified as having come from any known party, right?"

Clever. That question ensured that Dorian would give Terry a helpful answer *and* make Terry look smart.

"Correct. It's Locard's exchange principle: 'Every contact leaves a trace.' Meaning that every person takes some trace and leaves some trace of himself—or herself—at any location visited. So the unidentified hair could be from someone at the car wash, or a hitchhiker, or a neighbor."

"Or those unidentified hairs could have come from the person who framed Ian Powers?"

With any other witness I would have objected. But Dorian's answer would be better than any objection I could make. And this frame-up nonsense was the whole defense theory. I didn't want the jury to think it worried me.

Dorian raised an eyebrow. A big warning sign if you knew her. "I have no evidence to show that anyone was framed, Counsel. There were hairs in that car that were not consistent with either Jack Averly's or your client's hair. That's all I can say."

Terry's unfazed expression told me she'd anticipated that answer. She was just continuing to plant the conspiracy seeds. Now she paused and looked down at her notes, as though taking a moment to gather her thoughts. I knew she was simply making sure she had the jury's attention.

"You can't say *when* any of those hairs got into Averly's car, can you?"

"Which hairs, Counsel?"

"Any of the hairs you collected."

"No."

"And you can't say *how* any of those hairs got into Averly's car, can you?"

Dorian frowned. "Well, I can say that as many hairs as I found, it was likely they got there because your client sat in the car."

"Fair enough. But what I meant was, for all you know, the hairs that look like Ian's might have gotten there when Averly gave Ian a ride home one day, right?"

"True."

"And that day might've been two years ago, isn't that true?"

"Yes."

"Now, you said you found no evidence of forced entry into Averly's car, correct?"

"That's correct."

"But someone could have broken in without leaving evidence that force was used, right?"

"Yes, it's possible."

"So you can't rule out the possibility that someone broke into Averly's car at some point?"

"Not completely, no."

"Now, it's relatively easy to collect someone's hair without their knowing it, isn't it, Ms. Struck?"

"Well...it could be done. I'm not sure how easily."

"Then let me give you an example. If I held your jacket for you, I might find hairs on the shoulders that I could lift off with my bare hands, isn't that right?"

"You might."

"And if you used the courthouse restroom across the hall, I might find your hair in the sink?"

"It's possible."

"So wouldn't you agree that there are several ways someone could collect a person's hair without that person knowing it?"

"I haven't counted the ways, but I'd agree there are a few."

"And if I took hair off a person's jacket and put it into someone's car, you'd have no way of knowing that I'd planted that hair, would you?"

"Probably not."

"Thank you. So it's possible that the hairs you found to be consistent with my client's were planted in Averly's car, isn't it?"

"Counsel, it's possible we could be on a spaceship to Jupiter right now. Or I could be the next Miss America. Though I've yet to be nominated, hard as that may be to imagine."

At that, the jury laughed out loud. Short, squat, no makeup, inch-long-steel-gray-haired Dorian wouldn't enter a beauty contest if her life depended on it.

Judge Osterman frowned. "I believe Ms. Struck is interposing her own objection that your question calls for speculation. Which it does. Sustained. Next question."

Terry didn't miss a beat. She came straight back at Dorian. "You can't say someone *didn't* plant those hairs in Averly's car, can you?"

"No. I can't say they didn't, but I have no reason to say they did."

"And once again, you're not trying to tell this jury that the hairs in Averly's car are definitely Ian's hair— you're just saying they're *consistent* with Ian's hair, right?"

"Yes, right."

"So they might not be Ian Powers's hair, correct?"

"Correct, they might not."

"Thank you. Nothing further."

Before the judge could ask, I was on my feet. Terry's persistent questioning about planted evidence and frame-ups was, as she intended, having a water-on-rock effect on the jury. At first I'd seen only mild curiosity on their faces, but by the end of Dorian's cross, I'd begun to see real interest. I had to find a way to do some damage control. I took a shot in the dark.

"Ms. Struck, is there anything noteworthy about the hairs that was inconsistent with both Ian Powers and Jack Averly? Anything that might indicate whether they were deposited recently, or by someone who'd been in the car on more than one occasion?"

"What I can say is this: the unidentified hairs in Mr. Averly's car did not match each other. That indicates they came from different people—not one person—and probably at different times, or I would have found more hairs that matched each other."

It was as good as I was going to get. It didn't rule out the possibility that some unknown conspirator had gotten into Averly's car and planted Ian's hair, but no witness could do that. The only thing that could was common sense. I tried to look calm and confident as I said, "Nothing further."

"Defense?" the judge asked.

Terry looked unperturbed. "No, Your Honor, thank you. But I'd like this witness to remain on call."

Placing a witness on call means they have to come back whenever they're summoned—no further sub-poena required. Sometimes it means the lawyer has something to smack the witness with later—an inconsistent statement, or a prior screwup of some kind. Some-times it's a bluff. And sometimes it's just a way of making sure a witness will come back in case the lawyer forgot something. It would be just like Terry to bluff. But it would also be just like her to really have something up her sleeve—though what anyone could have on Dorian was hard to fathom. It made me every bit as nervous as Terry undoubtedly meant it to.

The judge turned back to me. "We have about fifteen minutes left. Do you have any short witnesses?"

Dorian, who'd just stepped down from the witness stand, gestured to herself and looked up at the judge. "How much shorter can they get?"

The jury laughed again. I'd heard she had a funny side, but this trial was the first time I'd seen it.

And on that note, the judge declared the court in recess for the day. Things wouldn't always go this well, I knew. But for now, just for this one moment, I let myself enjoy a brief surge of hope.

68

I would've preferred to take our end-of-day confab back to the Biltmore bar, where we could plot our next moves in comfort. But we couldn't talk in public. The only safe place, other than my room, was in my office with the door closed. And Eric had even questioned the security of that option. He'd offered to have our offices swept for bugs. So far, I hadn't felt the need. There was nothing we talked about that the defense didn't already know.

Bailey perched on a chair in front of my desk. "So who's next?"

"Have you heard from Janice?" She could give us some information on the feud between her brother Tommy and Russell, and just through her presence remind the jury that Brian had been a real person.

"She's still waffling," Bailey said. "She wants to show her support, but... it's a double whammy for her."

I nodded. Bad enough having to deal with agoraphobia, but she'd also have to be in the same room with one man who'd driven her brother to suicide and another who'd murdered her nephew. That didn't mean it was a lost cause, but I couldn't count on her.

"Have you taken a temperature check on Raynie lately?" I asked. I still wasn't sure what side she was on, and I couldn't afford to have the mother of the victim become a hostile witness. Better to do without her testimony than have the jury see that.

"Haven't had the chance," Bailey said.

"Why don't you let me give her a call?" Declan asked.

Why not? I didn't want to set him up to take any hits for being my "stooge," but I couldn't imagine Raynie getting ugly with Declan. Russell would, but not Raynie.

"If you're okay with it, I have no objection."

"You want to put her on Monday if she's…in the right frame of mind?"

I nodded.

"Then I'll take care of it right now." Declan stood to go.

"Hang on a sec. What's Vanderhorn been saying lately?"

Declan gave a little conspiratorial smile. "Not much. He's doing more listening than talking—"

"I hope you're recording this rare event—"

"It's going into my earth capsule. He keeps asking me how Russell's doing, what he's saying, that kind of thing."

"And since Russell isn't speaking to any of us, you tell him…?"

"That Russell's in a holding pattern and he'll be grateful when it's all over and done."

"If I had a daughter, I'd want her to marry you. Go make the call."

Declan laughed and headed for his office.

"We've got to put someone on to talk about Hayley's last days and hours. If it's not going to be Raynie, it might have to be Mackenzie," I said.

Bailey looked pained.

"What? She's pretty articulate, and she's likeable."

"It's not that I don't like the kid. It's just that she's not going to give us as much bang for our buck as the mom."

I nodded. No argument there. "But we're moving fast. Even if we don't put Raynie on Monday, we might very well be at the end of our case the day after. So, basically, we're out of time. If we can't use her, we go with Mackenzie . . . and someone from the studio for the screenplay issue."

"I'll line 'em up." Bailey stood. "And I've confirmed everyone for Monday. They'll be on deck at eight sharp." She left, and I started reviewing my notes on Mackenzie.

By eight forty-five Monday morning, I had all my witnesses lined up on the benches outside the courtroom. Declan hadn't been able to reach Raynie, which meant I'd have to use Mackenzie. When I said good morning to the jury, I got a couple of real smiles. Much more than the perfunctory nods I'd gotten up till now. Cheered (maybe more than I should've been) by that small sign of goodwill, I called Hayley's best friend.

Mackenzie, in a light gray skirt and white blouse that tied at the neck, looked like she was about twelve years old. As Bailey guided her into the courtroom, she darted a nervous look at the crowd that packed every square inch of seating, then cast her eyes back down and watched her feet all the way up to the witness stand. Even when Tricia administered the oath, she only glanced up briefly to say, "I do."

In as gentle a voice as possible, I told her not to be afraid to ask me to clarify any question she didn't understand. She nodded, and I took her through a description of her friendship with Hayley, how she was a new girl in school, lonely and friendless, how Hayley had taken her in, and how they'd become inseparable. Then I had to get into the less lovely part—information I'd learned only after the news of both Brian's and Hayley's murders broke.

Every witness, every single piece of evidence, is a double-edged sword. There's no such thing as a witness who doesn't have a downside. So the issue is whether the benefit is worth the cost. Mackenzie helped me humanize both Hayley and Brian. A big benefit. And I needed her to show that Hayley and Brian had cooked up the kidnapping scam—if only so I could prove that Ian Powers had stepped in and turned their amateur scheme into a double homicide. Proof that the victims had tried to pull a kidnapping scam was a necessary cost. But unfortunately, it wasn't the only downside to Mackenzie, so I'd thought long and hard about whether I really needed her. I'd decided I did. Now I hoped I wouldn't regret that decision.

If I have negative information about my witnesses, I bring it out myself. I don't want the jury to think I'm trying to hide anything, and if I'm the one who brings it out, I can sometimes cushion, or at least minimize, the impact.

"How did Hayley and Brian meet?"

Mackenzie swallowed and licked her lips. "He, uh,

Brian worked as a manager at a jewelry store in the Galleria near our school. I went in one day..."

"So you met him first?"

"Yeah...yes. The salesgirl had taken out some bracelets for someone and she left them on the counter." Mackenzie fidgeted with her skirt and looked down as she spoke. "I...uh, took one."

"You mean you stole it?"

She nodded. "I put it in my bra. But the security guard caught me at the doorway and brought me back." Suddenly she looked up. "I don't steal. It wasn't for me. I just wanted to give Hayley a present for her birthday. But I didn't have the money. At least, not enough to get her something really nice..."

Mackenzie dropped her head again and I waited a moment before asking the next question.

"Mackenzie? What happened after the guard caught you?"

She reluctantly looked up at me. "He brought me to the back room, to Brian's office, and told Brian. I gave him back the bracelet right away and I begged him not to call the cops. It would've killed my dad."

"And did he call the cops?"

"No. He said he'd seen me with Hayley and asked if we were friends. When I said we were, he said if I'd introduce him to Hayley, he'd let me off."

"And did Brian and Hayley become good friends?"

Mackenzie nodded. "At first just, like, friend-friends. But then they were, like, really tight. After that, I almost never saw Hayley alone anymore."

"Did you hang out with them when they were together?"

"Yes."

"Did Brian have a laptop?"

I needed to establish this, because the ransom note likely came from Brian's computer, though we'd never found it.

"Yes. He kept it in his car. He always had it with him."

"When was the last time you saw Hayley?"

"The night we went to Teddy's."

I had her describe their night out at Teddy's. It was a Thursday night. The "kidnapping" happened the following Monday.

"You spent Thursday night at Mr. Antonovich's house in the Hollywood Hills?"

"Yes."

"Was anyone else in the house? Any adult?"

"No. It was just Hayley and me."

"And did you see Hayley the next morning?"

"Yes."

"So actually that was the last time you saw her?"

"Yes."

"What did Hayley say to you?"

"That I wouldn't see her around or hear from her for a while, but not to worry about her. She said she'd be fine, that everything would be okay. And that I couldn't tell anyone she'd told me that. She made me promise." Mackenzie's face crumpled on those last words, and she delivered the rest between tears that fell like raindrops into her lap. "And I didn't! I should've told someone, but I didn't want to let her down! Now she's dead, and it's all my fault!" Overcome, she covered her face with her hands, and her sobs filled the courtroom.

I know some lawyers prep their witnesses to get emotional, even cry. I never do. Mackenzie's outburst was one hundred percent genuine, and the jury knew it. Several looked at her with pity.

I'd hoped Terry would leave her alone. No such luck.

"So you and Hayley stayed at her father's house all by yourselves?"

"Yes."

"And you did that quite a lot, didn't you?"

Mackenzie shrugged. "We did it sometimes."

"And sometimes you'd throw parties there, isn't that right?"

"Just a few times."

"But of those few times, the cops were called at least once, isn't that true?"

Mackenzie fidgeted with her skirt. "It was just because it was a little noisy. No one, like, did anything bad."

"But you had older boys at those parties, didn't you?"

"I—I don't know."

Terry pulled out a handful of photographs and passed them to me. I looked them over with a sinking heart. I wanted to object but knew it was pointless. The defense would claim that those older boys were potential suspects who might have used their access to frame Ian.

Terry had the photos marked as defense exhibits and placed the first one on the monitor.

"That girl in the skinny jeans and heels, is that you?"

Mackenzie visibly gulped at the sight and I saw her scan the audience nervously. I'd bet she was looking for her father. "Y-yes."

"And who's that boy—or, rather, man—standing with his arm around you?"

"I don't know. Just a guy."

"Isn't he a bouncer at the Viper Room?"

"I-I guess so."

Terry put another photograph on the monitor. "That blonde girl in the leopard tube top and sequined miniskirt, is that Hayley?" Between the hair, the makeup, and the getup, she looked at least twenty. A very experienced twenty.

At the sight of her friend, Mackenzie's lips trembled. "Y-yes."

"And who is this man standing behind her with his arms around her waist?"

"That's—that was her boyfriend. Before Brian."

"He worked for a casting director, and he was about twenty-five years old, right?"

"Yeah—yes."

Mackenzie looked down at her lap and blinked quickly. I hoped that Terry had pushed it too far, that this cross was starting to alienate the jury, but a fast glance in their direction told me otherwise. Nearly all of their expressions had hardened.

"Now, when Hayley told you she'd be gone for a little while and not to tell anyone, you didn't know what she was planning?"

"No."

"But now you know she and Brian were setting up a fake kidnapping to get money from her father, right?"

"I—yes."

"And when Detective Keller first questioned you, you

didn't tell her about your last conversation with Hayley, did you?"

Mackenzie shook her head.

"You have to answer out loud."

"No."

"You told the detective that you had no idea what had happened to Hayley after you left Friday morning, isn't that right?"

"Yes."

"But that wasn't exactly true, was it?"

"No."

"Thank you. Nothing further."

"—but I didn't know what to do!" Mackenzie continued, her voice trembling with grief. "I promised Hayley...I promised her..." Mackenzie's voice trailed off.

Terry went back to her seat and Bailey escorted Mackenzie out of the courtroom. I clenched my fists as a hard ball of anger burned in my stomach. Mackenzie didn't deserve this, but there was nothing I could do about it right now. It was on to the physical evidence and my next witness, hacker—or rather "sniffer"—Legs Roscoe.

He'd cleaned up considerably for his television debut. No spikes, no piercings—though I could see the telltale holes on his nose and ears. He even managed to look embarrassed about "cyber-sniffing" Brian's ransom note at the coffee shop.

"I'm not proud of this. It's just a game, you know? I do it because I can. I've never harmed anyone, blackmailed anyone, or anything sleazy like that."

"And you're sure the person you 'sniffed' was Brian Maher?"

"One hundred percent."

"And the girl with him was Hayley?"

"No doubt about it at all."

"Thank you, Mr. Roscoe. Nothing further."

And of course, no cross for Legs. Terry loved this testimony. It was further proof that our two victims were extortionists trying to squeeze a cool million out of Hayley's father.

The next witness was brief and easy: the LAPD computer expert who confirmed that the ransom note sent to Russell had indeed been sent from a laptop or desktop. No cross. No reason for it. And then it was on to our soil expert.

You know how voices can give you a sense of what a person looks like? Sterling Numan's deep, almost operatic-sounding baritone painted a picture of a large man, or at least a medium-sized man with a big barrel chest. Since I'd never met him in person, that was the mental image I'd been working with. So when a wiry little guy—five feet seven inches, tops—came bouncing into my office, tie swinging, schoolboy hair slicked to one side, and introduced himself, I'd had to bite my lip to keep from laughing.

I'd given him my standard advice for testifying, otherwise known as the KISS principle: Keep It Simple, Stupid. He'd assured me he was very comfortable with juries. My bad. I neglected to ask whether the feeling was mutual.

"Dr. Numan, please give us your credentials."

He swiveled in his chair to face the jury—which I hate—and proceeded to rattle off a list of degrees, accomplishments, and publications in a tone so condescending and self-congratulatory, I'd have thought it was a sketch right out of *Saturday Night Live*. I hoped things would improve when we got to the meat of the matter.

"Did you examine the soil samples removed from Brian Maher's car, Jack Averly's car, and Hayley's body?"

This time he turned to face the jury before I'd even finished the question. I was tempted to grab the baseball off the bailiff's desk and throw it at him—but I was afraid I might miss and hit a juror. My arm is a little unpredictable.

"First of all, the correct name for these 'soil samples,' as you call them, is *particulates*. It's important to use the correct terminology because each technical appellation has its own specific meaning…"

"Technical appellation." Kill me, just kill me. He started to roll through a list of all of these magic words. When he came up for air, I jumped in.

"Thank you, Dr. Numan. Did you determine the general location where those particulates came from?"

He shot me a look of annoyance at the interruption, then turned back to the jury. "Yes. I am able to determine the origin of particulates to a somewhat specific degree, though of course I cannot pinpoint the origin to a source within a small circumference…"

Blah, blah, blah. Incomprehensible. I badly needed this answer to be in English. It was the whole point of his testimony. I sliced in when he took a breath.

"Dr. Numan, forgive me. Those are a lot of big words. Could you help me out and give the *Soil*—or rather *Particulates—for Dummies* version?"

He shot me an imperious glance, then swiveled back

to the jury. "Of course. I was able to determine that the origin of these particulates was limited to a somewhat specific locale…"

And off he went once again, if anything, even less comprehensible than before. I gave up. There was just no way to make him juror—or human—friendly. Eventually, though painfully, I dragged him to his conclusion—I *think:* that both cars and Hayley's body showed signs of having been in the locale of Boney Mountain.

But by that time I thought I could hear jurors snoring. I hoped to wake them up with one last piece of evidence I hadn't mentioned during opening statements.

"I want to shift gears now and ask about another location: Fryman Canyon, the location of the ransom drop. Were you able to tell whether Jack Averly's car had been in Fryman Canyon recently?"

"I examined samples taken from that location using a variety of testing methods…"

Incredibly, he got more long-winded with every answer. I imagined calendar pages turning before he finally gave his conclusion: that he could not find soil or plant evidence to indicate that Averly's car had ever been in that location.

Translation: if Averly's car hadn't been in Fryman Canyon, Averly hadn't picked up the ransom money. Ian Powers had retrieved it.

By the time I was done, I suspected the jurors hated me for putting this guy on. I passed the witness to the defense, hoping they'd spend enough time with Numan to get their fair share of juror wrath.

Wagmeister did the cross this time—a clear sign that

Terry knew she didn't have to worry about this evidence. Unfortunately, Wagmeister kept it short and sweet. He had Numan admit again that soil analysis can't pinpoint exactly where in a given area the cars had been, then wrapped it up succinctly.

"And you cannot say, Dr. Numan, exactly when those particulates got on the cars, can you?"

Numan turned back to the jury. "No. I can only say it was recent enough that it had not worn off yet. But of course, cars run on wheels and wheels turn and when those wheels turn, they of course shed any material they may have picked up from any given area. And so the fact that I was still able to find the particulates that I did indicated to me that it couldn't have been very long— less than a year, certainly—since the cars were in that area…"

Seriously. What was so wrong with a simple "No"?

Wagmeister's expression went from amazed to amused, and when Numan finally wound down, he wisely threw in the towel. "Nothing further."

When the judge asked me if I had anything further, I wondered could there possibly *be* anything further? The soil should've been a nice piece of evidence to add to the big picture. But in the hands of "I'm comfortable with juries" Numan, all it did was confuse them and piss them off. The commentators would be dumping on us all night.

I had no time to dwell on the loss. The next witness would be Declan's inaugural run. I'd decided to let him take the print expert, Leo Relinsky. Relinsky had been telling juries about fingerprints for over thirty years, so I figured this was a foolproof witness to give a newbie who was getting his first taste of a high-profile case.

Declan had been studying his notes and getting ready half the night, though it surely wasn't the first time he'd put on a print expert. But this morning, in my office, he'd been a nervous wreck. He couldn't stand still. He was straightening his tie, adjusting his jacket, and fidgeting nonstop. I'd had to tell him to sit down three times. "If you don't relax, you'll pass out in front of the jury. Take some slow, deep breaths, and don't drink any more coffee. I'm getting the shakes just looking at you."

Now, as Numan left the courtroom, I sat down and whispered, "Go get 'em, slugger."

Declan stood, straightened his tie for the millionth time, and buttoned his jacket. He cleared his throat and barely managed to choke out, "The People call Leo Relinsky."

Declan started by having Relinsky state his credentials. It was a good way to warm up, because Leo's CV went on for a solid ten minutes. He'd won awards, published papers, taught classes—you name it, Leo had excelled at it. I could see that Declan was starting to relax. Excellent. Then Declan had Leo give his spiel about the uniqueness of fingerprints.

That out of the way, they moved on to the results: Jack Averly's prints on the interior driver's door handle of Brian's car, Ian Powers's prints on several areas inside Averly's car, and last, Powers's thumb and index fingerprints on the trunk of Brian's car, half an inch from the bloodstain.

It all went smoothly until Declan asked him about his findings on the nine-millimeter Ruger that'd been seized from Ian's house.

"Did you find any prints on that gun?"

"No, I did not."

"Did you think it unusual that someone would have a gun in his house that didn't have his prints on it?"

"Well, not necessarily."

"But doesn't the absence of prints indicate to you that the gun had been wiped down for some reason?"

"It could. I didn't particularly notice evidence that the gun had been wiped down, but then again, I wouldn't have thought much of it if I had. People frequently do clean their guns. Or they should."

"Did you find gun-cleaning fluid on the handle, or the trigger guard?"

Wagmeister stood up. "Objection! Assumes facts not in evidence—that he was looking for cleaning fluid."

The judge had been watching Declan with a mixture of pity and irritation. The questions about wiping the gun were a very bad idea for exactly the reason the witness had just explained. Declan had painted himself into a corner; now he was desperately trying to make something good come of it. A classic example of bad money after bad.

"Well, I'll allow it," the judge said. "But please move it along, Mr. Shackner."

Declan swallowed and his ears reddened. My heart ached for him. We'd all been there at some point—just not on national television.

"Shall I ask the question again?"

"No," Leo replied. "I remember it. The answer is that I always note the presence of cleaning fluid if it's there, but I did not notice any such fluid on the Ruger."

"Then, just to recap, you found Mr. Powers's prints on—"

Wagmeister was on his feet again. "Objection! Asked and answered."

"So it would seem from the way that question started," Judge Osterman said. "Are we going anywhere new, Mr. Shackner?"

Declan cleared his throat. Poor guy, I knew he'd just been trying to end on a strong note. "No, Your Honor, I guess not."

A brief scan of the jury showed a couple of mildly puzzled expressions, and our single black mom was suppressing a little smile. No harm done. In fact, we might've gained a few sympathy points. Nothing wrong with that.

Wagmeister did the standard cross. "With regard to the prints you found on the cars, you can't tell when the prints were put there, can you?"

Leo amiably agreed he could not.

As Wagmeister beat that dead horse for another ten minutes, I passed Declan a note for his redirect. He nodded, and when Wagmeister was finished, he asked that one question.

"You testified that you found Ian Powers's thumb and index prints on the trunk of Brian's car. Here's a hypothetical: Assume that those prints were found less than an inch away from a bloodstain that also matched Ian Powers. Assume further that the car was left in an outdoor parking lot near the airport for at least two days. With that information in mind, what if anything could you say about when those prints were deposited on that trunk?"

"Objection! Improper hypothetical!" Wagmeister shouted as though he'd been stung by a hornet.

"I assume there will be testimony to that effect regarding the blood?" the judge asked.

"There will," Declan said.

"Overruled."

"The short answer is that it means the prints were probably left fairly recently. Reason being, weather will break down blood evidence, and though prints are a little more durable, it can destroy prints too. So when you put it all together, the fact that you found identifiable prints near the blood indicates that both were most likely deposited recently. I can't be more precise than that, though."

"Thank you. Nothing further."

Declan had been pale after his earlier snafu, but when he sat down, I noticed there was a little more color in his cheeks now. A nice finish cures so many ills.

69

We still had an hour before the noon recess, so I asked Bailey to bring the New York contingent down to the courtroom. I had to put on the NYPD officers to prove that Averly had been in New York, under an assumed name, and that Hayley's iPad had been stolen from his hotel room.

"Okay, but who else are you going to call? The New York guys won't take that long."

She was right. And I couldn't afford to incur Judge Osterman's wrath. His latest edict: "Any party who runs out of witnesses before it's time to recess will find that they've rested their case." Since he really couldn't get away with forcing the defense to rest, I knew this warning was for me. "We could put on the airline records person to prove when Averly flew out of LAX and our computer cop to say that Averly used the iPad to buy that ticket to Paris."

"They're in the DA lounge, ready to go. But we still might come up short."

"That's all I can think of at the moment. We'll have to put on what we've got and hope for the best."

As it turned out, we were still ten minutes shy of twelve o'clock when I finished with my New Yorkers and records people, but the judge could see I'd done my best to use my court time. He let us go early without a fuss. When Bailey left to round up our next witnesses, I walked Declan to his office, knowing he needed some moral support. Sure enough, the moment I stepped inside and closed the door, he started to apologize for his screwup with Relinsky.

I held up a hand and told him to stop. "It can't have been the first time you got balled up in a witness and I promise, it won't be your last. We all have our days. And besides, the jurors loved you."

His eyes strayed to a small framed photograph on his desk. I looked at it more closely and saw it was a picture of a man who was beaming as though he were holding his newborn baby. Except he was holding an Oscar statue.

"Your father?"

Declan nodded and looked down at his desk. "The only good news about today is he'll never see it. I think the only reason he even knows I'm on this case is because one of his assistants told him."

"He didn't want you to join the DA's office?"

"He didn't want me...period."

"You mean, he didn't want children?"

"No. My older sister's the proverbial apple of his eye." Then he lowered his voice and spoke in a gruff tone that I surmised mimicked his father. "*Working* with fairies is one thing. But I'm not having any damn homosexuals in *my family.* And don't give me that bull about how you have no choice!"

Declan's admission, the pain in his voice, brought a lump to my throat. How could his father be such a Neanderthal? And how could he not see what a wonderful guy his son was?

"Declan, I can't say I understand that kind of mentality. I can only say that you're one of the best people I know. Smart, talented, charming, classy. If I ever have children, I'll feel like the luckiest woman on the planet if I get to have a son like you. Your father...needs help." I'd almost said his father was an asshat, but I stopped myself just in time. I could tell that Declan still wanted to find the good in him, still yearned for the day his father would accept and appreciate him for who he was. And who knew? Maybe one day he would.

Declan gave me a tight little smile. "Thank you, Rachel." He raked a hand through his hair. "Just what you need right now. My bullshit drama. What can I do for you? Is Gelfer up next?"

"Yep. So if you could organize the exhibits, I'll go back over my notes." I turned to go, then stopped with my hand on the door. "Thank you for telling me, Declan."

He gave a rueful smile. "Sure, any time."

"And that wasn't bullshit drama. If you want to hear bullshit drama, remind me to tell you about my last fight with Graden. If that doesn't make you feel like the model of sanity, nothing will."

I headed back to my office and reviewed Gelfer's reports for the millionth time. I'd saved our most damning piece of physical evidence for last: the DNA typing of the bloodstain on the trunk, which had shown a mixture of both Hayley's and Ian Powers's blood. I knew this would be a pitched battle.

Declan and I headed down to court early so we could get set up. I wanted to make everything as tightly organized as possible. Gelfer's CV was solid, but from what I'd heard, he wasn't super-smooth. I had to give him points for promptness, though; he showed up right on time, at one twenty-five. As always, he had that disheveled nutty professor look—badly cut mousy brown hair, wire-rimmed glasses, and a lopsided-looking jacket. I'd noticed before that even his lab coat seemed crooked on him.

"Hey, Tim. Ready to go?"

"Yeah, sure," he said in a breathless voice.

"Got your reports in there?" I gestured to the file in his hand.

"Uh-huh. Want to see?" He opened the file with shaking hands and started to take them out.

"No, I'm good." I'd gone over them so many times I could recite his findings in my sleep.

I wished he had time to take a walk around the block to calm down, but it probably wouldn't have helped. Even seasoned witnesses would find the pressure cooker that was this courtroom daunting. As usual, we were filled to capacity, every row tightly packed. The judge swept onto the bench and called for the jury. When everyone was settled, Judge Osterman asked, "People, ready with your next witness?"

"Yes, Your Honor. The People call Mr. Timothy Gelfer."

Gelfer moved up to the witness stand with stiff, self-conscious steps.

I took him through his résumé, which was actually fairly impressive. At first his voice quavered as he told the jury that he had a master's in microbiology and was in the process of getting his Ph.D. But he got a little steadier as he described the four articles that had been published in major scientific journals on various aspects of DNA testing and his work as a criminalist for the FBI.

"So you were stationed in Quantico?"

"Yes."

"For how long?"

"Five years."

"What made you leave?"

"My wife wanted to move back here to be closer to her family."

"And how long have you been a criminalist for the Scientific Investigation Division here in Los Angeles?"

"Four years."

Gelfer had calmed down now and seemed to have hit his stride. I established that he'd done the DNA typing on blood samples taken from Brian Maher, Hayley Antonovich, and Ian Powers, then had him describe the procedures for DNA typing. Declan started the disc that showed Gelfer in action in the lab, and Gelfer explained how each photo depicted the steps he'd performed in his testing. The visual aid made the testimony a little less dry and made it easier for Gelfer to break it all down. When he'd finished, I moved on to the crime scene evidence. I signaled Declan to run the disc that showed the photos of the bloodstain on the trunk of Brian's car and asked Gelfer what his analysis had shown.

"I found a mixture of two DNA profiles. The dominant profile matched the DNA of Hayley Antonovich, and the secondary profile matched the DNA of Ian Powers."

I briefly scanned the faces of the jurors to see how we stood. All were paying close attention, and a few were taking notes. Excellent.

"With regard to Ian Powers's profile, can you tell me how many other people might possibly have that same profile? Or to put it another way, what is the statistical likelihood that the bloodstain could have come from someone *other* than Ian Powers?"

"The odds of that are one in one quadrillion, four hundred and seventy-seven trillion, two hundred thirty-six billion—"

"I can't even picture a number as long as that, so just to cut to the chase: How many people are there on this planet?"

"Just over seven billion."

"So when you say the odds of finding another person with the same profile as Ian Powers's is one in one quadrillion, are you basically saying there's no one else on this planet with the same DNA profile as Ian Powers's?"

"In a word, yes. We would have to look through more people than there are on earth to find another person with the same profile."

"And in plain English, that means the blood that was found on Brian's trunk was Ian Powers's, correct?"

"Correct."

There was no topping that, so I didn't try. "Thank you, Mr. Gelfer. No further questions."

When I sat down, I noticed that Bailey was gone. "What happened?" I whispered to Declan.

"She said she had to take care of something and not to worry."

I wouldn't—I had enough to keep me busy right here. Terry moved a giant binder to the lectern.

"There are two forms of DNA testing: RFLP and PCR, correct?"

"Well...those are the tests relevant to this case."

"And you used PCR testing in this case, isn't that correct?"

"Yes."

"Isn't it true that PCR testing is more vulnerable to contamination?"

"Well...yes. If proper protocols aren't followed."

"When you say protocols, you mean there are things that should never be allowed to happen during PCR testing, right?"

"Yes."

"And that's because you need to follow certain procedures in order to ensure that evidence doesn't get contaminated, right?"

"Right."

"One of the biggies in terms of things you should never do is bring a suspect's blood sample into the lab while evidence is being tested?"

"Yes, that would be a very bad thing to do."

"Tell us why, Mr. Gelfer."

"Because PCR is a very sensitive testing method. If you bring a suspect's blood sample into the lab while you're testing an evidence bloodstain, you run the risk of contaminating the evidence stain with the suspect's blood sample."

"And that would make the suspect's DNA show up in the evidence bloodstain, wouldn't it?"

"Well...I...it could."

"To be more specific: If you brought Mr. Power's blood sample—the blood you removed from his arm—into the lab while you were testing the bloodstain on Brian's car, you could contaminate that stain with Ian's DNA. And that would make it look as though Ian's DNA was in the blood on the trunk of Brian's car when it really wasn't. Isn't that true?"

"Objection!" I'd had enough of this b.s. questioning based on shadows, smoke, and mirrors. "Improper hypothetical, Your Honor. There is no evidence whatsoever that there was any contamination here."

Terry didn't wait for the judge to rule. "Actually, Your Honor"—Terry brandished a stapled sheaf of papers—"These are the quality control and proficiency test results that just came in this morning on Mr. Gelfer and his lab."

"Does the prosecution have these reports?" the judge asked.

This had to be some kind of scam. Some smack written about SID by a defense hack so he could get his name in print and his butt on the witness stand in a high-profile case. I tried to look unconcerned as I answered. "No, Your Honor. I need time to review these reports before cross continues. It's unfair to allow questioning based on data I've had no chance to examine."

"I'm not going to take up this jury's time with a recess, Ms. Knight. You can review the documents briefly now and I'll give you some extra time to go over them during a regular break, before redirect—"

"But Your Honor, this is—"

"I've ruled! Ms. Fisk, give the prosecution—and the

witness—a copy of the reports and proceed with your cross."

A law clerk trotted over with the report. The top of the front page showed the ASCLD/LAB emblem—American Society of Crime Laboratory Directors/Laboratory Accreditation Board—telling me this was no sham. This was the real deal. And just issued that morning? How the hell had Terry gotten these reports? My knees suddenly felt like Jell-O. I sank into my seat. Holding on to a neutral expression as best I could, I skimmed the findings. The words "Errors" and "Unsatisfactory" jumped out at me. Oh, God. This was bad. Very, very bad. A roaring in my ears kept me from hearing the beginning of Terry's next question. I leaned over to Declan and whispered, "What'd she just say?"

Declan looked pale. "Just asked if he'd seen the report."

Gelfer adjusted his glasses. A fine sheen of sweat had broken out on his forehead. When he answered, he was short of breath.

"N-no. I didn't know it was out yet."

"But you can see that it's from ASCLD/LAB, right?"

"Yes."

"Please tell the jury what ASCLD/LAB is."

He explained that ASCLD/LAB is an organization that sets the standards for lab and tech procedures and administers the testing that determines whether a lab should be accredited.

"And just so the jury understands, Mr. Gelfer. Your lab, and all the criminalists in it, are tested every so often to make sure your labs are being run properly and you're all following standard procedures, isn't that right?"

"Yes." Gelfer's voice cracked.

"Then ASCLD/LAB writes up a report of how you all did on that test, correct?"

"That's right, yes."

"And a couple of months ago, all of you techs and your lab underwent blind or undeclared tests to check on whether proper procedures were being followed, right?"

"Right."

"These pages I'm holding appear to be a report on your last set of blind tests, don't they?"

"From what I've seen...yes."

"I'm going to let you look at this page for a moment before I ask a few questions." Terry glanced back at me. "Page seven, Counsel."

I flipped to the page, fighting the urge to squeeze my eyes shut, and forced myself to read. It was like having to walk through a curtain of razors.

Terry continued. "This page shows that one of your fellow techs didn't follow enzyme activation and cycling times. Without going into all the gory details, that's a big no-no, isn't it?"

"Yes. But it wouldn't cause the DNA in an evidence sample to change. I mean—"

"Not saying it would, Mr. Gelfer. But it would affect the validity of any result you got, wouldn't it?"

"It—well, more likely it would prevent us from getting any result."

"Fair enough. Another tech failed to wipe down the table with ethanol after using lab cleaner—also a big no-no, isn't that right?"

"It's...a problem, but—"

"But that didn't result in contamination, is that what you wanted to say, Mr. Gelfer?"

"Yes."

"I agree. Now turn to page nine."

Heart pounding, I found the page. When I saw what was written there, I wanted to bang my head on the table, then put my fist through a wall. Instead, I leaned back and doodled on my notepad. And tried not to look like I knew the biggest case of my career was about to explode in my face. When Gelfer finished reading the page, he looked like he was going to cry.

"That blind test did involve a contamination mistake, isn't that right, Mr. Gelfer?"

Gelfer swallowed, then answered. "It—it seems so."

It was almost physically painful to watch him up there. Like a man in the stocks, helpless to avoid the rocks being thrown at his head.

"And what happened was exactly what I mentioned earlier: a suspect's blood sample—blood that had been drawn from his arm—was brought into the lab where evidence was being tested. Right?"

"Yeah, uh, yes."

"As a result, the evidence sample did in fact get contaminated with the suspect's blood. Meaning the suspect's DNA showed up in that evidence sample, didn't it?"

Gelfer glanced down at the page again. "It...yes, it did."

"But it turned out that result *couldn't* be right. It couldn't be the suspect's blood in that evidence stain, because the evidence pertained to a cold case. The suspect hadn't even been born when that crime was committed. So when the suspect's DNA showed up in that evidence stain, there was no question that it had to have been caused by contamination. Correct?"

"Yes."

"Now, please turn to page ten."

Gelfer obediently turned the page, looking like a whipped dog.

"Tell us. Who is the tech that made that grievous mistake, Mr. Gelfer?"

Gelfer's eyes moved down the page. His face, already pale, now sagged as he stared at the report, slack-jawed. Without looking up, he replied in a choked whisper, "Me."

The moment the word left his mouth, a gasp went up in the audience. An unnatural stillness settled over the courtroom, like the calm before a tornado. I sat motionless, holding my body erect with an effort as shock waves ran from my numbed brain to my toes. Seconds later, the silence was broken by the rapid shuffling of feet in the spectators' gallery behind me. Reporters were running for the door. This was going to hit every television and radio station in the country in about five minutes. By tomorrow morning, it'd be front-page news. I could already see the headlines: "Cornerstone of Prosecution's Case Crumbles!" And the worst part of it was, I couldn't even blame the defense. This was all on us. The knowledge was almost too painful to process.

A pot of gold fell into Terry's lap somehow, and she used it well. Now, she co-opted the only comeback I had.

"You did all the DNA testing in this case, didn't you?"

Somehow, Gelfer found his voice again. But it was plaintive, pathetic—and entirely unconvincing. Like a child who crayoned the walls and then cried that he "didn't mean to."

"Yes, I did. But I know nothing like that happened here. I followed protocol, I—"

"You were very careful in this case. Is that what you want to tell this jury?"

"Yes! I *know* there was no contamination. I never had the suspect's blood anywhere near the lab when I was testing the evidence! I know it for sure!"

"But isn't that what you thought when you contaminated the cold case evidence in the blind tests?"

"I..." Gelfer's mouth was open but no words came out.

I had to admit, furious as I was, I felt sorry for him.

"Mr. Powers's life hangs in the balance, sir! After what you did in those blind tests, do you honestly expect this jury to take your word for it that these test results are accurate?" Gelfer stared at her, looking like he was about to cry. "Answer the question, Mr. Gelfer! *Do* you?"

"I...uh." Gelfer swallowed, opened and closed his mouth silently, then, his voice barely a whisper, said, "Yes, I guess so."

Terry looked at the jury and shook her head, her expression both mournful and angry. Her voice was laced with disdain as she said, "I have no further questions for this witness."

"People?" the judge asked.

Gelfer sent me a pleading look, but there was nothing I could do that wouldn't make matters worse. This bomb had obliterated the DNA evidence. There was nothing left for me to resurrect. And as I stood to answer the judge, I realized that the damage wouldn't be confined to the DNA. This case hinged on the physical evidence. We had no eyewitnesses, and our proof of motive had always been thin. A fuckup this gigantic on our most incriminating piece of physical evidence would burn through the credibility of every single expert we'd called—the hair, the prints, the soil. Now all of it would be laid to waste, leaving us with nothing but a few suspicious phone calls. And a sure acquittal.

"No. Nothing further."

70

It was only four o'clock. You'd think total annihilation would take a little longer than ninety minutes. I asked for a brief recess to gather my next witnesses and the judge reluctantly allowed it. He was probably wondering why we were bothering. It was a good question.

The jury filed out, and as I turned to speak to Declan, I heard Wagmeister and company excitedly whispering their congratulations to Terry. I glanced up and saw Ian Powers looking over a law clerk's shoulder at me with a smug little smile. An instant later it was gone, replaced with his usual solemn expression, the look he probably surmised an innocent man who was falsely accused would have. It wasn't a bad impression, and it got a big boost from the fact that you could still see the child star Mattie from *Just the Two of Us* in his features. I huddled with Declan on our end of counsel table and tried to ignore the backslapping jubilation coming from the defense side.

"How'd Terry get that ASCLD/LAB report?" he asked, looking shaken.

"She's got to have a snitch with connects high up. I'll ask Dorian when it's all over. And I'll check out this report to make sure we didn't miss anything, but right now, let's move on." I could always call Gelfer back to the stand if I found anything helpful. But I didn't really see any way of rehabilitating him no matter what else I saw in the reports. "Who've we got on deck?"

"I think that studio cop, Ned Junger."

I was about to go out and look for him when Bailey strode in.

"Not everyone thinks your case just blew up," Bailey whispered. "Raynie's on board."

I was stunned. She'd kept her distance through the whole trial, never even checked in to ask how I thought it was going. "You're kidding?" Now, of all times, I would've expected her to figure that Russell had been right all along. Speaking of which, he'd gone over to the railing to congratulate his good buddy, the murderer. They were all smiles and high spirits. It set my teeth on edge. But Raynie's defection was as good a consolation prize as I was likely to get. If I could trust it. "Is it possible she's pretending to be friendly so she can get up there and tank us?"

Bailey shook her head emphatically. "She was crying when she called me. Kept apologizing for not being more supportive."

Or supportive at all. Still, I was skeptical.

"Look, just trust me on this one, okay? What the hell do we have to lose?"

That point won the day. "Is she ready right now?"

"Yep. And if I were you, I wouldn't wait to let her change her mind."

"Okay."

Bailey hurried out to get her.

I needed a blockbuster ending to have any hope of making a comeback—unlikely as that seemed. The mother of the victim can be a very powerful witness if she's at all sympathetic. But Raynie was a wild card. I had no idea what to expect from her. The judge took the bench at four ten on the nose and called the jury out. As they filed in, Bailey brought Raynie up the aisle. Her tearstained face told me that either Bailey was right on the money or this was the best snow job I'd seen since the presidential primaries.

The entire gallery shifted to watch and whisper as she moved toward us. It was the first time they'd seen a family member take the stand. Russell's face was pinched with anger, and the entire Ian contingent seated around him gave Raynie, the traitor, cold-eyed looks of contempt.

Raynie seemed to have aged fifty years since I last saw her. Her shoulders sagged, and she clutched a handkerchief as she slowly walked to my side of counsel table. I guided her up to the witness stand and got her settled. Raynie sniffled into her handkerchief as she confirmed that she was Hayley's mother and Russell's ex-wife. Bailey brought her a box of Kleenex.

"I'm going to take you back several years to when your ex-husband, Russell Antonovich, was just a young writer on a teen show called *Circle of Friends*. Do you remember any problems between him and a fellow writer on that show named Tommy Maher?"

"Yes. Tommy claimed that Russell stole his screenplay."

I had her describe the nasty fight over authorship of *Wonderland Warriors,* how Tommy became so unhinged they had to move him to the edge of the lot. The story had spread all over Hollywood; it was widely known that not only wouldn't his contract on *Circle of Friends* be renewed, he'd probably never get hired as a writer again. So few had been surprised when he'd committed suicide. And after Tommy's death, Russell's fortunes had skyrocketed as *Wonderland Warriors* became a box office phenom.

I was watching Raynie carefully for any sign that this was a setup, but when she spoke of Tommy's death, a look of genuine sadness crossed her face. So far, so good. I wrapped up the background testimony and moved on.

"Did Hayley have an iPad?"

"Yes. I gave it to her for her last birthday." Raynie pressed her lips together. Bailey handed me the iPad, which was now encased in the standard evidence envelope. I pulled on latex gloves and removed it from the envelope. Then I turned it on and tapped the e-mail icon.

"Is this it?"

I held it up for Raynie, and the corners of her mouth trembled. Putting a hand to her lips to control the shaking, she choked out her answer. "Yes."

Raynie had been living with the reality of Hayley's death for some time now, but sitting on that witness stand, identifying something Hayley had held in her hands, brought it home on a visceral level.

"Did you know Hayley and Brian were dating?"

"I had no idea. I'd never met or even known of Brian."

"Did you know where Hayley was supposed to be when Russell got the text saying Hayley had been kidnapped?"

"She was supposed to be at her father's house in the Hollywood Hills, which was just a couple of miles away from where I live. He let her stay there when he wasn't using it for...entertaining."

"Is that where you last saw her?"

"No. The...last time...I saw her was at home...our home."

"When was that?"

Raynie teared up again and fought for composure. I swiped a look at the jury. There were some sympathetic looks, but a few, incredibly, looked bored. Of all the possible bad signs a jury can give, boredom during such emotional testimony was the worst.

"Thursday. She said she was going to her father's house and that she'd be there through the weekend. Russell was supposed to check on her." Raynie shot a look in Russell's direction through swollen eyes.

"Did you ever see the messages Brian sent to Russell?"

"Yes."

"I'm putting the first text on the monitor right now." The message, with Hayley's photo below, flashed up on the screen. "Is that what you remember?"

I've got your daughter. She'll be safe if you do as I tell you. If you call the police she'll be killed. I'll be in touch with my demand.

"Yes, that's it." She pointed to the photo with a trembling finger. "And that's...Hayley." A fresh wave of tears overtook her.

"You saw it on Russell's cell phone, right?"

"Yes."

"Could you tell where it was sent from?"

Terry could object to this, but we both knew I could get it in through other witnesses. She let it go.

"Yes." Raynie bit her lip and a slight tremor shook her body. "It came from Hayley's phone."

"I'm sorry, Raynie. Do you need a break?"

"No, no. Go ahead."

"What was the next communication about Hayley?"

"A few hours after that, Russell got an e-mail with a video."

"I'm going to show you that e-mail and video now. Okay?"

Raynie nodded. I put the e-mail on the monitor first.

One million dollars in cash in a duffel bag. Go to Fryman Canyon. Take the small path on the left for fifty yards, then turn right. Walk until you see two trees with white string tied around the trunks. Leave the bag between them. Go home and wait for the call. If you bring in the police, Hayley's dead.

"Yes, that's the second communication."

"Now I'm going to play the video that came with it. Ready?"

She nodded again, more slowly this time. It hurt to

look at her. The only thing I could do to help her was to get it over with.

Again, Hayley's sweet, almost unbearably young face looked steadily into the camera. For the first time, I noticed a look of sadness in her eyes as she spoke. "Dad, just do what they say and everything will be okay. Please."

With that, Raynie completely dissolved. And for the second time in this trial, racking sobs echoed through the courtroom. Even I had to swallow hard to keep my emotions in check.

"I have nothing further, Your Honor."

"Defense?" the judge asked. "Any cross?" His tone suggested what the answer should be.

Terry took the cue. "No. No questions, Your Honor."

"People?" the judge asked. I certainly couldn't find a stronger ending. I stood and forced a look of confidence.

"The People rest."

71

By the time I rested my case, it was a quarter to five. Not enough time to start the defense. Having the jury go out for the evening with a mother's sobs ringing in their ears was always helpful. I knew some jurors were unmoved, but there were at least two or three who'd clearly been affected by Raynie's testimony.

Terry was well aware of this. When the judge turned to dismiss the jury, she asked for a sidebar. "Judge, I know you want to take advantage of every minute of court time. I could do my opening now," she said, her voice low and tight with tension.

"We have less than ten minutes, Ms. Fisk. I can't imagine you'll be finished that quickly and I'm not inclined to make the jurors stay late. I can see they're getting tired. Besides, it'll be no favor to you if they're just sitting there wishing they could go home while you do your opening."

Terry had reluctantly agreed and the judge let the jurors go for the evening. I was taught early on to stand whenever the jurors enter and leave the courtroom as a sign of respect. But it has the added bonus of giving me a chance to exchange friendly nods and smiles—in other words, to get a feel for how they're responding to me.

The librarian looked coolly neutral as she gave me a short head bob. The Pac Bell worker ignored me. The single black mom gave me a little smile with sad eyes. Was that sympathy for Raynie? Or for me, because my case was history? Maybe both. The rest swept by us without a glance. General reading: not good. An alternate dropped his reading glasses as he passed by and I started to reach out and retrieve them for him, but he beat me to it and scooped them up without so much as a nod in my direction.

I watched him leave: a talent agent whose agency represented some of the actors and writers who worked for Antonovich and Powers. But he was smart, which was more than I could say for the remaining jury pool, so I'd tossed the dice. Maybe I'd made a mistake. But he was just an alternate, and none of the jurors was likely to let go of a front-row seat at the biggest show in town.

When the jurors were gone, Terry made the standard motion to dismiss the case for insufficient evidence, leaning heavily on the blood evidence that was supposed to be the linchpin of my case and was now its most likely demise. Though it was a routine motion that had no hope of succeeding, I knew her every word would be the top news story of the day. Ordinarily, this wouldn't bother me. The press changed screaming sides about who was winning or losing at least once a day. By now, even the *least* avid trial follower knew better than to buy into the stories. But this time it was different.

Because now they had real-time footage that showed

the bona fide disaster that was Gelfer's testimony—a bellyflop of graphic, epic proportions. If a picture is worth a thousand words, video footage is worth a thousand photos.

I walked out of the courtroom with head held high, but inside, I was leaden. The brief shot of hope-filled adrenaline I'd gotten from the unexpected appearance by Raynie had ebbed and was now a distant memory. I punched in the security code on the door to our wing on the eighteenth floor and dragged toward my office, feeling as though I were slogging through quicksand.

"Rachel! Wait up!"

I turned to find Sandi Runyon, director of media relations for the DA's office, trotting toward me.

"We need you in the conference room for a presser in five minutes," she said.

Talk about the last thing I wanted to do right now. "Sandi, I can't do it. I'm dead." And in a really shitty mood. I didn't need to add that because she could see it for herself.

"I know, but if you don't show up, it'll look bad."

"You mean worse than it already does? How would that even be possible?"

Sandi squeezed my arm. "I know, kiddo. I saw Gelfer. It sucks. But otherwise you'll be leaving Vanderhorn out there alone." She gave me a meaningful look. We both knew what that meant: brain farts and bluster. If anything could make matters worse right now, it'd be Vanderhorn fielding the hardballs alone.

I sighed and let Sandi lead me into the conference room. The press had already piled in and filled every available seat and square inch of standing room. Except

for the space where the podium stood—that was wide
open. Feeling as though I were heading for a firing
squad, I moved to that end of the room and stood next
to the flags of the county and state. Seconds later, Vanderhorn entered the room from his private side door and
walked to the podium.

His statement was brief but cheesy. "Every trial is a
long and winding road, and just like that road, it has its
bumps. But I have every faith that ultimately, justice will
prevail."

The press began to shout questions before the period
could even be heard at the end of that line.

"Do you still believe justice means Ian Powers gets
convicted?"

"How do you expect to get a conviction now that your
most important evidence has been discredited?"

"Wasn't the blood the only thing that really showed
Ian Powers was involved in the murders?"

Vanderhorn held up his hands. "I'm going to let my
lead prosecutor speak to the specifics." He stepped aside
and gestured for me to take his place on the hot seat.
"Ms. Knight?"

I tried to salvage what I could from the wreckage that
was our case. "While the blood is important, it's far from
the only critical piece of evidence that proves Ian Powers murdered these two young victims." I listed the rest
of the evidence we'd presented and tried to show that we
still had a strong case. The truth was, we didn't.

With no solid proof of motive, we were completely
dependent on the physical evidence. And the blood was
the strongest. No other piece of evidence tied Ian as
surely to the murders.

Even the fingerprints on Brian's trunk weren't a slam dunk. We couldn't prove they were left there at the time of the murder, and besides, after the drubbing Gelfer had taken, everything that came out of the LAPD crime lab would be suspect. All it would take now to blow down the house of cards was a couple of decent defense experts. There were thousands who'd jump at the chance for the free publicity this case would give them.

After I'd been grilled, baked, and fried for ten minutes, Sandi put me out of my misery.

"That's all for now, folks. Thanks for listening."

She escorted me out, and Declan, who'd been standing near the door, followed. Sandi gave me a pat on the back. "Ya done good, kid. I'll spare you the usual platitudes."

"Thanks, Sandi." I took out my key to open the door to my office.

"But you know, it ain't over till it's over."

"Couldn't help yourself, could you?" I said. Bailey opened the door from inside.

Sandi shrugged, gave Bailey a nod, and left.

"Have fun?" Bailey asked.

"Not as much as when a defendant tried to stab me with his pencil, but close."

"I don't know how you did it," Declan said. "I'd have lost it for sure. Especially with that *Times* reporter. What a dick."

"Yeah, they've been hating this office for a long time," I said.

"They're no fans of LAPD either," Bailey said. "Anyway, I have news . . . sort of."

I looked at her, puzzled.

"Cliff Meisner called, so I took it for you. He said to tell you he found an 'open port' on Ian's computer, whatever that is."

I didn't know either, so I called him back. Bailey's cell phone rang, and she got up and signaled she'd be right back.

Cliff had the unenviable task of trying to explain it to me, one of the computer illiterati. "It's...let me just put it this way. Most computers have only a few ports and they're all identified. Having an open port is a big red flag. So something's up with Ian's computer. I just don't know what, and I don't know how long it'll take me to figure it out. Could be a month or so."

I'd be out in Antelope Valley handling illegal fireworks cases by then. I thanked Cliff and hung up. The odds were that this "open port" business had nothing to do with our case, but long odds were all I had left. The only question was, how could I get some answers before the case ended? I folded my arms and hunched over. There had to be something. And then I sat up. There was.

72

"I'd ask what got me the pleasure and honor of this call, but I can probably guess," Graden said, a smile in his voice. "What do you need, Rachel?"

"Advice from a nerd."

"Fire away."

I told him what Cliff said about Ian Powers's laptop. "But he needs at least a month to figure it out. Said going through every possibility takes time, and I guess it's not his only case—"

"That sounds about right. And you've got, what? A couple of weeks?"

"I wish. Now that my case is in shreds, Terry'll want to get it to the jury as fast as possible." I told him about the DNA debacle. "My guess is we don't even have a week before I start rebuttal."

"Less than a week? That's..." Graden fell silent for so long I started to wonder if he'd hung up. "I was about to say that's impossible, and it might be. But the idea I just had... well, the problem is, you won't want to put this person on the stand. So if something does come of this, I don't know how you'll get it into evidence."

"I'll drive off that bridge when I come to it. I really can't be picky about anything at this point."

"Okay. I'll get right back to you. Hang tight."

"I have a choice?"

I sent Declan home. No reason why we all had to sit in Doomsville.

"But you'll let me know if you need anything, right? I'll just be sitting around—" Declan said.

"Hopefully getting drunk—"

"But first I'll be working on getting bios for these mystery defense witnesses."

Terry had finally given us her witness list just before we left court. As predicted, it was mostly defense experts who'd grind our DNA into even finer dust and trash most of the other physical evidence too. I recognized one of their names: Owen Poplar, a print "expert"—aka whore for hire—who surfaced whenever the price was right to show why prints didn't match and how they could be planted.

But there were a few names that had no title or description. Naturally, Terry hadn't taken any written statements, so we had no idea who they were or what they'd have to say. I planned to demand that the judge impose sanctions for this typical defense shell game first thing in the morning.

"Thanks, Declan. Let me know if you come up with anything. But don't feel obligated to stay sober on my account."

After Declan left, I went to work on my cross-examination for the experts. But regardless of the problems or issues they raised, the bottom line for my cross would be the same: You can't say it *isn't* Ian's hair, Ian's blood, or Ian's fingerprints, can you? The only weak spot was that the defense didn't have to prove it wasn't Ian's hair, blood, or prints. They only had to raise a reasonable doubt. And I'd already done that for them.

Bailey came back, which provided a welcome distraction from my morbid ruminations. I told her what Cliff had said, and that I'd put Graden on it.

"Great idea." She sat down and put her feet up on one of the storage boxes under the table where I kept old cases. "I checked out the mystery witnesses on the database. Nothing on them in California. I've got someone checking the national sources."

My cell phone played the first bars of "I Shot the Sheriff"—the new ringtone I'd given to Graden just for giggles. Who says I don't spend my time wisely?

"Can you and Bailey get over here with that laptop in the next half hour?"

"Gee, I don't know, we were going to go get manipedis." I rolled my eyes. "We'll be there in ten."

I called Cliff, and twenty minutes later we were in Graden's office, laptop in hand.

Graden was looking particularly sharp today, and I found myself momentarily distracted as I enjoyed the view.

"I assume you meant it when you said you were desperate," he said with a questioning look.

"Trust me," Bailey said. "She meant it."

I nodded.

"Okay, don't say I didn't warn you. I had a huge white-collar case a few years ago that involved a highly sophisticated computer hacking scheme. This group came from the Russian Business Network—ever hear of them?"

Bailey and I shook our heads.

"It started as an Internet provider that promised absolute security for any—and I mean any—business that paid their hosting fees: arms dealers, kiddie porn, didn't matter, they'd never give up client information unless there was a court order. Since they shielded the location of the IP addresses—I could explain how—"

"No, please don't bother—"

"They made it impossible to figure out what court had jurisdiction, which meant that their security really was impenetrable. The case I had involved a cybergang made up of former members of RBN. They were all Russians—most of the serious hackers are—and they hacked into Citicorp and stole millions—"

"How'd you break the case?" Bailey asked.

"Got lucky. I found and bit off the head of the hydra—a super-hacker named M. Parkova. They don't come any smarter or more conscience-free. The feds decided they'd rather cut a deal and find out how those hackers did it than go for the max, so Parkova got a sweet deal—"

The sound of raised voices just outside his office made him stop and go to his door. He looked out and I heard another voice ask if he wanted to be interrupted. "Yeah, thanks, Scottie." Graden stood aside. "Ms. Knight, Detective Keller...M. Parkova."

And in walked the master hacker. She was five feet tall if she stood up straight, and effortlessly pretty, though the "dare me" glitter in the eyes behind those dark-framed glasses and the severely pulled-back hair made "pretty" seem too frivolous a word for her. I held out my hand and she gave it one firm, quick shake, then sat down, pushed her glasses up her nose with one finger, and said in a thick Russian accent, "Who's going to pay me for this?"

"The DA's office," I said firmly, though I had no authorization. I'd just have to make it true. Hell, I'd pay her out of my own pocket if I had to. Assuming I could. I had no idea what evil-genius hackers were charging these days.

She gave me a short nod, the most important item now checked off. "I'm best in world, but your lieutenant says you have few days. No one else would try. So I make no promises. And you pay whether I'm successful or not. You understand?"

"Yes."

She pointed to the laptop. "This is it, yes?"

I nodded and handed it to her.

Graden said, "You're going to have to work here in the station. We can't let this laptop out of our custody—"

"I do most work at night. Many times, I work all night, but—"

Her nose wrinkled as she looked around her with disdain, then she reluctantly said, "It's not a problem."

I guessed police stations weren't her cuppa.

"And I'll need you to document every step you take," I said.

She sighed. "That will slow me down."

"Dictate it into a micro recorder while you're working," Graden said.

Parkova made a face. "Fine. What I'm looking for?"

"All activity on the day of the kidnapping." I gave her the date. The less she knew about the case, the less she could be accused of fabricating evidence. "I especially need to know about any activity between this laptop and Russell Antonovich's laptop or phone."

"Then I need this Russell's machine."

"Will his smart phone do?"

"It gets e-mail? Yes."

Bailey said, "I'll get it to you." She'd taken it from Russell the first time we went to the house, and she'd held on to it.

"Do it tonight." She turned back to Graden. "Take me to workroom."

Graden went to the door and called to one of the officers to give our newly hired expert a room. The officer gestured for her to follow him, and M. Parkova marched out, laptop under her arm.

"Did she do any time?" Bailey asked.

Graden nodded. "Three years in Terminal Island."

A federal prison in San Pedro. I'd just recruited the ex-con head of an international cybergang. Go team.

73

Graden asked me if I wanted to do dinner, but I was too keyed up to be decent company. I'd been so excited about a possible break in the case that I hadn't stopped to think about the fact that hiring Parkova was the one thing I'd done so far that could get me thrown out of the DA's office—and sully my name forever. It was an act of insubordination of high magnitude to hire an ex-felon hacker without prior approval. If I lost the case, there was no doubt about it, I'd be fired on the spot. Vanderhorn not only wouldn't hesitate, he'd relish the opportunity. But I was in it now, no going back. So I took my anxious self back to the hotel.

Too beat to deal with parking, I pulled up to the valet stand and tossed Rafi, the valet, my keys. The rare event brought a surprised smile to his face. The hotel elevator was packed, but I didn't want to wait for another one, so I squeezed in and held my breath. Toni once told me that breathing the air in those close quarters was a surefire way to get sick. Ever since, I reflexively stop breathing every time there're more than two people in an elevator. When I got off, I took a big gulp of air.

I headed down the hallway that led to my room, thinking about how I'd handle the Gelfer debacle in closing arguments. Just the thought of having to talk to the jury about it made my stomach churn.

Suddenly, an unfamiliar voice called out behind me. "Hey! Rachel!"

I turned to see the grinning face of a deeply tanned young man in his twenties wearing sunglasses on top of his head. A cameraman was standing off to his right. They quickly moved toward me, backing me into the wall, and in the next second, a blinding spotlight snapped on.

"I just wanted to ask you, how do you feel after to-day's disaster? Are you ready to throw in the towel?" He thrust a microphone under my nose.

Without conscious thought, I slapped the microphone out of his hand, shoved him as hard as I could, and ran down the hall to my door.

"Hey, come on!" he called out. They followed me down the hall. "We just want your reaction! What're you so afraid of?"

I scrambled into my room as quickly as possible, my heart beating so fast I couldn't catch my breath. I threw the dead bolt, slid in the security chain, and grabbed the hotel phone. "Get someone up here, fast! There's some lunatic in the hallway with a camera!"

Fortunately Gregor, head of security, was on duty. "Lock your door. I'll have someone up there right away, Rachel. Shall I call the police? Or would you rather do it?"

Finally able to draw a full breath, I thought a moment. "I'll take care of that end. Thanks, Gregor."

After I hung up, I listened for a moment. I thought I could still hear voices out in the hallway, but I couldn't tell if it was the same two jerks who'd accosted me. Two minutes later I heard Gregor's booming voice. "Are you a guest in this hotel?" A murmured voice responded, then Gregor, in a tone with enough menace to scare off any conscious biped, said, "Then I suggest you both leave immediately. And don't you *ever* let me find you on a guest floor again! Got it?"

More murmuring. Then Gregor shouted, "Move faster!" A moment later there was a knock at the door.

"Rachel? It's me. They're gone."

I opened the door. Gregor's solid rectangular frame filled the doorway. It was a reassuring sight. "Thank you so much. Those two just ambushed me." Now, in hindsight, I realized there'd been no real danger, and I felt sheepish. "Sorry to sound the alarm like that. I guess I overreacted."

"Please, you were more than justified. No apology necessary. Are you okay?"

"I'm fine, Gregor. Thank you again."

"I'll put extra security on your hallway from now on. I don't know why I didn't think of it sooner—"

"Maybe because you were thinking no one would be sleazy enough to hit me up where I live? Because I sure didn't think of it."

Gregor apologized—unnecessarily. I told him to knock it off and thanked him again. When he left, I called Mario, who'd just been promoted to senior investigator for the downtown DA Investigators Unit. He'd worked on the case that involved Lilah. I told him what had happened.

"You've got to be kidding me. That same hallway?"

Last year, one of Lilah's henchmen had jumped me in that hallway. Beat me up badly enough to put me in the hospital. I had a feeling that might've had something to do with my overreaction to those creeps tonight.

"Yeah. Seems to be my favorite meeting spot for assholes. What do you think I should do? Gregor says he's going to keep a closer watch, so maybe that's—"

"Uh-uh. Not enough. I'll have someone posted there for the duration. You want an escort to and from the courthouse?"

"God, no. These guys aren't trying to kill me." I told him I already had secure parking at the courthouse. And Rafi wouldn't let anyone get near my car at the hotel— he wouldn't take the chance of forfeiting a tip.

By the time I ended the call, I was feeling relatively normal. Exhausted, depressed, demoralized, but all things considered, that qualified as normal. One hot shower and a glass of wine later, I was in bed with a murder mystery. Three minutes later I was asleep with all the lights on. I woke up just long enough to turn them off. But I thrashed around all night, as one nightmare after another assaulted my subconscious. I woke up the next morning more tired than I'd been when I went to bed.

74

On Tuesday morning I forced myself to eat a real breakfast of scrambled eggs, toast, and fruit. I was going to need my energy. I found Mario himself standing guard in my hallway. "Nice," he said, gesturing to my beige cotton suit and silk tank ensemble. Mario was the quintessential metrosexual. He always looked fantastic—hip, but understated.

"Not too casual?" I asked.

"You might consider accessorizing. A gold necklace would brighten things up a little."

"Good point."

I went back, found a simple chain, got the thumbs-up from Mario, and headed for my car. As I drove to the courthouse, I planned what I'd say to the judge about the defense team's sleazy play in springing unknown witnesses on us at the eleventh hour. Bailey was in my office by the time I got there and she filled me in on what little she had.

"Terry's witnesses are all from Nevada, and none of them have rap sheets. They all seem to be hotel casino service-type workers—waitresses, maids, that type of thing."

"What on earth?"

"Great question."

By the time Declan and I walked into the courtroom, my temper was at full boil. The jury wasn't in yet, but the gallery was packed with reporters. And it appeared as though the Ian side of the courtroom was even more crowded than usual. It figured. Especially now that it looked like he'd win, everyone wanted to show their undying loyalty. There even seemed to be more law clerks at the defense counsel table. They were multiplying like rabbits over there. I told Tricia, the clerk, that we had something to handle before the jury came out, and when Judge Osterman took the bench, I fired with both barrels.

"The defense has insisted from day one that they had no witnesses to turn over. Now, at the last minute, they turn over a list of over forty witnesses, half of whom are experts they had to have contacted months ago. This is an outrageous flouting of the rules of discovery and an obvious effort to blindside the prosecution."

The judge scanned the witness list as I spoke, then he looked at the defense side of counsel table. "Defense? This does look like a rather extensive list. It's hard to believe you just contacted all these people—and, as Ms. Knight points out, especially all these experts—the night before the People rested."

Terry stood up.

"As the court is well aware, we don't have to turn over any names unless we intend to call them, and we weren't sure we'd be calling anyone. We only made that decision the night before last."

"I see," the judge said. "Well, then I'll have to accept your representation as an officer of the court—"

What? I lost it. My body rigid with anger, I fought to keep my voice from rising. "There most certainly is something you can do, Your Honor. Discovery laws were enacted to address exactly this kind of shell game. You have the power to prohibit the defense from calling those witnesses altogether. Or you can tell the jury that the defense improperly withheld their names. There is no reason to believe this...*ridiculous* story that they didn't know whether they were going to call these witnesses. In fact, I just learned from my investigating officer that ten of them are from out of state. The defense had to have made arrangements to bring them out here long before this. There is no way, *none,* that all these witnesses were just a last-minute idea!"

I heard myself in those last few seconds and saw by Declan's expression that I'd gotten much hotter than I'd intended. When I stopped speaking, it was so quiet I could hear the squeak of the bailiff's Sam Browne belt across the courtroom.

The judge glared at me. "First of all, Ms. Knight, you can tone down the rhetoric. I'm not prepared to find that the defense deliberately withheld anything. They may very well have thought they might not present any affirmative defense and only changed their minds at the last minute—"

"But Your Honor, every single one of these witnesses required advance notice and extensive—"

"Do not interrupt me, Counsel! There'll be no sanctions. Now, unless there's anything else we have to take up—"

"There is," I said, cutting off the judge and too angry to care. "I'll need a recess to prepare for cross for each and every witness."

The judge narrowed his eyes at me. "We'll see, Ms. Knight. I'm not inclined to waste this jury's time—"

"I wouldn't be asking for any if the defense hadn't deliberately hidden their discovery—"

"I warned you once not to interrupt me, Ms. Knight." The judge gave me a furious look. "Do it a third time and I just may hold you in contempt. I can't make myself any clearer than that. This is not a game of tit for tat. Just because the defense didn't turn over discovery soon enough for your taste doesn't mean you have the right to exact your idea of payback."

Payback? Was he insane? "This isn't about payback, Your Honor. It's about the People's right to a fair trial. If we can't subject defense witnesses to the same scrutiny our witnesses get, the jury won't have an accurate picture of the evidence. And that means we can't get a fair verdict."

"That was a very pretty speech, and completely unnecessary. The People will get their fair trial. You can ask for more time whenever you like, Counsel. But whether you get it or not will be up to me." He turned to the bailiff. "Let's have the jury."

I sat down and tried to get my temper under control. It wouldn't do to let the jury see me like this. The press was already a lost cause. They'd have a field day with "Courtroom Fireworks as Judge Threatens Prosecutor with Contempt!" I wondered for the hundredth time whether the jury was obeying the admonition not to read or watch any news about the trial. If they were, they'd be the first.

But it wasn't just about needing time to prepare for cross—though that was reason enough. I also had to give Parkova the chance to dig into Ian's laptop. This fight with Judge Osterman had shown me it was going to be an uphill battle all the way. One I might very well lose.

75

Terry gave an opening statement that was as effective as it was brief.

"Ladies and gentlemen, I'm a 'show me' kind of person. So I'd rather show you than talk at you. After all, as the judge told you, what I say"—Terry pointedly turned her body to include me—"what *any* of the lawyers say, isn't evidence." She pointed to the witness stand. "Only what comes from that chair up there is. And now you know there's a good reason for that rule." She half turned toward me again and pointed. "This prosecutor told you she would present DNA evidence that would conclusively prove my client's blood was on the trunk of Brian Maher's car. But as you've now seen—"

I couldn't restrain myself. I jumped up. "Objection! Counsel is arguing, not giving an opening—"

"Sustained," Judge Osterman said in an icy tone that made it clear he didn't like having to rule in my favor. "Ms. Fisk, please save the argument for later and get on with what you intend to prove."

Terry nodded. "I apologize, Your Honor. I got carried

away." But her smug tone implied she'd gotten all the mileage she wanted. I gritted my teeth to keep from saying what I thought of her. She turned back to the jury. "I really only need to tell you this: Ian Powers did not kill Hayley and Brian. I don't have to make empty promises right now. I'm going to *show* you that Ian Powers is innocent. And then I'm going to show you who the real murderer is."

Short, sweet, and dramatic, and it had the desired effect. The jurors were energized, their expressions engaged and intrigued. Mine would've been too, except I was busy showing the jury I didn't give a damn—and worrying about the bomb Terry was about to drop. She started, predictably, with the parade of experts.

First up: Dr. Anthony Kandell, a DNA expert who thumped on the LAPD crime lab in general and Gelfer in particular for slipshod practices that ran the serious risk of incriminating an innocent man. My cross was simple.

"You're aware that Gelfer testified he did not make those mistakes on any actual cases, just on one of the blind tests administered to check lab procedures?"

"Yes, but the fact that he—"

I cut off the rest, which I knew would be a repeat of what he'd already said on direct: that Gelfer couldn't be trusted about anything after having made such rookie mistakes on a lab test. "Objection, nonresponsive," I said. "That called for a 'yes' or 'no' only."

Judge Osterman wavered for a moment, but probably because Terry had already hammered the point, he gave me this one. "Sustained."

"Thank you, Your Honor." I turned back to Kandell. "And if Gelfer didn't make those mistakes in this case, then his conclusion that the blood on the trunk was a mixture of the defendant's and Hayley's is correct, isn't it?"

"Well, but the problem is, we can't assume he didn't—"

"Objection, Your Honor, again, nonresponsive—"

I acted irritated, but the truth was, I didn't mind. The more the witness sparred with me like this, the more it showed he wasn't a neutral scientist, he was a defense advocate—something I'd put to good use in closing arguments.

"It is. Sustained. Please just answer the question."

The witness sighed. "Yes, *assuming* he didn't make those mistakes, the conclusion would be correct."

"Nothing further."

The other experts only pointed out what I'd already conceded: the hair comparison couldn't pinpoint Ian Powers as the source, it could only include him among the group with consistent characteristics, blah, blah, blah; and the soil analysis couldn't prove when Averly's car was on Boney Mountain.

But I got to have a little fun with the defense print expert, Owen Poplar, the particularly obnoxious whore who didn't just take shots at Leo Relinsky's opinion— he also tried to imply that the prints found on the trunk of Brian's car were planted. Poplar didn't try to sell the planting theory too hard, so I decided to leave that subject for my rebuttal. What he did try to sell was that Leo was wrong when he declared that the prints matched Ian Powers's. Knowing what was coming, I'd had Leo prepare separate blowups of the prints from the trunk and Ian's exemplar. Now I flashed them up on the monitor. What had been an abstract concept during testimony was now splashed across the screens in sharp relief. The prints were so identical they were virtually indistinguishable.

"Now, would you please point out the differences you were describing during your testimony for Ms. Fisk?"

Poplar cleared his throat nervously. He obviously hadn't been expecting this. Why, I have no idea. Eventually he pointed to a break in the ridge on the thumbprint found on the trunk. "If you look over here, you see that this break isn't on Mr. Powers's exemplar."

"I do see that. But isn't it true that prints found at a crime scene, especially prints found on an item that's been outdoors for some time, usually do have less detail than an exemplar?"

"Not necessarily."

"Really." I let my expression say what I thought of that answer before continuing. "Then you're saying that prints rolled by an expert under pristine conditions are of no better quality than prints that a murderer leaves at a crime scene by *accident?*"

He really couldn't say that or he'd get laughed out of court, let alone his own profession.

"No, I'm not saying that. I'm just saying that sometimes the prints found at crime scenes don't have such breaks as are shown here."

"Not *breaks,* plural, right? There's only one."

Poplar looked at the monitor again, probably hoping to find more, but eventually conceded, "Yes, I only see one at this time."

"At this time? You've had weeks to look at these prints before coming to court today, haven't you?"

"Yes, I looked at the prints before, obviously, and no, I don't see any other breaks."

His tone was now petulant, and I noticed a couple of jurors were frowning.

"But you stand by your conclusion that these prints don't match?"

Saying that, with the prints right there on the monitor in front of everyone, was the death knell for Poplar's credibility. Even laypeople could see the match.

Poplar sat up straighter, and now his tone was downright bitchy. "I'm not saying that, I'm just saying I don't see enough points of identity to declare a match."

"But that's not what you said on direct, Mr. Poplar, is it? You said on direct that these prints didn't match."

"No, you must have misunderstood, Ms. Knight. That is not what I said."

I knew the jury remembered it too, because a couple of them were shaking their heads. So I was gracious.

"Well, if that's true, then I apologize, Mr. Poplar. But I'm sure Ms. Hogan, our talented court reporter, will be able to resolve this for the jury if they have any doubts." I paused and smiled benignly as, out of the corner of my eye, I saw a couple of jurors make notes. "How many points do you need to declare a match, Mr. Poplar?"

"I don't have a specific number. I just have to be convinced that there's enough to dispel any reasonable doubt."

Spoken like a well-coached defense witness. "I see. In other words, you have a sliding scale?"

He narrowed his eyes, looking for the trap he knew was lurking in that question. "Well...yes."

"And that sliding scale means you can always give

the defense the opinion they want if they're willing to pay, isn't that true?"

"Objection! Argumentative!" Terry declared.

"Nothing further." I strode back to my seat and tried to act nonchalant. Not easy to do when you want to jump on the table, pound your chest, and do an end zone victory dance.

My triumph was short-lived.

At the five o'clock recess, I told the judge I'd need at least a day to prepare for the remaining experts.

The judge had retreated a few steps since our heated exchange. "I'm inclined to grant that request since Ms. Knight only learned of these witnesses a couple of days ago."

"No need, Your Honor," Terry said. "I'm not going to call any more experts."

"Well, that solves that problem, doesn't it?" the judge said.

Not hardly. I'd counted on using those experts to buy us some time for Parkova—and for me to figure out what those Nevada casino witnesses were going to say. I'd been worried that Terry might rest without putting on a defense. If she had, I might've been screwed. But she'd decided to put on witnesses, and that gave me a fighting chance.

It's what I always called "defense to the rescue." Although the defense doesn't have to prove anything, once they try to, the jury gets to see what they've got. And if what they've got is garbage, the jury sees there's no real defense at all. Basically, the worse their witnesses are, the better my case looks. I can't count the number of times the defense bailed me out by putting on a weak case. And it could work for me here too. If I could show that the defense was a sham, the jury might forgive me for the DNA debacle.

But now, thanks to Terry's move, I'd not only lost the opportunity to trash more defense witnesses, I'd just lost crucial time.

76

After court, the three of us met in my office and tried to figure out what the Nevada witnesses had to do with the case. I'd turned on my cell phone so I'd hear it if Graden called, but the default ringtone started playing almost immediately, telling me the reporters hadn't given up.

"How long's it been since you answered any of their calls?" Bailey asked.

"Weeks?" I had no idea. "You'd think they'd give up." I shook my head and turned the ringer back off.

"I couldn't come up with anything Powers or Antonovich was doing in Vegas. No film shoots... *nada*," Bailey said.

"Me either," Declan said. "The only thing I heard was that they were looking into investing in a casino, but that was a while ago."

I hated not knowing what the defense was up to. Because when it comes to a jury trial, what you don't know can and usually will hurt you... badly. The case was a roller coaster, and all I could do was lean out of the car to try and see the tracks a few feet ahead. But when

I walked into court the next morning, I stepped into a minefield no one could've anticipated.

Judge Osterman took the bench five minutes early. Jimmy called the court to order, and the loud buzzing and milling in the gallery came to such an abrupt stop, it made my ears ring.

"Juror number four left a message with my clerk," the judge said. "If the parties would come to sidebar, I'll let you all read it."

Juror number four was the black single mother who was my favorite. I looked at Bailey and Declan and shook my head as I rounded counsel table and moved to sidebar. This couldn't be good.

It wasn't. Her mother had been rushed to the hospital last night. The doctors said it was a heart attack and they didn't know if she'd make it. The juror needed to stay with her mother; she was the only family her mother had left. She provided the names of the doctor and the hospital, in case the court needed verification. She apologized and said she deeply regretted causing the inconvenience.

"I did have my clerk verify all the information, and it checks out," the judge said. "Obviously we have to let her go."

"Oh, I agree, Your Honor," Terry quickly replied.

The speed of her response told me she'd figured out that juror number four was probably in our camp. But there was nothing I could do. This was legitimate cause to excuse her.

"Yes," I said, feeling as though I'd been kicked in the gut...again. Every time I started to feel like we were back on our feet, some new disaster fell out of the sky to knock us flat.

The judge called the jurors out, explained that a personal emergency had come up for juror four, and said that the clerk would now draw an alternate at random to replace her. I held my breath as Tricia mixed up the name cards for the five alternates in a glass bowl and pulled one out. She opened the card and read. "Alternate number five."

It was the talent agent. He'd been my big gamble. We could be golden, or we could be totally screwed now. It was anyone's guess.

As I pulled out my legal pad, Terry called her next witness. "The defense calls Suzanne Forester."

A plain-looking, heavyset woman in her forties with steel gray hair and no makeup took the stand. I recognized her as one of the Nevada witnesses.

Bailey leaned over and whispered, "Here we go."

I nodded. Whatever she had to say would give us a good idea of what the rest of the Nevada witnesses had been summoned for. As she raised her right hand and took the oath, I was almost more curious than nervous about what was to come.

Terry established that Ms. Forester lived in Las Vegas and had worked for the past ten years as a hotel maid. "Are you a member of a union?"

"Yes, a hotel workers' union."

"And did you work for the Pink Panther Hotel and Casino approximately five years ago?"

"Yes. I worked there until it got sold."

"What happened when it was sold?"

"The new owners shut down the hotel and laid us all off. They said they were going to renovate, and when they were done, they'd hire us all back."

"Did they renovate?"

"Yeah."

"And did they hire you back?"

"No. They didn't hire none of us back. They went non-union."

"I see. And who were these new owners who refused to hire you back?"

Her eyes scanned the courtroom. "Him," she said, pointing to Ian Powers. "And him." She pointed to Russell in the audience.

"So they broke their word and never rehired you or any of the rest of the employees?"

"No. And then, a little while after they reopened, they sold the place."

"They don't own it anymore?"

"Far as I know, they're out."

"And have you found other work?"

Suzanne Forester shot an angry look at Ian Powers and huffed, "None of us have. Ever since those two dumped all their union workers, all the casinos been finding ways to get rid of us."

I leaned over to Bailey and whispered, "So this is the conspiracy? How...?"

Bailey shook her head. Terry spent the rest of the morning calling the other Las Vegas workers, but there was little for me to do on cross. She wasn't trying to show that any of these people were involved in setting up Ian Powers. Terry was just using these people to lay the groundwork for the "real" straw man. A quick scan of the jury told me most of them seemed confused. I knew they wouldn't be for long.

Back in my office at the noon break, Bailey and I tried to figure out how the defense would do it.

I opened my container of yogurt and stirred up the fruit. "They've got to show that someone in Russell's inner circle who could've known about the kidnapping is tied in closely with the union—"

"*And* that there's someone in the union crazed enough to commit two murders just so he or she can set Ian up. It's so…out there." It was. But I'd seen worse theories find traction in the jury room.

77

By the time we got out of court, I was wrung out. Too many curveballs in too short a time. I unlocked my office door, flopped into my big, cushy chair, and let my head fall back as I closed my eyes.

"You were right about where the Vegas witnesses were coming from," I told Declan. "But I did not see that union thing coming."

"They bought the casino under another name," Bailey said. "Andower Limited. And of course, they got rid of it a couple of years ago. The thing is, you'd have to know what you were looking for to find out about it. I only figured it out now because the witnesses gave us the name of the hotel."

"Makes sense. Explains why the media didn't catch it either."

"But they'll be all over it now. Might even give those jerks a little well-deserved bad press."

I sat up. "Come to think of it, when did *you* have a chance to get all that?" She'd been in court with us all day.

"I did a little checking on my cell while you were bouncing around with those witnesses."

"Your cell? Are you suicidal?" I asked. The judge had said he'd confiscate any cells that weren't turned off.

"The advantage of sitting behind you guys—he can't see what I'm doing."

"So how are they going to connect this union business to Russell on the day of the kidnapping?" Declan asked.

That was the question of the day—or more accurately the trial. We found out soon enough.

The next morning, when the jury filed in, I tried to suss out my talent agent, now known as juror number four. But he didn't look at me or the defense.

"The defense calls Angela Mosconi," Terry announced.

Dani's personal assistant? I turned to look at Bailey. She shrugged and shook her head. Angela walked in looking as confused as we were. For some reason, that made me feel better.

Terry quickly established that Dani was Russell's current wife and Angela had been Dani's assistant for the past three years. Asked if her employer was in the courtroom, Angela pointed to Dani, who looked both stricken and confused. Asked if she sometimes spent the night in the house, Angela said that she did, and generally had the run of the place.

"And you were at the Antonoviches' house the night Hayley got—for lack of a better word—kidnapped, right?"

"Right."

"You remember that Dani and Russell spent most of that evening in the study together, don't you?"

Angela frowned and thought for a moment. "I'm not sure. They may have."

"Well, you saw them there when you brought Dani her green tea, didn't you?"

"I really don't remember, to be honest."

"But you generally do bring her a cup of green tea every evening, isn't that right?"

"I usually do. But that night was so weird…I don't exactly know whether I did or not."

"If Dani or Russell says you brought her tea in the study that night, would you agree they were probably right?"

Looking mildly perplexed, Angela said, "I guess."

I had a feeling I knew where this was going. A glance at Bailey showed me she did too. Declan had on his poker face, but I could see his wheels were turning. If I was right, this was about to get ugly.

"Your father is currently retired, is he not?"

Angela looked startled at the abrupt shift. "Yes."

"Before he was retired, what did he do?"

"He worked in the restaurant of a casino in Las Vegas as a maître d'."

"And what else did he do?"

"I'm sorry?"

"Wasn't he also the president of the hotel workers' union?"

"Y-yes."

"You're very close to your father, aren't you?"

Now Angela looked worried as well as confused. "Uh, sure."

"And isn't it true that you called him on the night of Hayley's kidnapping?"

"I—no. No, I didn't."

Terry brandished a cell phone bill and one of her law clerks handed a copy to Declan. "Who pays for your cell phone, Angela?"

"The Antonoviches."

I quickly scanned the bill. It looked legit and I doubted Terry would pull a bush-league trick like trying to dummy up an exhibit. I wasn't about to object and let the jury think this worried me. But I'd have it checked out later, just to be safe.

Terry approached the witness stand. "I'm showing you the phone bill. Do you recognize the number at the top?"

"Yes, it's my number."

"I've highlighted a phone call on this bill. Do you recognize that number?"

"Yes. It's my father's number. But I—"

"That's enough, you've answered the question."

And she'd established who the "mole" was—the one who connected the union to Russell and the kidnapping.

"So you *did* call your father the night of the kidnapping, didn't you?"

"I . . . yes."

"Now, since your father was union president up until about a year ago, you know that he was very vocal—along with many other union officials—about his anger with certain casino owners who laid off their union staff and rehired non-union workers, don't you?"

"I know they didn't like it."

"Didn't some of the casino owners get death threats?"

"My father would never—"

"In fact, Russell Antonovich and Ian Powers were

among those casino owners who received death threats, isn't that right?"

I jumped to my feet. "Objection! No foundation, assumes facts not in evidence, and it calls for speculation! There's no evidence this witness knows anything about that!"

"Counsel is allowed to inquire, Ms. Knight. If the witness doesn't know, she can say so."

"It's also hearsay, Your Honor!"

"That's enough, Ms. Knight. I've ruled. Take your seat."

I might've fought the ruling a little harder, but I knew that Terry would get it all in anyway. And now I knew how.

"Isn't it true that your father's union made death threats on Russell Antonovich and Ian Powers?"

"No!"

"And isn't it true that when you called your father that night you told him about the kidnapping?"

"No! My father just had open-heart surgery! I called to find out how he was doing!"

"You didn't tell him about the kidnapping? Something as outrageous as that happens and you don't mention it?" Terry's incredulous tone said it all. No one would believe she hadn't at least mentioned it.

"I didn't even know about the kidnapping till the police came! And I didn't talk to my father after that—I never had the chance!"

"So you deny having seen the message about the kidnapping on Russell's cell when you brought Dani her tea that night?"

"Yes!"

"And you deny having told your father about the kidnapping that night?"

"Yes! I absolutely deny it! And my father would *never*—"

Terry cut her off with the wave of her hand. "I have nothing further."

I used my cross to let Angela repeat her denials in full sentences, but the damage was done. When she left the stand, red-faced and teary, the jury was awash in frowns and skeptical looks.

The judge announced the mid-morning recess, and as the jurors filed out, I saw Wagmeister and Ian exchange surreptitious congratulatory nudges, elbow to elbow, as they stood and pretended to watch the jurors exit with solemn expressions. After the jurors were gone, we huddled at counsel table.

"We'll need to line up our rebuttal witnesses for tomorrow," I said.

"You think they're done?" Bailey asked.

"Just about. They've got one more. But they'll be done by the end of the day."

"Let me put a call in to Graden and see if Parkova's made any progress."

"Don't bother. We're out of time." Tomorrow was Friday. We didn't have enough witnesses to fill up more than half a day, so there was no way I could push to the weekend to buy ourselves time. "Besides, we'd have heard from her if there was something to report."

Declan asked if there was anything he could do, but I shook my head. "It's over."

The coup de grâce was coming now.

78

As Terry walked to the lectern, it seemed to me that she took special pleasure in pronouncing the name of her final witness. "The defense calls Russell Antonovich."

Just the fact of the victim's father testifying for the defense has huge emotional impact. If even the father doesn't believe the defendant is guilty, then...But in this case, the emotional significance was the least of it. This father would be their star witness, who'd deliver the cornerstone of the defense case.

From the moment he stood up, the entire courtroom was glued to his every move. The gallery of spectators stared and the reporters took notes as they watched him approach the stand. The jurors, who up till now had been careful to keep a neutral appearance, leaned forward eagerly. This was a real Hollywood star, and he was just a few feet away.

Russell, his expression intense, stopped in front of the witness stand and raised his right hand with a stiff, jerky motion. Tricia read him the oath and he practically cut her off midsentence as he impatiently replied, "Yes, yes." He'd dressed up for the occasion, in a navy blazer, crewneck T-shirt, and jeans. No baseball cap. For him, it was practically black tie.

Terry started by having Russell describe Ian's personal history and the history of Russell's relationship with Ian, taking care to show in great detail how close they were, and especially how close Ian had been to Hayley.

"Ian was only eight years old when he starred in *Just the Two of Us*. Sounds glamorous, but he had a rough life. His dad was a drunk and his mom was…a mess. He and his two sisters raised themselves, and Ian was the sole support for the whole family. But as soon as he started making money, he really gave back. Sponsored Big Brother–type clubs for underprivileged children, founded that summer camp program for kids in gang territory, and he got that law passed to protect child actors from abuse. Lots of people talk, but Ian really walked the walk."

"Was he close to your family?"

"He was like a second father to Hayley," he said solemnly. "I never worried about my family when I left town for a shoot so long as Ian was around."

Terry covered the meteoric rise of the Antonovich-Powers partnership quickly. A smart move because everyone already knew they were top-tier players. The less said, the better, about a level of wealth and power the jurors could never even imagine, let alone experience.

"You guys have done okay since *Wonderland Warriors*, haven't you?"

"Yeah, you know, we're comfortable," Russell

replied. The "aw shucks" was palpable. It made me want to gag.

"Now, you recall the problems you encountered with your joint venture in the Las Vegas casino?"

"Oh, yes." Russell shook his head. "We were in so far over our heads—had absolutely no idea what we were getting ourselves into."

"So if you had it to do over again, what would you do differently?"

"Well, for sure, I wouldn't listen to the business manager who told us to fire all the union workers. But probably I wouldn't do it at all. We just weren't meant for a cutthroat business like that." His tone was sheepish, his expression a picture of remorse.

I glanced at Ian and saw he was nodding his head, sharing in Russell's mea culpa. Poor, poor Russell and poor, poor Ian. They weren't ruthless jerks who'd dumped service industry veterans out on the street so they could fatten their profit margin. Oh, heavens no! They were just a couple of country bumpkins who'd listened to bad advice. Was the jury buying this fairy tale? I snuck a look at them as I pretended to take notes. They were all leaning forward, engrossed. Some even wore benign smiles that seemed to say, "See? These are just regular guys—they screw up just like me."

"When you didn't rehire the union workers, what happened?"

Russell's expression shifted from remorseful to worried. It was a better performance than he'd ever coaxed out of his stars. He answered in low, serious tones. "They were vicious. We got death threats nearly every day. Someone sent Ian a dead snake with a threatening note, and I got physically attacked when I was out at dinner with some business associates."

I made a note to get him to name those associates, but Terry saw me coming.

"And who are those associates?"

"They're all Japanese businessmen, no longer in this country. But I can get their names for you."

How convenient. I glanced at Ian out of the corner of my eye. He had his elbows on the table and was leaning forward, a look of sorrow on his face. These two should take their act on the road. But the shocked expressions on the jurors' faces told me they were eating it up.

"How long ago was this?"

"It's been almost two years, but I'm still getting threats on my listed phones."

"Did you keep a record of those calls?"

Russell shook his head, his expression frustrated and sad. "I didn't take them seriously. Especially after we sold the casino. I really never thought…" He blinked rapidly and looked away for a few moments. "But I did bring some of the threatening letters." He pulled some envelopes out of his jacket, and Terry moved to the witness stand to retrieve them.

I stood up, angry as I'd ever been during a trial. I was fed up with this trial-by-ambush tactic and I was sick of this judge who repeatedly let them get away with it. I controlled my voice with an effort. "Your Honor, I've never seen or heard of these letters."

What should have drawn a sidebar and serious sanctions merely drew a nod and a mildly stated question from Judge Osterman. "Ms. Fisk, why was this not turned over in discovery?"

"I didn't know he had these letters, Your Honor. I can promise the court that if I had, I would've gladly turned them over."

"Your Honor, I find it impossible to believe—"

Judge Osterman held up a hand and spoke sternly. "Well, I don't, Counsel, so have a seat." He turned back to Terry. "Ms. Fisk, when we break for the day, you'll give them to Ms. Knight and she will have the evening recess to examine them."

"Of course, Your Honor," Terry said. "And I just want to add that I'd never intentionally withhold discovery—"

"Let's not do this here, all right, Counsel? This jury's time is precious. Please continue."

I tried to calm myself with slow, deep breaths, deliberately keeping my eyes down so the judge wouldn't be able to see the fury in them.

Terry walked back to the lectern and made a show of reading the three letters, then put two of them up on the monitor. They were threatening, no doubt about it. *You're dead, you bloodsucking asshole.* The other one got more creative: *I've got arsenic. And I'm still a food server. Enjoy your dinner.*

"Were they all like this?" Terry asked Russell.

"Yes. Some were worse. They threatened my family, said that—"

I forced a calm tone. "Objection. Hearsay."

"It's borderline," the judge said. "But I'll sustain the objection."

Terry frowned to telegraph her disagreement but quickly resumed. She had real momentum going with the jury now, and she knew it.

"And how many of these threatening letters did you get?"

"I don't exactly remember. I know it was a lot more than that." He gestured to the few Terry now held. "But I gave the rest to the Las Vegas police. I actually thought I'd given them all to the police, but when you asked me to make sure, I discovered I'd missed these. They may have come in after the police said they'd closed the case."

I'd check with the Las Vegas PD to see if they had a record of this, but I was certain they did. I believed Russell and Ian did get threats. And I didn't much blame the people who'd sent them after the crap those two had pulled.

"Moving forward to the night of the kidnapping, do you remember what you did when you got the first note, the text message from Hayley's phone saying she'd been kidnapped?"

"Yes, I went into the study."

"And did someone join you in the study?"

"My wife, Dani."

"Did you tell her about the text?"

"Yes, and I showed it to her on my cell phone."

"Did you make any calls at that time?"

I sat up. The call to Ian Powers.

"I know the records show I made a call to Ian. I just can't remember why..."

"So you didn't tell him about the kidnapping text?"

"No." He shook his head. "Absolutely not. I was afraid to talk about it on the phone. I thought whoever had Hayley might have me bugged. I know we'd been having some production problems on...something. But why would I bother to call him at a time like that?" Russell spread his hands, his expression perplexed and contrite. "All I can say is, I must have been on autopilot. I know I was about out of my mind." Russell shrugged and shook his head.

I'd predicted that answer, and it was a convincing performance. I didn't buy a second of it.

"What did you do with your cell phone after that?"

"I'm not exactly sure. I think I set it down on my desk. Periodically we would pick it up and look at it." Russell shook his head. "It was so unreal...even now, I can hardly believe it." He dropped his head and pinched the bridge of his nose, squeezing his eyes shut.

"Would you like to take a break?"

Russell nodded. "It's okay. I'm okay."

"Do you remember anyone else coming into the study that evening?"

"Yes."

"Now, to be clear, I'm talking about the period of time before you got the second note with the ransom demand."

"Yes, I understand. Angela was there. I remember her coming in to bring Dani her tea."

"Do you know where the cell phone was when she came in?"

"I'm pretty sure Dani was holding it, staring at it. I'm not even sure she knew Angela was there. She was kind of in shock. We both were."

"But you noticed Angela? Why?"

"Because, like I said, I was paranoid. I was worried that if the kidnapper found out that anyone else knew, he'd..." Russell swallowed, then continued. "So I wanted her to get out. But she kept fussing, setting up the tea and the brown sugar and who knows what."

Terry paused and gave a sweeping glance across the jury to make sure she had their attention before asking her next question. She needn't have worried. The jury was riveted.

"So...Angela had both the time and opportunity to see the text on your cell phone."

"Yes, certainly."

"Now, you're here testifying for the defense. I take it you don't believe Ian had anything to do with this?"

I could've objected. What Russell believed was irrelevant. But why bother? The jury already knew it by now.

"No. There is not one doubt in my mind about this. Ian Powers is not guilty."

"Thank you, Mr. Antonovich. I have nothing further."

Declan tried to give me an "atta girl" look of encouragement. But as I stood up and walked to the lectern, I saw the jury sit back in their chairs—a clear sign they'd made up their minds. It was over. But I didn't care. As long as they were still sitting in that jury box, I intended to keep on fighting, no matter how lost the cause.

"Mr. Antonovich, how many times would you say you've spoken to me since this case first broke?"

"Several. I don't remember."

"Yet you never told me or the lead investigator on this case, Bailey Keller, anything about your trouble with the union in Las Vegas, did you?"

Russell leaned forward and fixed me with an angry look. "Because you never asked. You focused on Ian Powers right from the start. I tried to tell you he couldn't have done it. But you didn't care about the truth. You just had to have someone go down for this—it didn't matter who."

I could tell he'd been waiting to unload that one on me for some time. But I was ready for it.

"You honestly believed that I wouldn't look into the possibility of another suspect?"

Russell set his jaw. "Yes."

"So let me get this straight: You were willing to let your best friend stand trial for the murders of your daughter and Brian Maher rather than give the police even *one shot* at exonerating him by investigating your theory?"

A few jurors looked mildly interested, and Russell shifted uncomfortably in the witness chair, but he remained resolute. "Yes. I guess I didn't trust them to really follow through."

That was a lame answer. Either this was a weak spot Terry couldn't cover or a blind spot she'd forgotten to cover. I went after it.

"And so you never even tried. You, as his best friend, didn't do everything possible to see your friend exonerated? Because you didn't think the police would do a good enough job?"

"How do I know you wouldn't try to scare off the witnesses?"

"Who would I scare off, Mr. Antonovich? The union workers? They didn't look like the type to get scared off to me."

Russell became even more truculent. "But you might've gotten to Angela. I don't know. And maybe the person who really did this got to Jack Averly. Maybe that's why Averly never showed up in court. Someone knew Averly was going to clear Ian and he wasn't going to let that happen."

This particular defense spin had swirled around a bit before the trial started, but Terry had never delivered on it. I noticed that the low buzz coming from the defense table had just picked up tempo. Either Russell's last answer had been programmed and they were pleased, or he'd gone off script. Whatever the reason, it meant they were distracted. I launched my final salvo.

"So now we have yet another conspiracy? One to silence Jack Averly?"

"Yes."

"Because Averly was going to exonerate Ian Powers?"

"Yes, that's right."

"Averly, the guy who drove Ian Powers to Boney Mountain, who wound up in New York with your daughter's iPad, who bought a plane ticket in Brian's name to frame Brian for Hayley's murder, *this* was the guy who was going to prove that Ian Powers—"

Terry jumped to her feet and shouted, to drown out the rest of my question. "Objection! Argumentative!"

"Your Honor, this is cross—"

"And it's argumentative," the judge said with a disapproving glare. "Move on, Ms. Knight."

But a sidelong glance at the jury showed me there was no point. Three were leaning back, arms folded, two looked irritated, and the rest were simply stone-faced. I knew I was violating the cardinal rule that you never spar with a victim, but I had no choice. I had to take the risk. Now, I could see that my gamble hadn't paid off. I'd lost. "Nothing further, Your Honor. But I ask that Mr.

Antonovich remain on call." If by some chance those threatening letters turned out to be bogus, I'd put him back up there and shove them down his throat.

"Your next witness, Ms. Fisk?"

Terry stood, and I heard the note of triumph in her voice. "None, Your Honor. The defense rests."

79

"Rebuttal, Ms. Knight?"

"Can we have a brief sidebar, Your Honor?"

The judge nodded and turned to the jury. "Why don't we take our afternoon break, then? It's three o'clock, I'll see you back here at three fifteen."

Declan and I stood as the jury filed out. Not one of them looked in our direction. Bailey leaned toward me. "Nice cross, Counselor."

"Not that it mattered."

Bailey sighed. "I'd like to tell you you're wrong…"

I moved toward sidebar with leaden feet. I knew I probably shouldn't even bother with rebuttal, but I couldn't let go. If there was any way to rescue this case, I had to find it. "Your Honor, as you know, the defense had said they intended to call many more witnesses than they did, so I expected the defense case to take at least a couple of days longer—"

"And you don't have witnesses ready for today," the judge said. "Is that where you're going?"

"In a nutshell, yes. I can get them in tomorrow, I believe."

Terry's chin jutted out as she leaned toward the court reporter. "This court has made it very clear that we had to have witnesses standing by every day, and that if either of us ran out, it would require us to rest our case. The defense has abided by that rule and I'm urging the court to enforce it for the People as well. If Ms. Knight doesn't have her witnesses, then there should be no rebuttal. The case should go to the jury."

"Ms. Fisk is right," the judge said.

I started to respond, but he held up a hand and cut me off. "I've heard your position; it doesn't require any further explanation." The judge folded his arms and pursed his lips as he looked down at the space between us. The court reporter's hands hovered over the keys, waiting to hear what he'd say. I reflexively crossed my fingers, my heart in my throat. Finally, the judge made his decision.

"I'm going to allow the People to start their rebuttal tomorrow. I want to make it clear that the only reason I'm doing this is because Ms. Knight is correct: the defense witness list was extensive, which created the impression that it would take a great deal more time than it has. Ms. Fisk, you've dropped at least seventy percent of the witnesses you originally indicated you'd call. I really can't, in all fairness, punish Ms. Knight for relying on your representations. So I'm granting the People's request. But I warn you, Ms. Knight, I won't brook any delays tomorrow. I want this case to go to the jury as soon as possible, so make sure you have everyone here."

"Thank you, Your Honor," I said.

I walked back to counsel table and gave Declan and Bailey the news.

"I'm outta here," Bailey said. "I'll tell 'em all to be here by eight thirty."

"I'll be in my cave," I said.

I spent the rest of the day in my office getting ready for my last witnesses. There wasn't that much to do. They were all crime lab people. I intended to put Leo back on to give the defense fingerprint whore, Poplar, another thrashing, and Barry Feinstein, the head of the DNA section, who'd supervised Gelfer's work on this case. He'd say that from what he'd seen, Gelfer had followed proper procedures during the testing in this case. He wouldn't be able to say he'd watched him every second of the day, but it was better than nothing. I'd already had Russell's threatening letters sent to the crime lab to see if I could do anything with them, but I wouldn't have an answer on them until tomorrow.

The only thing left to do was work on my closing argument. If everything went according to schedule, I'd be doing it by tomorrow afternoon. I made bullet points of the evidence we'd presented and made a separate list of the zingers I'd save for rebuttal. Since the prosecution has the burden of proof, I'd get to argue twice, once before and once after the defense. That final rebuttal is the golden opportunity where we always stash our "gotcha's" because the defense can't respond.

Engrossed, I lost track of the time until Declan checked in. "It's seven o'clock. Want me to bring you some dinner?"

"Damn. I didn't realize. Thanks, but no. I'm just about ready to go."

"Then I'll wait and give you a lift. You've got to be tired."

Bailey had given me a ride to work, so I didn't have my car. I knew I should turn down the offer. I needed the exercise and the evening was beautiful. The sky was still bright, but the sun's rays were low, giving the air a soft, balmy warmth. But I was wiped out. "That'd be great. Just gimme a sec."

"No rush. Call me when you're done."

I called Bailey, just to check in. I got her voice mail and left a message saying I was heading back to the hotel.

When Declan dropped me off, I decided to hit the bar. I needed the break and I hadn't seen Drew in a while. Being in trial means living in a tunnel, with the courtroom at one end and home at the other—nothing in between. There's just no time. Anticipating a very dry martini, I opened the heavy glass door and swung into the cool darkness.

And stopped dead in my tracks. Sitting at a table with two other men, just twenty feet away, was the same jerkweed who'd hit me up in the hallway outside my room. Sunglasses and all. I quickly backed out and headed up to my room before they could see me.

I called Drew and told him about my encounter with the asswipe reporter now sitting at his bar, whom I'd nicknamed Sunglasses. "You see him?"

Drew was silent for a moment. "Yeah. What do you want me to do?"

"Would you consider watering down his drinks?"

"Sure, but…" Drew paused a moment. "You know the two dudes sitting with him?"

"No."

"Call you right back."

Five minutes later, my cell played Drew's ringtone, "One for My Baby."

"Tell me you gave him a water martini."

"I did you one better."

"What?"

"Can't tell you right now. But just to warn you: those other two guys with him? They're reporters. I hate to say this, but you might want to steer clear of this place for a little while. At least till the trial's over."

Damn. Now I wasn't even safe where I lived. I sighed. "Okay. Thanks, Drew."

"Oh, and just so you know. I heard them talking. This guy, Sunglasses, is only a freelance. My guess is he's going guerrilla on you so he can get some footage that'll score him a real gig. So watch out for him."

"Will do. But please, whatever you decide to do to this douche bag, make sure it hurts."

"Trust me."

I knew I could. Just the thought that payback was being delivered—even if I wasn't there to see it—was enough to lift my spirits. I was fed up with feeling hunted and powerless to do anything about it.

I'd showered and gotten into my comfy sweats and poured myself a glass of Ancien pinot noir by the time Bailey called me back.

"Hey, where've you been?" I asked. "I'm sitting here drinking all alone. Which isn't all bad since it means more for me—"

"I've got good news and bad news." Bailey's voice was tight and low.

"Good news." I'd had enough of the other to last me a lifetime.

"Parkova's got something."

I put down the glass of wine and sat up. "What?"

"She called it an MITM attack. 'Man in the middle.' It's a way of intercepting someone's e-mail without them knowing it."

"Ian was intercepting Russell's e-mail?"

"Yep."

"How?"

"The only words I understood were 'man in the middle,' so I think I'll let her explain."

"So that's how Ian knew about the kidnapping."

"And why he didn't have to be in Russell's house at the time the kidnapping e-mail came in."

"If I call her to the stand, can she prove this?"

"That's the bad news. Right now, it's an educated guess. She needs to firm things up—"

"So she needs more time. How much?"

"A few days. I know we've only got enough witnesses to fill up tomorrow morning, but if we can stretch them out, we'll make it. Monday's Labor Day—"

"Right." I'd forgotten. But getting there was another story. There was no way the judge would give me tomorrow off. I'd have to stall. "I'll do my best, but..."

"I know." Bailey sighed. "Okay, I'm going back in there. Parkova'll be working all night and I need to follow whatever the hell it is she's doing so I can write a report for your girlfriend Terry."

My girlfriend. "Yeah, Fisk and I just booked a spa weekend together."

Bailey snorted. "For the mud baths."

"No, she's got those at home."

"Anything you want me to tell Parkova?"

"Yeah. Hurry."

80

I spent the rest of the evening dreaming up ways to stall. Call in sick? Dicey. Shoot Terry? Tempting, but the judge would just make Wagmeister take over. And he'd probably be delighted to do it now that they looked like sure winners. Give some of the jurors food poisoning? Hard work. They weren't sequestered, so they could go wherever they wanted. Bailey would need to tail them. Bailey might not approve of this plan. I fell asleep with no workable ideas.

But I woke up with a couple. Idea number one: pray for rain. It was far from foolproof, but there *were* clouds in the sky. Rain was good. Rain meant slow traffic. Slow traffic meant a late start. I did a mental rain dance as I got dressed. I even threw a trench coat over my shoulder to give the weather a little encouragement. As I walked up Broadway toward the courthouse, I looked at the clouds, tried some visualization exercises. Come on, you suckers, pour. But by the time I arrived at work, not a drop had fallen. Proof that the clouds were on the defense dole.

Since the weather had crapped out on me, I was forced to put idea number two into action. I went to Declan's office and found him hunched over a legal pad.

"Hey, Rachel. Need anything?"

"Yes, but first I have some news." I told him about the latest development with Parkova.

"Awesome! Finally, the good guys get a break!"

"Doesn't sound like a game changer yet. First of all, we have to hope the trial lasts long enough for her to firm it up—"

"But if she can, I'll take it."

"Me too. But we've got to stall, and I think we both know that the judge is not my biggest fan."

"He's a tool."

"This is true. But a tool who still likes you…"

Declan's eyes widened.

"I'm putting you in, slugger. All you have to do is remember to talk slowly. But I mean, really, really slowly." Declan's brow creased with worry. "You can do it. I know you can."

The truth was, he had to do it. There was no other choice. If I suddenly slowed my pace and meandered around the courtroom, everyone would know it was an act and I was just stalling for time. But they hadn't seen enough of Declan to really know what his style was. And after his stumble with Leo's testimony, if he moved slowly, everyone would think he was just being extra careful. Declan nodded and then he gave a little smile. "Okay, put me in, Coach. We all know I can drop the ball. That should eat up some time."

His willingness to look less than stellar for the sake of

the case was a real sacrifice, and it showed me yet again what a mensch he was. I told him so.

"Just promise that, whatever happens here, you'll tell everyone that I took the hit for the team."

"You better believe it. You'll be the stuff of legend. A current-day J. Miller Leavy—"

J. Miller Leavy was the most famous L.A. prosecutor of all time.

"More like a J. Miller Leavy on downers," Declan said.

Declan got into character by walking slowly on our way to court.

"You're killing me, dude," I said. The slow pace was sheer agony for me.

"You want me to sell this?" I nodded. "Then don't argue. It's my *process*."

"You hang around too many actors."

We walked into the courtroom and set up at counsel table…slowly. "I'm busy, don't distract me," Declan said. Slowly.

When the jury was seated, Declan stood deliberately, reviewed his notes with great care, and then called our first rebuttal witness. Leo Relinsky. He then reshuffled through his notes for as long as he dared.

"Good morning, Mr. Relinsky. How are you today?"

"I'm well, and you?"

"Just fine, thank you for asking. Mr. Relinsky, is it common to see fingerprints planted at a crime scene?"

Leo stated it was not. Declan consulted his notes, then opened his binder, flipped through some pages, then closed his binder. Finally, he asked his next question. "Why is that?"

While Leo explained, Declan garnished every answer with "Thank you for that, Mr. Relinsky" and "Very interesting, sir." Then he'd pause and consult his notes before asking the next question.

And when it came time to put exhibits on the monitor, he dropped them, put them in upside down, and then spent minutes readjusting the focus. Each question, punctuated by pauses, took almost a full minute to get out. Only I knew what a great act this was.

And because it was Declan, an obvious newbie whom they hadn't seen much of, the jury was forgiving and even somewhat entertained by his puppy-like display of nerves. But I knew their goodwill had its limits.

"Mr. Relinsky, are there set standards for how many points must match before you can declare that a print was made by a particular person?"

"Yes, the commonly accepted standard is eight points. I personally won't declare a match with less than ten, though."

"Do you know of any expert in the field who doesn't have a set minimum number of points?"

"Not one who's qualified, no."

"Then you don't ascribe to the Jackson Pollock style of print analysis?"

It was what they call a two percenter—just two percent of the country was likely to know that Pollock was a famous abstract artist—but apparently about four percent of our jury knew, and they laughed. One of them was the Hollywood agent.

Somehow, Declan managed to stretch Leo's testimony out till almost noon. I knew Terry couldn't let it go without some cross-examination. Otherwise it'd look as though she'd conceded the fingerprint battle. So Leo was ordered to come back after the lunch break.

"You are, quite simply, my hero," I said as we ate our turkey and Swiss sandwiches.

"I can pull it out for another hour after Terry's cross, I think," Declan said. We exchanged a conspiratorial grin.

"And I'd think our crime lab director's testimony will take some time. No way they can let him off easy." No matter how strong the defense was right now, they couldn't afford to let us off the ropes on the DNA evidence even a little. "But just to be on the safe side, want to take him too?"

"Uh...sure...though if I'm being entirely frank, Your Honor, I must admit...this is slightly embarrassing...I do have some...ah...difficulties with the finer points of deoxyribonucleic acids."

We laughed. It was the best either one of us had felt in days.

When we resumed after the lunch break, Terry did as minimal a cross-examination of Leo as she dared, but as promised, Declan dragged his feet on redirect. By the time he called Barry Feinstein, our crime lab director, it was almost three o'clock—just as we'd hoped. Judge Osterman called for the afternoon break. That would take us to three fifteen. Every minute helped. Plus, the brief recess gave me the chance to bring Barry in on my strategy. Barry and I went back a long way—to the days when he was a new tech and I was a baby DA. Fun and smart, with a casual style, he knew how to make DNA sound simple. It'd been a real loss to us in court when he went into management. "Take your time, Barry. Explain at length, and talk slow. We need you to be ordered back to finish your testimony on Tuesday."

Barry raised an eyebrow. "Want to tell me why?"

"Yes, but then I'd have to kill you."

Barry turned to Declan. Declan gave him a wide-eyed look. "All I heard was the lady telling you to speak clearly so the court reporter and the jury would catch everything."

I smiled at Barry. "Any further questions?"

Judge Osterman came out and Jimmy called the court to order.

Barry smiled as he faced the judge and spoke under his breath. "No. But I'd just like you to remember this little exchange when you need a rush on your evidence, or you insist on getting Dorian on your next case."

I winced. Point taken.

The judge called for the jury, and when they were seated, Barry walked over to the witness stand and took the oath. Declan came through once again, slow as molasses and as thorough as could be. And Barry's testimony was helpful.

"You are familiar with, ahh, Mr. Gelfer?"

"I am."

"He works in your lab, does he not?"

"Yes, he does."

"Do you observe your lab workers during testing?"

"Yes, I frequently watch them." Barry went into a lengthy description of his job duties and the importance of monitoring the actual casework.

"Thank you, sir. That was very interesting," Declan replied.

If there was a way to string out the questioning any longer, I sure couldn't think of it.

"Were you in the lab the day Mr. Gelfer performed

the DNA analysis on the bloodstain found on Brian Maher's car trunk?"

"I was."

"I see."

Declan shuffled through his notes before he continued. "Could you see whether he brought Ian Powers's blood sample into the lab at that time?"

"Yes, I would've seen that if he'd done it. And no, I did not see Mr. Gelfer bring Ian Powers's blood draw into the room at any point during testing."

"I see. Thank you. Could you describe what you saw Mr. Gelfer do that day?"

Barry could. In excruciating detail.

"Are you confident that there was no contamination?"

"Yes, I am."

Declan nodded. Slowly. "And are you confident that the results were accurate?"

"Quite confident."

"Thank you very much, sir."

On cross-examination Terry predictably asked, "You mean, as far as you could see, Mr. Gelfer followed proper protocols, correct?"

"Yes, that's correct."

"And he didn't bring Ian Powers's blood draw into the lab *as far as you could see,* correct?"

"Correct."

"But since you didn't see his every move, there is a possibility that the evidence sample from the car trunk was contaminated, isn't there? You can't rule it out completely."

"Completely? I don't know that I can rule out anything in this world completely."

"So the answer is no, you can't rule out that possibility, correct?"

"Yes, I can't completely rule it out."

Terry raced through her cross. Even on a slow day, she talks faster than anyone I know. But today she was setting a new land speed record. More than once, the court reporter had to stop her and get her to repeat her question. Finally, the reporter lost it. "Counsel, I didn't get one word of that! If you don't slow down, you're going to have to start writing your questions out!"

Terry obviously hoped to force us to rest before the end of the day so the judge would declare the evidence closed. But she didn't reckon with the awesome powers of Declan Shackner. When Terry finished cross at four o'clock, Declan immediately requested a break.

"Counsel, we've already taken our afternoon break," Judge Osterman said.

"I'm sorry, Your Honor. Some aspects of life just aren't in my control."

Judge Osterman sighed. "Fine, we'll take a ten-minute break. And I don't mean eleven. Understood?"

"Yes. Thank you, Your Honor."

Declan made a big show of leaving the courtroom with a fast stride. Barry stepped off the witness stand and came over to us.

"He has a bright future with the DA's office, doesn't he?" he asked.

"If I have anything to say about it he does."

"So what's the story?"

I told him. He shook his head sympathetically. "Talk about down to the wire. Well, I'm glad to do what I can to help the cause."

The judge took the bench at ten minutes past four and called for the jury. Barry gave me a private wink and moved slowly up to the witness stand. Declan stalled by scanning his notes for as long as he dared, then had Barry go over every single move he made on the day of the testing in such excruciating detail that even I wanted to pull my hair out. But he did it wisely. Not once did he repeat a question he'd already asked. And at five minutes to five, Declan looked up innocently and told the judge, "I'm about to move into a whole new area, Your Honor. Perhaps the court would prefer to recess now? If not, I'm happy to continue..."

"No, I don't think that will be necessary. If you've got a new area we may as well start fresh on Tuesday. We could all use the holiday break, I'm sure."

Declan was the man of the day, and when we got up to the office, I poured us all shots of the scotch I kept in my bottom drawer. "Here's to our champion!"

It would've been even nicer if I'd known whether there really was anything to celebrate.

81

We all weighed in with our opinions about which way the jury was leaning. The unsurprising consensus was that most of them looked ready to acquit.

"I think there might be a few on our side, but they don't look strong," Bailey said.

Meaning, they'd be easily talked out of their inclination to convict by the others. I agreed.

"So, what do we do now?" Declan asked.

It was a fair question. Our rebuttal was largely over. The crime lab hadn't come up with anything on Russell's letters. The postmarks on the envelopes were authentic, and the letters didn't appear forged. All of our hopes now rested on Parkova's findings, which weren't in yet. But I couldn't just go back to the Biltmore and wait all weekend. I'd go crazy. I should go to the gym, but I wasn't in the mood for that either. I knew what I wanted to do.

"I want to go watch Parkova."

"Me too," Bailey said.

"It's unanimous," added Declan.

We walked out into the early evening. The sun had painted rosy streaks through the clouds and the sky was just beginning to fade to indigo. I watched low shafts of sunlight grow on the horizon as the clouds retreated over the mountains to the east. I enjoyed the short walk to the Police Administration Building, knowing it was my last chance to breathe in the warm, smog-filled air for several hours. Then it occurred to me that most of us downtown dwellers had the lungs of dedicated smokers. The thought made me take shallow breaths until we were inside the building.

Parkova was hunched in front of Ian's laptop, talking into her recorder in an accent so thick I could barely pick out three words. If we had to play that thing back to the jury, we'd need an interpreter. Parkova turned and took us in. "I have cheering section now?" She glared at us through her heavy glasses and noted Declan, our new addition, but showed no interest in him whatsoever.

"We're just here to help," Bailey said.

"You expect to be able to help, how?"

I shrugged. "We could bring you food, coffee...methamphetamine?"

"Just be quiet, is all I ask." And with that, Parkova turned around and went back to work.

After an hour, the hollow feeling in my stomach reminded me I hadn't eaten in a while. "I'm going to raid the vending machines. Anybody want anything?" I gestured to the half-eaten PayDay next to the laptop. "Another PayDay?"

"Yes," Parkova said without looking up. "And a Coke. Not diet."

Bailey asked for Doritos—a personal favorite of mine also—and Declan asked for an apple.

"An apple?" I was incredulous. "Really?"

Declan laughed. "It's Speedo weather and my homies are not forgiving."

"Don't even think of asking me for sympathy." I gestured to his slender, perfect-looking body.

When I returned with provisions—and Declan's sad little apple—I settled in and watched for a while. But there wasn't much to see, unless you find watching someone type, swear at the computer (that part of her English vocabulary was rich and varied), and scowl an intriguing sight. For the next four hours Parkova worked while we kept whispers to a minimum. I made notes on my closing argument and tried not to think about how this case was likely to end. On occasion, one of us would nod off.

At ten o'clock, Parkova spoke her first non-swear words. "Hah! I knew it. There."

I sat up, rolled my head to unkink my neck, and rubbed my face to get circulation going. "What? There . . . what?"

"Original e-mail."

I couldn't process that. "What are you talking about?"

Parkova turned around in her chair to face us and pushed her glasses back up the bridge of her nose. "I found MITM attack. This Ian set up so he intercepts Russell's e-mails—"

"So all of Russell's e-mails go through Ian's server first? He can see everything Russell gets?" Declan asked.

"Correct."

"How on earth did he do that?" I asked.

"Probably bribed engineer at data center. Put Russell's server behind his, put his server closer to router. Everything Russell's server gets, it has to go through Ian's before it reaches router. Clear?"

Not really, but I didn't care at the moment, so I lied. "Clear. Go on."

"Once e-mails go to Ian's computer, he has choice. He can stop it, change it, let it through. Whatever he wants. So I look at ransom e-mail from kidnapper. I can see it comes from computer. It goes into Russell's server, goes to Ian's computer, then…changes. E-mail that goes to Russell is different." Parkova paused and looked at me for recognition. "You get it?"

"I—maybe," I said. "The e-mail got changed…?"

Parkova nodded impatiently. "E-mail originally sent out to Russell is not e-mail Russell got. E-mail changes after it goes to Ian's server."

"Changes how?" Bailey asked.

Parkova quickly scrolled through Russell's phone, then held it out. "Here is e-mail on Russell's phone. One you give me."

We read the ransom demand and the description of where to drop the money in Fryman Canyon—the e-mail we all knew about.

Then Parkova turned the laptop so we could see it. "But that was not original. Not e-mail that was sent. Here is original e-mail."

My heart began to pound as I read the original ransom note.

We don't want money. All we want is for you to make a DVD admitting that you stole Tommy Maher's screenplay for "Wonderland Warriors." Bring it to God's Seat on Boney Mountain at 7:30. If you do not comply within twenty-four hours, we will tell every media outlet about what you and Ian Powers did to Brittany Caren.

"Here is e-mail you have." Parkova showed us the e-mail on Russell's phone. The one we'd presented in court:

One million dollars in cash in a duffel bag. Go to Fryman Canyon. Take the small path on the left for fifty yards, then turn right. Walk until you see two trees with white string tied around the trunks. Leave the bag between them. Go home and wait for the call. If you bring in the police, Hayley's dead.

Bailey and I turned from the screen and stared at each other for a long minute. The "original" e-mail had raised so many questions I didn't know which one to ask first.

"So did the original e-mail get altered *before* it reached Russell?" I asked.

"Yes. Has to be." Parkova pointed to Ian's laptop. "E-mail you see on this computer"—she then pointed to Russell's phone—"is *not* e-mail received here on this phone."

"So Ian Powers altered the e-mail before it got to Russell?" I asked.

"I cannot tell you *who* did it. I can say only someone

who has access to Ian's server, or his computer. But correct—it was changed before Russell got it."

Someone with access to Ian's computer. Who besides Ian himself? No one we knew of. We'd found it locked in his desk drawer. And who else would've had the opportunity? Or, more important, the motive? No one. I said as much to Bailey.

"No, you're right. It's gotta be Ian," Bailey said. "So, at least now we know why everyone wound up on Boney Mountain—"

"Yeah, but Brittany Caren?" Declan asked. "How does she fit in?"

I said, "Well, Ian obviously knows—"

"And so would Russell," Bailey said. "The original ransom note says 'you and Ian'—meaning Russell—"

"Right," I said. "Something both Russell and Ian did 'to' Brittany."

"What the hell would they have done to her?" Bailey said.

"That is the question. But whatever they did, it's got to be ugly, or Hayley and Brian wouldn't have used it. We need to find Brittany, like, yesterday. You said she was MIA?"

Bailey nodded. "She had that big blowout on the set and took off before Hayley turned up dead. Problem is, if she's at the heart of this thing, then Ian Powers may've had something to do with her vanishing act."

"And if so, any move we make in her direction is only going to cue his people to push her further away," I said.

"Assuming she's still alive," Declan said.

We all fell silent. I turned the question over in my mind, looking at it from all the angles.

"I'd bet she's alive," I said. "Ian can't afford to have any more bodies land on his doorstep. Not this soon. Besides, whatever it is she knows, she's kept it quiet this long. So there's no pressing reason to make a move that risky at a time like this. But the question is, how do we find Brittany?"

We didn't have much time to hunt her down. And I couldn't think of anyone we could tap to help us. I remembered how cagey and uncooperative Brittany's mother had been. Was she in on whatever this was? Or was she just being an obnoxiously jealous gatekeeper? One thing was certain, though: she was tight with Russell, and that meant she was tight with Ian. We couldn't take a chance on asking her for help. We had to find Brittany, but we had only seventy-two hours left and no leads. I stood up and began to pace. For a change, Bailey was too distracted to give me any grief.

There was an old desktop computer in the office they'd requisitioned for Parkova, and while we'd been talking, she'd started it up. The home page had a banner that flashed the news of the day, and the story on the top right was a wrap-up of the trial. I stopped to look at it.

"Kind of amazing how much coverage—" Declan began.

The news story…I had an idea. I quickly pulled out my cell phone, found the number I was looking for, and made the call. This had to work. It had to. I crossed my fingers. "Please pick up," I silently prayed.

"Well! Ms. Knight. What an unexpected pleasure." The British accent of tabloid reporter Andrew Chatham was music to my ears.

"As I recall, you said you could be useful," I said.

"And I was, was I not?"

"You were. But this time is for the big money." I took a deep breath. "I need to find Brittany Caren, ASAP."

"Why?"

"I can't tell you that. Can you find her within the next seventy-two hours?"

"Well...yes."

"Are you sure?"

"Quite."

Success. I couldn't believe it. My heart soared. But the calm, absolute certainty in his voice made me curious. "How? No one's that good."

"First of all, I am that good, and second of all, because I already know where she is. So, as your people say, 'What's in it for me?'"

"I'll owe you one?"

Andrew was silent for a moment. "Very well. I believe you're honorable."

Wow. I just got called *honorable* by a tabloid reporter. What a great day.

82

The next three days were the most hectic I'd ever had. Declan and Bailey and I worked nonstop. But on Tuesday morning, as I drove up Broadway to the courthouse in the already warm early morning sunshine, I was energized and ready for battle.

The minute I got to my office, I called Tricia and told her we'd need to see the judge in chambers before we began. Then I went to Declan's office.

He was reviewing his notes from our past three days. "Got a minute?" I asked.

When he looked up, I saw there were dark circles under his eyes—which were red. But he looked pumped. That pretty much summed us all up at this point, I thought.

"Of course. What's up?"

I stepped in and closed the door. "I didn't want to do it, but I have no choice. I have to put Parkova on the stand, and if we lose, I'll be fired for it. If you're sitting next to me when she takes the stand, you'll get blamed for being in on it. You'll be fired too, or at the very least, you'll get stuck out in the hinterlands trying misdemeanors for the rest of your career. I can't let you take that risk. It's not fair. So I don't want you to come to court with me this morning. If you're not there, I can claim you didn't know anything about it—"

Declan held up his hand. "Save your breath, Rachel. I'm not hiding in my office. I totally agree with everything you've done and I'm not going to pretend otherwise. I just hope that if I get to keep my job, I'll have the smarts to do the same thing under the circumstances." He paused and gave me a little smile. "Though I can't say I ever want to be in the same circumstances."

I smiled briefly. "I can't say I blame you." I looked him in the eye. "Are you sure?"

"Very sure."

This kid had the heart of a lion. It'd kill me if he had to pay the price just because I'd put my own neck on the line. But I couldn't stop him. It was his choice to make and I had to honor it. I went back to my office and sat down to finish my cup of coffee—not that I needed the caffeine—but Bailey called and told me to meet her in front of the courtroom right away. "I can't handle any bad news—" I began.

"Just get here."

I hurried out, and when I approached the courtroom, I saw a familiar figure seated on the bench near the doors. "Janice!" Brian's aunt was clutching the arm of a nice-looking man in glasses and a well-cut beige suit with one hand and a colorful-looking book with the other. We exchanged greetings, and though hers was warm, her strained expression told me what this trip was costing her.

"I...want to apologize for not being able to get here

sooner," she said. "Bailey tells me it's too late for me to testify."

I confirmed that it was. Rebuttal is confined to the points raised by the defense. Terry hadn't made a big issue of the screenplay theft or gone into anything about Brian that Janice might've been able to speak to, so I couldn't justify putting her on the stand. "It is, but I'm glad you're here. I'll go arrange for you to get a seat." Especially now, at the end of the case, there was heavy competition for space in the gallery. I looked at the man she was holding on to and introduced myself. "Would you like a seat also?" I had a feeling Janice wouldn't be going anywhere without him.

"I'm so sorry," Janice said. "Rachel, this is my agent, Elden Brademeyer."

We shook, and he confirmed that he'd very much appreciate it if I could find him a seat. I saw Terry march toward the courtroom and glance at us as she opened the door.

"I'd better get inside—"

"I'll take care of the seating," Bailey said. "You go ahead."

I set up at counsel table, and two minutes later the judge called us all into chambers. Wagmeister was running late, so it was just me and Terry. I told the judge about the new information we'd obtained over the weekend and intended to present in rebuttal. The battle in chambers was heated. Terry fought hard to keep it out. But Judge Osterman shut her down. "No, the evidence is relevant and admissible. And it's very clear that the prosecution had no way of finding it any sooner. Motion to exclude is denied. And I assume you're also moving for mistrial?" Terry confirmed she was. "That will be denied as well. If you need time to prepare for cross, let me know and I'll consider it." Before we left chambers, Terry asked for time to speak to Ian in lockup. The judge frowned. "You may, but make it fast. I'm taking the bench in fifteen minutes."

Terry emerged after ten minutes. I expected to see her go and talk to Russell. But as I watched her out of the corner of my eye, she didn't so much as glance in his direction. I huddled with Bailey.

"Notice she didn't say a word to Russell?" I asked. "I have to believe he already knows what we've got. Otherwise, she'd be over there telling him about it."

Bailey nodded. "If only to warn him. So I guess you were right. Russell knew. He's been covering for that asshole the whole time." She shook her head. "But somehow...I don't know."

I nodded. I didn't want to believe it either.

When the door to lockup opened, Terry stood and noticed me looking at her. A very slight, almost imperceptible smile crossed her face. It was so brief, I wasn't entirely sure I'd seen it.

It was a very different Ian Powers who emerged this time. No more bright smiles, no more waves to his loyal fans. White-faced, eyes hooded, he walked stiffly to his seat and kept his back to the crowded gallery.

When the judge took the bench, Declan declared he had no further questions for Barry Feinstein after all, and Terry declined further cross. The jury looked tired and unhappy about having to come back after a three-day weekend. I'd have to cut to the chase fast.

I started with Parkova. When Tricia asked her to state

her name, she said, "M. Parkova." Tricia raised an eyebrow but recorded the name without further comment.
Parkova sat, scowled at the packed gallery, took one
glance at the jury, then pushed her glasses up her nose
and turned to me, stone-faced.

I started with her federal hacking conviction, established that she'd served her time, then quickly got to the
point. I had her describe how she'd located the original
e-mail and how it had been intercepted by Ian's computer on the way to Russell.

Then I put the original e-mail up on the monitor.

> We don't want money. All we want is for you to
> make a DVD admitting that you stole Tommy Ma-
> her's screenplay for "Wonderland Warriors." Bring it
> to God's Seat on Boney Mountain at 7:30. If you do
> not comply within twenty-four hours, we will tell ev-
> ery media outlet about what you and Ian Powers did
> to Brittany Caren.

The jury stirred, confused but interested. A wave of
whispers spread across the gallery like rustling leaves.

"This was the original e-mail that was sent to Russell,
correct?"

"Yes."

Here in court, Parkova's terse style was a blessing.

"But it was intercepted along the way by Ian's computer, correct?"

"By his server, yes."

"And did that original e-mail go through to Russell
Antonovich's e-mail?"

"No."

"What happened to it?"

"E-mail was altered before it reached Antonovich."

"Can you tell who may have done that?"

"I cannot, no. Someone with access to Ian Powers's server, or computer."

Parkova explained about the man in the middle attack, and how Ian's server was placed in a position to intercept all of Russell's e-mail.

"So when the e-mails intended for Mr. Antonovich passed through Ian Powers's server, did that give Ian Powers the chance to alter them before they got to Mr. Antonovich?"

"Yes. Whoever controls Ian Powers's computer can decide whether to let Antonovich e-mails go through or change them...or delete them."

"And in this case, the original ransom note that passed through Ian Powers's server was altered?"

"Yes."

"Nothing further."

I'd deliberately left the original ransom note up on the monitor throughout my questioning where the jury could read and reread it. I expected Terry to take it down when she started cross. But for some reason, she didn't.

Terry bounced Parkova around a little about her felony conviction and shady past, then took aim at the most damaging part of her testimony.

"Now, being an expert hacker yourself, not to mention a convicted felon, you could have altered that e-mail yourself, couldn't you?"

"Yes. But why would I do this?"

"To curry favor with the police? I imagine you could use a favor or two from them."

"I need nothing from police."

"You're on parole, aren't you?"

"Yes. So?"

"So, you still need to make nice with the police, don't you?"

"Make nice? I don't know what you mean by this. I do this job because I get paid. Just like you."

Surprisingly, I saw Judge Osterman suppress a smile at that.

"So you wanted to give the prosecution what they needed so you'd get paid, isn't that right?"

"No. They have to pay me no matter what. Doesn't matter. I find, I don't find. Still, I get paid."

Stymied on that front, Terry went for the jugular. "But you still could have altered that e-mail yourself. Isn't it true, Ms. Parkova, that the jury has to take your word for it? The word of a convicted felon?"

Someone else might've been offended. Parkova just looked annoyed. "Don't have to take my word. Easy to check. Just go look at computer." Parkova shook her head, her expression a mixture of disdain and irritation. "And how would I know to write such a thing? I know nothing of this case." Parkova added in a voice laced with boredom, "I don't know why this original e-mail is such big deal anyway." She gestured to the monitor, which still showed the original e-mail.

"Well, someone in law enforcement could've told you to write that, couldn't they?"

Parkova frowned. "They could tell me to do this, yes.

But why they want me to write *this?* Better I write a confession, no?"

The answer drew titters from the audience and a few smiles from the jury. Terry went on a little longer, but sparring with Parkova was like hitting a tennis ball into a rubber backboard. Every question Terry lobbed bounced right back with equal force. I'd planned to get into the issue of Parkova's ability to fabricate the original on redirect, but now I didn't have to. Parkova had made all the points for me. And besides, the issue would be resolved—or not—when I called my next witness.

Finally, Terry gave up and released Parkova. But as I stood to announce my next witness, suddenly a strangled yelp burst from the gallery.

Russell was standing, his eyes fixed on the monitor. "No! It can't be!" He was shaking, and his voice trembled. "I don't believe it! It can't be!" The agony in his voice was raw and painful, like the grinding of a rusty hinge. He turned toward Ian, whose back was to the gallery, his expression a mixture of wounded shock and anger. "How *could* you?! How could you do this?!" Ian never turned around. Raynie let out a wail of anguish. "You bastard!" she cried out, then put her head down and sobbed. A woman sitting next to her put an arm around her shoulders. Suddenly, Russell bolted from the courtroom. A few reporters jumped up to follow him.

Caught off guard, even Judge Osterman was rendered momentarily speechless by the outbursts. Now, the entire gallery erupted in a loud buzz as the impact of Parkova's testimony—and Russell's reaction—set in. No one knew exactly what the original ransom note meant, but it was clear that Ian had gone to great lengths to keep it hidden. And Russell's reaction told them it had something to do with Hayley's murder.

Bailey and I exchanged a look. Russell's reaction told us something too: he hadn't been covering for Ian after all. He'd truly believed in Ian's innocence until Parkova's testimony sank in. Bailey mouthed, "Told you so." I nodded. For once, I was glad to be wrong.

Judge Osterman banged his gavel and shouted, "Come to order!" But the gallery wouldn't be tamed. The buzz continued to build in wave after wave. The judge banged his gavel another three times, but it wasn't until he shouted, "I'll have you all thrown out!" that the crowd finally settled. When a semblance of peace was restored, the judge glared at the gallery. "I won't warn you again. This is a court of law, not your living room!" Then he turned to the jury. "I am ordering you to disregard those outbursts. They are not evidence and they are not competent proof of anything. You are to completely dismiss it from your minds. Do you understand?"

The jury nodded. "Yes," they said in unison.

"Sidebar, Your Honor!" Terry demanded with barely controlled fury.

But the judge refused. "I'll deem you to have made a motion for mistrial, Counsel. You can put all of your thoughts on the record later. For now, your motion is denied. People? Please proceed."

I stood up slowly, but my pulse ratcheted up into high gear. No matter how a civilian witness behaves before walking into court, there is no predicting what will happen once they get there. I've seen strong ones fall apart like a cheap suit, and I've seen timid ones come through like Braveheart. So the moments before a witness begins to testify are always nerve-racking ones. But I had good reason to be nervous this time: the entire case hinged on the testimony we were about to take. I took a deep breath and said as calmly as possible, "The People call Brittany Caren."

The response in the courtroom was visceral and immediate. "What?" someone whispered loudly in the back of the courtroom, as another said, "Brittany?" and "Did you hear that?" Again, a loud buzz rolled through the gallery as reporters and spectators reacted to the name.

Judge Osterman banged his gavel. This time he made the threat more immediate. "The next sound I hear from *anyone,* anyone at all, I'm clearing the courtroom and that person will be held in contempt! Do I make myself clear?"

The audience immediately fell silent. No one wanted to miss this show. Into the sudden hush walked Brittany Caren. Ashen-faced, wearing little if any makeup, and dressed simply in a pale yellow summer shift and an off-white cardigan that was draped loosely over her shoulders, she came up the aisle leaning on the arm of a goateed and mustached man in his forties.

I snuck a look at the jury. They were straightening up in their seats, watching intently as Brittany approached. Bailey opened the swinging gate that separated the lawyers, judge, and jury from the spectators and escorted Brittany to the base of the steps at the witness stand. Brittany took the oath and I helped her get seated, then adjusted the microphone. I looked her in the eye and whispered, "Okay?" She said, "Yes," and glanced at the man who'd escorted her. I nodded. "I'll take care of it."

I stepped back to the lectern. "Your Honor, Ms. Caren is here today courtesy of her therapist, Dr. Shepherd." I indicated the man, whose goatee and glasses gave him the prototypical look of a shrink. "I ask that he be allowed to remain and sit with me at counsel table. Since the only relevant information he has is privileged, he can't be called as a witness."

"I don't have a problem with that," the judge said.

I knew Terry certainly did, but she couldn't say so. There was no legal reason to exclude him. And objecting to this shaky girl's lifeline would not endear Terry to the jury.

I began by having Brittany briefly describe her early work as a child actress, and how that led to her getting the leading role in *Circle of Friends*.

"How old were you when you got that part?"

"Twelve."

"Did you know the writers on that show?"

"Yes, of course. We saw them at lunch, at table reads...yes."

"Was Tommy Maher one of those writers?"

"Yes."

"Was Russell Antonovich one of those writers also?"

"Yes."

"Did Tommy have a dispute with Russell Antonovich?"

"Yes."

"When did that argument arise?"

Brittany frowned. "I believe the show was in its second season."

"Did you witness the argument?"

"Everyone on the lot witnessed the argument—it

went on and on. Tommy accused Russell of stealing his screenplay."

"And did he claim that screenplay was the basis for *Wonderland Warriors,* the film that became Russell's first big hit?"

"Yes."

"You say the argument went on and on. Did Tommy make his accusation more than once?"

"He made it a hundred times. But Russell always denied it. Tommy kept trying to tell everyone that Russell was a thief, that he'd find a way to prove it."

"And did he?"

"Not that I ever knew. Tommy always wrote his scripts by hand. I know because it always took him longer to get scripts done for the show. So I assume he wrote the screenplay by hand too."

Terry barked, "Objection! Speculation!"

Brittany jumped in her seat.

"Sustained. Ms. Caren, you cannot assume when you testify. If you did not personally observe something, then you can't speculate about what you believe. Okay?"

Brittany nodded. "Yes, Your Honor."

I continued. "Now as far as you know, Tommy threatened to find a way to prove it, but he never did?"

"Not as far as I know, no."

"At the time Tommy was making these accusations, was the film deal for *Wonderland Warriors* being negotiated?"

"Objection. Again, calls for speculation."

"It doesn't, Your Honor. I'll lay the foundation."

The judge nodded. "Please do."

"Were you involved in discussions regarding your possible role in *Wonderland Warriors*?"

"Yes. But the talks were tentative because they hadn't closed the deal with Russell and Ian yet."

"And at the time you were involved in those negotiations, was Tommy making his accusations about Russell stealing his screenplay?"

"Yes."

"If Tommy did come up with proof that Russell had stolen the screenplay, would that cause a big problem for the studio that produced it?"

Again, Terry objected, but I pointed out that since Brittany had been in the business most of her life, she knew enough to testify on the subject.

"I'll allow it," the judge said. "The jury can decide what weight to give her opinion."

"You can answer, Brittany," I said. "If Tommy came up with proof the screenplay had been stolen, would that cause problems for the defendant, Ian Powers, and Russell Antonovich?"

"Yes, big problems. Because Tommy could sue for a share of the profits, and he could tie them up in lawsuits forever. And of course it would make Russell and Ian look really bad—possibly be the end of their careers, at least as filmmakers."

"So could Tommy's complaint that Russell stole the script stop the studio from going through with the deal?"

"It definitely could. They wouldn't want the headache."

"How long did this argument between Tommy and Russell go on for?"

"About a month, maybe a little more."

"Did the argument ever get physical?"

"Once. It was toward the end. They got into another one of their fights and Tommy socked Russell, knocked him down. It was pretty gnarly. After that, they put Tommy at the far end of the lot to keep him away from Russell."

"But they didn't send him home?"

"No. Everyone knew they weren't going to let Tommy come back next season, but I guess the studio didn't want to make more trouble for themselves by breaking his contract."

I waited for an objection, but this time it didn't come. I moved on to the heart of the matter.

"Did Tommy eventually get sent home?"

"Yes."

"When was that?"

"About a week and a half after he punched Russell. It was the day after the holiday party."

"And do you know why he got sent home at that time?"

"Yes." Brittany teared up and bowed her head as her shoulders began to shake. I brought her a box of Kleenex. She wiped her eyes, then lifted her head. With a voice choked with emotion, she said, "Because of me."

83

I **waited until** Brittany raised her head, and gave her a questioning look. When she offered me a confirming nod, I continued. "How is it that you caused Tommy to be sent home?"

"Because I—" She stopped and bit her lip.

The hush in the courtroom was so complete I could hear the jurors in the first row breathing.

"Do you need a break, Brittany?"

Her next words came out in a rush, but they were clear enough.

"No, I have to finally say this. I have to tell the truth." She glanced at Ian with sad, angry eyes, then turned back to me. "Because Ian told me to say that Tommy raped me at the holiday party. He said if I didn't, Tommy would ruin everything. And he promised me if I did that, he and Russell would make sure I always had work. Actually, he promised I'd always have a starring role in Russell's films."

Someone in the gallery gasped, but otherwise the courtroom was completely still. I could feel the tension in the jury box. There was something particularly monstrous about Ian, a former child actor himself—and one who'd made himself their *champion,* no less—putting a young actress in this hideous position.

"And did he? Did Tommy rape you?"

"No—no, never!"

"Did you see him at the holiday party?"

"Yes, I ran into him when I was heading back to my trailer. He was really drunk, and kind of, you know, teary and sad. He said he knew he wasn't coming back next season and he said he'd miss writing for me. That's all that happened!"

"Now, when Ian said you had to tell that lie, what did you say? Did you agree to do it?"

"No. I was scared, I—I didn't know what to do. I didn't say anything to Ian. I went back to my trailer. But then my mother came and got me. She said she'd heard what happened to me and that I had to tell Chuck—"

"Chuck?"

"Chuck Viener, the head of the studio."

"Did your mother ask you if it was true that Tommy raped you?"

"No. She just grabbed my hand and the next thing I knew, I was standing in Chuck's office and my mom and Ian were there and they were telling Chuck that they wouldn't let me be on the lot with that...rapist."

"Objection, hearsay!"

"Overruled. It's an admission, or at least an adoptive admission," the judge said.

"And what happened next? Did Chuck ask you whether it was true?"

"Objection! Hearsay!"

"It's a question, Your Honor. A question can't be hearsay," I said, annoyed.

"Again, thank you for the evidence lesson, Ms. Knight," the judge said acidly. "Overruled."

Brittany nodded, at first unable to speak. Finally she choked out, "Yes."

"What did you do?"

"I didn't know what to do, I was scared." She looked around the courtroom beseechingly, her sorrowful expression a heart-wrenching portrait of a broken spirit. "I-I did it. I told him it was true." Brittany stopped to catch her breath.

"Brittany, at that time, who was supporting the family—financially, I mean?"

"Um...me."

"And you knew that if you didn't go along with Ian's story, you might lose your job?"

"Yes—I *knew* I'd lose my job, and I might never work again."

"So you went along with the lie because you felt you had no choice?"

"Yes."

"What happened next?"

"Ian and my mother said that if Tommy was removed from the lot that day, we wouldn't call the police."

"So Mr. Viener never knew that it was a lie?"

Brittany shook her head. "No."

"Was Tommy removed from the lot that day?"

"Yes."

"Did you see Tommy again after he left the lot that day?"

"No."

"Why not?"

"Because…" Fresh tears rolled down her face, and Brittany had to struggle to get the words out. "Because the day they sent him home, he shot himself. He killed himself. And it's all because I lied!" Brittany covered her face with her hands, and her choking sobs filled the courtroom.

This time an audible gasp went up from the audience. The jury sat absolutely still; they seemed to be barely breathing. The energy in the courtroom had shifted completely as the awful implications of Brittany's testimony sank in. I glanced at the defense table. Ian's shoulders were hunched around his ears and he stared down at the legal pad in front of him. Terry and Wagmeister had their poker faces on, but the law clerks looked shell-shocked.

"Shall we take a break, Brittany?"

After a few moments, she reached for more Kleenex, wiped her eyes, and took a deep, ragged breath. "No, that's okay."

"Is this the first time you've publicly admitted that you falsely accused Tommy of rape?"

"Yes."

"Was Russell Antonovich in on this lie about Tommy?"

"Objection, calls for speculation!"

It might, and Russell wasn't on trial, but I wanted the whole truth of this sordid story to finally be told. Brittany looked at me, a deer in the headlights. She opened her mouth to continue, but the judge spoke first.

"Unless she has personal knowledge, the objection is

sustained," the judge said. "But I do see the relevance, Ms. Knight. So ask your next question."

The judge was signaling me to take another tack. I wasn't sure there was one.

Brittany looked deflated. I flashed her a supportive smile as I mentally regrouped.

"Was it after Tommy committed suicide that you began to have...emotional trouble?"

"Yes. I got into drugs and drinking. Anything to make myself forget what a horrible person I am, and what I'd done."

"Brittany, how old were you when all this happened?"

"Thirteen."

"And you're how old now?"

"Twenty-three."

"So you started drinking and drugging when you were thirteen?"

"Y-yes. That's when it started."

"And did you begin to have problems at work as a result of your drug and alcohol problem?"

"Yes. I'd be too hungover to make it to the set. Or I'd get to the set and forget all my lines..." Brittany sighed and hung her head.

"What about after *Circle of Friends*? Did you continue to have drug and alcohol problems?"

"Yes, it only got worse."

"But you continued to get work, didn't you?"

"Yes, Russell put me in all of his films. Gave me starring roles. But I couldn't get insured, so no one else would cast me."

"And that has continued to the present time?"

"Basically, yes. Until I walked off the set of Russell's new production, so I'm not working at all now. But... yes, he's still the only one who hires me."

"And it's been that way since the day you lied about Tommy raping you, since the day Ian Powers promised you'd always have work, right?"

"Yes."

That was probably as close as I could get. I consulted my notes to give the jury a chance to catch the underlying message: that Russell was the only one who'd hire her because he was in on the deal that promised Brittany job security for life in return for her lie about Tommy. That wrapped up the history of things.

"I'd like to move on to events just before Hayley's... death. Do you remember when was the last time you saw Hayley?"

"I think... you showed me a phone bill, right? It would've been around that time because she called me to ask if we could get together and then we met up at a club."

I brought out Hayley's cell phone bill, and Brittany identified her number as one of the calls.

"So that would've been about three weeks before she was killed, then?"

"I guess so, yes."

"Did you know that Tommy's son, Brian, was involved with Hayley at that time?"

"No, she never told me about him."

"And when you met her at the club, did you tell Hayley about accusing Tommy of rape?"

Brittany's face crumpled and slow tears rolled down her cheeks. "See, that's the thing. My memory's... not so good. A lot of things are still hazy, because I was drunk and stoned almost all the time. I know she started asking me stuff about the past, about what happened with Tommy when I was in *Circle of Friends*. And so I think I must have. Because, if Hayley knew about it, I was the only one who could have—or would have—told her."

"Objection, speculation," Terry said in a flat voice.

"Well…sustained," the judge said.

I tried again. "Brittany, to the best of your knowledge, who besides yourself knew that the story about Tommy Maher raping you was a lie?"

"For sure?" Brittany asked.

I nodded.

"For sure, only Ian. But possibly also my mom…and Russell."

Terry could have objected to those *possibles*, but there was no point to it. Mother Caren and Russell were none of her concern.

I paused to let the jury reach the obvious conclusion: that no one but Brittany would have told Hayley, because they'd be implicating themselves in the plot to frame Tommy for rape. But just in case, I made a note to drive the point home in closing argument. "One last area, Brittany. You did not come forward to volunteer this information to the prosecution, did you?"

"No. The last time I spoke to you, I knew Hayley was…missing. But I didn't know she was…" Brittany stopped, unable to say it.

"And a little while after we spoke, you left the country?"

"Yes. I'd been fighting with almost everybody on the

set for weeks. I was just sick of…everything, mostly myself. I couldn't stand my life anymore. Valerie, my dresser, my only friend on the set, told me about this rehab center, called—"

"You don't have to tell us the name. It's not in this country, correct?"

"Yes."

"So you checked yourself in?"

"Yes."

"And do they allow you to see newspapers, news programs, things of that nature at the center?"

"No. When you came this weekend and told me about Hayley…" Brittany began to cry softly.

"It was the first you'd heard that she was dead?"

Brittany wiped her eyes and nodded. "Yes."

"When you finish your testimony, will you go back to the center?"

"My therapist is taking me back." She nodded toward the doctor, who was sitting nearby. "I still have another two months to go and I'm not allowed to be out alone."

"Thank you, Brittany."

The cross was minimal. Terry tried to get Brittany to admit that Russell had continuously given her work because he felt sorry for her, not because of any deal Ian had brokered, but there wasn't much else Terry could do. She couldn't go on the attack with a witness this vulnerable, and there was no point to it in any event: Brittany's honesty was obvious, and there was no witness who could contradict her testimony. Trying to discredit her was hopeless.

I finished the case with those who had witnessed Brittany's downward spiral. Studio head Chuck Viener, who was devastated to find out he'd been lied to about Tommy, the other actors on *Circle of Friends,* and one of the few directors who'd worked on a film with her early in her career.

"She was unemployable," the director said. "No insurance company could afford to take a risk on her. So no one wanted to touch her with a ten-foot pole."

"Except Russell Antonovich."

"Right. She was in all of his films."

84

I rested my case, and Terry had no further evidence to offer.

"Ladies and gentlemen, that will conclude the evidence portion of this trial. I'm going to excuse you for the day while the lawyers and I work out jury instructions. We'll begin closing arguments at nine o'clock sharp tomorrow morning. I again remind you of the admonition: do not discuss this case with anyone, do not listen to or read any reports or commentary about this case, and do not form any opinions until the case is finally submitted to you. Have a great night, and I'll see you tomorrow."

As the jury moved past us toward the door, I searched their faces for some sign, anything that would tell me what they'd made of all that testimony. But the jurors were more buttoned up than ever. I glanced at Terry, who, like me, was standing at attention, watching the jurors leave the courtroom. Now, even more since I knew Russell hadn't been covering for Ian, I wondered why she hadn't warned him of what was coming when we got out of chambers this morning. That at least would have given him a chance to leave in time to avoid being hounded by the press. As the last juror walked out, Terry turned back to counsel table and caught me looking at her. I raised an eyebrow. She tossed her legal pad into her briefcase. "Guess Ms. Brittany's about to clean up her act," she said. "And she won't be doing any more work for Russell Antonovich."

"Seems so."

"Good for her." She gave me the tiniest of conspiratorial smiles, snapped her briefcase closed, and walked off.

When Bailey and Declan and I got upstairs, I told them about my last exchange with Terry.

"Well, I'll be damned." Bailey smiled. "She did it on purpose."

I nodded. "Payback to Russell for screwing Brittany over all these years." Who knew? Terry had a human side after all.

We turned on the television in Eric's office. News programs on all channels were on fire with the story of how Ian and possibly Russell had muscled Brittany into making the false rape accusation.

"They're toast," Declan said. "No matter what happens with this trial, it's over for both of them."

"You think so?" I knew I sounded skeptical.

"I know what you think of Hollywood," Declan said. "But trust me, there're a whole lot of decent people in the industry who'll never do business with those two— or even speak to them—again."

It was good to hear, if true. But it wouldn't be enough. Not for the slaughter of two innocent children.

*   *   *

When I went down to court early the next morning, I again found Janice on the bench in the hallway. I'd asked Bailey to bring her up to my office when she arrived, but Janice had declined. "Too many windows, too high up," Bailey explained. Janice was in the same position as yesterday: sitting next to her agent, Elden, whom she held by the arm, and clutching in the other hand what appeared to be the same book. I told her I'd secured them a front-row seat for closing arguments.

"Ian Powers is guilty as sin," she said. "Do you think the jury will do the right thing?"

I sighed and told her I hoped so.

"Can you get that hideous Russell Antonovich for...anything?" she asked.

Elden intervened. "Janice, she's got a closing argument to give right now," he said. "Let her be."

"I'm so sorry." Janice squeezed her agent's arm. "You're right, Elden." She gave me a shaky smile. "Good luck, Rachel. Do they say break a leg in this context?"

"Not unless they really want you to," I joked. "I'll see you in there."

When we finished in chambers, I saw that the courtroom was packed tighter than ever. There wasn't even an inch between the bodies seated on the benches. The air was so thick with tension it was hard to breathe. The jurors had dressed up for the occasion; some of them were even wearing suits. It was impossible to tell if that was a good or bad sign. It might just be a sign of celebration, because one way or another, their travails would soon be over.

I gave my first argument—a meat-and-potatoes, no-fireworks description of the evidence.

Terry made a strong pitch for her conspiracy theory, pointing out that the threatening letters and calls Ian and Russell had gotten were "undeniably real" because "the prosecution would've been happy to show they were fake" if that had been the case. She was right about that. The only mention she made of the altered ransom e-mail was the brief statement that "Ian Powers is not on trial for tampering with e-mail—or for whatever Brittany Caren claims happened over ten years ago." She theorized that the henchmen sent by Angela's father somehow got hold of the original e-mail and showed up on Boney Mountain. How they might've done that, she didn't say. But the way Terry laid it all out, it didn't sound as preposterous as I would've liked. And the jury was soaking up every word. For conspiracy buffs, this argument was practically edible it was so delicious. Did I have any of those on the jury? No one had admitted to it during voir dire, but jurors seldom did. This case was far from won.

"Ms. Knight, your rebuttal argument?"

I thanked the judge, then I thanked the jury for their patience through what was a much more difficult case than we'd expected. I made sure to hit the points Terry had made, then I moved on to my conclusion.

"In the end, this is all about ambition. It started with a screenplay. A screenplay Ian Powers knew had 'blockbuster' written all over it. But then Tommy Maher surfaced, screaming to anyone who'd listen that Russell Antonovich had stolen the script from him. Suddenly, the dream was about to go up in smoke. Instead of going to the Oscars, they'd be going to court, maybe for years. And if Tommy could prove that Russell had stolen that screenplay, not only would they lose in court, they'd lose in Hollywood. They'd be branded as thieves and liars. Ian Powers had to make Tommy go away.

"His solution? Frame Tommy for the rape of their child star. Tommy would have to shut up or risk exposure for that heinous crime. And the studio head, Chuck Viener, would never talk. Everyone looks bad if it comes out that a pedophile has been allowed to work on a set with child actors.

"And then, Ian Powers got luckier still. Tommy committed suicide. For Ian, it was a dream come true. Because now, not only were they rid of his haranguing, but any suspicions Tommy might have raised would be dismissed as the ravings of an unbalanced, jealous mind.

"The defense wants you to remember that Ian Powers is not on trial for what he did to Brittany. That's true. Sad, but true. But what he did to her tells you so much about who this man is. Think about it: Ian Powers was himself a child actor. And as the defense was so proud to bring out, he was the sole support for his family at the tender age of eight. Who could know better the kind of pressures Brittany endured as sole support for her family? And yet, knowing full well the enormous stress of being a child forced to shoulder that weight, he willfully, unconscionably destroyed a child actress for his own personal gain."

I pointed to Ian Powers, who sat rigid in his chair, staring straight ahead. "That's who this man really is. Now, did Russell Antonovich and Ian Powers steal Tommy's screenplay? I think the answer must be yes.

Just the fact that Ian Powers would go to such lengths to silence Tommy proves it."

At that, several jurors turned to look at Ian for a long few seconds. I waited until I had their full attention, then continued.

"The fact that this perfect 'solution' begat not only Tommy's suicide but also a lifetime of misery for young Brittany was of no concern to Ian Powers. Nor, I should mention, for Russell Antonovich, who got the ball rolling when he stole that screenplay. As far as they were concerned, it'd all worked out perfectly. Ian and Russell were making millions—the sequels, the merchandising, the video games. Everything was beautiful.

"Right up until Hayley and Brian threatened to expose both of them for the lie they'd perpetrated. And what did those kids ask for? Not money. Not a cut of *Wonderland Warriors* proceeds. All they asked was that Russell admit the truth. But Ian Powers couldn't let Russell admit he'd stolen that screenplay. It would undermine their credibility all over town. And beyond that, how could Ian be sure it would stop there? Even if Russell admitted he'd stolen the screenplay, Hayley and Brian had shown they had possession of an even bigger threat. They knew that he'd set Tommy up with the false rape charge. And if that ever got out, everyone would know he had Tommy's blood on his hands. Between lawsuits for the profits on *Wonderland Warriors* and the wrongful death suit for Tommy's suicide, he'd be ruined. Good-bye beautiful life.

"So Hayley and Brian had to be silenced. There wasn't much time to plan this out, but Ian wasn't dealing with a Mafia don. He was dealing with two innocent young kids. It wasn't hard to get the drop on them. Just leave a DVD in a bag by the side of the road, wait for Brian to come pick it up, and then put a gun to his head—a .44 Ruger gets anyone's attention—and force him up the mountain, to a remote spot where no one would find his shallow grave.

"As for Hayley, Ian Powers likely believed he could control her. With Brian gone, she had no ally. Brittany was still on the bottle and unable to cope with even a shooting schedule, let alone a pitched battle against two of the most powerful figures in Hollywood. If Hayley was isolated, she could be persuaded not to expose him and her father.

"But once again, Ian got 'lucky.' Hayley sent Brian texts that night. Texts that showed Hayley was right there, under Ian's nose. She made it so easy, that poor little girl. All he had to do was send her a text from Brian's phone, telling her to come out and meet him. Think for just a moment how cold-blooded this man has to be. This young girl had been like a daughter to him for most of her life. But that didn't matter. With cold, calculated deliberation, he lured this child out—deceived her so he could hunt her down like an animal, slit her throat, and dump her body into the trunk of a car."

I paused and turned to look at Ian Powers. His face was pinched with fury, but also fear. He met my eyes for just a second, then looked away. I turned back to the jury. This time, I noticed only one or two of them had been watching Ian.

"And I must say, the plan, as hastily made as it was, nearly worked. If it hadn't been for that freak storm, we might never have found Brian's body. We would have believed what Ian Powers wanted us to believe: that Brian killed Hayley and flew to Paris to live large on the ransom money."

I paused, taking a moment to let it all sink in, as much for myself as for the jury.

"Before I sit down, I want to leave you with one final thought.

"Pearl Bailey said that a man with ambition but no love is dead. In Ian Powers you have just such a man. A man whose overweening ambition left him with not a single shred of humanity. An ambition so all-consuming, he willfully, knowingly destroyed four lives. Not only the lives of Hayley and Brian, but also the life of a talented writer and a thirteen-year-old girl, whose remorse for what Ian Powers made her do sent her into a downward spiral that may yet prove to have ruined her for life. Ladies and gentlemen, it's too late to ask for justice for Tommy Maher, or for Brittany Caren, but it's not too late for Brian and Hayley. I ask you to do justice for them and convict their murderer, Ian Powers."

85

The jury went out at three o'clock. With the whole country watching, there was no way they'd come back with a verdict before tomorrow, but I intended to stay in the office. I wasn't going to take any chances.

As I left the courtroom, I found Janice waiting for me.

"You did a magnificent job," she said.

I thanked her. "You're welcome to come up to the office with us."

"Thank you, but no. I'll just wait here, if that's all right."

"Of course, Janice." I noticed she was still carrying that same book. She never seemed to be without it. "Do you mind if I ask you about that book?" I gestured to the one in her hand.

Janice smiled sadly. "Tommy gave it to Brian when he was little." She held it out. It was a child's book, titled *Fifty Famous Fairy Tales*. Janice handed it to me, and it fell open to a well-worn page about halfway through. I noticed handwriting in the margin. "That's Tommy's writing," she said. "Brian never let it go. When I saw that he didn't take it with him to Los Angeles, I thought it meant he intended to come back." She looked away, then said softly, "Now I know he did. He just came out here on a mission."

"Janice, would you mind letting me hang on to this for just a day or so?" I asked.

Janice was reluctant. "I suppose so. But I will want it back."

"I promise. In fact, I'll bring it back to you tonight if you like—"

"No, tomorrow's fine." She looked down for a moment, her expression thoughtful. "I don't know whether I ever told you this, but Tommy loved Brian so much. I think Brian was one of the only bright spots in his life. That's why it never made sense to me that he'd...leave...over the theft of a screenplay. Now I understand it a little better. After all the hell he had been through over the script, this false claim about Brittany was just too much. Knowing Tommy, he felt doomed." She sighed and shook her head. "Anyway, I wanted you to know that Tommy really was a good father..."

I told her I believed her, and how sorry I was, for all of it. We spoke for a few more minutes and then she and Elden left.

Bailey and Declan and I headed upstairs.

"So what do you think?" Declan asked. "Did we get him?"

"We don't do that," answered Bailey.

"I never bet on a verdict," I said. "Bad luck."

Declan raised an eyebrow but said nothing. I pulled out bottles of water and sodas from my fridge and set them on the table. Bailey took a bottle, leaned back, and put her feet up on the table next to my desk.

"No doubt about it, Russell was in on the phony rape scheme," Bailey said.

"Had to be," Declan agreed. "Like that director said, no one risks a film budget on an actor as dicey as Brittany." He shook his head. "What a sleazy dick."

"True, that." Russell Antonovich was every bit as consumed with greed as Ian. The only difference was, he had his pit bull, Ian, to do the dirty work while he got to stay in the background and reap the benefits. It killed me to think he'd pay no price for his part in all this.

The justice our system metes out can be such an imperfect thing. We had no solid proof that he knew about the false rape claim. There was no legal way to go after Russell. But there's more than one way to skin a bottom-feeding, parasitic worm. And I intended to find it.

After the jury went home for the evening, we decided it was safe to take the night off.

"How about a drink at the Biltmore?" Bailey suggested.

I knew she'd been missing Drew. None of us had had any kind of life since this trial had started. I called Drew ahead of time just to make sure we wouldn't get ambushed by reporters.

"Coast is clear," Drew said. "And when you get here, I'll tell you why."

I'd told Bailey and Declan about Sunglasses, the jerk-weed reporter who'd shown up in my hallway and then at the bar. Now, on the way over, I told them Drew had the rest of the story for us.

In spite of Drew's assurance, I entered the bar warily.

But it was a quiet night and easy to see that there was no one there who looked like a reporter. Declan ordered a beer just to join us in a toast—he had to drive—but Bailey and I cut loose and ordered martinis. Drew poured himself a shot of Oban, a really nice sipping scotch.

"Here's to a job well done," Drew said, raising his glass.

We all clinked and sipped.

"Okay, I'm dying to hear it. What happened?" I asked.

Drew smiled. "I poured him a martini with about four shots in it—"

I nearly choked on my drink. "Four straight shots in one tiny little glass?"

"We have big beauties for special occasions," Drew said.

"Oh, man," Declan said. "I'd be in a puddle on the floor."

"That was the general idea," Drew said. "Dude drained it in two swallows. Who the hell does that with a martini, anyway?"

"A classless douche like that," Bailey said. "Go on."

"He started getting so loud and obnoxious, customers were complaining. Even his buddies were embarrassed. So I told him he'd have to leave. He stood up." Drew slammed his palm down on the bar. "Face plant. They had to carry him out and put him in a cab."

We all laughed.

"So much for the wannabe reporter," I said.

"Hang on for the finale," Drew said. He went to the register and came back with his cell phone. "Check it out."

And there it was in glorious Technicolor: guerrilla freelancer Sunglasses being hauled out between the two men—toes dragging along the floor, eyes at half-mast, mouth hanging open.

"Hey, what's that on his face?" Bailey asked, pointing to the photo.

"That's drool!" Declan said.

"Sure is!" Bailey said, chuckling. "Nice job, honey."

"He who lives by the camera, dies by the camera," Drew said.

We all drank to that.

After two sips, Declan called it a night. But he pointed to the book I'd borrowed from Janice, which I'd taken with me. "You have a chance to look at that?" he asked.

"No."

"Mind if I borrow it for tonight? I'm coming in early, so I can give it back to you in the morning before court."

"Sure, but guard it with your life. It's got heavy sentimental value." And other value as well, I had a feeling. But I could look it over tomorrow. It was a slim volume.

Declan tucked it into his jacket. "Get ripped, you guys. You deserve it."

I turned to Bailey. "I hadn't thought of that. But since he insists..."

Bailey and I stayed and caught Drew up on the past few days. By the time we called it a night, we were both fried. Drew had a few more hours until closing, so Bailey crashed with me. The following morning, we treated ourselves to a real breakfast. I indulged with pancakes and bacon, a splurge for me, and Bailey ordered French toast—just another day for her.

I let Bailey give me a lift to the courthouse, and I was in pretty good spirits for most of the morning. But by lunchtime I started to worry. Declan stopped by and dropped off the book I'd borrowed from Janice. We talked briefly and then he asked if I wanted to go out—now that we had time to live like real people—but I had no appetite. When I still hadn't heard a peep from the jury by two o'clock, my stomach began to knot.

I foolishly called Bailey to share my angst.

"Shouldn't they be back by now?" I asked.

"Juries should do a lot of shit they don't do," she snapped.

"They haven't even asked a question, though."

"Probably still voting on what to have for lunch."

By four o'clock, I was pacing in front of my desk. The three square feet forced me into tight circles. I was getting dizzy, which kind of felt good—until dizzy turned to queasy. At a quarter to five, the court called. The jury had a verdict. We had a half-hour lead to give the defense time to get back to the courthouse. I called Bailey and Declan. "They're in," I said, in a voice so strained I barely recognized it.

"Breathe," Bailey said. "Whatever happens, you did a hell of a job. Vanderputz can't blame you."

"He can. And will."

"Then I'll shoot him."

On that cheery note, I grabbed a legal pad and stepped out into the hallway. And bumped right into Toni.

"Hey! Good thing I bounce," she said. She peered at me. "Well, don't you look all hot and sassy."

"Really?"

"No. You look like a bird that stuck its beak in a socket. Where're you heading?"

"To court. We've got a verdict."

"You are not going down there looking like that. Come on." She took me by the hand and dragged me down to her office.

When I got a look at myself in the mirror, I realized she was right. My hair was all over the place and my makeup was a smudgy mess. But five minutes later, I looked presentable enough to be set loose on the world.

"I don't know what I'd do without you," I said.

"You'd go around looking like a Cabbage Patch doll."

"Want to come?" I asked.

"Want me to come?"

I nodded. If I was about to crash and burn, I wanted Toni and Bailey to be there. Toni and I picked up Declan and we rode down together. Just as we got off the elevator, Bailey emerged from the stairwell, lightly sweaty, out of breath, and in a foul mood.

"Goddamn press is a mile deep all the way around the courthouse."

Declan nodded. "I caught a look at the television in the lounge. They've got helicopters flying around, traffic is blocked off on Temple—it's a zoo out there."

Declan looked pale and I noticed a tremor in his hand as he reached for the courtroom door. I was glad I didn't have to show my hands. The courtroom was packed and thrumming with loud chatter and tension. I kept my eyes down and made my way to counsel table.

I dropped my legal pad on the table in front of my chair, then turned to make sure there was a seat for Toni in front of the railing next to Bailey. I scanned the gallery. No sign of Russell—no surprise there. I expected he'd be at an undisclosed location for some time to come. Dani was a no-show as well. But Janice was in the front row, and she and Raynie had apparently met and hit it off, because the three of them—Janice, Raynie, and Elden—were sitting together. I returned the book of fairy tales to Janice and we spoke for a few seconds before Jimmy called the court to order. Everyone quickly squeezed into a space on the benches in the gallery and Judge Osterman came out. From that moment, I registered every single sight and movement as though it were a film playing in slow motion. Judge Osterman mounting the steps to the bench, his face solemn. Tricia standing at attention, nervously twisting her wedding ring. The bailiff moving toward the door the jury would pass through to take their seats in the box. I wasn't conscious of breathing, only of my heart pounding in slow, heavy thumps and a sick feeling in the pit of my stomach.

"Let's have the jury," Judge Osterman said.

The bailiff went through the door, and seconds later, the jurors filed out. I studied each of their faces for some sign, some clue of what was to come. But they were more stone-faced than ever before. Then one juror—the librarian—looked across the room at the defense side of the table. And smiled. Spots danced before my eyes, nearly blinding me as I registered what that smile meant. It couldn't be. They couldn't do this. They couldn't let this murderer go. I heard the judge's next words as though I were under water.

"I understand you have a verdict, ladies and gentlemen."

The Hollywood agent, who'd been elected the jury foreman, answered. "We do, Your Honor."

The bailiff took the folder containing the verdict forms from him and brought them over to Tricia, who handed them up to the judge. I watched the judge's face as he pursed his lips and read the forms, but his expression gave away nothing. Slowly, he went through them, organizing the pages. I put a hand on the table to steady myself as I realized that this might be the last time I tried a case in the Special Trials Unit. Or downtown. Or forever, for that matter.

"Will the defendant please rise?"

Terry and Wagmeister flanked Ian Powers, six law clerks behind them, as they all rose together. Terry put a comforting hand on Ian's arm and Wagmeister gave him a brief pat on the back. Ian looked like a cadaver—hollowed, sunken cheeks and dark rings under his eyes. The Armani suit hung on his gaunt frame like a shroud. If nothing else, it comforted me to know that I'd cost him some peace of mind. I snapped back with the judge's next words.

"The clerk will now read the verdict."

And in that moment, all of the air was suddenly sucked out of the courtroom. My heart was pounding so loudly I had to struggle to hear the clerk's voice as she read the verdicts.

"As to count one, the murder of Brian Maher, we the jury—"

I found myself following each syllable in slow motion, a beat behind every word.

"—find the defendant, Ian Powers...guilty. We further find that the murder was willful, deliberate, and premeditated."

Someone in the audience gave a yelp that was quickly silenced by a glare from Jimmy. I felt the blood rush to my head. All I could think was, We got him. We got him.

"As to count two, the murder of Hayley Antonovich, we the jury find the defendant, Ian Powers, guilty, and we further find the murder to have been willful, deliberate, and premeditated.

"As to both counts one and two, we further find that the defendant personally used a deadly and dangerous weapon, to wit, a knife."

My lungs filled with air for what felt like the first time since I walked into the courtroom. I looked at the jury, my eyes filled with gratitude. Not one of them looked back at me. A careful bunch, they kept their faces neutral. And when Judge Osterman polled them, at Terry's request, they affirmed that these were their verdicts in voices that were loud and proud. I'd thank them later... if they let me. Chances were, they'd want to get out of here as fast as they could go.

The judge thanked them for their service, told them they were allowed to talk to anyone they wanted about the case now, but were free to decline and should not feel pressured to do so. Then he warned the press to be civilized and respectful of jurors and all parties and declared that the court was in recess.

In an instant, a loud roar erupted as everyone in the courtroom jumped to their feet and began to talk at once. I pulled Declan in and we wrapped Bailey and Toni in a group hug, as I let the relief wash through me. As much as possible in a court of law, justice had been done.

EPILOGUE

The next morning, I got word that Jack Averly had finally turned up. He'd made his way to a quiet seaside resort in Puerto Vallarta, no doubt traveling on a share of the ransom money. (We'd figured Ian must have picked it up while Averly flew to New York.) Averly probably could've hidden there forever if he'd had half a brain. But he got drunk at a campfire party on the beach and mouthed off about his days as a PA/drug dealer at RussPow Studios. An alert guest, who just happened to be a producer for CNN, called the Los Angeles bureau. He'd be back in pocket soon, facing flight and accessory charges that would keep him locked up for at least a couple of years.

And I soon learned that Declan was right: Hollywood had its own unique but very effective way of dealing with its own.

The *Daily Inquisitor* led the charge at first: "Wife Leaves Superstar Director—'I Can't Take His Life of Lies!'" According to the story, Dani had left Russell and "confidential sources" claimed it was because of what she'd learned during the trial. "Dani said she was sure Russell had been in on the rape setup that led to Tommy's suicide." Dani was never quoted anywhere, but the fact of her separation and impending divorce turned out to be true. It was all downhill from there.

Some of the actors who'd carried the signs in front of the courthouse claiming Ian had been framed now admitted that they believed he was guilty and were "glad justice had been done."

But the hardest blow was delivered by Brittany herself, in an exclusive interview with the *Inquisitor* that I might—or might not—have helped make happen. A front-page cover showing a tearful Brittany carried the headline "They Ruined My Life! Russell Deserves to Be Sitting Next to Ian in That Jail Cell!" She told the whole story, no holds barred. And now, without the constraints of a courtroom, she could say, "Russell was in on all of it: the lie about Tommy raping me, the deal to give me work for life—he was on board because he stole that screenplay and he'd lose his deal if the studio found out. He and Ian made my life a living hell! I'll never work for Russell again and I don't care if that means I'll never work for the rest of my life."

Of course, we soon learned that it meant just the opposite. I heard from Andrew Chatham that a hot young director who'd been through rehab himself had offered Brittany a supporting role in his next film.

"Mark my words, Ms. Knight," Andrew said. "Russell Antonovich is through in this town. In the coming months, you'll see that one deal after another will fall apart. Russell's studio will close down by the end of the year."

It wasn't prison in the traditional sense. But it was hell on earth for Russell Antonovich. I'd have to make my peace with that.

Declan and I got the official summons to see Vanderputz for congratulations two days after the verdict—once he finished taking bows on every channel but Animal Planet. Eric came with us, and I was glad he was there to witness it. Our fearless leader managed to make it sound like we'd won a third-grade attendance award. "That was very nice work," he'd said. "Of course, the evidence was overwhelming..." Translation: even my pet shih tzu could've won it.

"He never fails to disappoint," I said to Eric on our way back to my office.

"Like I said, consistency is his strong suit." Eric smiled. "But he did let your felonious expert slide."

There was that. Not one word was said about my having hired Parkova without prior approval.

When Declan and I were safely behind the closed door in my office, we exchanged views.

"What an asshat," Declan said.

"A real chowderhead," I added. "But I've been meaning to ask you what you made of that book."

"The fairy tales?" he said. I nodded. "Did you read the notes in the margins?"

I had. "I've got my theory," I said. "But I want to hear yours."

"That was Tommy's inspiration for *Wonderland Warriors*," Declan said. "Nothing specific, but I saw the movie. Did you?"

"No. But I heard it was part fairy tale."

"It was. And his notes had some of the ideas that wound up in the movie."

"But it wouldn't have been enough to prove he wrote the screenplay," I said.

"No. But it is for me. I'm glad I got to see it."

What you know and what you can prove. They can be very different things. "Me too."

"Well, I've got a stack of case files screaming my name," Declan said. He stood to go, but paused at the door. "I... just want to thank you for writing that note to my folks."

I'd written to tell them what a talented lawyer Declan was and that his star was going to rise quickly in the office. "I just told 'em the truth."

Declan gave me a long look that acknowledged another truth: I'd also done it to give his father a wake-up slap. "Thank you, Rachel."

After Declan left, I thought about all the fathers in this case.

Nietzsche said, "When one has not had a good father, one must create one." This case proved it in ways even Nietzsche might not have predicted. Brian wanted not only to vindicate his father, but also in some measure to justify his father's suicide, by proving he'd written the screenplay that launched Russell's empire. Hayley wanted to create an honorable father by forcing him to admit his misdeed and give the credit where it was due. And Declan, whether he was aware of it or not, had taken a civil service job that was all heart and small pay, in part to force his father to accept him on his own terms—in essence, to create the loving father he needed.

And as for me, what was a prosecutor if not

someone who stood up and fought back against the predators of the world? Only now, during this case, had I fully understood how the lessons I'd thought of as games were actually my father's way of teaching me how to fight back—both physically and emotionally. "Never hesitate, Rachel. Always shoot to kill," he'd said. I now saw that in becoming a prosecutor, I'd put his lessons, his final gift to me, to good use. And so I had found the good father I thought had abandoned me.

With the trial over, my fatigue hit me like a brick wall. I needed some serious R and R. I'd racked up an impressive amount of comp time and I intended to use it. Bailey said she planned to do the same. Graden had offered to kick off our vacation with a dinner for everyone— including Declan and his plus one—at his place.

"Declan, you've never had better cooking," I said. "You've got to—"

"I'm in, you don't have to sell me. It sounds perfect. And besides, a good meal will be a refreshing change. My cooking skills end with Top Ramen."

Toni's trial wrapped up just in time—with a conviction of course—and she and J.D. were picking up Bailey and Drew.

I got there early, intending to help—or at least put out the hors d'oeuvres. But Graden was all set. He asked what I was drinking.

"What are you having?" It looked good. Cool and refreshing. At six o'clock it was still fairly warm outside.

"Ketel One and soda with a lime."

"I'll have the same."

We took our drinks out to the patio and shared a lounge chair. The ocean air was fresh but still warm, and the fading sunlight bounced a golden light off the water of the infinity pool. It was heavenly. We sat in silence for a while and enjoyed the view of the ocean.

"I did thank you for Parkova, didn't I?" I asked.

"Repeatedly." Graden chuckled.

"She was a great witness." I told him how she'd handled Terry's question about her fabricating the original ransom note.

Graden laughed as he shook his head. "Only Parkova."

Then I remembered what I'd been meaning to ask. "What does the 'M' stand for?"

"You promise never to tell? She'll definitely hunt me down and kill me." I promised. "Miriam."

This was the big state secret? "She can change it legally if she's that twizzled about it."

"Legal isn't really her thing, but I'll let her know." Graden paused. "I had an idea I wanted to run by you."

I waited.

"I thought it might help if we let Parkova track those reports Lilah sent you—"

My nemesis, who'd almost gotten Bailey and me killed. And who'd sent me previously undiscovered reports on my sister, Romy.

"But I thought you already checked them out and they were legit?"

"They are. I'm not talking about that part. I'm talking about having Parkova see if she can track down Lilah by seeing how those reports were accessed."

The sheer poetic justice of having the genius hacker

go after the brilliant sociopath brought a smile to my face.

"It's brilliant. I love it."

The doorbell rang and we went to answer it. Declan was there with a tall, sandy-haired surfer-looking type whom I knew very well.

"Kevin Jerreau!" I said. "I haven't seen you in…a year?"

Kevin and I had been baby DAs together, and friends ever since. He'd helped me on a case a couple of years ago involving the murder of my dear friend and fellow prosecutor Jake Pahlmeyer.

We hugged. "Your fault, not mine," Kevin said.

I looked from Kevin to Declan. "I didn't know you two knew each other."

"He taught my evidence class in law school," Declan said.

Kevin smiled. "Actually, I'm the one who suggested Declan try clerking at the DA's office."

"Then I have you to thank yet again," I said.

Graden took the drink orders, and as he went to prepare them, J.D.'s car rolled up and the four of them—J.D., Toni, Bailey, and Drew—descended on us.

It was a magical night, with laughs, great stories, and the best steaks I'd ever had. Declan and Kevin were the first to leave.

I looked at them knowingly. "You've got another party to get to."

"No," Declan said.

"Yes," Kevin said.

But Toni, J.D., Drew, and Bailey weren't far behind them. As I walked them out to the car, I hugged Bailey and Toni and told them we had to make plans. "You're taking some time off, aren't you?" I asked Toni.

"Oh, yeah." She leaned in and whispered, "Listen, if you dare go home tonight, I will personally make your shrink appointment."

I grinned. "No appointments necessary."

As I waved good-bye, Bailey and Drew gave me a smile.

Then Graden put his arm around me and we walked back inside. And closed the door.

ACKNOWLEDGMENTS

Scientific advancement offers opportunities to both sinners and saints, and so the new frontier of cyberspace has proven to be both the gift and the bane of our existence. But the world of computer crime is a complex one and its depiction requires specific expertise that I do not possess. For the computer-related crime in this story I was fortunate enough to be able to call upon a true expert: Gregg Housh. My undying gratitude goes to Gregg for the time he took to answer my endless questions and for the fascinating background he provided about the world of cyberspace crime.

The DNA testimony in this story was reviewed for technical accuracy by Barry A. J. Fisher, former crime laboratory director for the Los Angeles County Sheriff's Department and current senior forensic adviser for the Department of Justice International Criminal Investigative Training Assistance Program. My profound thanks go to Barry for his help.

All credit for the accuracy of the computer crime and DNA aspects of this story goes to Gregg Housh and Barry Fisher. All credit for the errors goes to Yours Truly.

Once again, I am forever indebted to Catherine LePard. I would never have taken the leap into novels had it not been for her. To Marillyn Holmes, I again thank you for your excellent help, keen eye, and knowledge. To beloved friends Lynn Reed Baragona and Hynndie Wali, who are still performing the yeoman task of keeping me sane.

I love you all!

Dan Conaway, I will never stop marveling at my ridiculous luck in having you for an agent. Please believe me when I say I'm grateful for you every single day. And to fantastic assistant Stephen Barr, you are such a pleasure. What a team! I couldn't love you more.

My deepest thanks to wonderful editor in chief Judy Clain, and CEO Michael Pietsch. I am so fortunate to be working with you. And thank you to the new, fabulous assistant Amanda Brower, a rising star. To senior production editor Karen Landry for saving me from myself yet *again*—thank you, Karen, for another great job.

To the publicity all-star team, Nicole Dewey, Sabrina Callahan, Miriam Parker—aka, my buds—and to all the wonderful people at Mulholland Books, a million thanks to you for all your hard work, creativity, and brilliance.

ABOUT THE AUTHOR

Marcia Clark is the author of *Guilt by Association* and *Guilt by Degrees*. A former prosecutor for the state of California, she is now a frequent media commentator on legal issues. She lives in Los Angeles.

...AND HER NEXT BOOK

In July 2014, Mulholland Books will publish Marcia Clark's *The Competition*. Following is an excerpt from the novel's opening pages.

PROLOGUE

Christy Shilling rolled over and squinted at her nightstand for the fifth time. Why hadn't her alarm clock gone off? She pushed the Kleenex and can of Icy Hot spray out of the way. *Still* too early, but at least she could get up now. Christy didn't think she'd slept more than two hours total. And what little sleep she did get had been riddled with anxiety. Nightmares of waking up, going to her closet, and finding it wasn't there. Echoes of the devastating pain of that moment still hurt so badly she was afraid to look at her closet door.

But there it was. The plastic dry cleaner's bag, hanging in front of the mirror, right where her mother had left it. Christy's heart soared. The Marion J. Fairmont High School cheerleading uniform in that bag was the realization of a dream she'd had since third grade, when the Newport Junior High cheerleading squad came to her school. She'd never forget the moment those girls ran out onto the auditorium floor. Christy had watched in openmouthed awe. Always the smallest in her class, she'd kneeled on her chair to take it all in. And from the very first shout, Christy had known she'd do anything to be one of them.

She'd made the junior high squad, and those tryouts had been tough. But they were nothing compared to varsity. Weeks of practice in the school gym, the rec center gym, her backyard. The sore hamstrings, the bruises, the falls, the constant anxiety. She'd been so nervous the first day of tryouts she'd had to run to the locker room to throw up. And after Christy made the first cut, the pressure only got worse. At that point, just the cutthroats were left. She'd been proud—and a little amazed—to find herself among them.

Throughout the next two weeks of practice, rumors flew about what the judges were looking for. Hair in ponytails, hair in pigtails; no makeup at all, light makeup, glam makeup; rail thin, muscular thin, "healthy"—whatever that meant; short, medium, tall; blonde but not bottle blonde, brunette, auburn. Christy threw up so often her clothes got baggy. Her mom had threatened to make her quit if she got any thinner. Christy tried using safety pins to make her clothes look tighter, but her mom had seen right through it. She'd retaliated by instituting morning weigh-ins. Desperate, afraid to ask anyone for help—if the coach found out she'd be cut for sure—Christy had searched the Web. She'd found her salvation in protein shakes and Ensure. After a few days, the needle on the bathroom scale held steady at 103 pounds. Christy's eyes had filled with tears of relief. But nothing worked when it came to sleeping. She'd tried melatonin; warm milk; long, hot baths; even counting sheep. Nothing had helped, and by the last four days of tryouts, she was running on fumes.

But she'd made it. The varsity cheerleading squad.

Today would be her first pep rally. In just a few hours, she'd run out onto the gym floor to do her first routine in front of the whole school. Christy's breath caught as she pictured the packed bleachers, heard the roar, the stomping of feet, the whistles. She saw herself yelling to the crowd, taking her first run for her handspring-roundoff combination—and her final move, a climb to the top of the pyramid, then a somersault through the air into the basketed hands of the bigger, base girls. Christy thrilled to the imagined cheers and fist pumps, hugged herself as she savored the moment. Her cell phone rattled on her nightstand. It was a text from Harley Jenson. They'd been besties since they pulled their nap-time rugs together on the first day of preschool. *The big day! Break a leg—KIDDING. You'll be awesome! Xo, Harley.* Christy hugged the phone, jumped out of bed, and headed for the shower.

7:42 a.m.

"Honey, don't stress. You'll do great—"

Harley Jenson looked up and forced a smile as he sprinkled more brown sugar on his oatmeal, then dropped back into his world history notes.

"Harley, listen to me." His mother pulled out a chair and sat across from him. "I don't want you to pressure yourself. If you don't get the scholarship, we'll find a way to make it happen, I promise." She squeezed his arm. "Okay?"

Harley covered his mother's hand with his own. "Sure, Mom." He tried to give her a genuine smile. "I just want to give it my best shot, that's all."

His mother sighed. "Of course, sweetheart." She squeezed his hand, then got up and moved to the sink to hide the tears that burned in her eyes. The truth was, she didn't know that they'd find a way to make it happen. With Andrew laid off, nothing was certain anymore. At least, nothing good. They'd planned a family trip to Greece that summer, knowing it might be their last chance to travel together before Harley went off to college at MIT in the fall. Now, those plans were a taunting, bitter memory. Family vacations? A pricey, prestigious school for Harley? That was for rich people with steady incomes. *This* family would be lucky to keep the house. But she didn't mourn for herself or her husband. They'd had their youthful chances to shoot for the moon. It was Harley she mourned for. The unfairness of it all made her heart ache. He'd done everything right. Made the grades, done the extracurricular résumé builders—and he'd been duly rewarded with early admission to MIT. But that was back when they'd been paying customers. Now, the only way he'd get in was on a scholarship. And the competition for the few slots that afforded a full ride was breathtaking. Harley never complained, but she knew he was working night and day, seven days a week, to make it happen.

Harley closed his notebook and forced down one last bite of oatmeal—it was hard to get food past the knot in his stomach—and brought his bowl to the sink. He rinsed it quickly before his mother could see how little he'd eaten. He'd studied hard, but he still didn't feel ready for his exam. And he had to ace it. If he didn't, he'd ruin his perfect 4.2—and probably his one shot at the scholarship for MIT. He needed more time. Even one more hour would help. His cell phone buzzed with a text. It was Christy. *"Thx, Scooter! See you there! Xoxo."* Scooter—as in the opposite of Harley-Davidson—had been his nickname in elementary school. Only Christy still called him that. He didn't love it, but it was better than Vespa. Harley frowned at the phone. He hated to miss her pep rally, but it was his only chance to sneak in more study time. Besides, she'd never know if he didn't tell her.

Harley leaned down to kiss his mother's cheek. "Bye, Ma. Don't work too hard."

As was her habit, she walked Harley to the door.

He slid into his backpack. "Love ya!"

"Love you back!" His mother swallowed hard as she watched him head out, his heavy backpack swinging behind him. He still moved like the little boy who'd given her a nervous-brave smile as he left for his first day of school—a side-to-side roll that reminded her of a skater. She smiled with wistful eyes as he headed down the front walk and out into the world.

1

10:45 a.m.

Principal Klavens's voice blared through the classroom loudspeakers. "As you know, it's Homecoming, and I'm sure you're all as excited about it as I am. Pep rally starts at eleven a.m. sharp. Show your school spirit and greet our new cheerleaders. See you there! Go, Falcons!"

Groans went up in nearly every classroom as the students rolled their eyes and traded disgusted looks. The truth was, they didn't mind the break in their routine. Any excuse to get out of class.

10:59 a.m.

The gymnasium buzzed with heat and raucous energy; the bleachers, designed to hold three thousand, were nearly packed to capacity. Girls' high-pitched notes and boys' hornlike, cracking bleats mingled and snowballed into a roar. Wincing at the din, geometry teacher Adam Findley leaned toward Hector Lopez, the Spanish teacher. "Bet you wouldn't mind having library duty today."

Hector nodded. "Yeah, no kidding. Sara totally lucked out."

Finally, Principal Dale Klavens walked out to the center of the floor, the wireless microphone invisible in his large mitt of a hand. He still carried himself like the linebacker he'd been when he was in high school. The principal loved these rare opportunities to see all the kids together like this. To him, it was a family gathering. He tapped the mic and waited for everyone to settle down, then thanked the crowd for coming—as if they'd had a choice—and read off the announcements: a bake sale for the Woodland Hills Home for the Elderly, the job fair next month, and the upcoming performances of the junior and senior orchestra and jazz bands.

"And since our fantastic jazz singer Sheila Wagner has graduated, it's my pleasure to announce that her replacement will be Dimitri Rabinow—"

Girls shouted out, in singsong tones, "We love you, Dimitri!" and "Dimitri's so hot!"—sparking a wave of laughter.

Principal Klavens chuckled along with them. "Seems we've made a popular choice." Then he pushed his hands down, gesturing for them to be quiet. "And now, the moment we've all been waiting for: Fairmont High's new, world-class varsity cheerleaders—I give you...the Falconettes!"

The locker room door at the far end of the gym opened, and a single line of girls in blue-and-gold pleated skirts and blue sweaters bearing the gold outlined image of a falcon in midflight came bursting out, cheeks shining.

They went into their V formation. Christy Shilling tilted her head and smiled at the crowd, just as she'd been trained. Captain Tammy Knopler, in position at the apex of the V, shouted the cue for their windup chant, "Hey, Go! Hey, Fight!" They clapped out the rhythm for four beats, then started to yell the words. The students joined in, stomping and pounding the wooden bleachers as they shouted, "Go!" and "Fight!"

After a few rounds, the squad threw their arms straight up in the air and called out, "Go, Falcons!" The crowd obediently roared back, "Go, Falcons!" The V stretched out into a line, and Christy took the brief run to start her first tumbling pass. Just as she launched into her handspring, the double doors behind the top row of bleachers flew open. At first, no one noticed the two figures who stood there, rifles in hand. The crowd continued to clap and shout; Christy went into her roundoff. As she turned in the air, the shorter of the two figures raised an assault rifle and fired off four rapid shots. The blasts ripped through the noisy gym. A hush fell, and for an instant, wide-eyed students turned to stare at one another. Christy landed heavily and stuttered backward on her heels.

Then heads began to crane, searching for the source of the foreign sound. They found it at the top of the bleachers. Two figures clothed in camouflage coats and black balaclavas, assault rifles held high. Shrieks rang out.

The figure on the right, the shorter of the two, shouted, "Time to die, motherfuckers!"

The taller figure yelled, "Run, assholes! Run!"

One of them gave a weird, high-pitched laugh. Then the gunmen aimed their weapons down at the crowd. Staccato gunfire pierced the air. Screams of terror filled the gym as students hurtled down the bleachers, pushing, falling, trampling over one another as they desperately searched for cover. The acrid smell of fear mingled with panicked shouts as the black-hooded gunmen fired into the sea of bodies. Bullets tore through arms, legs, torsos, sending bright-red sprays of blood through the air.

Tammy ran toward the locker room. Christy knew she should run too, tried to make her feet move. But her body and brain felt disconnected. *Run! Run!* Christy sobbed to herself, even as she thought, *This can't be real, it has to be a nightmare.* Finally, feeling as though she were moving underwater, she began to follow Tammy. As she reached the locker room door, Christy stretched out a hand. She started to push the door open. She was nearly inside, nearly safe, when the shorter of the two gunmen turned to his left and fired. Christy's head exploded in a red mist as she dropped to the gym floor.

Somewhere, someone had pulled a fire alarm, and the shrill clanging underscored the frenzied screams of the crowd.

The killers moved down the bleacher steps in tandem at an almost leisurely pace, shooting into the crowd below as they went. They yelled at the students with a vicious glee, "Fuck the jocks!"

When the gunmen reached the gym floor, a bloodied hand groped the air blindly. "Help me, please...," the boy whimpered.

One of the killers laughed. "Sure, no problem." He put his gun to the boy's temple and pulled the trigger.

The bleachers had turned into a battlefield. Bodies everywhere—flung over benches, splayed out on the steps, curled under the seats, crumpled in heaps on the gym floor. Blood, bone, brain matter, splashed the walls, the bleachers, the floor.

The shorter killer gave a sign to his partner, and now they began to move more quickly, heading for the main entrance, which was clogged with teenagers clawing and scrambling over one another to reach the doors.

Angela Montrose, the girls' soccer coach, threw her arms around as many students as she could, shielding them with her wide, sturdy body. Another barrage of shots rang out. Just ten feet to her right, three boys and a girl spun and fell to the floor. Angela stretched her arms to the breaking point and pushed the students forward with all her might. If she could get them past the bottle-neck, out to the open hallway, they'd have a chance.

She'd just crossed the threshold when another wave of shots rang out. Searing fire spread through Angela's right side. Suddenly, her knees buckled. She stumbled as black spots swam in her eyes. Mustering her last ounce of strength, she shoved the students out from under her wing and yelled, "Run!" Then, clutching her side, she crumpled to the ground. One of the gunmen walked over and looked down at her. They locked eyes. He raised his gun and pointed it at her face. Angela closed her eyes and silently said good-bye to her sister, her partner, their dogs. Bracing for the shot, she startled at the sound of an empty metallic click. The gunman cursed. Something heavy clattered to the floor next to her. Angela opened her eyes and looked up. The gunman was gone. Her eyes fluttered closed.

Students screamed as they poured out through the double doors of the gym. The gunmen moved behind them like deadly sheepherders and took in the chaotic scene. Another high-pitched laugh, then the shorter gun-man calmly took aim at a group of girls running for the main entrance, fired a few shots. Without looking to see if anyone was hit, he again signaled his partner.

The taller figure nodded and fell in behind him, pulling a handgun out of his jacket as they headed for the wide staircase that led to the second floor and the library. At the foot of the stairs, they stopped and fired at the students fleeing up the steps. Hector Lopez, who had just cleared the landing, cried out, "No!" He'd led a group of students to the stairway, hoping the gunmen wouldn't come this way. He dropped back and pushed the two girls nearest to him up the stairs. "Go! Go!" Hector deliberately slowed, praying that the gunmen would take him, the easiest target, giving the girls more time to escape. More shots. Hector could feel his back muscles go rigid as he anticipated the sting of bullets, but he kept moving forward.

Up ahead, he saw that the girls had made it to the top of the stairs and were sprinting down the hallway to the right. As he reached the last step, he heard another set of shots. Closer, much closer. Hector grabbed the handrail to pull himself up, but his fingers slipped off and he nearly tumbled backward down the stairs. He teetered, arms windmilling to regain balance. At the last second, Hector managed to pull himself back and climb up the last step. Only then did he notice the blood running down his side. He glanced over his shoulder, saw the gunmen had reached the landing. He took the hallway to the left, hoping to draw them away from where the girls had fled. Hector's stomach lurched, and he felt bile rise in his throat. Stumbling past the library, head-first, body almost parallel to the ground, he held the wall for support. Had they followed him? Where were they?

As he neared the boys' restroom, he risked another glance over his shoulder. Saw them behind him, heading toward the library. Hector leaned into the lavatory door and fell to the floor inside. Using his left hand, he slid his cell phone out of his pocket and pushed 9-1-1. He managed the words "Fairmont...shooting." The last thing he saw before blacking out was the time on his cell phone: 11:08.

Harley had been in the library, head down, desperately cramming factoids on the War of the Roses, when the fire alarm began to ring. He'd ignored it. Probably just a prank or an accident. But the shrill clanging persisted. Harley looked around, sniffed the air. No smoke. He got up and headed toward the windows that looked down on the front of the school to see if they were being evacuated. He'd gotten only halfway across the library when he heard screams, pounding footsteps—and then a voice bellowing from somewhere out in the hallway. "Hey, assholes, have a nice day!"

A series of loud pops—they sounded like firecrackers, but...were they *shots?* Then laughter, ugly and brutal. Another shot. Then another. Closer this time. Just outside the library door. Harley frantically turned to Ms. Sara Beason, the teacher on duty. She stood at the front counter, staring, wide-eyed, at the doorway. He started to move toward her, when she suddenly screamed, "Hide!"

Harley quickly scrambled behind a bookcase and ducked down. A blonde girl he didn't know was standing near the storage cubbies at the front of the library, frozen, mouth hanging open.

"Get down!" Harley whispered to her. "Down!" He gestured to her wildly.

She stared at him, uncomprehending at first. Harley yanked at her hand, pulling her to her knees. She dropped woodenly to all fours and crawled under a nearby desk. Harley scurried back to his hiding place.

Seconds later, a mocking voice came from the doorway. "Where're all the good little kiddies? Helloooo?" Footsteps, then the same voice, closer now. "Hey, who's got library duty? Guess what? It's your lucky day!" Harley heard Sara Beason scream. Then, the boom of gunfire. It rattled the windows, shook the desks.

Harley thought that only a bomb could be that loud. More footsteps, Harley couldn't tell exactly where, and more shots. How many? It was impossible to know. It all blended together in one continuous, deafening roar. From the other side of the library he heard moaning, then a low swishing sound. What was that? Harley heard a weird, high-pitched laugh. Someone—one of the killers?—snickered and said, "Losers." Again footsteps, this time moving his way.

Harley swallowed hard, pressing his lips together to keep from screaming. He peeked through a gap in the books and saw someone—a killer? It had to be—walk over to the desk where the blonde girl had hidden. Shaking with terror, Harley tried not to breathe. He couldn't think beyond the words *Go away, go away, go away* that ran through his brain on a continuous loop. The killer moved past the desk. Harley briefly closed his eyes in gratitude and dared to take a shallow breath. Then, without warning, the killer doubled back and rapped sharply on the desk.

"Knock, knock, anybody home?" He laughed, leaned down, and looked at the girl cowering on the floor.

The girl sobbed, "No! Please! Please don't—"

"Please don't," the killer mocked in a high falsetto. "Well, since you said *please*." He took two steps away, then abruptly turned back. "Then again, that's a stupid, bullshit word." He swung the barrel of the gun under the desk. Fired point-blank into her face. Blood and brains splashed the wall behind the girl.

Harley jammed a fist into his mouth and clutched his chest with the other hand to muffle the pounding of his heart. Ears ringing from the deafening sound, he squeezed himself into a ball and took shallow little breaths. He knew he was next. A warm, wet trickle made its way down his right leg.

He heard footsteps, the brush of pant legs. It sounded like they were near the windows, but he couldn't be sure. Could they see him from there? Harley didn't dare turn his head to look. He thought of his mom, his dad, pictured them during one of their last happy dinners together, and squeezed his eyes shut to hold on to the memory. One of the killers was speaking. The voice seemed very close. Just feet away. Harley willed the ringing in his ears to stop as he strained to make out the words.

One of the killers spoke again. "Ready?"

An affirmation. "Yeah."

Then both voices. "Three...two...one."

A beat of silence.

This is it, Harley thought. He curled up knees to chin, wrapped his arms over his head, and sobbed silently into his chest.

2

I glanced at the clock on the courtroom wall for the fifti-eth time. It was seventeen minutes past eleven, which meant I'd been waiting exactly twenty-seven minutes for my case to be called. I hate waiting. Especially in a noisy courtroom where I can't get anything else done. Usually I could stay in my office until the prosecutor assigned to the courtroom called me with a five-minute warning—it was all I needed, since my office was just upstairs—but this particular home-court deputy district attorney wasn't exactly a fan of mine. We'd locked horns when he screwed up the murder of a homeless man. Deputy DA Brandon Averill was just too big a hotshot to be bothered with low-rent, pedestrian crimes like that. I'd grabbed the case away from him in front of a packed courtroom and wound up proving he'd had the wrong guy in custody. My bestie, fellow Special Trials prosecu-tor Toni LaCollier, says Brandon's a dangerous enemy. I say Brandon's a tool. We're probably both right.

I could've asked the court clerk to give me the five-minute heads-up, but that's a risky proposition. Even if they're willing to help, clerks are busy people. And some might even "forget" to call just for the pleasure of seeing a judge ream you. But I knew Sophie wasn't like that. And besides, I'd run out of patience. I headed for her desk, but at that moment Judge J. D. Morgan glared down at the packed courtroom and made an announcement. "Since I can't seem to find a single case where both sides are up to speed, we'll be in recess." He banged his gavel. "Get it together, people. I expect a better showing when we reconvene at one thirty."

Damn. Now I'd have to come back for the afternoon session. I refused to get stuck down here for another hour. Better to take my chances with the clerk. I moved toward the line of attorneys queueing up at Sophie's desk, but the judge gestured for me to approach. He leaned over the bench and covered his mic. "Rachel, where's your worthy adversary?"

"My worthy...you're kidding, right?" I nodded toward the back of the courtroom, where defense counsel Sweeny was schmoozing (i.e., wheedling) for more cash from the defendant's family. He had put the case on calendar so he could postpone the trial for another month. Guess why? I'd told the clerk I wanted a full hearing on Sweeny's reasons for delaying the trial. Again.

The judge sighed. "Look, I'm giving him the continuance this one last time. So agree on a drop-dead date for trial and stop busting my chops."

I gave him a sour look, but I nodded. He was right. The endless delays pissed me off, but another month wouldn't matter. The case was basically all physical evidence, and my experts were local. My cell phone vibrated in my purse. I reached in and sneaked a look. The screen said "Bailey Keller." My other bestie, who also happened to be a top-notch detective in the elite Robbery-Homicide Division of LAPD. Her call might mean she was free for lunch—a welcome distraction from the irritating morning I'd had so far. I turned back to the judge. "Okay if I have someone stand in for me if I get His Nibs to agree on a date?"

"Sure." The judge started to head off the bench, then turned back. "Hey, by the way, you and Graden still on for dinner Saturday?"

Graden and I—Graden, the lieutenant of Robbery-Homicide—had been dating for over a year now. And Judge J. D. Morgan had been dating Toni for the past two years. It's a cozy, some would say quasi-incestuous, group. But we work seventy-hour weeks—at least. Where else are we going to meet someone? The parking lot?

"Absolutely."

"Good. Now go make nice to Sweeny and pick a date."

J.D. trotted down off the bench and headed for his chambers. I did my lawyerly duty, then called Bailey back.

"Hey, Rachel," Bailey answered, her voice tense. "You get pulled in on that school shooting yet?"

I had just pushed my way into a packed elevator. "What school sh—?" I managed to close my mouth before saying "school shooting" out loud.

"Just happened."

"Oh my God. How bad?"

"We still don't have a body count. I'm putting a team together."

Body count. We used the term all the time, but about children? Never. The words brought up horrifying images. I squeezed my eyes shut, trying to will them away.

"Rachel? You still there?"

"Yeah, I just…give me a sec." I made myself push away from the horror of it all and think. If the case was already big enough to justify bringing in the Robbery-Homicide Division, then District Attorney William Vanderhorn, affectionately known by me as the Dipshit, would insist that we have a presence in the investigation. It gave him a chance to show up at the scene and get free publicity. And if Bailey had anything to say about it, that presence would be Yours Truly. "You on your way out there now?" I asked.

"Yeah. You may as well let me pick you up. One way or another, you'll wind up getting sent out."

Bailey was right. Vanderhorn's obnoxious press grab aside, it was SOP for the Special Trials Unit to show up at the crime scene, because we usually get our cases the day the body is found. That means we're involved in the investigation, which makes for a lot more work— normally prosecutors don't even get the file until they start picking a jury—but it lets us put together a much tighter case. It's an honor to be chosen for Special Trials, but it's not a job for anyone who wants normal working hours. Free evenings? Free weekends? Fuggetaboutit.

The elevator bounced to a stop at the eighteenth floor of the Criminal Courts Building, one of the two floors occupied by the district attorney's office. It's a long-standing, not so funny joke that the contract for the elevators went to the lowest bidder. They operate like one of those cheapo carnival rides. "Okay." My voice was as leaden as my heart. I didn't even want to imagine what I was about to see.

"We think we've already identified the shooters."

I punched in the security code on the door that led to my wing and headed for my office. "Then why...?" If they already had the shooters, there wouldn't be much for me to do. I unlocked the door to my office and dropped the case file on my desk.

Bailey sighed. "Yeah, now that I think about it, Rache, maybe you don't need to come. This one's gonna be...really bad."

I wanted to take a pass on this crime scene. Though homicides are always grim, nothing compares to the tragedy of a child victim. Let alone a mass murder involving children. I *didn't* want to see it. I *didn't* want to know about it. I *didn't* want it to be true. But it was. And I had to do something about it. Even if it was too late.